Ghost Walk

G William Smith

DARK HEART

Copyright © G William Smith 2023

First paperback edition 2023

Book design & Illustrations by Maytree Design

ISBN 978-1-7395-2250-6

darkheartpublishing.com

What are ghosts but whispers and shadows? And all the things that might have been.

John Chancel

20 Signs Your House May Be Haunted

Are eerie noises keeping you awake at night? Have you been experiencing disturbing dreams? Maybe your pets are displaying odd traits or you've caught your young child talking with a new imaginary friend. Do you constantly feel unsettled or ill at ease? Perhaps you feel you're being watched or sense a dark presence close by, when you know you're all alone.

Then you may well live in a haunted house.

Paranormal activity can present itself in a variety of different ways. No two hauntings are identical. Some can feature just a single phenomenon, such as a flickering light or a particular door that slams shut for no apparent reason. While other hauntings can display a wide variety of phenomena, ranging from strange noises to full-blown apparitions.

In order to help determine whether you're experiencing a genuine haunting. Here is a list of the most frequently reported phenomena and manifestations associated with paranormal activity.

1. A History of Darkness

History and the paranormal are intrinsically linked. Therefore, locations with a noted historical past are more likely to experience some form of paranormal activity than those without. If you suspect your home may be haunted, then the first place to look for a clear indication is into its past.

Most haunted houses are usually located on the site of some kind of historical tragedy or emotional trauma.

A forgotten murder or suicide, an unexplained history of tragedy. Sometimes other fatal catastrophes occurring near a property have been known to affect a building.

These traumatic events seep into a building's structure, saturating it with layers of spiritual residue.

The more traumatic the event; the deeper the shadow left behind.

***

'Hear me!'

I wake with a start. My heart pounding like a fist inside my chest. Gulping for breath, I struggle to breathe.

Deep breath in. Hold. Deep breath out.

The air tastes musty and there's a dull stench of decay with every mouthful.

Deep breath in. Hold. Deep breath out.

I repeat the process until my heart calms to a steady pace. I have to remain calm. It's far too easy to get lost down here. To get lose yourself to the darkness.

I drag my hand down my face. My fingertips tracing each and every texture. From my clammy brow to the rough stubble on my chin. Unfurling my fingers in the cold air, I can feel the gentle tingle of sweat clinging to the soft skin of my palm.

As I stare into the blackness, the last moments of the dream return.

The ash trees swaying overhead, the early morning dew. The damp leaves clinging to my bare feet.

The face of the policeman.

He's out of breath, clasping his side. Sweat saturates his mud spattered shirt. He's on the verge of speaking, but as usual, he says nothing. He just stares at me with that same look of utter hopelessness I recognise from a thousand different nightmares. Even after all these years. It never changes.

Shaking my head, I try to focus on something more tangible. The cold has dulled my reasoning and numbed my senses. It's hard to tell what is real anymore.

Across the cellar, the bulb on the camcorder blinks in the dark. I lean back in my chair and watch the tiny light as it flashes.

On, off. On, off. On, off.

Even now, I'm not entirely sure I'm actually awake. If it wasn't for the musty smell of mould, I could easily believe I was still dreaming. Without this wretched stink, I could easily slide off into oblivion. Drift away into nothingness—

'Jesus!'

I jerk upright as the battered cooling unit on the wall clatters into life with a rasping shudder.

Every fucking time!

Annoyed and tired, I slump back in my chair as the pitiful thing rattles through another laboured cycle of activity.

As my eyes grow accustomed to the dark, more of the cellar's contents reveal themselves to me.

Emerging from the darkness like familiar ghosts.

The whole cellar's vibrating. Loose objects rattle in the gloom. After so much sensory deprivation, the sudden activity cuts through my psyche like a knife.

Twisting in my chair, I glance at the neon green display on the travel clock:

03:53

Right on time. The first Central Line train of the morning. Racing through an adjacent tunnel, just metres from where I'm sitting now.

Flipping the switch on the camping lamp, a tight cone of light encircles my chair, intensifying the darkness beyond. Gripping the corner of the bar towel, I tug it away from the monitor screen.

The image on the little portable is still the same. A locked-off wide-shot of the pub cellar, illuminated by the camcorder's night vision mode. A chaotic mass of twisting pipes, gas cylinders and scattered bottle crates. And huddled in the centre, a forlorn, hunched figure in a surplus army jacket and oversized Ushanka hat. Arching my back, I watch my movements replicated on the tiny screen.

All around my chair, glowing in the lamplight, loose sheets of newspaper fan out across the floor, like giant newsprint petals.

Nothing moves here that I don't know about. But then again, nothing moves.

Fuck it! An entire week in this dump, with nothing to show for it. No visual anomalies, no temperature changes. No nothing!

Groaning, I reach across the camping table next to my chair and reactivate the laptop from standby mode. The audio program I've been running during the night reappears on screen. I catch sight of a small audio spike caused by my loud groan as it scrolls off the side of the graph. The line drops flat as the silence returns.

God, I feel alone.

05:57

I stand and stretch my bones, trying to shake the stiffness from my cramping muscles.

Over in the corner, a single blade of daylight catches my eye. A thin slit of sunshine squeezing through the cellar drop doors. Slicing through the darkness, it falls upon the large black crash mat at the base of the drop. Although it's encased in a tough plastic cover, the fortified foam cushion still looks comfy enough to grab a few hours' kip on.

Not that there's much chance of that. Because I know, if I do, I'll be crushed to death in my sleep. Killed by a falling barrel.

Irrational, but there it is.

All week I've sat staring at that mat. Reassuring myself, this could never happen. That it would be virtually impossible to die that way. That I'd hear the trapdoors open above me or the shouts of the delivery drivers unloading the lorry. But still I'm unable to even sit on the bloody thing, let alone lie upon it. In fact, I'm already feeling anxious just thinking about it now.

Turning away, a sheet of newspaper scrunches underfoot. Glancing down, I spot a headline in the gloom:

BLAIR FURY AT PEACE MARCH

The country's in revolt while I skulk here in the dark.

Sighing, I take another step. Arriving at the edge of my incandescent boundary. The glow from the lamp has created a tangible barrier between light and dark at the very edge of the paper fan, which I feel unable to transgress just yet.

Turning, I return to my base. The flimsy camping chair creaks under my weight as I drop back into it.

Shivering, I wrap my jacket across my chest. God it's cold. My feet feel like ice in my damp Hush Puppies. Trying to distract myself, I reach for my journal.

The gold embossed lettering glistens in the lamplight:

Executive Diary 2003

I open it to the page marked by my pen:

Saturday: February 15

With a despondent growl I dash a coarse line across the empty page and toss the diary aside. Slumping back in my chair, I pull a crumpled packet of B&H from my jacket pocket.

Striking a match, I savour the taste of nicotine in my dry throat.

Leaving the cigarette hanging from my lips, I tug my jacket sleeve back to the elbow and unbutton my shirt cuff. Taking the cigarette from my mouth, I dangle it over my forearm. The burning ambers hovering just above the sallow skin.

Holding my breath, I stub the cigarette down.

Over on the laptop, the audio graph spikes again, as it registers the sound of air sucked through clenched teeth.

For a moment, I feel something again, as fresh blister appears amongst a cluster of older scars.

The minutes tick by; tick-tock, tick-tock.

Everything stays the same. Nothing moves. Except for the thin sliver of daylight in the loading bay. Which silently glides across the wall. Glistening against the yellow mould on the damp bricks.

The blister continues to throb, but already its intensity is waning.

Maybe I sleep, maybe I don't. My life descends into nothingness.

The dull thud of footsteps echo overhead. Moments later, the trapdoor at the top of the staircase opens and Jerry McGilvery leers down into the gloom. 'You still alive down there?' he chuckles.

I don't know, I really don't know.

I sit at the end of the bar packing my kitbag. Another acquisition from the army surplus store in Euston Road. I check and count each item as I place it back into its correct pocket. This repetitive discipline helps me focus. Keeps my anxiety at bay. Helps me cope.

Out in the kitchen, t.A.T.u. is playing on the radio over the sputter of a steaming kettle. Behind the bar, Jerry is hanging an A3 flyer for an Elvis tribute act. It's immediately consumed by the glut of supernatural paraphernalia already swamping the bar. Cobwebs, plastic skulls, giant spiders, rubber skeletons, every kind of spooky codswallop you can think of. The whole place looks like a crap Halloween display at Poundland. There's even an enormous banner hanging from the ceiling:

THE MOST HAUNTED PUB IN ENGLAND

Underneath the banner Martyna, the bar's Polish cleaner, is dragging a threadbare mop over a worn area of parquet flooring Jerry optimistically calls *'the dance floor'*.

Jerry places a coffee mug on the bar in front of me. Like everything else in this place, it's plastered with a tacky ghost emblem.

As another tube train rumbles under the building, I nestle the mug with the palm of my hand. It's an automatic reflex I've now adopted to counter the intrusive effects of each passing train. I stare rigidly at the tiny ripples rolling across the surface of the milky brown liquid, as I wait tensely for the train to pass. Jerry, as usual, is taking it all in his stride. It's almost second nature to him now. Stooping behind the bar, he picks a folded beer mat from the floor and replaces it back between two vodka bottles on the top shelf, to stop them rattling together.

Although he appears nonplussed, the continued effort of having to counter these ceaseless assaults is having its effect. Haggard and distracted, he looks almost as drained as I do.

Barely acknowledging today's post, he tosses the envelopes onto a thick heap of unopened mail behind the bar. Another persistent assault he's doggedly ignoring. He's up to his eye-balls in debt. If it wasn't for the fact, it's a listed building. He'd have sold this dump to a property developer years ago.

As the train fades away, my hand continues to shake around the mug.

The neck of a Chivas whisky bottle taps gently against the rim.

'I don't know how you do it!' Jerry says, screwing the cap back on the bottle. 'I wouldn't spend the night down there, not after what I've seen.'

Acknowledging Jerry's gesture, I take a quick sip from the mug and wait for the inevitable.

'I'll never forget it.' Jerry continues predictably, his tone taking on a strange ethereal lilt. 'I was taking some empty crates down to cellar, when there it was in the darkness, just floating there. All deathly pale like, with its hand held out towards me, beckoning me...'

Glancing across the bar, I have to suppress a smile as I spot Martyna mouthing along to Jerry's outlandish anecdote. God knows how many times she's had to hear it. It's my third time and I've only been here a week.

Unperturbed by my apparent disinterest, Jerry continues on with his story. 'Whispering and groaning, like it was trying to communicate with me.' He pauses a moment to enhance the suspense. 'Then poof! It disappeared! Just like that. But I could still hear its distant moaning echoing in the dark...'

I've been far too amused by Martyna's comic antics to notice Jerry has concluded his recital and is now waiting, like some ham actor, for someone to acknowledge his performance.

With no recognition forthcoming, Jerry snatches up a bar towel and leans across the bar, his expression turning dour. 'I tell you there's something bloody scary down there.' His fingers tighten around the towel, forming a taut fist.

Cash wise, things must be a lot worse than he's letting on, but I'm too tired to give it any further thought. 'Jury's still out on that one,' I tell him dismissively.

'Now don't start that again.' Tossing the towel aside, Jerry pokes a stubby finger in my direction. 'I know what I saw. Doors don't just open by themselves...'

Right on cue, the kitchen door creaks open as a fresh wave of vibrations ripple through the bar.

'See,' he says unflinchingly, as if it's all the work of some malevolent spirit and not the seven twenty-five out of Bethnal Green. It's all too ridiculous for words.

Hoping that's put an end to it, I resume my packing, but Jerry's not letting up. 'What about the moaning?' He asks, forcing himself back into my eye-line.

My shoulders sag. I can't face another debate with Jerry right now. 'Wind?'

But my tone's way too flippant for Jerry's liking. 'Don't tell me it's fucking wind! I thought you were this great ghost hunter?'

Now I'm annoyed. 'I'm not a bloody ghost hunter!' I snap,' I'm a parapsychological and paranormal investigator.'

He pulls a 'whatever!' expression. Ignoring my attempt to side-track the conversation. 'And the noises from the other night?'

It's a fair question, but he's just thrown me off my count, forcing me to start over. 'Mice?'

'Mice! You said it sounded like a voice.'

He's trying to put words into my mouth. 'Sometimes the microphone wire acts as a mini antenna. Which can cause it to pick up fragments of radio transmissions.'

Jerry's frustration overtakes him. 'Look! I'm not paying you for dodgy fucking wiring and mice! This ghost means money to me! And God knows I need it.' His eyes widen despairingly, as I begin laying my equipment back out across the bar. The intense scrutiny makes me even more flustered. The moment everything is out of the bag, I immediately start repacking it again. 'Nobody's going to come to a poxy haunted wine bar with no poxy ghost in it!'

As Jerry rages on, I can't get the numbers in my head, to run in sequence…. E.M.F. detector; six. Infra-red thermometer; seven. Micro cassette recorder; seven—no eight. The spare batteries for the…

Jerry snatches the kitbag and drags it over the bar, forcing my focus back onto him. 'You promised me a fucking ghost, and that's what I want!' He tosses the bag back at me. 'So if you want paying for this gig, you'd better come up with something fast!'

The early morning commute is in full flow. The opposite platform packed with disgruntled commuters.

I can feel their eyes upon me. Sense their condemnation.

Tugging my collar up around my neck, I catch a glimpse of the gapping space between the platforms and I'm again gripped by the irrational fear I will somehow topple and fall onto the exposed tracks.

Reaching behind me, my fingertips touch the station wall.

The cool surface of the tiles reassures me. Makes me feel safe. Once the train is in the station, I'll be okay. Once the void is gone, I'll be able to move again. I'll be able to cross the platform and enter the carriage.

I try not to get ahead of myself. Try to remain calm until that moment arrives.

A gust of warm air bellows from the tunnel mouth as a train rumbles in the darkness.

Iraqi war dead everywhere. The tube's rammed with them. Dozens of murdered civilians, crushed between a throng of irritated commuters. Their faces, painted deathly white with children's face paints. Large black circles darkening the hollows of their eyes. Broad red gashes etched across their foreheads. One considerate corpse has even brought along his own coffin. It's propped against the central partition, blocking access to the sliding doors. Its cardboard frame, already disfigured by the steady stream of commuters forced to squeeze around it.

Anti-war demonstrators heading to the rally in Hyde Park. Men, women and children clutching colourful home-made placards and chattering in excited tones about the upcoming event.

A couple of teenage girls in matching tutus are standing by the centre doors, carrying a giant peace emblem made from a plastic hula hoop and some ribbon.

The whole carriage has a buzz of expectation about it, except for the old soldier sat opposite me in his faded army uniform, who's eying my fatigue jacket with palpable disdain.

At the next station, a sour-faced woman in a business suit pushes through the carriage. Struggling over my kitbag, she gives me a '*some people*' glare, but I'm not getting into all that bollocks. If you have an issue, love, take it up with Saddam Hussein over there. I stare instead at my Hush Puppies, wishing this journey was already over.

What the fuck!

Sourpuss is glaring at me in absolute horror. Even Corporal Jones is looking rattled.

Glimpsing my reflection in the window opposite, I'm not surprised. My eyes are wide and demented. An abundance of white staring back at me from the dark glass. I look like a crazy man.

Fighting the impulse to panic, I run through the last few moments in my head.

I'd been dozing off when I had felt the train decelerate.

It's a section of line where two tube lines converge and where for a few seconds, you can sometimes glimpse of another train running parallel in the adjacent tunnel.

I had glanced up, expecting to see a random face on the train opposite.

But it was her.

She was screaming; her face contorted with fear. Her hand thrust toward me, pleading for help, her tormented scream infused with the shrill screech of breaks.

Then she was gone. Snatched away by the intervening platform wall, as the train slammed into the next station.

Fuck knows what happened then; maybe I screamed, maybe I howled in shock. Maybe in my delirium I jumped from my seat and did the hokey-fucking-cokey. Whatever it was, it's prompted Sourpuss to relocate herself pronto.

Can't say I blame her.

The train comes to a shuddering halt and I have to fight the urge to leap from my seat and run screaming through the station.

Furiously gripping the armrests, I hold myself in place.

Because it's not real, it can't be. It's all in my head. It's the lack of sleep, or the meds, or just my sodding subconscious having a fucking breakdown. But...

The carriage doors slide open and I stare out across the platform. Petrified, she'll appear among the transferring passengers. Afraid she will find me cowering here, hiding amongst the Iraqi war dead.

My heart is racing. I need to get a grip. Control and disguise the physical symptoms of my panic.

I am safe. I am safe!

My fingernails dig into the armrest.

Breathe deep, breathe slow. In and out, in and out.

I stare wide-eyed at the mass of unsuspecting passengers piling through the open doors of the carriage, each one blissfully unaware they're stepping into a train carriage with a certifiable headcase.

Slouching down in my seat, I attempt to hide amongst the mayhem of the anti-war campaigners, hoping their particular brand of crazy will mask my own.

The doors slide shut and the train moves on again. Grabbing some tranqs from my jacket, I gulp them down dry. I can't stop shaking. Every breath feels like it's ripping a fresh gash through my lungs.

Sensing the eyes of the other passengers upon me, I force my chin off my chest and turn toward my accusers.

Nothing.

No one is looking in my direction. No one seems to care. Even the old soldier appears to have lost interest. I suspect he's seen worse.

I let out a sigh. The moment passes. The world goes on. No one nudges their friend or mutters my name. They all ignore me.

Dismissed as just another lunatic on the tube.

One of the few benefits of living in Central London.

***

Mid-seventies television footage: A young boy shuffles nervously on a threadbare velvet settee.

'How do you know there's a ghost in your house, Tony?'

The interviewer sits just off-camera. His tone, clipped, clear and articulate.

'I've seen it,' the young boy replies, his voice barely a whisper.

While Tony looks uncomfortable, his older sister, who is sitting next to him on the settee, is all too eager to speak. 'But I've seen it most!' she says in an earnest, yet excited voice.

The reporter tries to prompt the boy again. 'And are you not frightened by this ghost, Tony?'

As Tony draws away from the reporter's microphone, his sister is more than happy to elaborate on his behalf. 'Well, sometimes, but not all the time.'

Giving up on Tony, the reporter turns to the girl. 'And why do you think this ghost is in your house, Tracey?'

Tracey bustles with enthusiasm and is all too eager to express her opinion. 'Well, I think God doesn't know about it. You know, I think he's so high in heaven that sometimes it's hard for him to see everyone.'

As his sister continues talking, Tony slumps further down on the settee.

Tracey is now in her element, with new notions and conceptions leaping through her mind. 'And sometimes; I think God's so busy and has so much to do. That some people get over-looked completely.'

Tony disappears from shot.

2. Strange Dreams

Frequent repeating nightmares or continued sleep disturbances, including sleepwalking, could mean a spirit is attempting to contact the sleeper.

When we're asleep, our brains are at their most relaxed and vulnerable and are more susceptible to paranormal influence.

So any frequent dreams in which people or events unknown to the dreamer appear, or visions in which the dreamer reacts to some kind of past occurrence they have hitherto unknown knowledge of, should not be ignored.

***

Qamra Mishal shifted anxiously on the sofa, as a loud, piercing scream rung through the lounge.

'These last few months, it's been like living with different person.'

Across the room, Qamra's teenage daughter Lila gibbered incoherently as she thrashed on her bed. The image on the

TV continually losing focus, as the camcorder battled with its own night vision mode and the cameraman's erratic camerawork.

Placing her teacup on a nearby packing case, Jo Kalman turned to the fraught woman by her side. Qamra looked tired and haggard. Despite her natural olive complexion, Qamra's face looked drawn and pale and there were dark circles under her eyes. 'Sometimes I not recognise her anymore,' Qamra continued. 'She used to be such a gentle child.' On the video, Qamra had just appeared by her daughter's bedside, attempting to subdue the convulsing teenager. As another high-pitched screech echoed from the TV, Rafeeq, the Mishal's pet Labrador, hauled himself off his mat and lolloped out toward the kitchen extension.

Jo couldn't blame him.

Between the disturbing imagery on the Mishal's wide-screen TV and the disorienting nature of the cramped front room. Jo's own head was reeling.

The giant television, along with all the other furniture had been packed together down one end of the narrow lounge, to allow space for redecoration at the other. Loose electrical fittings hung from large holes in the ceiling while bare floorboards ran throughout the house.

'She started getting moody and difficult straight after move,' Qamra said, nervously twisting her hands together in her lap. 'She hardly eats and agues all the time. We thought she just being teenager. You know how they are. Then she attack another girl at school because of argument.' The more Qamra's voice faltered, the more pronounced her delicate

Middle Eastern intonation become. 'She has these dreams. She says things in sleep, horrible things! Some nights it's like she's fighting someone, screaming and shouting. And the scratches, her arms are covered in scratches. My nerves are gone. It's like living in a nightmare.' Qamra flinched as another shrill scream rang around the room.

On the video, Qamra was now grappling with Lila's wrists, attempting to stop the child from clawing at her own face. Reaching a new, heightened state of frenzy, the teenager howled. A deep, agonising howl of despair.

'There's money in this, right?' Belo Mishal pushed the pause button on the camcorder and lent toward Jo. 'Your magazine pays good money for this sort of thing?'

'Belo!' Qamra squirmed at her husband's blatant crassness.

'Well, it's why she's here isn't it?' A look of pained be-musement appeared on Belo's face. With Qamra's trauma clearly etched across her face, Belo's continence displayed no such afflictions. Even in what must be his mid-forties, he still possessed all of his boyish good looks with only a slight trace of grey in his thin chin strap beard and a slight paunch betraying his true age.

Surprised by the unexpected question, Jo found herself trapped between Belo's expectant stare and Lila Mishal's frozen grimace. 'Well, if we ran the story, I guess we could arrange some kind of payment. But I wouldn't like to say—'

That was enough for Belo. Leaping from his seat, he clapped his hands together. 'Well, why wouldn't you run it? It is *the* house, after all. I mean that's gotta be worth something.' Despite being born and raised in England, Belo was still prone to the occasional syntax error, which Jo had quickly learnt to ignore. But with Belo's elated glare now fixed upon on her, she was forced to reassess the subtle inflection in his last statement.

'I'm sorry. What do you mean *the* house?'

Belo seemed surprised by her question. 'Here, look,' he said, jabbing the fast-forward button.

With Belo preoccupied with his camcorder, it was left to Qamra to elaborate further. 'We didn't know who else to tell. We couldn't go to priest. He would say that we were mad. Or Lila was! Or worse, she was possessed.' Whispering the last word, Qamra looked close to tears. 'The doctor just kept prescribing sedatives. We didn't know who else to turn to—'

'There you go,' Belo punched the play button triumphantly. As the jerky images on the video juddered to a sudden halt, a large man with a ruddy complexion appeared on the TV screen, conducting what appeared to be some kind of séance in the Mishal's home. There were tiny cardboard pyramids and slips of paper spread across the floor in odd patterns. Qamra could be seen sitting quietly in the background, alongside another couple, who Jo took to be friends of the family, while Lila sat by herself in the middle of the candlelit room.

As the teenager squirmed anxiously in her chair, the large man loomed ominously behind her, his hands hovering either side of her head. 'So we called clairvoyant,' Qamra said. 'To see if he could *do* anything. He held séance here. That's when he told us...'

The clairvoyant's hand came to rest on the nape of the young girl's neck.

'Told you what?' Jo asked.

Again, Belo's impatience got the better of him. 'This is the *Babcock* House. They changed the name of the street, but this *is* it! This is where they were all murdered! Right here! Look!' He grabbed a thick book from the sideboard and pushed it in front of Jo. The illustration on the open page displayed a full-page facsimile of a 1973 edition of *Strange Frontier Magazine*, featuring a cover photograph of a grey council house under the headline:

INSIDE THE HOUSE OF HORRORS

'This is your magazine right. Well, this is the same place.' Belo's voice had reached an almost euphoric timbre.

Across the room, Qamra sounded less enthusiastic. 'I never would have moved here if I had known,' she said, wrapping her arms across her body. 'A good deal you said. No bloody wonder it was good deal! I knew it wasn't right! From day we moved in, it never feel right! There are constant problems and noises. Voices muttering in dark. Banging on floors and windows. I'm getting headaches, backaches. I'm living in pain all the time. It's house, it's not right. You feel it, don't you? Like someone is always watching you...' Breaking down Qamra buried her face in her hands. With a heavy sense of obligation, Belo attempted to console his wife, only for his embrace to be harshly rebuffed by a furious Qamra.

Unsettled and embarrassed, Jo turned her gaze away from the squabbling couple, only to find herself the object of intense scrutiny.

Through the half open lounge door, Lila Mishal held Jo's eye a moment before stepping back into the shadows.

'No chance!' Jo's proposal landed with a dull thud. The folder's contents spilling out across Frank's desktop.

'You haven't even read it!'

'Don't have to!' Frank sneered. 'There isn't a chance in hell I'm ever running *that* story again.'

Jo had been expecting some resistance from her father, but the sheer ferocity of his refusal had rocked her. 'You've got to be kidding?' she protested sourly. 'This was the biggest story we ever ran.'

'It was the biggest mistake we ever made! That story nearly destroyed me. I'm not likely to make that mistake again?' Frank slumped back in his chair and pulled a crumpled handkerchief from his trouser pocket. Through the opaque glass partition behind him, several faces in the adjoining conference room turned in their direction. 'So this is it, then? This is what you dragged me out of my meeting for.'

Despite her indignation, Jo couldn't help sounding deflated. 'I thought you'd be happy.'

'Happy!' Frank rubbed the hanky around the back of his sweaty neck. 'See those men in there?' He jabbed his thumb over his shoulder. 'They're trying to close me down and here you are, wanting to bang another nail in my coffin.' Grimacing, Frank twisted his neck and thumbed his chest. Reaching downward, he retrieved a half empty bottle of Pepto-Bismol from a desk draw. Unscrewing the cap, he gulped a mouthful of the bright pink liquid.

Judging by his pained expression, Frank Kalman wasn't just feeling the weight of his failing company on his broad sloping shoulders, but also the entire Kalman publishing legacy.

Once a prominent German publishing house, Der Kalonymus-Verlag had only survived after Frank's father had fled with his family to England in the nineteen-thirties following the Nazi party's seisure of all Jewish owned newspapers and publishing houses in the country. Reestablishing the business as Kalman Publishing in his new homeland, Ezra Kalonymus had quickly rebuilt the company into a thriving and profitable enterprise, with a slew of successful book and magazine titles to their name.

Following Ezra's death in the early seventies, Frank had taken control of the company, but rapid social change and recent upheavals in the publishing industry had seen the company's fortunes drastically decline under his stewardship. With book sales down and circulation of their few remaining magazine titles on the slide, Frank had already cut back on office staff, while most of his long-term contributors had long since called it a day.

For months, Jo had been campaigning for a change of focus, badgering her father to move away from the company's more traditional portfolio of unexplained mysteries and real crime periodicals, in order to attract fresh readership. New technology; Health and wellbeing; Celebrity news and fashion: Frank had doggedly dismissed everyone of Jo's ideas, demanding she concentrate on her actual job and leave the running of the company to him.

Normally this would have suited Jo fine. If truth be told, she quite liked her 'actual' job, which consisted mainly of selling magazine space to prospective clients, most of which she did over the telephone from her own home. But recently, with companies looking toward different platforms for their advertising, Jo had been struggling to drum up potential clients. As a result, advertising revenues had plummeted. So when, by chance, Jo had answered a call from Belo Mishal, she had seized the chance to redeem herself in her father's eyes and instead of passing the story to *Strange Frontier's* features editor; she had followed it up herself.

The Babcock connection had been an unexpected bonus.

She knew of the Babcock Haunting, of course. Everyone at *Strange Frontier* did. But Jo was also knew her father had shelved all the original Babcock articles and tie-ins way back in the seventies. With nothing left at the office to go on, Jo had spent the whole of the pervious evening researching the case on-line instead. But now, under her father's scathing glare she felt painfully ill-prepared.

'But it was our story,' she cooed. 'Why should we let anyone else have it—'

'And you can knock all that crap on the head!' Frank snapped. 'The days when you could just walk in here and demand whatever you like are long gone my girl.'

'That's not fair!' Jo's lip twisted into a sour pout. 'You know, next month is the thirtieth anniversary of the haunting. And what are we running?' She craned her neck in order to read a fresh print proof on her father's desk. 'Some tired old gumpth about crop circles and the mystic art of satanic levitation! No wonder sales are down the drain!'

Frank's palms slammed against the desktop. 'Enough of this crap!' He barked, heaving his heavy frame from his chair. 'A couple of years at university and you think you've got all the answers?'

Stunned, Jo gaped at her father. 'I'm trying to help!'

'You can help by leaving me to run my own business!' Frank growled dismissively, turning his back on his daughter. 'Now, if you don't mind. I've got a real meeting to get back to.

'This isn't fair,' Jo objected, striding around the side of her father's desk, incensed by Frank's abrupt dismissal.

She'd hardly taken a step before she collided with the tip of Frank's finger. 'No, life isn't fair is it? And it's about time you realised that.' Frank jabbed his fingertip a second time against Jo's chest bone, causing her to wince. 'I've been way too soft with you. For far too long.' Twisting his arm aggressively, he turned away again. 'Letting you get away with whatever you wanted.'

'Whatever I wanted!' Jo's voice rose an octave. 'That's rich! Considering I've had to fight you for everything. You never listen to me. You dismiss all my ideas without a second thought.' Jo threw her hands in the air. 'Sometimes I don't even know what I'm doing here.'

'I ask myself the same question.' Frank huffed angrily, glancing back at Jo with a belligerent scowl.

Quashing her animosity, Jo assumed a defiant posture. 'I worked hard for my degree. I think I deserve a little more than just selling advertising! I'm capable of so much more.'

'Capable,' Frank scoffed. 'You can't even organise your own life. You're a dreamer. You've spent far too long with your head in the clouds. You're just like your moth—' trembling with rage, Frank cut himself off, as a cold, angry silence fell between them.

Jo glowered at her father. 'Just like my mother, that's what you were about to say wasn't it?'

Unable to hold his daughter's eye, Frank turned away.

Infuriated, Jo lurched forward. 'I don't need this!' Snatching back her folder, she strode toward the door. 'And I don't need you!'

In her unbridled fury, Jo completely missed the sudden slump of her father's shoulders and the violent tremble of his hand. 'I'll tell you this. I'm nothing like my mother! Because I won't give up, like she did!'

As the door slammed behind her, Frank dropped back into his chair. Tossing the Pepto-Bismol angrily into the desk draw, he thumped it shut. 'Fuck it to hell!' he growled, twisting his neck.

'An official spokesman for the Prime Minister said he had no doubt the protesters' views were sincerely felt. But pointed out the planned mass demonstration in Central London today would be punishable by torture, imprisonment and death had it been taking place in Baghdad instead. Many see this announcement to be a definite hardening of the government's pro-war rhetoric, which has branded Saddam Hussein's regime tyrannical and evil.'

Flipping a fluoxetine tablet into her mouth, Jo glared impatiently at the computer's sluggish progress bar, while across the flat, *Good Morning Britain* played to an empty lounge.

'The official later claimed the reported one million people due to take part in today's demonstration would match the number of Kurds forced to flee from the regime's ruthless ethnic cleansing.'

The disc tray sprung open with a loud ping. Checking her watch, Jo grabbed the disc and slipped it straight into a paper sleeve. She could still make it, with time to spare, if she left straight away. Jo had already endured a fitful night, worrying about today's meeting and the thought of being late was already making her nauseous. Picking up a half-eaten piece of toast, she studied it a moment before dropping it back onto the plate.

'Onto local news now. Police have launched a fresh appeal for information concerning the whereabouts of missing teenager Ashley Hooper. This follows a new sighting of the seventeen-year-old getting into a white van in the Pine Hill area of North London on the day she disappeared. The teenager who vanished nine months ago was last seen wearing a light tan suede jacket and—'

Jo hit the off switch on the remote. Throwing the DVD into her handbag, she hurried across the lounge. Twenty minutes from Belsize Park to Embankment, she was cutting it close even by her standards. As she reached the apartment door, a small excited Havanese dog rushed from the kitchen, wagging its tail. 'Not now, Bruno. Mummy's in a hurry. I'll take you for a walk later.'

With one hand on the door catch, Jo checked herself in the hallway mirror, assessing her outfit. A smart new Stella McCartney jacket trouser combination, offset by her favourite H&M blouse. It had taken three attempts to reach this combination, but finally Jo felt satisfied. The suit's colour complimented her own delicate olive complexion and dark hazel eyes. The blouse was a little lively. But Jo hadn't wanted to appear too formal. She'd left her long black hair loose and it brushed pleasingly over her shoulders while still remaining presentable.

Her dark intelligent eyes showed no trace of tiredness from the sleepless night. She could even detect a subtle hint of determination on her long, almond-shaped face. She turned her head in the mirror, reassured by the quiet resolution conveyed by the gentle slope of her aquiline nose and soft square jawline. Buoyed by her appearance, Jo blew Bruno a playful kiss and slipped out the door.

Only to have her path immediately blocked by a large cardboard placard emblazoned with the words:

SAY NO TO WAR

'Is that what you're wearing?' the man holding the placard asked. 'Very official?'

Jo let out an exasperated sigh.

Greg Campbell lived in the apartment above Jo. After discovering their mutual disgust for the proposed invasion of Iraq, they had agreed to attend today's anti-war march together. It had completely slipped Jo's mind. Greg had even brought his seven-year-old daughter Hanna with him, who was now beaming up at Jo in her usual ebullient fashion. And she wasn't the only one.

Jo had to suppress a smile as she caught Greg, casting an admiring glance over her new outfit. A compliment Jo felt unable to reciprocate. Greg had on a loose pair of denims with a large graffiti motif across the thigh and a baggy hoodie under his blazer. Greg's fashion sense had always been woeful, but since his recent divorce it had veered dangerously close to full-blown mid-life crisis.

Aware Jo had noticed his interest, Greg tried to deflect attention elsewhere. 'I don't think Blair will be able to ignore this, do you?' he chuckled, waving his placard in a mock conformational manner. After a quick sideward prompt from her dad, Hanna held her own homemade placard up for Jo to inspect. The board was a riot of multi-coloured flowers and unicorns. 'Here, I've made one for you too. It has flowers on it, just like mine.' Hanna held out another smaller board decorated in bright felt-tip pen.

DON'T ATTACK IRAQ

'Oh, that's lovely, it really is,' Jo smiled. 'I'll make sure everyone gets to see it.' With a slight tilt of her head, she motioned Greg to one side. 'I'll have to meet you at Hyde Park. I have something to do first.'

'Must be important.' Greg sounded a little put out.

'Job interview.'

31

Greg's eyebrows arched in surprise, then comprehension. 'Hence the outfit.'

'Hence the outfit. But I promise to come and find you at the demonstration afterwards.'

Expressing a slew of hasty apologies and assurances, Jo darted toward the stairs. 'Well, good luck with the interview,' Greg called after her as she skipped down the stairwell. 'We'll be eager to hear how it all went.'

But Jo had already disappeared out through the lobby doors.

Intolerable! Jo glared angrily at the tiny clock on her Blackberry, as yet another new arrival was greeted, then escorted from the reception area. In all fairness, she had arrived early for her meeting, but even so; to be left festering in the lobby for the best part of an hour was beyond a joke.

Dropping the phone back into her handbag, Jo caught sight of an open packet of Silk Cut in the inside pocket. Although desperately craving a smoke, Jo promptly dismissed the idea. It would be just her luck to have Gillian finally appear only to catch her puffing franticly on a ciggy in the street.

Dispirited and annoyed, Jo gave her surroundings another critical reappraisal. Designed in an ultra-modern loft style, the small reception area had barely enough space for the reception desk, tuxedo sofa and water cooler. It's claustrophobic feel, accentuated further by the looming presence of celebrity psychic Max Schaffer. The giant wall graphic advertising the new season of *The Max Schaffer Experience* was doing very little to ease Jo's seething frustration. It was with the show's production head that Jo was due to meet that morning.

Unless, of course this all turned out to be just some cruel ruse by Gillian, designed to humiliate her. Tapping the back of her hand furiously with her index finger, Jo tried to reassure herself. No, this was just typical Gillian behaviour. Letting you know, she was in charge. She had always been the same. Even at university, while Gillian Bishop had bristled with limitless self-assurance and confidence, she'd also exuded an unpleasant aura of arrogance and self-importance. But it had been precisely this abrasive quality; mixed with her relentless determination, that had allowed Gillian to transform a small struggling production company churning out cheap documentary programmes for a niche satellite channel into a modern vibrant business concern with a slew of popular reality and paranormal investigation shows behind it.

The most popular being *The Max Schaffer Experience*. Its heady mix of real-time paranormal investigation and elaborate séance set pieces had resinated with The Mystery Channel's key democratic, quickly becoming the channel's highest rated show. There was even talk of the show transitioning to a mainstream terrestrial channel.

It had been several years since Jo had spoken with Gillian, so it had been a surprise when she had answered Jo's call on the first ring the previous evening. True, Gillian had sounded her usual brusque self during the call. Emphasising her own importance by constantly breaking from the conversation to bark orders at some poor underling. But this had abruptly changed the moment Jo had mentioned The Babcock Haunting. Almost immediately Gillian's tone had transformed. Immediately, attentive and inquisitive, she'd lost no time in arranging a meeting with Jo for the following morning. In fact, Gillian had sounded so enthusiastic over the phone, Jo had half-expected to find Gillian waiting expectantly in reception to greet her.

Okay, maybe not to that extent. But Jo certainly hadn't expected to be left stewing in the lobby all morning.

Jo cast another plaintive glance out through the glass doors. It was still a madhouse out there.

When she'd arrived, the streets around the Dark Dimension offices had thronged with excited protestors, bewildered tourists and weary looking police officers. All gradually migrating toward Embankment for the start of the anti-war march. The sheer size of the turnout had been a surprise. Even now, a steady flow of animated protesters were still milling past the doorway, cheering, chanting and waving placards.

Jo felt a momentary pang of conscience as she remembered Greg and Hanna would be among the crowd somewhere. Hanna still clutching the homemade placard she had made for Jo.

Jo checked her watch again. She still had time to meet them both in Hyde Park. If she could just get things moving. She was just on the verge of asking the snooty receptionist to call 's office again when a young man with an apologetic expression came bounding toward her.

'Jo Kalman,' he said, extending a welcoming hand, his wrist a mass of bead bracelets and colourful charity bands. 'I'm Jacob. I hope you haven't been waiting long.'

Not waiting for a response, Jacob immediately began directing Jo from the reception area. 'Did you get caught in the demonstration? It's been bloody crazy here today.' Chasing behind Jacob, Jo barely had time to register the erratic nature of the interior office layout as she was briskly ushered through. The whole place was a riot of of bold graphic designs and vibrant colour schemes, which Jo immediately found refreshing and fun.

Rounding a corner, they arrived at a huge open workspace, which Jacob dubbed 'The Forum'. A vast eclectic workroom cluttered with a bizarre muddle of odd chairs, tall industrial lamps and arcade games. At its centre, a tight group of people were gathered around a cluttered table tennis table, deliberating over a slew of production papers and concept sheets.

Spotting Jo, a tall, angular woman with short cropped hair broke from the group and strode purposely toward her. 'Well, hello stranger,' she gushed, wrapping her long arms around Jo and giving her a strong, lingering hug. 'Oh my God look at you, you look fantastic.' Taking her firmly by her shoulders, Gillian gave Jo the full head-to-toe appraisal. 'But there was really no need to dress up. We're very informal here.' Jo cringed as Gillian ran her eye over her new Stella McCartney outfit. 'And you've put some weight on too I'm glad to see,' Gillian added in an insinuating tone, her hands still squeezing Jo's shoulders.

Unsettled, Jo gestured toward her surroundings. 'Well, this is all very modern.'

'I know, I know.' Gillian rolled her eyes in mock exasperation. 'Activity-based working, if you can believe it! Guess that's what happens when you hire straight from the kinder-garden.' Gillian gave a forced chuckle and shrugged. 'At least they haven't replaced the fire escape with a slide and ball pit.'

Deciding she'd expressed enough obligatory pleasantries, Gillian lent closer to Jo, staring deep into her eyes. 'So...' she purred furtively, 'what have you got for me?'

A sharp scream rang around the small glass office. As Lila Mishal thrashed wildly on her bed, Gillian leant forward in her chair. Unable to hear the teenager's tortured jabbering over the persistent parade noise, she jerked her head irritably. 'Jacob, will you shut that damn window?'

Propelling himself across the floor on his swivel chair, Jacob slammed the window shut, reducing the noise to a muffled thumping. 'It's a big turnout,' he observed, scooting back across the office.

'The good it will do 'em,' Gillian sneered. 'Blair will do whatever Bush tells him to do. He's got absolutely no backbone that man!'

'Surely he wouldn't dare, not after this turnout.'

Gillian shot Jo a disparaging glance. 'Ever the optimist,' she huffed, turning back to the small TV monitor on her desk.

On the video, Qamra was now struggling with Lila on her bed. The picture froze as Gillian thumped the remote and sat back in her chair. She took a prolonged drag on her cigarette. 'And you're absolutely sure this *is* the old Babcock house? I thought they knocked it down years ago.'

Jo pulled a photocopy from the card folder on her lap. 'I checked with the land registry office. They changed the road name years ago and the building's been renovated; but it's basically the same house.'

'And they claim to have seen a shadow man in the house?'

'Well, the stepfather has, on the upstairs landing.'

Gillian clapped her hands together, startling both Jo and Jacob in the process. 'This is terrific! No, it's more than that. It's *fucking* terrific!' Leaping to her feet, she began pacing the room. 'Of course we've already covered The Babcock Haunting on our *Mysteries of the Paranormal* show, but this is a whole new angle and it's perfect for Max. He loves all that swivelled eyed possession stuff.' Gillian turned abruptly to Jo. 'What's the girl like? You know when she's not all...' Crossing her eyes, she twirled an index finger in a tight circle next to her temple.

'I don't know,' Jo admitted. 'I haven't really seen her, well I've seen her, but I haven't really spoken to her.'

'We'll get our own therapist to look at her of course. And what do we know about this...?' Gillian glanced down at the printed sheet Jo had given her. 'Mishal family?'

Jo explained how Qamra and Lila had been refugees from Iraq in the early nineties. How Qamra had met her husband Belo while living with her aunt in London and how they now had their own five-year-old child.

Without being prompted, Jacob begun scribbling furiously into his notepad.

Gillian nodded sagely. 'Definitely a lot of human interest there. It might even play well considering the currant climate. What's their English like?'

'Very good. Perfect, in fact.'

'Great, because I can't be doing with all that subtitle stuff. Makes it harder for people to relate to them. What about the stepfather? What's he like?'

'In general?'

'With the stepdaughter?'

To be honest, Jo had taken an immediate dislike to Belo. There was an inherent crassness about the man, Jo found intrinsically distasteful. 'Good, they seem close,' Jo said in a non-committal tone. 'He's a little overprotective I suppose, but that might just be the culture.'

Satisfied, Gillian nodded her head. 'I'll need to see all the unedited copies of these tapes. Then we can set up some meetings and arrange some shooting dates.'

'Shooting dates?'

'Of course. The anniversary of the tragedy is just a few weeks away. And we've got a repeat haunting in the same bloody house. It's all too good to miss. We've got to get a crew in there, a full investigation. And a séance, of course.' Gillian snapped her fingers as another notion struck her. 'Even better; a *live* séance on the actual night of the anniversary. My God; Think of the ratings.' She clapped her hands together again. 'Right, I need to get Max in and set up some trails—'

Gillian cut herself off, misreading Jo's perplexed expression. 'What? Do you think they'll object?'

Jo wasn't sure what she thought. Having spent years laboriously dragging her ideas past her father, this sudden flood of enthusiasm was a bewildering change of pace.

'Of course there won't; *they* came to you after all,' Gillian said, dismissing Jo's hesitancy with another dramatic hand gesture. 'Jacob, I need you to get Malcolm Rice and Dave Parish in here as quick as you can and Dan Phillips if he's about.' Jacob jumped from his seat and headed for the door. 'And tell Jasmine to get Max on the phone for me.' As the door closed behind Jacob, Gillian turned back to Jo. 'Of course we'll have to get you on board straight away.'

'What just like that?' Jo exclaimed, surprised by the sudden urgency.

'Of course, why not? We'll set you up as a freelance for now, then sort you out something more permanent later.'

'Later?'

'Of course, why not? That is unless you would prefer to stay with *daddy*!'

Jo bristled at Gillian's churlish intonation. 'No, there's nothing for me there anymore.'

'Well, that's all decided then,' Gillian declared emphatically, while stretching to retrieve a packet of Marlboro Lights from her desktop. 'You'll come and work with us. And it's about time. Print publishing is dead on its feet. God knows why you even went back there.'

Jo's feelings regarding her father were still a raw mix of conflicting emotions. 'He needed me...'

'Did he? Or did you just need *him*?' Gillian said brusquely.

This time, even Gillian couldn't miss the hurt on Jo's face. 'Okay, that was below the belt,' Gillian admitted in a softer tone. Lighting her cigarette, she tossed the lighter aside. 'I'm sorry, but if truth be told. I'm right against the wall on this one. We've been trying to pitch the show to one of the larger networks. But we've been stuck for something big to start the season with.' Crouching by the side of Jo's chair, Gillian placed her hand over Jo's. 'And then here you are. Turning up out of the blue. With exactly what I need. Just like the old days.' Gillian forefinger rubbed against Jo's wrist as she held her gaze. 'We made a good team back then didn't we? You did the right thing coming to me. Now you can be somewhere where your talents will be probably appreciated.'

Jo gave a weak smile, if only to reassure herself.

'That's more like it.' Squeezing Jo's hand, Gillian leapt to her feet animatedly. 'Right then, I've got a lot of people I need to introduce you to.'

'What right now?'

'Unless you've got something else, you'd rather be doing.'

And there it was. The same callous assumption that everyone would just jump to her command and fall into line behind her.

'No, no, it's fine,' Jo heard herself saying.

Outside, the muted sound of the protest march echoed further into the distance.

***

Contemporary news footage: Standing by the entrance to a large industrial estate, a local news reporter addresses the camera directly. 'The last known movements of missing teenager Ashley Hooper were reconstructed by police today, nine months after the seventeen-year-old disappeared.'

The shot changes to footage of the earlier police reconstruction. A young girl with a passing resemblance to the missing teenager walks along a pathway close to the industrial estate, shadowed by several reporters.

'This follows the launch of a fresh appeal, following the emergence of new video footage taken on the day Ashley disappeared.'

The shot cuts to grainy CCTV security footage. A young woman wearing a striped beanie hat and scarf can be seen walking past the chain link gates of a wide delivery bay, just as the roof of a dirty white van glides into view at the bottom of the image.

At first, the teenager seems unsettled by the van's sudden appearance, but relaxes after talking with the unseen driver. She disappears around the front of the vehicle. Moments later, the van disappears from view.

'Ashley is described as white, about 5ft tall, blond with dyed streaks of pink hair. She was last seen wearing a tan coloured suede jacket, a red and black striped woollen hat and scarf, grey trousers and brown boots. Metropolitan Police are asking for anybody with information about her whereabouts to come forward.'

3. Unexplained Noises

One of the most common ways paranormal beings manifest themselves is through sound, whether through music, human voices, or the sound of mysterious knocking on doors and walls.

At night, you may even hear footsteps or whispers in the dark. Hearing things being moved or dropped is not uncommon either. Neither is the sound of distant moaning or crying. These noises can be quite subtle and other times terrifyingly loud.

The household may also experience unexplained voices or 'animal growls' on audio or videotapes recorded in the house.

***

Heavy fists pounding on my front door. I can hear them half a block away.

Lighting up a cigarette, I sneak another peek across the road. It's the usual thing. Black leather jackets, white shirts, slicked back hair. Debt collectors. The early morning wake-up call. Probably the only benefit of working nights. You're never in when people expect you to be.

The taller of the two lumps is out in the road, staring up at the block. Judging by his eyeline, he knows exactly which studio is mine. Not a comforting thought.

Propping my kitbag against the cycle barrier, I take a seat on my camera case. This could take a while. Watching the knuckleheads, I wonder who's sent them this time and what they're after. Not that it matters much. They'll have a hard job getting something out of nothing.

Down by my feet, the local stray brushes against my leg. 'How you doing, Scruff?' I give the cat a friendly scratch as I rummage in my satchel for the remnants of last night's ham and cheese sandwiches, which he snatches eagerly from my hand.

The lump in the road is now yapping on his mobile, while the other continues to thump the entry phone button; ever the optimist.

Finishing his conservation, the lump waves to his mate. I watch as they reluctantly walk away.

To be on the safe side, I finish my cigarette where I am. Some of these sods can be proper sly when they want to be.

I check the time on my Moratoria. Ten minutes; should be enough. Flicking the butt into a hedge, I sling my bags over my shoulder and stroll across the road. As I rummage for my keys, I contemplate removing my business card from the sleeve next to my buzzer:

Anthony Vail: Professional Commercial Photography: Studio 9

But what would be the point? If they already know where I live, not knowing which doorbell to push is hardly going to deter them much.

As I enter the lobby, Leo's door opens and the big man lumbers out. He's got the studio on the ground floor and acts as an unofficial doorman for the block. He's not actually called Leo, that's just what I call him. The sign on his studio says:

Leandro Bonelli: Artist

I call him Leo, after his compatriot, Leonardo da Vinci. I think it suits him better and he doesn't seem to mind. If anything, he looks more like an ageing street fighter than an artist, with his broken nose and lumpy forehead. But as I don't know the names of any Italian boxers, Leo will just have to do.

'Your friends were here again,' Leo grumbles, his teeth clenching the lip of his pipe. The smell of tobacco mixes with the pungent smell of turpentine wafting from his studio.

'You give 'em anything?'

'Just my middle finger, when they tapped on my window.' Laughing, I give him a wink. He's a good bloke is Leo and not a bad painter either. 'One of these days, though, they're gonna catch up with you,' he calls after me as I load my bags into the old traction cage lift in the lobby. 'They always do.'

Like I say, he's alright is Leo, not the judgmental kind. He's an artist, so he knows all about being broke. And from the state of his face, I'd say he's had his fair share of hard times as well.

This entire building is like that; full of odd bods. It's an old furniture warehouse converted into artist studios each with their own living space ancillary. Bought mine years back when I still had money. Back when Hoxton was a dump. Now they're doing the place up, house prices are soaring. It'll be worth a fortune in a few years. That's if they haven't kicked me out by then.

It's mostly bills in my mailbox and I stuff them into my jacket as I drag the lift gate closed. Pushing the button for the top floor, the old deathtrap rattles into life.

I clock the answerphone flashing straight out, but I resist the urge to tap the message button until I've stacked today's bills neatly on the telephone table. They're all the same date, so I only have to arrange them by size. Amongst the bills, there's a folded menu for a local Chinese restaurant, which I place on the menu pile by the microwave. I quickly unpack my kit bags and return all the equipment to their allocated spaces on the studio shelves before returning to the answerphone. It's my business line, so who knows, maybe they'll be a job for me. Who's the optimist now?

I push the play button.

'Mr Vail this is Scott Purgavie from The First Allied Bank. This is now the third message I have left for you now. I must caution you if we don't receive your loan payment by the end of the week, I will have no choice but to suspend your business account. Thank you.'

Well, so much for that. Leaving the machine playing, I wander over to the kitchenette and flip the switch on the kettle. As the water boils, I heap some coffee granules into a mug.

Several hang-ups, followed by another message. It's from a photographic wholesaler I sometimes deal with. Payment bounced. Another curt 'thank you'. This is getting repetitive. One of these days, I'm going to have to get rid of that bloody machine.

The milk smells a bit iffy, but not enough to be concerned about. I slop a drop into the mug and top it up with boiling water. Slurping the coffee, I pull my breakfast from the fridge. Frozen lasagna. Working nights can really mess you up. How else could you explain frozen lasagna as a viable breakfast option? I throw it into the microwave and punch the cook button.

Another beep on the answerphone.

'Tony B-b-b-babcock. It's im-imperative that you call me back. My n-n-umber is 079—'

Striding from the kitchenette, I grab the answerphone and slam it against the wall, cutting short the stammering fool. The trailing wires snatch across the telephone table sending my mail pile flying.

Now I'm mad. Dropping to my knees, I snatch at the scattered envelopes, franticly stacking them back onto the table. Oldest at the bottom, newest on top, large below small. Once they're all back in place, I crouch by the telephone table and wait for the anger to subside. 'This will pass,' I mutter, over and over. 'This will pass.'

Over on the kitchen counter, the microwave pings. Breakfast is ready.

I swig back a palmful of pills with a gulp of raspberry flavoured Panadol Syrup.

20mg of olanzapine. 50mg of sertraline.

The olanzapine keeps me sane. The sertraline gets me through the day. The Panadol because I like the taste.

Staring at the haggard reflection in the bathroom cabinet, I struggle to recognise the bloated face gazing back at me.

A crack of daylight squeezes through the blackout curtains. I lay transfixed by this single blade of light cutting through the darkness. My body feels hollow and lifeless. Watching the drifting dust motes caught within the bright shaft, I can't help but wonder how much of that stuff I inhale every day. How much filth is gradually filling my empty core?

I guess time is passing.

On my bedside cabinet, the MiniDisc recorder is spinning, continually recording every sound.

Two figures moving behind the crack of a door, screaming and swearing. My heart pounding as I creep forward. The lino, cold beneath my bare feet.

A sudden groan, then silence.

I freeze. The sudden calm is worse than the anger. My body trembles.

She bursts through the door, her eyes bulging, wild with terror, knocking me aside as she runs down the hallway. Petrified, I turn toward the open door.

He's slumped on the kitchen floor, an open gash across his throat. Feet twitching as blood trickles across the floor. I inch forward, transfixed by the horror. Sensing my approach, his head slumps back. His eyes bore into me. 'You,' he whispers. 'You did this to us.'

The blood on the floor touches my toes.

I wake with a jolt, my heart thumping. The sound of the old lift echoes through the wall.

The dream was so vivid, so real. If I close my eyes, I can still see the embossed motif on the kitchen lino. All its tiny indents and scuffed scratches. The blood tracing the shape of its repetitive faux tiling.

I don't even know if these memories are real, or just the product of my own tormented psyche. Memory embellishment. The act of filling half-remembered recollections with your own imagination. Like a child's colouring book. But the colours in my memory book have long since merged. Seeping over the lines, blurring and distorting the picture, until all that's left is a dark, chaotic mess.

Three hard buzzes on the intercom. Tensing, I grab the handset. Staring at the fuzzy grey image on the security screen, all I can see is an empty street.

I wait for someone to drift back in front of the camera.

Nothing. Just empty static and road noise. Yanking open the door, I stick my head out into the hallway. There's no sound from the lift or the stairwell. Probably just kids fucking about. Slamming the door shut, I've barely taken two steps before the buzzer blares again. I snatch up the handset. 'What!'

'Delivery.'

I hesitate before pushing the lock release button. All I can see is the top of some fella's baseball cap. Like I say, some of these sods can be proper sly. 'Yeah, from who?'

He tells me, and I relax. It's a job I've been expecting.

The courier gives me a funny look as I sign for the package. It could be for any number of reasons. The bloodshot eyes, the mad bed hair in the middle of the day. But right now, it's because he's just spotted the scars on my forearms.

I ignore him, of course. What else can I do?

He tells me he's going to return for the package later that evening so it must be sensitive stuff.

Inside the box, they're the ugliest looking trainers I've ever seen. Chunky, impractical, and adorned with a colour scheme envisioned by a hyperactive child during a fever dream.

Probably worth a fortune then.

I spend the next two hours arranging and rearranging the trainers on the pedestal. Readjusting the lighting for each new angle so the product will look its best against the plain white backdrop. Even my trusty Hasselblad struggles to capture the radiant majesty of these monstrosities but I get all the shots I need by the time the courier returns.

He checks the box's contents before resealing it.

Don't worry pal there's no chance I'm going to pinch those sweet kicks.

Passing him the package, he glances down at my forearms, which I've now covered with a long-sleeved sweatshirt.

I don't move until I'm certain the room's in total darkness. Only after my eyes have stopped wrestling with the inky blackness, do I reach out and pull the safelight cord, filling the small darkroom with its comforting warm glow.

I set the trays, developer nearest to the enlarger, then the stop bath, and finally the fix. Each tray, exactly the same distance away from its neighbour. It reassures me to see them all lined up and ready for use. I even have a different colour for each one. Not that it makes any difference in the red safelight, but it's good to know.

After measuring out the chemicals, I wash my hands in the sink.

I place the negative in the enlarger carrier, checking the shiny side is upward and all the numbers are pointing away from me. I set it to the correct height and focus the image on the masking frame. I expose a thin test strip of photographic paper, slide it into the developer and hit the timer.

I wash my hands in the sink.

I stare at the luminous second hand as it travels around the clock face. I watch each second tick by.

Ding.

I remove the strip from the developer and drain it off. I slide it into the stop-bath, gently rocking the tray from side to side. Removing the strip from the stop-bath, I drain it and slide it into the fixer tray. Rocking the clear liquid again to make sure it covers all the strip. I use one set of tongs to lift it from the developing solution and another pair for the fixer. I remove the test strip from the fixer and only then do I flick the white light on.

I wash my hands in the sink.

If the test strip looks good, I do the final print. If not; I make the necessary adjustments to the exposure and contrast and try again. Each step in the process follows the next. It can't happen any other way. If you don't follow the steps exactly, you don't get a perfect print at the end. I'm comforted by the regimental order of the exercise.

It takes a couple more hours to expose and develop the final proofs before I'm able to turn my mind to other things.

I plug the headphones into the MiniDisc player. As there's nothing written in last night's log, I check the readings on my decibel sensor. If there is anything there, it's usually a passing car in the street above, or a wandering drunk careering home from the pub, but it's still worth a try.

Three triggers.

I take the timings from the sensor and match them to the recordings. The first two are lorries passing around midnight. The third is not until six in the morning. I forward the recording to the time code and push play.

A cry and the sound of my own muttering, repeating my calming exercises over and over.

Christ almighty! Why do I even bother! Pulling the headphones from my head, I throw them aside.

The sound from the television echoes across the lounge. A lifetime of insomnia does that to you. You leave the damn thing on just to mask the silence. It's nice to hear another voice in your home. Even if that voice belongs to Eamonn 'sodding' Holmes.

'It now looks certain today's anti-war march was the largest public rally ever held in British history. Scotland Yard still cannot confirm exact figures, but they have stated the turnout will probably exceed the numbers seen during last year's Golden Jubilee weekend celebrations.'

I rinse my face and knock back a couple of Nurofen. My head is pounding. I've gone over last night's recording so many times I can't think straight anymore. I pull my dinner from the fridge. Frozen lasagna. It's the same tray from this morning; only a little more crispy. I slam it in the microwave and punch the timer button. The old Samsung groans into life as the dish spins inside. I've dislodged the top menu on the pile next to the microwave. I nudge it back into place as I pull the milk carton from the fridge and give it another suspicious sniff. The glass plate rattles on the turntable, drowning out the sound of the television.

As I watch the ready meal spinning, I'm struck with a sudden sense of unreality. As if I've become detached from my own surroundings. The microwave, the kitchenette cabinets, the breakfast bar all distort into a characterless flat image I no longer feel connected to. I feel myself drifting...

Ping.

The microwave breaks the spell and I'm back in the moment. Tugging open the door, I pull out the ready meal. As

I stare at the reheated lasagna, a shiver runs down my spine. But it's not because of the food.

Some words you can distinguish over any other noise. No matter what you're doing, they'll always catch your attention. Your own name, being the most powerful. Striding across the studio, I grab the remote control and punch up the volume. The TV's tuned to one of the filler satellite channels located somewhere between the porn and God Channel.

Washed-out seventies news footage. A semi-detached council house with the unmistakable signs of fire damage. A Ford Anglia police car parked outside. The obligatory nosey neighbours. The tired old misleading rhetoric. It's all here. Every one of my nightmares parading through my lounge. My fingers grip the remote, as a middle-aged man with a shock of white hair replaces the grainy news footage. Max Schaffer; a painfully camp thespian masquerading as a spiritualist. The compulsory black polo neck and sink-plug medallion, the mystical waving of the hands. The man's a walking cliché.

'Was it, as sceptics have been claiming for thirty-years, just an elaborate hoax by an attention-seeking four-teen-year-old?' The shot changes to a faded photograph of a family standing together in their living room. A middle-aged couple; their teenage daughter. A small boy huddling at his mother's side. 'Or were more sinister forces to blame for the Babcock family haunting? That was to ultimately claim the lives of both Chris and Ruth Babcock and their teenage daughter, Tracey? Stay with us after the break; when we delve into another *Mystery of the Paran*—'

Blackness.

I squeeze the remote in my hand, staring at the blank screen. My mind feels numb. But it doesn't last.

Shaking violently, I drop to my knees. As the panic consumes me, I hear myself scream.

'We should consider therapy again,' Sharman tells me in that nauseating, non-confrontational tone of his. He pushes his glasses up onto the bridge of his nose. 'These feelings need to come to the surface. You can't keep suppressing them.'

I know where he's going with this.

'I don't need more therapy.' My raw tone jars harshly against the Sharman's soothing West Country lilt. 'I just need something stronger. Something to stop these feelings!'

'These feelings, or all feelings?'

Christ! I twist in my chair. 'You don't know what it's like. Having to live like this. With all these...' I have to search for the right words. 'These fragments; lurking here.' I tap the side of my head in frustration.

Sharman nods his head solemnly. He's sitting in front of the window, the daylight streaming through the blinds behind him. His face, little more than a dark outline. He does this on purpose of course. It's supposed to keep the focus on me. It's not just his fashion sense that's archaic, even his technique is outdated. Stuck in the past is Dr Sharman, playing the part of the stereotypical psychiatrist, even down to the corny corduroy blazer and tan elbow patches. But he seems to think it's working for him.

They all have their own style and their own way of doing things. I should know I've seen enough of them. Each one believing they've developed their own unique form of analysis. Their own personal insight into the human psyche. But it's all bluff. They're all just groping in the dark. If there's one thing I have learnt over the years. It's that there's no instant fix, no magic solution. I've learnt the hard way that miracles don't just happen overnight. If someone is going to help you, they have to stay the course. They have to be there for you.

Which brings me back to Sharman. He's a little conventual in his thinking I grant you. But he understands me. And he's always been there for me. I was lucky. By the time I got to him, I was a total mess. Batted from one frustrated shrink to the next. Trapped in an endless circle of psychiatrists, psychotherapists and care workers. No one knew what to do with me. They just stuck me on the meds and passed me on. Then I landed on Eric's doorstep.

In them days, he was only just getting started. Fresh out of grad school and dropped straight into a council internship. Saddled with all the head-cases and outcasts no one else wanted. But he wasn't like the others. He wasn't trying to score points. He just wanted to help me. To make me better. Which was something new for me.

'Tony, are you ghost haunting again?'

Rocked by the unexpected question, I'm immediately on the defensive. 'What's that got to do with anything?'

'Because I believe these things are linked. Whenever you feel overcome by, as you say 'these feelings', you also feel the need to conduct your investigations.' As he speaks, he taps the end of his pen on his clipboard. I'm sure the frequency of the tapping changes, depending on how much he's trying to annoy me. 'Which only contributes toward heightening and intensifying your negative feelings.' He holds my eye. 'They feed off each other until you're left feeling the way you do now.'

'And how is that?' I snap.

He searches for the right word before he replies. 'Lost.' I shake my head. I'm not having this, but Sharman isn't letting up. 'Something has happened hasn't it? Something has triggered these recent attacks. It's been a long time since you've experienced anything so severe.' I look away, unable to hold his eye. 'You know we have to deal with this issue. We have to talk about it.'

I've heard enough. 'I just need something to set me straight, get me back on track.' I glare back at him even though he's practically just a silhouette against the sunlight. Like a priest, barely discernible behind his confessional screen. And just like a priest, it's now his turn to remain silent as he waits me out.

'Just this once,' I plead.

He takes a deep breath. 'You know I can't do that, Tony.'

He's started with the patronising monotone. It's meant to calm me down, but it does anything but. 'You can, you have before.' Tears are welling in my eyes.

'That was a long time ago. Things are different now.'

'Why's it different? You said you'd always be there if I needed help. And I need your help now! For Christ's sake, it's your job isn't it? Don't you have to help me?' I hate myself for begging, for whining like a kid. I shouldn't be like this anymore. I should be stronger.

He leans forward, distorting the pattern of sunlight around his silhouette. 'I want to help you, Tony. But I need to understand what's happening to you. Why there's been this sudden change? Thirty years is a long time to bury your feelings. To repress your memories. You have to try to release them naturally, or they'll just keep forcing themselves to the surface. We need to talk about it.'

Here we go again. 'That's all you ever do. Fucking talk! I'm in pain here! How can I talk about it? It wasn't me then. I'm no longer that person. I don't even remember who that person was.' Sharman is silent as he waits for me to calm down. 'Will you just help me? Please.'

'Of course Tony, that's what I'm here for.' He tilts his head to the side. 'How about we take a fresh approach?' he suggests. 'In order to find out what's going wrong now. I suggest we first go back to where it all began.'

And there it is. He's like that is Dr Sharman. He always wants something for something.

So we go back. To the one place I don't want to go.

***

Mid-seventies news footage: A rain soaked reporter stands in front of a limp police tape cordon. Behind him, a solitary policeman lingers by a parked patrol car. Far in the background, a woodland path leads off into the trees.

In stark contrast to his bedraggled appearance, the reporter's tone is keen and precise. 'Today police confirmed the two bodies discovered at the base of the Ashwood Forest Viaduct were those of Ruth Babcock and her teenage daughter Tracey. This follows yesterday's confirmation that another body found at the Babcock home was that of Ruth's husband, Chris Babcock.'

Footage of a fire-damaged semi-detached council house briefly replaces the shot of the reporter. 'These recent events have reignited the media frenzy that has surrounded the family following a series of popular articles run by the sensationalist magazine Strange Frontier.'

The image changes to a man in his mid-thirties with shoulder length hair and long sideburns. Dressed in a smart flecked wool jacket and waistcoat, he pushes through a throng of excited reporters as he leaves a smart London office. His exit is further hindered by several huge piles of rotting rubbish stacked along the pavement.

'The magazine's editor Lawrence Ashby has so far been unavailable for comment.'

4. Rouge Shadows

Dark areas where there should be light. Fleeting shapes and unexplained shadows that seem to move when all else is still. Many times these shadows have vaguely human forms, although they may appear less distinguishable or smaller in physical statue. These so-called shadow people come in a large variety of manifestations. Dark spectres, vague coalescing outlines, eerie black masses, menacing silhouettes in human form. Some are clearer, with more distinct features. But even then; only a brief fleeting glimpse of a moving shadow is likely to be seen.

***

A torrent of filthy rain water cascaded down through the gutters of Bull Inn Court, toward the open grates of The Strand below. The narrow passageway, squashed between the high walls of the Adelphi and Vaudeville theatres, widened out just enough in the middle to allow a small group of rain drenched tourists to gather around a tall, imposing tour guide.

While most of the tourists shivered under soaking Kagools or emergency macs, the charismatic guide had dressed more appropriately for the volatile English weather. Donned in a full-length Stockman wax coat and matching wide-brimmed hat, he spoke clearly and eloquently, as he recounted the sinister history of the group's current location.

With evening creeping in, a string of Edwardian, wall mounted gas lamps had flickered on, illuminating the walkway with a spooky, yet atmospheric ambience, despite the alleyway smelling unerringly like a urinal.

Sheltering under her compact umbrella, Jo wandered closer to the edge of the group, just as the guide was concluding a colourful tale of a murder and vengeance, concerning a nineteenth century actor, who, according to the guide, had died, 'just yards from this very spot.' Although judging by his careful use of the phrase '*just yards from this very spot*'. Jo felt it more probable the unfortunate performer had, in fact died '*a fair distance from this very spot.*' Presumably at a location with far less atmospheric lighting.

Announcing a brief break in the tour, the guide swiftly disappeared around the end of the alleyway. Following him out into The Strand, Jo spotted the tall figure disappearing behind two red phone boxes by the side of the road. Moving up behind him, Jo tapped the guide on the shoulder. 'Uncle Lawrence.'

Caught unawares, the guide gagged on the whisky he'd been slyly sipping from an ornate hip flask.

Swinging around, Lawrence displayed only the briefest flicker of uncertainty before an enormous grin broke across his face. 'Jo-Jo. I thought we were meeting in the pub afterwards?'

Amused by the use of her old childhood nickname, Jo smiled awkwardly as Lawrence furtively slipped the hip flask back into his coat pocket.

'I thought I'd swing by a bit early and catch you in action.'

'You should have said. You could have tagged along for the entire walk. 'London Ghosts by Gas Light' is one of my best tours.'

With no real initiation from either side, they hugged.

Still clasping her hands Lawrence took a step back as he gave Jo a full head-to-toe appraisal. 'My God,' he said poignantly, 'You look just like your mother.'

Jo had accompanied Lawrence on the last part of the tour. Which had culminated in a small bar close to Covent Garden. A garish modern refurb decorated to resemble a traditional 'Ye Olde English' pub, right down to the hanging yard of ale glasses, horse brasses, and reproduction fox hunting prints. After a quick glance around, Jo had found a couple of empty seats by the imitation log fireplace.

Up at the bar, a small group of lingering tourists were busy plying Lawrence with several large whisky drams, in exchange for a few extra ghostly anecdotes.

As Lawrence laughed and joked, Jo was pleased to see her godfather had lost none of his old vigour, charisma, or charm. His wild hair had thinned a little, but his clothes were still as bold and eye-catching as she remembered. As a child Lawrence had always reminded her of a flamboyant school teacher or eccentric university lecturer. Elegant and urbane. An unbridled mix of spontaneous enthusiasm and calm authority.

Right now, Jo couldn't help but wish for a little of his apparent bonhomie. She felt drained and exhausted, having spent the entire day being dragged from one long production meeting to the next, being introduced to an endless procession of Dark Dimension personal and contractors.

After Belo Misha had jumped at the chance to get his house on television, Gillian's team had burst into a flurry of activity. Preparation for the shoot had begun in earnest and a location recce organised for later that week. Jo had been welcomed enthusiastically into the fold. Due, no doubt, to the fact she was now known to be an old friend of Gillian.

The only person Jo had yet to meet had been Max Schaffer himself, but according to Jacob, Max never came in for production meetings as he preferred to keep himself 'untainted' for the filming dates. Whatever that meant.

Gillian had decreed her team would deal with all aspects of the shoot, while Jo would concentrate on research. As she had, as Gillian had termed it, *a certain history* with the story. She'd been particularly keen for Jo to dig up as much background on the events surrounding the original haunting as she could, presumably in order to tie those events with the current paranormal activity occurring in the house.

Over at the bar, Lawrence made an apologetic gesture, which Jo waved away affably. Having already concluded this post tour drink was probably as much a part of the evening's entertainment as the walk itself.

Hearing Lawrence's voice resonating across the bar brought back a flood of pleasant memories for Jo. Not a real uncle by birth, but an adopted uncle by choice. Lawrence had been a prominent figure in Jo's childhood. Whilst most of her parents' friends had been dour and serious. Lawrence had always found time for her. Indulging in all her childish games and interests.

In those days, he'd had flair and panache by the bucket load. He would come to their house, either working with her father or socialising with other colleagues. Drinking and laughing with her parents until the small hours of the morning. On these nights, Jo would creep out onto the landing and listen through the ornate wooden balustrade to the grownups downstairs. Enjoying the sound of their laughter and feeling part of their adult lives.

Then it had all changed.

Jo still recalled that last night. She'd been sitting in her usual place by the balustrade. There had been no laughter that night, instead a heated argument had raged below. She remembered feeling scared and disturbed by the loud cursing as Lawrence and her father had raged at each other.

Only after Lawrence had stormed from the house had Jo sensed her mother's presence behind her on the landing. She'd turned to her, confused and shaken, unable to understand why she had just stood by and done nothing? Jo's mother had barely acknowledged Jo's concern before gently touching her daughter on the shoulder and turning away.

There had been an expression on her mother's face that night that had puzzled Jo, even to this day. A distant look of painful resignation.

With that, Lawrence had left their lives forever.

Well, not entirely. Jo still received the odd birthday or Christmas card from him and on the day of her graduation she'd received an enormous bouquet, along with a brief note of congratulations. It wasn't excessive or overbearing but in this considered way Lawrence had remained a peripheral presence in Jo's life.

Plying himself away from the remaining tourists, Lawrence took his seat by the 'Ye Olde' gas fire. 'Sorry about all that,' he apologised with a vague *what can you do* shrug.

'Not a problem. I was early anyway.' Glancing around the pub, she smiled. 'This is all rather cosy.'

'Isn't it,' Lawrence agreed. 'I occasionally stay on here after a walk.' His playful smirk implying that by 'occasionally,' he actually meant 'always.'

Outside the rain was now hammering against the window-panes. 'I hope you don't mind me calling you out of the blue like this,' Jo asked as Lawrence settled back in his chair and took a sip from the whisky glass he was cradling in his hand. 'Of course not. It's been far too long. In fact, I haven't seen you since...' he fell silent.

'The funeral,' Jo said with a humourless half-smile.

'Ah, has it really been that long?' Lawrence said wistfully.

Although her father had requested a small, intimate burial for Jo's mother, the church had been packed with a swathe of literary and publishing luminaries. Scouring the benches

64

for a friendly face, Jo had spotted Lawrence sitting in a far corner. He'd given her a reassuring smile but had declined an open invitation to return to the house afterwards. To the best of Jo's knowledge he and her father hadn't even acknowledged each other during the service.

'So how did Frank take your leaving the firm?'

'Well, you know,' Jo said with a dispassionate shrug. Lawrence nodded solemnly, grasping the undertone implied by Jo's dismissive answer.

In actuality, Frank had accepted Jo's resignation with the same gruff indifference he had received all of Jo's suggestions and proposals. He had barely glanced at it before callously discarding it to one side. 'It was just a matter of time,' he had huffed, turning his attention to a folded print proof on his desk. 'Another rat deserting the sinking ship.'

Fuming and overwhelmed with guilt, Jo had bitten her lip and marched from her father's office.

And that had been that. She had cut herself loose from her father's world. Only to be back, just days later, digging through it all again. An ironic twist she was sure had not gone unnoticed by Lawrence. 'It looks popular, the walk,' Jo remarked glibly, as she attempted to break the mood and move the conversation away from her father, if only momentarily.

'People love a good ghost story,' Lawrence said, relieved at the change of topic. 'Especially the Americans. They love all the history. The dark, luscious Victorian melodrama. All those creaking floorboards and creepy gas lamp séances.' Lawrence smiled as he took another sip of whisky. 'And talking of ancient history.' He gestured toward the card folder

Jo had placed on the table between them. 'How's the research going?'

'To be honest, I've only just started,' Jo admitted. 'This is all I've got so far, but I'd be glad of anything you can tell me.' She passed Lawrence the thin file of photocopied articles. 'I'm trying to get as much background on the original haunting as I can.'

'Let me guess, you're especially interested in any personal stuff that wasn't made public.'

'That's right.'

It took a moment for Jo to decipher the mischievous grin on Lawrence's face. 'They want this stuff for their psychic.'

'Bingo.'

Jo groaned, not only because of the obvious rouse Gillian had sent her on but also the ease Lawrence had tumbled it. 'Lawrence I didn't...'

Lawrence held his palms up in mock submission. 'Don't worry about it. It comes with the territory. But in all honesty I don't think there's much I can tell you that isn't in here.' He tapped the folder with his knuckle. 'I hardly had any direct contact with the family and we only ever published what Patrick Milgallon gave us.'

'So there was nothing you didn't publish?'

'Nothing at all, any extra stuff Patrick used for his own book.'

'Means I'm gonna have to finish this then,' Jo said, reaching into her handbag. Lawrence huffed as she produced a frayed copy of *Broken Spirits* and passed it over the table. With an amused smile, Lawrence turned it over in his hands, as if he hadn't seen a copy in years.

It had taken only a quick search in a second-hand book-store in Tottenham Court Road for Jo to unearth a frayed edition of Patrick Milgallon's book. Barely into Chapter Four, she was already struggling with it. Constantly losing its way with endless contradiction and needless speculation, the book continually veered off into elaborate conjecture and unwarranted supposition.

A bemused smile appeared on Lawrence's face as he spotted the large black-and-white photograph of Milgallon printed on the back cover. An outlandish image of an eccentric-looking man, flamboyantly dressed with a full bouffant of hair and a lush Zapata moustache.

The photographer's aim had clearly been to portray the book's author in a mysterious, yet charismatic light, but ultimately Milgallon had come off looking weirdly camp and uncomfortable. 'You probably don't remember but you met him quite a few times,' Lawrence said, noticing Jo's own curiosity at the image.

'I did?'

'Your house was a bit of a working commune back then. We did as much work there as we did at the office. Plus, it was just around the corner from the Royal Free Hospital, so it never suffered from the power-cuts in the evenings. I should think you were about four or five then. I remember your father liked to spend as much time at home with you as could back then.'

That came as a surprise to Jo. Her own memory of her father from that time was somewhat different. She always recalled him as rather grumpy and distant back then, with little interest in her childish pursuits.

'Come to think of it,' Lawrence continued. 'He occasionally let you sit in on some meetings. Reaching down into a worn canvas bag he had retrieved earlier from behind the bar, Lawrence produced a thick, dogeared reference book:

HAUNTED LONDON

'I use this for my tours,' he said in a conspiratorial tone as he opened it to a page marked with one of his tour flyers.

Chapter 17

The Babcock Haunting

'This one's far more concise than Milgallon's thing, plus it goes into much more detail about the aftermath of the hauntings. There you go.' As he passed the book over to Jo, he tapped a photograph of Jo's father, taken in the seventies, along with Lawrence and the man Jo now recognised as Patrick Milgallon. They were all sitting together in the front lounge of her parents' house in Hampstead.

The image was surprising enough, but nothing compared to the appearance of the young child sitting on her father's lap.

'Oh, my God!'

'Thought you might like that.'

Jo was genuinely surprised by the photo and by her own appearance in it.

'And these may be of help to you.' Lawrence pulled a thick binder from his canvas bag and passed it to Jo. Inside Jo found several copies of *Strange Frontier Magazine*, each featuring an article about The Babcock Haunting. 'There's not much in there that isn't in Milgallon's book, but you might find them useful.'

'This is fantastic,' Jo admitted. 'There was none of this stuff back at the office.'

'I'm not surprised. I shouldn't think your father would consider it one of the magazine's finest moments.'

'Was it really that bad? Dad refuses to talk about it.'

Lawrence shrugged. 'Well, for a while it looked like he might lose the business over it,' he said solemnly. 'But Frank, being Frank, managed to save himself in the end.'

Jo immediately bristled at Lawrence's sudden animosity toward her father. Although there may have been some merit to Lawrence's hostility, Jo knew for a fact that her father hadn't been solely responsible for Lawrence's ultimate undoing. Over the years, she'd heard numerous stories about his unreasonable behaviour. That he was difficult to work with, belligerent, stubborn and uncompromising. She'd also heard the rumours of his recreational drug use and extra material affairs, which had all contributed to his inevitable downfall.

Pushing aside her rising animosity, Jo tapped the file appreciatively as she placed it on the table. 'Well, this is great. It could give me some real insight into what happened.'

Lawrence flashed Jo a dismissive half-smile. As he held her eye, there was a haunting familiarity to his gaze, almost as if he was gazing at someone else entirely. Feeling a tad uncomfortable, Jo gulped down the last of her vodka and orange and begun crunching on the few remaining ice cubes.

Snapping out of his brief malaise, Lawrence gestured toward the barman. 'Here, let me get you another.'

A few minutes later, two fresh drinks arrived at their table. Which, like their earlier order, were conspicuously free of charge. The result, no doubt, of some unvoiced agreement between Lawrence and the management. Remunerations for providing the pub with a regular succession of tired and thirsty patrons, three times a week.

'As I say I'm not sure I can tell you much about the haunting that isn't already known,' Lawrence said, reaching for his glass. 'Well, nothing that's going to interest Max Schaffer, that is.'

A distinct edge had crept into Lawrence's tone, but Jo let it slip. 'I'd still like to hear about it from you. If you don't mind.'

After a moment's contemplation, Lawrence gave a conciliatory shrug. 'Well, I suppose I have time for one last ghost story.'

As Jo waited, Lawrence lent back in his chair. Milking the moment for all it was worth. 'We can separate the events into two distinct events,' he finally begun. 'The haunting itself and the tragedy that followed. If you don't mind, I'll contain myself to just the haunting, as it's the only part of the story I have any real firsthand knowledge of.'

Placing the base of his glass in his palm, he began slowing rotating it. 'During the summer of seventy-three, an old couple living next-door to the Babcock's called the police to complain about the terrible screaming they could hear coming through the wall of their council house.'

As Lawrence spoke, Jo glanced down at a photograph in the book he had just given her. An elderly couple standing in front of their sixties style council house. The old man's hand, pointing toward the neighbouring house, an identical semi-detached with large square windows.

'Normally, the couple would've just ignored the commotion. They knew the family far too well. Their neighbour, Chris Babcock, was known to drink and the occasional violent argument with his wife was not uncommon. However, on this night, the screaming had been so extreme it had been too much for them to bear.

'But when the police arrived, it turned out Chris Babcock hadn't even been at home that night. He'd been working a late shift at a local dairy. The noises the old couple had heard had been coming from the Babcock's oldest child, Tracey. That's when it all came out. For months the family had been tormented by a poltergeist.'

Lawrence lifted his glass and took a quick sip before continuing. 'The disturbances had been occurring on and off for several months and had always centred around Tracey, although other members of the family also claimed to have witnessed strange activity in the house. The youngest child had even given the poltergeist a name. He called it 'Mr Nox', because of all the banging noises he made. The children also claimed it would appear to them as a black silhouette. They said it would watch them from their bedroom doorway.

'Well, I had a source in the Met who put me onto the story. The whole thing was ideal for us. It had everything we could ask for; family turmoil, paranormal activity, plus all the extra menace that accompanies a poltergeist haunting. Of course Chris Babcock didn't want to know at first, but a little negotiating and a sly cash deal persuaded him to allow one of our people into the house.' Lawrence lent forward and tapped the back of Milgallon's book. 'Patrick Milgallon was a paranormal eccentric we used on some of our features. *'An expert in the occult says'* that sort of thing. Harmless enough, or so we thought. We paid him to pad out the story a bit, jazz it up for the magazine and give it a bit of colour.'

Lawrence held his hand in the air to quell any potential condemnation from Jo. 'Now, before you jump to any conclusions; we didn't fabricate anything, but....' he tilted his head to one side. 'We were required to tidy the story up a bit.'

A disapproving glare from Jo forced Lawrence to elaborate further. 'Understand, back then people were looking for escapism. The early seventies was a bleak time. Everything was in turmoil. The country was being ravished by rampant inflation, mass unemployment, IRA bombings and football hooligans. Everyone was on strike. Rubbish was rotting on the pavements and London was being overrun with rats. The country seemed to be on the brink of disaster. We couldn't even qualify for the World Cup.

'Up to this point, *Strange Frontier* had been publishing a lot of stuff on archaeology, folklore, myth and magic. Quite dull and with a limited readership. I'd been pushing for more sensationalist content, UFO abductions, conspiracies, weird sex cults, and the fresh approach was paying off. Our sales were on the rise. People were looking for the extraordinary. A tatty little story about a mentally unstable teenager screaming at a bedroom wall wasn't going to sell many copies.'

Ignoring Jo's reproving expression, Lawrence quickly continued. 'Well, the articles immediately resonated with our readers. The family's fear and uncertainty seemed to reflect the worry and pessimism the entire country was experiencing at the time. We began running a feature in every issue. Updating the readers on the investigation. Concocting possible identities of the ghost. It was all going very well.'

Lawrence shifted uncomfortably in his seat. 'The only thing we didn't bank on was Milgallon.'

'He overdid it?'

'That's an understatement,' Lawrence huffed. 'He turned the whole thing into a sodding circus. He got all sorts of people involved from his *psychic* institute and then the television companies picked up on it and we lost control of the story completely.

'Not that it mattered to Patrick. He thought the whole damn thing would be his ticket to scientific validity. He was forever cropping up on various TV shows, peddling one outlandish theory after another. For a while he became quite the paranormal mainstay. That is until, by sheer stupid bad luck he got himself nabbed for gross indecency in the gents' toilet in Paddington Station.'

Jo couldn't help but notice the obvious glee in Lawrence's tone as he described Milgallon's abrupt fall from grace. 'That put an end to both his media career and his academic aspirations right there and then. God knows what he's doing now. If he's even still alive.'

But any satisfaction Lawrence may have been experiencing regarding Milgallon's past misfortunes evaporated the moment he glimpsed the obvious disillusionment on his god-daughter's face.

Lawrence gave a deep sigh and his voice became sullen. 'Well, considering what happened to that family, I guess we all got what we deserved in the end.'

Jo leant forward, clearly stifling the urge to enquire further into the circumstances of the tragedy Lawrence had alluded to earlier. After a moment's solemn reflection, Lawrence gave a consenting tilt of his head.

'So what happened?' Jo asked.

Lawrence shrugged. 'We allowed ourselves to ignore the obvious. The fact it was a poltergeist case should have rung some alarm bells for a start.'

'I don't understand.'

A thin smile appeared on Lawrence's lips. 'Remember those apparitions I mentioned earlier? The ones the Victorians loved so much. Ethereal spectres, seen only by gaslight. Well, in reality, those apparitions were merely the result of the gas lamps themselves. It was discovered the carbon monoxide emitted from the lamps could provoke hallucinations and delirium.' Jo still looked unsure as to the relevance of this information. 'My point is,' Lawrence went on. 'We all get the ghost our environment provides for us.'

'And what kind of environment produced the Babcock poltergeist?'

'Not a very pleasant one.' Lawrence slumped back in his chair dolefully. 'You have to understand that a poltergeist haunting is a very different animal to your normal run-of-the-mill ghost sighting. With a ghost we simply observe it. It's just there, like an echo of the past. Whether we choose to engage with it or not is our own choice. But a poltergeist haunting is an intrusion, an assault. You're not only observers of the event, you're part of it, you're a victim of it. While the aristocracy love to revel in their ancestral ghosts, working class hauntings are more of an affliction.'

Falling silent, Lawrence let his gaze drift toward the imitation flames flickering in the fireplace.

'What were they like?' Jo asked wistfully.

The question took Lawrence by surprise until he noticed Jo's gaze had fallen upon another photo illustration in the book on her lap. An awkward family portrait of Babcocks posing together in their living room, the youngest child hiding his face behind the pleats of his mother's skirt.

'The Babcocks? Well, now there's a question,' Lawrence said, rubbing his thumb against the side of his glass. 'On the surface they appeared to be a typical working class family, which I suppose was part of their appeal. It was also the image we tried to cultivate in the articles. We wanted them to be relatable to the average reader.'

'I take it from your tone they were far from that.'

'As I mentioned earlier, there were certain aspects about the family we had to conceal. Stuff that would have made them, well, less sympathetic. Chris Babcock liked a drink. He also fancied himself as a bit of a ladies' man and had quite the reputation for it. In fact, he didn't care who knew. He could turn on the charm when he wanted to and he used to sing at a local working men's club, where he revelled in his newfound notoriety. He also had a volatile temper, especially after a few pints, which would land him in all kinds of bother. But like I said, he had a certain charm and always managed to wangle himself out of any serious trouble.'

'Even with his wife?'

'Well, that's where he had an advantage and why he got away with as much as he did. Ruth was an agoraphobic.'

'Agoraphobic? As in, she couldn't leave the house?'

'Well, she could, but it depended on how bad she was feeling. The condition got better or worse depending on how much anxiety she was experiencing.'

'Which I imagine would have been quite considerable.'

'To put it mildly. Can you image a worse scenario? An anxiety riddled agoraphobic trapped inside a haunted house.'

Pleased with the witticism, Lawrence left it hanging a moment before taking up the story again. 'But agoraphobia was only one symptom of her condition. Where Chris was outgoing and sociable, Ruth was the complete opposite. She was insecure, skittish and oversensitive. She was never diagnosed, but I would guess she suffered from some form of social anxiety disorder. Back then, most physiological disorders in the working class were simply dismissed as an inevitable consequence of their situation. Many differing conditions were just lumped together and treated with one course of medication.'

'So what? They just prescribed drugs for her?'

'To her and to the children. We didn't make that public, of course. We played down Ruth's mania and never mentioned Chris's philandering.'

With a solemn shrug, Lawrence gestured for Jo to flip to the next page of her book. Printed on the page was a photograph of Ruth Babcock praying at home with members of the Hackney Christen Society. The harsh glare of a magnesium flashbulb undermining any intended ethereal ambiance.

'Of course, the whole thing had a detrimental effect on Ruth's mental health. Her anxiety transformed into delusional paranoia. She became convinced evil spirits were possessing the children. She and the family begun attending a local christen society, letting them hold spiritual meetings in the house. The society put an end to the magazine articles and Milgallon was refused entry into the property. So that, from our point of view, would have been that!'

Lawrence paused a moment for dramatic effect. A trick, no doubt honed from his many ghost tours. 'About a month later, Ruth had a complete breakdown and what would have remained a minor tabloid story became a major media sensation. The police, social services, the local authority, all got dragged into it. Everyone blamed everyone else. The whole thing was a total mess.'

Jo flipped the page again. The last page of Chapter 17 displayed a police photograph of two blanket covered bodies laying at the base of a tall railway viaduct. Lawrence had again fallen silent but this time it wasn't merely for effect. He appeared genuinely saddened by his own disclosure.

'What caused her to do it?' Jo asked in a tentative tone.

'Ruth? Do you mean what finally tipped her over the edge?'

Jo wasn't sure if Lawrence had intended this pun as a joke. With each whisky, his attitude had become increasingly cavalier. 'Who knows?' Lawrence huffed dismissively. 'There was the inevitable backlash of course. The public; who only a few months before had been lapping this stuff up, were suddenly outraged by it all. Milgallon was ridiculed and rebuked as a gullible crank. As editor of the original articles, I was thrown to the wolves. Within a year, I'd lost my job and all my credibility.' Lawrence's head sagged downwards, as the combined effect of his excessive self-pity and alcohol consumption finally took its toll.

As Lawrence stared morosely down at his whisky, Jo took a delicate sip from her own glass. The first time she had done so, without him accompanying her.

'And that, as they say was that,' Lawrence concluded glumly, twisting his glass in his hand.

'Until now.'

'Oh, let's not get carried away here,' Lawrence sniped irritably. 'The whole Babcock haunting was nothing more than an elaborate hoax perpetrated by Tracey Babcock and exaggerated to ridiculous lengths by Patrick Milgallon!' Huffing, Lawrence lent back in his chair. 'But this new haunting does lead me to the obvious question, though.' He fixed Jo with a long, ponderous glare. 'Is this something you should be doing?'

Jo felt her hackles raising. '*Me* personally or as part of the television programme?'

'Either,' Lawrence shrugged.

'And why should that matter?'

'Because sometimes, the best thing you can do with a mistake is to leave it alone.'

'It wasn't *my* mistake.'

Lawrence tilted his head ruefully, refusing to be put off by Jo's sudden indignation. 'Well, not yet.'

'I think that's down to me don't you?' Jo countered, with far more animosity than she had intended.

'Hey,' Lawrence said in a surprisingly placating tone. 'I'm only thinking of you here. I mean I wouldn't want you to rush into anything now, only to regret it later. I mean, have you seen any actual proof other than this family's say so?'

'They've made some videos.'

'Of?'

'The girl sleepwalking, having nightmares. I know it doesn't sound like much I admit, but it's very compelling.'

'And you say there's been no other activity in the house since the Babcocks?'

Jo was more prepared for this question. 'Well, maybe be-cause in the intervening years the house was occupied by a couple of pensioners. Maybe they just didn't notice or they put it down to something else.'

'Like dementia?'

In a fit of frustration, Jo threw her hands in the air. 'I would've thought you of all people would be more receptive to the possibility of the paranormal.'

'Because of the ghost walk,' Lawrence scoffed. 'See that lot over there,' he nodded toward the last remaining tourists, still lingering up at the bar. 'For them, it's all a bit of fun. They just like the idea of the supernatural. They like all the spooky stories and the history. But deep down they know it's all just hogwash.' Lawrence shrugged as his demeanour hardened. 'But there are people who take this stuff seriously. For them, it's very real. And no amount of rational explanation will ever persuade them to the contrary.'

Jo shook her head dismissively. 'But you should see the girl. The family seems genuinely freighted.'

'And you think putting them on television is going to help them any?'

'No more than splashing them across the cover of a magazine!'

It took a moment before Lawrence accepted Jo's jibe with a conciliatory tilt of the head. 'Touché,' he muttered gruffly, draining the last of his whisky. 'I'm just saying you should be cautious. These people may be frauds or they may actually believe they have a ghost in their house. But you must be certain what you're dealing with before you get too involved. You don't have to take my advice. But do yourself a favour. Before your TV crew gets in there and messes everything up, do your own research. Here...' he rummaged in his pocket and pulled out a crumpled business card. 'Give this guy a call and get him to have a look first.'

Jo threw a cynical glance at the card. 'A paranormal investigator?'

'Believe me, if anyone that can tell you what's going on in that house. It's this guy.'

Mid-seventies television footage: The camera follows a tightknit group of researchers as they conduct an scientific investigation in a suburban living room.

Over the shot, we hear the voice of a male reporter. 'The investigation has been ongoing for several nights now. The children particularly have been enjoying the attention.'

The shot cuts to a suave-looking man in a silk shirt and cravat, as he records the reactions of two young children with a Super 8 movie camera. 'Patrick Milgallon is a noted psychic researcher and a self-proclaimed expert on the occult and supernatural. We can see him here with other members of the Paranormal Research Institute, setting up for tonight's vigil.' Behind Milgallon other researchers can be seen adjusting equipment and taking readings from small handheld devices.

The shot switches to a face-to-face interview with Patrick Milgallon.

Milgallon is smoking during the interview and appears confident and relaxed in front of the camera. His polished diction and lofty bearing the product of a privileged Oxbridge education. 'I think people's conception of reality is changing. Traditional barriers are being broken down. People are becoming more responsive to all the different aspects of existence.'

'You've come under a lot of criticism recently, concerning the validity of your research here.'

'Let me be clear, this is a very real and important scientific study.' Milgallon leans towards the reporter, his manner increasingly defensive. 'It's easy for people to jump to any number of incorrect conclusions when they don't understand what they're actually witnessing.'

'And what about you? Have you witnessed anything yourself?'

This question annoys Milgallon, but he's all too aware he's on camera. 'That's not how the spirits have chosen to reveal themselves,' he answers in a haughty tone.

'So other than the children's say-so. Has there been any actual evidence found?'

'We are collecting new information every day. It's still an ongoing investigation.'

'But you're convinced what you're investigating here is real.'

'After extensive testing, I can categorically state these are genuine occurrences and I am convinced that very soon we will have undeniable proof of paranormal activity in this house.'

The shot cuts to the reporter standing outside the house speaking directly to camera. 'For the time being, the mystery surrounding the strange, unexplained phenomena occurring here at number twenty-seven Clifton Close remains unresolved. But who knows, in the future, maybe the truth will reveal itself. That is; if the *spirit* is willing.'

5. Cries and Whispers

Hearing muffled voices or music can be a sign spirits have entered your home and are trying to communicate with you.

The person experiencing this kind of phenomena may also hear names being called, or a conversation happening in the next room or even the sound of breathing in the close vicinity.

Even hearing your own name whispered is not uncommon and can be a clear indication that a spirit is close by and is trying to communicate directly with you.

***

The Virgin Mary stares off into the rafters, oblivious to my presence.

Ain't that always the way?

Gazing away from her water damaged cheeks and peeling paintwork, I glance down at the E.M.F. detector.

Zilch.

Rubbing the back of my neck, I stare despondently around the old church.

There's no real reason I'm here. Just hoping to catch something by chance, before they convert this dump into luxury apartments. Judging by the state of the place, I'm not the only lost soul to have found their way in here. There's graffiti splashed across the wall and a stained mattress in the presbytery. Filthy syringes lay scattered in the aisles and there's a dark pool of liquid by the pulpit that I'd rather not think about.

It's late evening. Already the light is fading beyond the boarded windows. There's a certain consensus amongst paranormal investigators that the human psyche is more susceptible to psychic influence during the nighttime, that our senses become more heightened during the hours of darkness. Not that I'm likely to spend the night in here. Far too scary. Even for me.

I take one last look at the Blessed Mother. She's almost life-sized. Perched upon a waist-high pedestal. It's a fine piece of work and I can see how she would've inspired the faithful back in the day. Not that I've got much time for that sort of thing. When you've been through what I have; you can't help but question the existence of a benevolent Almighty.

Still, it would be nice to believe life isn't merely a series of cruel, random, unpredictable occurrences. That there is purpose and meaning to everything. I follow the Virgin's gaze. But there's nothing there. The space behind the altar is empty. They're gutting the church bit by bit. Looks like Jesus was one of the first things to go. Apart from Mary, the only other effigy left is a statue of St Joseph. He's also gazing mournfully at the space behind the altar. His despondent chagrin, cruelly ridiculed by the addition of a brightly coloured hard hat, precariously balanced on his head. A callous portent to the church's and his own eventual fate.

Kneeling down to replace the E.M.F. back into my kitbag, I'm struck by a sudden compulsion. I'm drawn again to the space behind the altar, where Jesus should be suffering on the cross. And even though he's doing his suffering some place else now, for a moment I'm tempted. But in this same instant, I'm aware of my own hypocrisy. My unequivocal belief in an afterlife, conflicting with my ardent disbelief in a compassionate god. If I can accept one exists, surely I have to accept the existence of the other, however begrudgingly.

Tentatively, I my hands come together. If only I could believe there was someone there. Someone watching over me...

Shuffling footsteps behind me. I turn and there he is. Shabby donkey jacket and dungarees.

The fucker!

His face twitches as he approaches. With his greasy hair and thick-rimmed glasses, it's like he's trying to make himself look ridiculous. 'Tony, Tony B-b-babcock. I've b-b-been trying to reach you.'

He's avoiding direct eye contact, which only annoys me more. Snatching my kitbag from the floor, I toss it over my shoulder. 'I told you before you've got the wrong man. My name is Vail, Antony Vail.'

As I bundle past the fat bastard, he turns and yells after me. 'Oh, it may be now b-but that's not what it used to be.'

Behind the church, a tube train rattles over a neighbouring overpass. Cutting through a row of the grubby spray-shops, Norris isn't far behind. 'I know everything a-bout you,' he wheezes, as he struggles to keep up with me. 'I know what really happened to you and your family.'

'How could you possibly know what happened to me?' I yell back at him.

'Because your sister told me!'

Grinding to a halt, he barrels straight into me. Snatching his filthy jacket, I slam him backwards against a filthy buttress. Struggling to break free, he topples over. My knee slams into his gut as we both hit the dirt.

Scrambling to my feet, I leave him groaning on the deck. 'Listen, you fat shit! My sister is dead. Do you understand me? Dead!' I freeze on the spot, as I hear my own words. 'She's dead.' Glaring down at Norris, I stagger backwards. From the state of his face, I must have hit him. And hit him more than once. His lip is spilt and there's blood gushing from his nose. I stare at my raw knuckles, my mind a muddled blur.

A couple of mechanics appear from one of the archway garages, drawn by the sound of confrontation. Overwrought, I turn on my heel and stride away. Clutching his face, Norris calls after me. 'She needs you, To-tony! She needs you...'

My walk turns into a run.

I'm speeding through the trees, my heart racing. I can feel the wind against my face; the exhilaration of speed. The euphoria of freedom. Tracey's behind me on her bike, whooping and laughing. We race each other into the woods.

Later, we climb through the broken railway fence and play hide and seek amongst the signal boxes and equipment sheds.

As evening creeps in, we lay together in the long grass watching the trains on the viaduct. It's getting dark and the sun has dropped behind the trees. In the autumn twilight, she turns her head and smiles. 'Don't worry. One day we'll never have to go back. It'll just be me and you.' She pulls me close and cradles me in her arms, as tears well in my eyes. 'But until then, you've got to be brave. Like this.' She opens her notebook. On the page is her drawing of me dressed as a soldier, with a tin hat and gun. 'See,' she says, rocking me gently, 'That's you. You're my little soldier. My brave little soldier.'

A tube train rattles overhead, barely masking the sound of my retching.

Every muscle in my body is throbbing. I gulp for breath as my head continues to spin.

It happened again. I lost control. I lost myself again.

I keep my fingertips pressed against the wall tiles as the train pulls into the station. The platform's clear so I'm able to make the carriage first try. Looking for something to occupy my mind, I grab a discarded newspaper and read a piece about Saddam's alleged nuclear arsenal under the headline:

Losing interest, I turn to the back page. Fulham beat West Brom three - nil. Not all bad news then. Tossing the paper aside, I turn toward the window and watch the cables snaking up and down on the tunnel wall.

A loud yell as I leave the train. Some fella dressed like a colour-blind forties gangster, complete with fedora and two-tone shoes. Laughing and singing at the top of his voice.

'I'm sitting on top of the world. Just rolling along, just rolling along.'

Darting across the platform, I touch the wall. Staring over at the daft spiv, my stomach churns.

At least he's happy in *his* mad world.

At Finsbury Park, Jeff's standing in a doorway, trying to look inconspicuous. It's late evening and he's attempting to use the shadows as camouflage. He's decked out in a riot of ridiculous streetwear, in an ill-judged attempt to blend in with the urban aesthetic. Yanking down his bandit scarf, he peers over his new Ray-bans. 'I'm in disguise!' he whines, miss-reading my sarcastic sneer.

'As what? My Little Gangster.'

He jumps on the spot as I hand him a wad of banknotes 'Christ, man, not out in the open!' Casting a panicked glance over my shoulder, he quickly pockets the cash and tries to slip me a pill bottle.

Seizing the opportunity to further mock the pretentious Oxbridge prat, I lift the bottle into the air and give it a quick rattle, pretending to inspect it. Jeff looks like he's about to have a stroke. Now I'm intrigued.

'What's wrong?'

'They're auditing the lab again. Asking questions. It's getting too risky. I think they're getting suspicious.'

I've already heard enough of his bullshit. 'So!'

A stray glance from a random passer-by cranks Jeff's anxiety up another notch. '*So* I'm going to have to cool it.'

That's it! Time to stop playing the fool. I grab Jeff's arm and twist him around to face me. 'We had an agreement. I need this stuff.'

'And I need to stay out of prison geeza!' He pulls his arm free and gives me a firm '*I'm serious*' glare. I hold his gaze, waiting for him to break, which he does within seconds. 'Look I'm up for a position in R&D and I can't avoid to fuck it up now. I've got my future to think of.'

'Yeah, well as long as you're okay!'

Fuck this twat! With his stupid disguises and his fake 'mockney' accent. Like I need this fucking clown. But I guess my face is telling a different story.

'Listen, man,' he says in a softer tone. 'Maybe when things cool down a bit.'

But I'm not having any of that bollocks.

'Don't do me any favours,' I snap, as I turn on my heel and stomp away.

Footsteps behind me. Dull heavy thuds, keeping step with me. I glance back.

Nothing. The road's empty. I prick my ear to the silence. Only the echo of distant traffic. Thrusting my hands deep inside my pockets, I keep walking.

There they are again. Footsteps. Deliberately trying to match my own to avoid detection. But I can clearly hear them over the soft tread of my Hush Puppies. Afraid to look back, I increase my pace as the footsteps match my stride. Soon I'm striding at a fast trot. Turning a corner, I barge straight into some fella coming the other way. 'Watch where you're going, mate,' he growls, as he pushes past me. Shaken, I mumble a weak apology and stare back down the road.

There's no one there. Turning I walk away.

Now all that follows me is silence.

I'm getting the evil eye from the Indian woman in the corner shop. She watches me like a hawk as I take each item from the shelf. In the corner, a small video camera is recording my every move. I can see myself on the monitor behind the counter. Scruffy and bedraggled, it's no wonder the woman's eying me with suspicion. I drop my groceries next to the till and she rings them up. Attempting to look less shifty, I force a smile, but I get nothing back.

Out in the street an angry drunk is shouting abuse at passers-by. Staggering and stooped he rages incoherently at a young couple as they hurry around him. Desperate to avoid confrontation, I keep my head down and stare at the pavement, but he lunges forward, catching my eye with a hostile glare. To my surprise, he remains silent and allows me to pass unmolested. As I reach the corner, he's still watching me. Maybe he doesn't know what to make of me. Or maybe he simply senses a kindred spirit.

The rattle of the old lift startles me awake. The television has entered standby mode and the studio is dark. I stretch in my chair. It must be two in the morning. Who the hell is creeping about at this hour? My bet is the graphic designer on the floor below. I've met her a few times in the lobby, heading out to some gaudy nightclub or restaurant.

I wait for the lift to stop on her floor, but it keeps on coming, shuddering to a halt on my landing with a dull thud. Who the hell is this? Mine is the only studio on this level. Listening for the occupant to realise they are on the wrong floor, I wait for the sound of the lift to descend back down again. Instead, the scissor gate clatters open and heavy footsteps echo along the hallway. Leaping from my chair and wearing only my T-shirt and boxers, I pad to the door in my bare feet.

I lean toward the peephole...

The entire door shudders from the impact of a heavy fist.

Christ almighty!

I leap backwards, my heart pounding.

A second bang, followed by another and then another, growing in strength. The whole door shakes in its frame as the banging becomes a mixture of violent punches and kicks.

What the actual fuck!

Reaching out, I grab the closest thing at hand; an unextended tripod from the rack. Hoisting it over my shoulder,

I take a defensive stance opposite the door, expecting it to burst open at any moment.

The banging stops, as abruptly as it started. Stunned into inaction, my arm muscles spasm and twitch as I wait for the next assault.

Nothing.

Creeping forward, I unhook the security chain. Turning my ear to the door, all I can hear is the harsh rasp of my own stunted breathing. Gripping the door handle, my hand freezes on the catch. Whoever it is. They could still be there. Hiding just out of sight of the peephole, waiting for me to appear. I'm tempted to push something heavy against the door and leave it at that. But a part of me needs to know what's out there. Forcing myself forward, I flip the catch and yank the door open. Wielding the tripod, I leap out into the hallway.

Nothing.

I spin around, searching the dark shadows, but the hallway is empty. Creeping along the landing, I stare into the lift. Empty; as is the stairwell.

What the hell!

I wait, motionless in the dark, the tripod shaking in my hands. Everything is silent.

Trudging back to my flat, I turn at my door. Something doesn't feel right. Something I'm missing.

Then I realise.

The lift gate is open.

Sharman taps his pen against his notebook. He always taps his pen when he's thinking. Either that or he just likes to piss me off.

The tapping stops.

'You've heard of hypnogogic visions?' he says pompously. 'They're hallucinations or vivid dreams that seem real. And they're usually experienced when we're at the point of just waking or falling asleep. Many people mistake these visions for ghost...'

I know where he's heading, so I cut straight to the chase. 'You're saying I want to see these things?'

Although riled by my interruption, Sharman continues in his usual measured tone. 'Maybe your subconscious is trying to tell you something. Remember all your natural defences are down while you're sleeping.'

'But why now?'

'Tony, you've spent a lifetime burying your feelings. Suppressing your memories. It's been your method of containing all the pain and confusion you hold within you. But the more you bury these emotions, the more they're forced to manifest into other forms.'

'You're asking me to do something I can't?'

'It's for your own good, Tony.'

'No, this is not helping me.' I shake my head. '*You're* not helping me.'

'I am helping you.'

'You know what I mean.'

He sits back in his chair. 'I can't prescribe you anything stronger,' he tells me bluntly.

'But I need it.'

'No, what you need is to—'

'Talk about it! That's all you ever want to fucking do!'

'That's all I can do.' Sharman smiles sympathetically as he waits for me to simmer down.

'Tony, what are you afraid of?'

It doesn't take me long to find a suitable answer.

'Everything.'

My heart sinks as I gaze around the cellar. This absolutely has to be the last time.

But I know I'll be back.

Upstairs Poundland Elvis is slaughtering *Guitar Man* with fierce determination. While down here in the dark, I run through my own tedious routine.

Flipping open my laptop, I reactive each of my recording programs. Sony PCG-705: It's a thin lightweight notebook with a long-battery-life. It cost a fortune and I'm still paying it off. But the notebook's DV connector allows me to capture high-quality images straight from the Handy-cam via a DV cable. And unlike most of my other stuff, it's extremely portable. Jerry lets me store all the bulky stuff down here during the week. All the tripods, extension leads and hard cases. Which means I don't have to keep lugging it all back and forth every night.

Unwinding a piece of cotton, I pin it across the bottom of the staircase. Standard procedure on an investigation. If it's broken in the morning, I'll know I've had visitors of a corporeal nature during the night. I also dust all the cupboard handles with talc, as well as the latches on the busted dumb-waiter. Again, it's less about identifying spirits and more about eliminating pranksters.

I leave the MiniDisc player for the moment. There's no chance of recording anything just yet, not with the constant din from upstairs. But I still make sure I've got a new disc in the cradle and the microphone and headphone jacks are inserted correctly. An audio recorder is essential. You think you hear all sorts of things during the night, only to play the recordings back in the morning to find there's nothing there. The same applies for the Handy-cam. What you see and what you think you see are far from the same thing. Shadows, orbs, fleeting shapes. Without hard evidence, it's all worthless. You can't rely solely on your own senses in this game. In fact, they're your biggest liability. You're constantly fighting your own expectations. You can deceive yourself a thousand times over. It's easily done.

Once I've finished setting the equipment, I take a moment to survey my handiwork. It's less than a minute before I have to retrace my steps and check everything again. Only after the second sweep can I relax. Leaning back in my camping chair, I listen to the monotonous dirge echoing overhead.

Are you lonesome tonight?

Well, there's a question.

I'll just rest my eyes a bit.

Tracey is laying amongst the long grass. The summer daisies dance in the breeze around her head. Her eyes open and she smiles. Staring directly at me, her lips move.

'Hear me!'

My body jolts as my eyes snap open. Apart from my own hoarse gasping, the cellar is as silent as the grave. Looks like Elvis has left the building.

I drag my hand across my face. Cold, clammy sweat clings to my palm. Christ, these dreams, they're gonna be the death of me.

'Hear me.'

I twist in my chair, my heels kicking up the scattered newspaper under my feet. I'm afraid to breathe. Somewhere in the dark; moaning. Weak and muffled, but it's there. Trying to remain calm, I check my equipment. I haven't even started the camcorder yet. There's a fresh tape laying on the table still in its shrink wrap. It'll take too long to open now. Cursing myself for falling asleep, I snatch up the headphones and grab the microphone from its stand. I push the record button on the MiniDisc player.

Silence.

No, please, just this once. I swing the microphone around in a slow arc. It's a powerful hyper-cardioid microphone, it has great range and cuts out a lot of unwanted ambient noise, but for the best results it has to be pointed directly at the sound source.

There!

A deep low moan. My heart skips a beat.

No, don't get carried away. I've been here too many times before. The hope, followed by the inevitable disappointment. It's probably nothing more than stray radio transmissions or echoes from the train tunnel.

But still...

Fumbling in my pocket, I pull out my E.M.F. detector and check the dial.

Nothing! Fuck!

I move closer to the sound. Of course, it has to be coming from the darkest, dankest corner of the cellar, where all the junk is stored. There's nothing much back there but rat shit and norovirus. Trying to ignore my usual sanitation concerns, I step forward.

The moaning stops.

I freeze on the spot, holding my breath.

Silence.

I crank the gain on the MD player as far as it will go. Straining my ears for any sound.

Still nothing.

My heart is thumping. Should I wait, should I move? If there is something manifesting back there, the last thing I want to do is spook it. Ignoring the obvious irony of not wanting to frighten an entity which is currently scarring the shit out of me, I resist the urge to pull my pocket torch from my jacket pocket. Instead, I stand in the darkness waiting.

As one minute follows another, I can feel my legs cramping. Maybe if I got closer? I take a step forward. Then another. I creep past the gas cylinder bank, with its mare's nest of valves and twisting plastic tubes. I can smell the hoppy sweet aroma of the kegs and the sharp tang of sterilising chemicals. This place is a nightmare for a paranormal investigator, with all the vibrations, smells and the constant cold. I peer into the dark corner, focusing beyond the twisted shadows cast from a pile of broken bar stools.

A noise. A low melodic horn?

I clasp the side of my headphones, just as the opening bars to *If I Can Dream* echo around the cellar.

Fucking Elvis!

I adjust the settings on the microphone, trying to filter out as much of the grating squall as I can. But all I'm getting is a constant thumping. Clutching the microphone, I stare at the far wall, waiting for the song to finish. As silence returns, I push the volume up as far as it will go, hardly daring to breathe. Hoping beyond hope I can still catch something on tape.

There! there it is! Something soft, almost like muffled footsteps, growing louder.

I strain my ears, trying to distinguish the sound from the ambient noise. The persistent rattle of the air cooler, the gentle hum of the beer pumps, the jangling guitar rift....

Fuck sake!

Burning Love. Will that man ever shut up?

Still cursing, I fumble with the MiniDisc player, attempting to hear past the rolling bass line, but it's hopeless. Letting out an anguished sigh, I turn back toward—

Jesus Christ!

Yanking the headphones off my head, I leap backwards, the woman's shrill screeching still ringing in my ears. 'Fuck!'

'Mr Vail? I'm so sorry,' she yelps. 'I'm Jo Kalman; we spoke on the phone.'

What the hell is she talking about? My head is spinning. Stumbling back against the cylinder bank, my fingers grasp the damp tubing in a reflexive spasm. Stretching across the surface, searching for any nook or crevice.

Find something to focus on; examine the details. Remind yourself what is real.

As I attempt to steady my breathing, she's still blethering. 'You said it would be okay to meet here.'

'Yes, yes, I remember. You wanted to speak to me about a haunting.' My heart is still racing, but at least I've got my bearings back. I remember she called earlier today, something about a poltergeist.

Edging past her, I hit the switch on the camping lamp and a tight pool of light appears around the folding table. Digging in my satchel, I grab my pill bottle and dry swallow a handful. Unsettled, she searches for a distraction. 'So this is how you do it, then?'

'Do what?'

'Catch ghosts?'

'I don't catch ghosts,' I correct her sternly. 'I'm a paranormal investigator, not a bloody Ghostbuster!'

She raises her hands in mock submission. 'To be honest, I didn't even know people did this for an actual job,' she says awkwardly.

Huffing, I thrust the microphone back onto its stand. I'm not about to tell her this isn't actually my full-time occupation. It's hard enough getting people to take me seriously as it is. Turning toward her, she still looks uncomfortable. My strange behaviour must be making her nervous.

'Tony.'

'Pardon?'

'Just call me Tony.' She smiles and nods. 'We're not all cranks, you know,' I tell her in a petulant tone, but her smile has disarmed me somewhat. Attempting to look busy, I start to reset my equipment. 'I have a degree in sociology and a master's in psychotherapy. I've also studied at the Institute for Psychical Research and have written several papers about the paranormal.' I'm laying it on thick now, but I don't want her to think I'm just some oddball that jumps at his own shadow. 'My primary field is parapsychology, which is the study of paranormal activity on the mind. But I also collect evidence of paranormal activity from locations where such phenomena have been reported in the past. Like this cellar, for instance—'

Fuck's sake! She's not even listening to me. She's staring down at my laptop, with a quizzical look on her face. 'So what does it all do?' she asks.

I want to slap the screen shut on her, but I need it open to run the sensors. 'It monitors changes in the temperature. The other program records vibrations. Not that they're much good down here.' She throws me an inquisitive glance. 'Because it's a beer cellar, it's kept at a constant twelve degrees celsius.' I nod toward the battered cooling unit bolted to the wall above the beer kegs. The fan inside rattles behind the rusty grill. 'Plus, we're smack bang next to the Central Line, so we don't get all that excited by vibrations either.'

'And this?'

She picks up my E.M.F. detector from the table, which I promptly snatch back. 'It's an electro-magnetic field meter, and it's extremely sensitive.' I carefully return the device to its original position on the table.

'Really.' She gives me a funny look.

'Well, I'm sure you didn't come all the way down here just to manhandle my equipment. You said on the phone you had a DV tape for me.'

Ignoring my churlishness, she takes the tape from her handbag. Making no attempt to take it from her, I glance toward the old felt noticeboard I'm using as a makeshift table. Taking the hint, she places it there instead.

'Is she pubescent?'

'I beg your pardon?'

'You didn't mention the girl's age on the phone. Is she pubescent?'

'She's fifteen. How did you know?'

'Oh, I can tell you more than that. I can tell you the house she lives in is probably a council house.'

Now she's intrigued. 'It used to be, the pervious owner bought it from the council in the eighties.'

Close enough. Cocking an eyebrow, I step causally toward the table. 'And I take it the family is suffering some kind of emotional discord at the moment?'

'Yes, the husband's a building contractor. He buys run-down properties, moves in and does them up for profit. But he's got stuck with this one and he's up to his neck in debt. It's causing a lot of tension. How did you know?'

Shrugging, I nudge the DV tape so that it's laying perfectly parallel with the side of the laptop. 'Classic poltergeist criteria. There's nearly always a pubescent child; usually female, suffering from some kind of emotional turmoil. It's thought poltergeists are attracted to volatile or stressful environments. A pubescent child can emit a huge amount of energy which a poltergeist can feed off.'

'But why a council house?'

'Council properties attract a higher percentage of poltergeists.'

'Not a draughty Scottish castles, then?'

She's trying to lighten the mood, but I don't feel like cutting her any slack. 'Ghosts maybe, but not poltergeists. They prefer to terrorise the poor and the working class!' If she realises I'm being sarky, she doesn't show it and simply shrugs away my comment. 'So why's he stuck with it?' I ask.

'Sorry?'

'You said he was stuck with the house. Why?'

'Because of the haunting?'

'I'm sure he hasn't listed it on the house's fixtures and fittings.'

'Well, it's a little more complicated. Turns out the house has a history.'

'Most haunted houses do.'

'This one has a specific history.'

A chill runs down my spine as an uneasy feeling coils in my stomach. 'Where did you say this house was?'

She routes in her bag and hands me a slip of paper. 'That's the address there. Do you know it?'

Even with the change of street name; It's fair to say, I know it. 'Is this some kind of joke?' I snarl.

She takes a step back, surprised by my sudden anger. 'I don't understand. You mean you know the house?'

Two figures moving behind the crack of a door. The sound of a groan as a body falls to the floor.

The force of the memory sends me reeling backward. Knocking against the table, it topples to the ground. The sight of all my possessions strewn across the concrete floor only heightens my anxiety. Stooping to gather them up, I lose all focus, until suddenly, like a spark in the darkness, I realise what's going on here.

Turning sharply, I jut my finger in her direction. 'Did he put you up to this? Did he send you here?'

Shocked, she stumbles backward. 'Did who send me?'

'Who! Roy Norris! That's who! The psychic bloody bin-man! The bloody bastard!' Directing my anger away from the woman, I kick my chair across the cellar. 'You think this is funny, don't you?' I can hear my voice shaking with fury.

As I grab her wrist, her shock transforms into panic. 'I don't know what you're talking about,' she pleads. 'I'm a researcher.'

'A researcher?'

Now the walls are shaking.

'For a television company!'

'Television company?' Releasing her wrist, I stare down at my hands. They're still moving by their own volition. Clenching my fingers, I try to maintain control.

'We're doing a programme about the house.' She's still talking, but I need to block her out. There's already too much chaos in my head. I try to use my calming techniques, but I can't control my breathing. I can't control anything. It feels like I'm choking as I fight the rising panic. With the blackness closing in, I fumble with my pill bottle, scattering the contents across the cellar floor. As my legs buckle, I'm hit by a sudden wave of nausea. Grasping for the edge of a keg, I topple forward.

Then blackness.

***

Mid-seventies news footage: Two female social workers led a traumatised child away from a council building. A throng of reporters jostle around the group as they make their way down the steps. The young boy tries to hide himself, but he has nowhere to go.

6. Glimpses of Things

Similar to unexplained shadows, these are fleeting physical images caught from the corner of your eye. Odd reflections in mirrors or darkened windowpanes at night. Strange movements reflected on shiny surfaces, like metal kettles or large kitchen appliances. A brief motion behind a door crack, or the momentary glimpse of some darting shape across the floor.

Any sighting of fleeting shapes and movements could be a sign of paranormal phenomena.

***

No one could say Johnny 'the King' Da Prato didn't give good value for money. Even offstage, he remained the consummate professional. The walk, the gait, the attitude. He was the total package, was Johnny. Not until he had totally shed the bedazzled jumpsuit, the lavish sideburns and Pompadour wig; would he return to his normal persona; John Da Prato bottle plant operative.

Until then, he remained the 'King of Rock 'n' Roll'.

Uh-huh-huh!

Besides you never knew when you might bump into one of your adoring fans backstage. Which on this night was exactly what happened.

Johnny had only just arrived at his dressing room (or in this case the kitchen larder where his regular clothes and personality awaited him) when the door suddenly burst open and a hysterical woman ran straight into his arms.

'Whoa there, little lady,' Johnny declared in Elvis's distinctive Southern drawl. 'You nearly knocked over the 'King' there.'

Flung unexpectedly into the arms of no-less than Elvis Presley himself, Jo gaped dumbstruck at Johnny.

'Look's like you've just seen a ghost,' Johnny crooned cooly as he gave Jo a complimentary twist of the hips.

Jo's hand shook as she dropped the lighter back into her handbag. Gazing through the pale wisp of smoke curling from her cigarette tip, she glanced along the bar. Jerry and Johnny were both still huddled together over two pints of Guinness. Johnny was still wearing his neon white jumpsuit, but had thankfully lost the wig and glasses. Behind them, Tony Vail sat slumped over an empty whisky glass, Johnny's sequined cape draped over his hunched shoulders. He looked drawn and pale and his hands were shaking worse than her own.

Jo couldn't get over how quickly everything had escalated. She took another shaky puff on her cigarette and tried to realign the events of that evening in her mind.

It had started innocuously enough. Jo had called the mobile number on the business card Lawrence had given her and Vail had agreed to meet her in the wine bar later that night. She had allowed herself plenty of time to find the place, but as it transpired, it would've been hard to miss.

THE MOST HAUNTED PUB IN ENGLAND

Garish as it was, the enormous banner hanging across the front of the pub had at least concealed much of the building's noisome façade. The tavern's once dignified Victorian decoration, having been marred by several layers of glutinous black and silver paint.

The interior of the pub had fared little better, with the same tenebrous colour scheme daubed throughout.

As Jo had entered the bar, an over-the-top Elvis impersonator had been in the process of winding up his set with a rollicking rendition of *Suspicious Minds,* for the benefit of a few disinterested patrons. It had taken several long minutes before an equally apathetic barman had appeared behind the bar. Explaining she'd come to meet Vail, the barman had given her a long, dubious stare. 'Yeah, he's down in the cellar now,' he had conceded. 'Investigating our ghost. You *do* know this *is* the most haunted pub in London don't you?'

Jo had cast a sardonic glance toward a second huge banner hanging across the bar. 'Yes, I had gathered that.'

'So what do you need to see him about? You got a ghost as well?'

Annoyed by the man's condescension, Jo had told him she was a researcher for a television program. 'A television program?' The man's whole demeanour had transformed in an instant. 'Jerrold McGilvery, by the way, proprietor of this fine establishment. Call me Jerry.' A sweaty hand had been thrust in her direction. 'Can I get you a drink or a packet of crisps? On the house, naturally?' His voice had dripped with sickly reverence. Jo had declined his offer, but Jerry had poured her a drink, anyway.

'So you're here to see our resident ghostbuster,' Jerry had chuckled as he had directed Jo around the end of the bar toward the kitchen. 'Best not to call him that, though. He gets really shirty about it. There you go.' He had tugged open a large trapdoor in the larder floor, revealing a steep wooden staircase leading down into complete blackness. Jo's apprehensive glance had been met with an unapologetic shrug. 'I would accompany you myself,' Jerry had said. 'But I can't leave the bar. You know, in case there's a sudden rush or something.' Jo had cast a sceptical glance back toward the half-empty bar, just as Elvis had attempted a rather questionable, high falsetto. 'Probably be a rush for the door, mind.' Jerry had grimaced.

Jo had barely begun her descent down the rickety old staircase before Jerry had called her back. But any hope she was about to be handed a torch had been quickly dashed. 'There you go,' he had said, pushing a crumpled flyer into her hand. 'The most haunted public house in London. All the

108

information is there; plus all the contact details if you want to make arrangements.'

'Arrangements?'

'Well, I'm thinking you'd want to film Vail as he reveals our resident ghost to the world. Because I'd be extremely welcome to that. I'd make it very easy for you guys, whatever you needed.' He had lent forward in a conspiratorial manner. 'I mean, between you and me this kind of exposure can be great for business. There was this hotel up north that was doing terrible business until it appeared on one of those *Ghost Chasers* shows. Now it's packed twenty-four-seven with amateur ghost hunters and barmpots. So I'm thinking, why not here? This place would make great TV. You wouldn't believe the history this place has seen. Loads of people got murdered here. They used to pile the bodies up down there.' He had nodded toward the dark abyss at the bottom of the staircase. 'That was in the nineteenth century mind,' he had lamented just as another dubious high note had reverberated around the bar. 'And let's not forget about Elvis. He dies here every Friday night.'

The cellar had been pitch black, apart from a few tiny appliance bulbs glowing in the darkness. Overhead, an air-conditioning unit had been rattling somewhere in the gloom. With her eyes still adjusting to the blackness, Jo had spotted a figure moving silently across the cellar. She had called out, but the figure hadn't responded. He'd been wearing a large Russian Ushanka cap and gazing intently into a dark corner. Moving toward him, Jo had just been about to tap him on the shoulder; when the figure had spun around. Screaming, they had both leapt backwards. If it hadn't been so startling, it would have been comic.

After they had both got their bearings back, they had talked a bit. Tony's tone had been strained at first, but Jo had been immediately taken by him. Unshaven and blurry eyed, dressed in a baggy army jacket and crumpled trousers. She'd found him strangely compelling. They'd been discussing the Mishal family when... Well, even now; Jo wasn't entirely sure what had happened.

'Is this some kind of joke?' he had yelled, after she had handed him the Mishal's address.

Had he already been to the house? Had the Mishals already explored other avenues before they had called her? Before she could ask, the whole cellar had started to shake. Then Tony had collapsed to the floor.

'What do you think happened?' Johnny asked in a hushed tone as he and Jerry sidled up to Jo.

'What do you think!' Jerry said, taking a stool next to Jo. 'He saw the ghost.'

'He had a panic attack,' Jo corrected him.

'Caused by seeing the ghost.'

'No. I think it was something I said.'

'About the ghost?'

Jerry was really getting on Jo's nerves now. Even more than the incessant train rattle.

Ignoring Jerry, Jo tried to replay the events in the cellar back in her mind. Had it been the address? No; that had just made him angry. He hadn't totally flipped until she'd mentioned the television programme. Had that been it?

'Kalman?'

'Pardon?'

Tony sat staring down at his drink. 'You said your name was Kalman.'

'That's right.'

Tony shifted on the stool. 'As in Frank Kalman? *Strange Frontier*?'

'Yes, he's my father,' Jo admitted cautiously.

'Jesus, what is it with your family!' Jumping down from his stool, he strode purposely toward Jo, his tired, bloodshot eyes burning with fury. 'Well, I've already had my thirty-seconds of fame thank you very much.' His mouth twisted into a vicious snarl. 'So how about you find someone else to torture for a change?'

He lunged forward, prompting Jerry to leap between them. 'I don't know what is going on,' Jo pleaded, as Tony glared over Jerry's shoulder.

'I think it's best you go luv,' Jerry said, while Johnny offered to escort her back to the train station.

Jo's gaze fell upon the large 'No Smoking' decal on the grimy window opposite.

Fuck it! She lit the cigarette anyway.

Immediately feeling self-conscious, Jo cast a furtive glance down the carriage. To her relief, no one in the near-empty tube train had even battered an eyelid. Jo relaxed a little. The last-minute rush down the escalators had left her breathless.

She'd just made the leap onto the final north-bound tube, with barely seconds to spare. And in doing so, had narrowly avoided the embarrassing prospect of having to accept a lift home in Johnny's battered Bedford van.

As she idly watched the tunnel wall speed past the carriage windows, Jo thought again about the sudden change in Tony Vail after she'd handed him the Mishal's address. '*Is this some kind of joke?*' He had shouted. '*Did he put you up to this? That bloody bastard!*'

A name came to Jo's mind. Rooting through her bag, she found her Filo-Fax and opened it to that morning's production notes. Written across the page, the name Roy Norris.

'The psychic bloody bin-man!' Jo muttered.

That morning's production meeting had begun well. Preparation for the live show had been progressing well. The only contention had been raised by Jazmin, one of Gillian's production assistants, following a call from Belo Mishal. 'They'd like to use their own medium. Apparently, he's already done several readings at the house. They'd like him to hold the séance.'

As she'd been speaking, a middle-aged man sporting a short goatee beard had rushed into 'The Forum', dumping his grey messenger bag down on the ping-pong table. 'Nice of you to join us,' Gillian had quipped surlily.

'Sorry I'm late, traffic out there is bloody murder. This new congestion charge thing is causing absolute chaos.'

Gillian had introduced him to Jo as Dan Philips, the show's resident paranormal investigator. While Dan had settled himself on one of the many bewildering objects used for chairs around the office, Gillan had impatiently lit a cigarette.

'They're very insistent.' Jazmin had said, fearing the issue with the séance had been forgotten during the lengthy interval.

Gillian's eyes had narrowed. 'Jo, I need you to handle this.'

'You want me to call him?'

'No, speak to him face-to-face. See what he's like. He's probably a charlatan, but he might know something about the haunting that we could use.'

'Okay, but I would've thought someone else might be better suited...'

Gillian had closed her down with a curt, 'I'd like you to do it.'

'Well, okay,' Jo had conceded. Not for the first time; Jo had got the distinct feeling she was being steered away from the Mishals. She had already noted with some annoyance that Jasmine had been assigned all the liaison duties with the family.

Relieved, Jazmin had passed Jo the contact details, which Jo had copied into her Filo-Fax.

'If you could do it first thing in the morning. We'll have something to tell the Mishals when we do the location scout.' Gillian had written a reminder in her own agenda, underlining it decisively. 'And Jo, how's that extra background coming along?'

The inquiry had been so abrupt it had caught Jo off guard. Having already discussed this issue with Gillian, she had assumed the matter settled. 'As I told you, I believe everything was published at the time.'

'Well, maybe there's stuff your father and Ashby didn't want to make public.'

Jo had bristled at Gillian's casual reference to her father. 'As I said, I don't think there was anything else.'

Gillian had rebuffed Jo's assurances with a dismissive wave of her hand. 'Well, see what you can do, anyway.' At that point Gillian had abruptly changed the subject. As Carl Baxter, the show's editor had run through a list of archive clips for the show, Jo had sat silently brooding.

'Discounting the odd television feature about the family there's no actual footage of the haunting itself.' Carl had lamented. 'And as you know, all the family photos went up in the house fire.'

'Do we know what caused the fire?' Posey Campbell, the shows co-presenter and so-called paranormal historian, had asked from the far end of the table.

'No one knows for sure. But the father had been stockpiling petrol illegally in the house. It's thought a fallen candle might have caught against a leaky canister.'

Gillian had pursed his lips as she had run through Carl's list. 'No, no, you're right, this won't do.'

'We've sawn programmes together on less.'

'But this is different. With the increased runtime we'll need a lot more padding.'

'There was one thing,' Carl had added almost as an afterthought. 'In one of the *Nationwide* features there was an interview with...' he' glanced down at his notes, 'Patrick

Milgallon; the paranormal investigator. During the lead up to the interview, there was footage of him filming the children with a Super 8 camera.'

'Jo? Any chance your father would still have a copy of that film?'

Jo had glared across the table at Gillian. 'I shouldn't think so.' Several curious glances had turned in her direction. Until then, Gillian had been the only one aware of Jo's connection with *Strange Frontier*. 'I don't see why Milgallon would have even given him the film. The magazine would have had no use for it, anyway.'

'Do we know what happened to that footage?' Gillian's question had gone out to everyone but her gaze had inevitably fallen back onto Jo. 'Do we even know if Milgallon is still alive?'

Jo had hesitated. Sensing where Gillian was heading. 'I'm not sure.'

'Do you think your father would know where he is now?'

'I really wouldn't know.'

Gillian had given her a dissatisfied glance. 'Might be still worth looking into,' she had insisted, turning back to her production notes.

Across the table, a hand had risen in the air. It had been Dan. 'So your father is Frank Kalman, then?' It had been less of a question and more a statement of fact. With the knot tightening in her stomach, Jo had braced herself for the next inevitable question.

Posey had lent forward on her stool. 'So your mother was *Rachel Graham*, the novelist?' Her voice had resonated with astonishment.

Every head had lifted at the mention of Rachel Graham's name, while Jazmin had stared in awe at Jo. 'So you're *the* daughter.'

'*The* daughter?' Jacob had asked from across the table.

'You know, the one she wrote the book about.' Jazmin had not been unable to contain her excitement. An uncomfortable silence had fallen over the table, following Jazmin's blunt revelation, which Jazmin herself had been the first to acknowledge. 'Oh, sorry. Is this a bad thing to be talking about?' She'd made a naive grimace.

'What do you think?' Gillian had snapped, but her chagrin had sounded anything but genuine.

He was crying again, pleading for his life, begging her. This was the worst part, seeing the desperation in his eyes. The look of betrayal, as despair had turned to hatred. But that was to be expected. After all, she'd just sentenced him the death. He screamed her name one last time...

'Mummy!'

Qamra woke from her dream, her mind dazed and foggy. It took a moment before she realised Kyra was standing by her bedside.

'Kyra, what is it?' Qamra asked tiredly.

'Lila is dreaming again,' the young child said, wiping the sleep from her eyes, her demeanour more annoyed than frightened.

Qamra signed, Lila's bad dreams were becoming increasingly frequent, but judging from the Kyra's grumpy expression, tonight at least it wasn't anything worse. 'I don't know what's wrong with that girl,' Qamra grumbled as she pulled back her bedsheet. Having the two girls share a bedroom was causing more problems than it solved.

'It's probably the man,' Kyra said with a yawn as she snuggled alongside her mother.

'I've told you before there's no man.' Qamra draped her arm over the small child. She'd have to have another word with Belo in the morning. All this talk of shadow figures on the landing was only giving Kyra nightmares.

'No not *that* man, the *other* man. The man that looks in the window.'

'Sorry what?' Kyra was already closing her eyes. 'Kyra what man!'

Behind Qamra, Belo shuffled in his sleep.

'The man that looks in the window when I'm in bed,' Kyra muttered sleepily.

'When did this happen? Kyra, this is serious. When did you see this man?' Qamra struggled to hold herself in check, her voice already sounding fraught.

'Some nights.'

'Kyra, how often is he there?'

The child shrugged. 'I don't know. Sometimes I'm asleep and I don't see him.'

'I'm telling you no one's been up here.'

Qamra crossed her arms sceptically. 'Have you checked the windows?'

'Yes, they're fine.' It had been a battle to get Belo to take Kyra's claims and Qamra's concerns seriously, but now he was up on the extension roof he had to admit Qamra had a point. Despite having used his own ladder to reach the rooftop. He could have just as easily clambered up via the building supplies heaped on the patio. Still unwilling to submit completely to his wife's raging paranoia, Belo attempted a fresh line of defence. 'How would anyone even get into the garden? They'd have to come through the wood.' A withering glare from Qamra told him he had just answered his own question, right there. 'Okay, as soon as I get delivery of the panels, I'll fix the fence,' Belo grumbled, as he climbed back down the ladder.

'You better!'

'I'm telling you she's just imagining it. Kids do that.'

'And I tell you, it's this house. It's driving everyone in this family crazy! It's driving me crazy!' Throwing her hands into the air, Qamra turned back toward the kitchen. 'And you can move all that crap off patio before you come back in!'

As Qamra stormed away, Belo glanced back at the old wire fence at the end of the garden. Despite his earlier re-assurances, he found himself reaching for his mobile phone. Maybe he would just call the building merchant and chase up the fencing panels. If only for a little peace of mind.

'Hello, Mr Norris...' After several minutes of fruitless knocking, Jo had decided upon a more direct approach. 'Mr

Norris...' Peering through the letterbox, Jo could just make out a bulky shadow at the end of the hallway. 'Hello?' Jo glanced anxiously over her shoulder. The teenage bike gang were still eying her with palpable suspicion from across the street.

Any stranger entering the estate would probably attract some degree of attention. But someone attempting to gain entrance to a dilapidated bungalow with the word 'nonce' spray painted across the front door would no doubt attract particular scrutiny. Jo had seen plenty of graffiti splashed around the Manor House Estate, but this branding seemed particularly specific to the occupant of the bungalow. Although a vigorous attempt had been made to scrub the scrawl away, the original message had remained very clear. And if the thick plywood board nailed across the lounge windows was anything to go by, it had not been the only message the bungalow's owner had recently received.

Stepping back from the front door, Jo cast a scathing glance over the bungalow. With its discoloured pebble-dash and peeling drainpipes it looked a sorry state. But to be fair; the entire estate wasn't much better. Most of the houses appeared to be in a similar state of disrepair, while split rubbish bags and broken furniture littered the verges and driveways.

Feeling increasingly exposed on the doorstep, Jo knocked again on the front door. 'Hello, Mr Norris. If I could just speak to you for a moment?' She had emphasised *Mr Norris* for the benefit of the loitering teenagers behind her, hoping a more official demeanour might help distance herself from the occupant of the bungalow. But the request had sounded so formal Jo immediately felt compelled to undermine it. Crouching down, she flipped open the letter plate again. 'It's about Lila Mishal,' she said in a more amiable tone. 'And the séance you conducted at the Mishal's house. It won't take a moment I assure you—'

The door opened a crack and the face of a thickset man, with a pensive expression appeared over a hefty security chain. Gazing through a pair of heavy rimmed glasses, his cautious eyes flickered nervously between Jo and the lurking gang behind her. 'The séance?' He repeated cautiously.

Roy Norris shuffled into the lounge carrying a large decorative tea-tray, on which rested a pair of Golden Jubilee tea mugs and an open packet of Rich Tea biscuits. He smiled awkwardly as he placed the tray on a small pouffe next to the sofa.

Based on its exterior appearance, Jo had expected the inside of the bungalow to be in a similar state of neglect. But to her surprise and relief, the interior had been the exact opposite. Every item in the lounge appeared to have been scrupulously polished and dusted. The dainty floral birch-arm sofa on which Jo now sat hardly looked used. Even the vintage crochet lace covers on the arms appeared to have been freshly pressed.

Roy politely passed Jo a mug of tea before manoeuvring his heavy frame into the ornate armchair opposite. Thickly built, with sloping shoulders and a round, corpulent face, there was an almost childish simplicity to the man. In his coarse dungaree trousers and a heavy ribbed jumper, Jo couldn't help but notice how out-of-place Roy appeared in his own home. The room's quaint ornamentation felt much more suited to a far older person. An assumption supported by a large button television remote resting on the arm of the sofa.

The only thing that didn't match the bungalow's refined decor had been a heavy framed bicycle, propped in the hallway. That and a heap of broken house bricks piled neatly on a plastic sheet over in the corner of the lounge, which Jo had been eyeing uneasily ever since her arrival. 'Do you live here with your parents?' Jo asked in a somewhat stilted tone.

'No, it's just m-me now.' Although Roy's eyes were constantly moving, they had as yet to settle directly on Jo. 'Mother d-died two years ago.'

'Oh, I'm sorry to hear that.'

'Don't be. She's in a b-b-better place and she still visits w-whenever she feels the need.'

Unnerved by Roy's apparent sincerity, Jo glanced nervously toward the lacy floral curtains, which were now tightly drawn; presumably to hide the wooden boards covering the windows. The air inside the room smelt stale. An old-fashioned air freshener stood on a table by the armchair. The gel inside, little more than a dehydrated husk. 'Kids can b-b-be so cruel.' Roy said, sensing Jo's unease.

'Pardon?'

'I used to throw them into the street,' he explained, nodding toward the brick pile. 'But they just threw them b-back again. So now I just keep them. Who knows, maybe one day I'll have enough to b-b-build an extension.' Having finally made eye contact with Jo, Roy seemed reluctant to let it go.

'Why do they do it?' Jo asked with an awkward smile.

Roy thought for a second. When he spoke, it was with a deep sense of melancholy. 'People fear what they d-don't understand. I'm afraid I b-belong to a different age. It was different with my mother. They used to come from m-m-miles around to hear her speak. She had a rare gift. She could touch people and understand how they felt even when they didn't know themselves. You could say I inherited it from her; God b-bless her soul. She passed peacefully just where you're sitting now. Biscuit?'

As Jo tentatively reached for the packet, a loud yell rung from outside. Tensing at the sound, Roy glanced nervously toward the window. As the shouting echoed away he flashed Jo an anxious half-smile. 'Sorry,' he said, plunging a Rich Tea into his mug. 'I can't stand sudden noises.'

'So is that how you became a clairvoyant, because of your mother?' Jo asked, ignoring Roy's sudden unease.

'I'm a clairaudient,' Roy corrected her. 'I hear spirits. I d-don't see them.'

'You hear voices?'

A broad smile appeared on his Roy's face in response to what must have been a fairly familiar reaction.

'It's Georgie. I know it's Georgie.' Dolly Pearson lent forward in her armchair, a look of elation illuminating her wrinkled face. Her eyes gleamed as she glanced over at a large photograph of her late husband standing on the mantelpiece, next to a decorative plate engraved with the words:

George & Dorothy 50th Wedding Adversary
May 5th 2001

Taking Dolly's frail hands in his, Roy smiled. 'I can hear him b-better now. Yes, it's George. He says he visits you from time to time. Keeping an eye on you, he is.' He gave the old lady a partial nod and a wink before adding. 'He says things will get b-better for you soon and that next year will be lucky for you.' Roy flinched as if the spiritual connection had just wavered. 'He says someone is calling him now. But he'll visit you again soon.' Roy's manner relaxed, as if released from the burden of contact. With tears welling in Dolly's eyes, he patted the old lady's hands reassuringly.

'I knew it was Georgie. I knew he was here.' Dolly's eyes glistened through a veil of fresh tears. 'I could feel his presence. I knew it.' She smiled as she turned toward the only other person in the room.

Jo could barely mask her revulsion.

On the doorstep, Dolly took hold of Roy's hand and slipped a folded banknote into it. 'That's for you,' she purred.

'It's not necessary, you know that,' Roy said, while deftly slipping the note into his back pocket.

'I want you to have it,' Dolly insisted. 'You know what a comfort it is to me.'

They'd barely made it back to Jo's car, before Jo was unleashing her displeasure at Roy. 'I can't believe you took money from that old lady? For that....' She searched in vain for a better word. 'Lie!'

Roy appeared genuinely affronted by the accusation. 'I d-d-didn't lie!' he protested. 'I may have em-embellished a few points, but I d-d-didn't lie.'

'What would you call it then? She's totally vulnerable! She's just lost her husband.'

Feeling cornered, Roy mustered the courage to confront Jo straight on. 'Exactly! What d-do you think she's got left in this world? Only the hope that one day, she'll be with him again. She's scared and lonely. She just n-needed someone to tell her she wasn't alone. I gave her hope and reassurance that's all.' Forcing home his point, Roy lent over Jo. 'And that's not b-bad for twenty quid!'

Pulling up outside Roy's bungalow, Jo turned to Roy. 'Do you know a Tony Vail?' Roy's expression hardened as he reached for the door handle. 'I thought maybe you might know him,' Jo added quickly, worried Roy was about to spring from the Mini and run for home. Jo had been putting off the question all afternoon. and now she was glad she had. Roy's entire demeanour had transformed in an instant. 'He seems to know the Mishals. I thought maybe he'd been there before?' The intensity of Roy's stare was now making her feel uneasy. 'Is there a problem?' she stammered.

'You d-don't know who he is do you?'

Up at the bar, Lawrence was holding court in his usual spot, surrounded by another group of rain sodden tourists. Exchanging more ghostly tales for his usual remittance, if the large whisky in his hand was anything to go by. Engrossed by his own storytelling, he failed to notice Jo marching toward him until she was almost upon him. 'Jo-Jo—,' he beamed, opening his arms wide.

'Bastard!' Jo thumped Lawrence hard against the chest, rocking him back against the bar. 'You knew all along who he was, didn't you?' she yelled, ignoring the stunned faces of the assembled tourists standing around her. 'What the hell did you think you were doing?'

'What could you possibly mean?' Lawrence protested, raising his hands in mock admonition. An action which immediately sent him sliding along the edge of the bar.

'Tony-bloody-Babcock!' Jo raged, turning her back on a smiling Japanese tourist who was now attempting to capture the whole altercation on video.

'I thought it had a certain irony to it,' Lawrence chuckled, while fiercely gripping the bar rail.

'A certain irony! He had a panic attack, for Christ's sake!' Jo's voice was now rasped with emotion. 'How could you do that to me? What have I ever done to you?'

'You; nothing!' Lawrence sneered. 'It was never about *you!*'

'So what? This is all about my father! And what you think he did to you thirty years ago?' Jo retorted, having jumped to the most obvious conclusion.

'No, not your father,' Lawrence mumbled morosely.

But Jo was no longer listening. 'Oh my God, you're pathetic! I thought you were better than that!'

Lawrence twisted his head in a surly fashion. 'I am better than that,' he barked. 'I am better than all of *this!*' Struggling to regain some of his lost decorum, Lawrence attempted a more dignified posture, only to lose his grip completely on the bar rail. Sliding down the bar, he crashed to the floor with a heavy thud. Wallowing on the ground, Lawrence's demeanour became more despondent. 'You don't understand,' he bemoaned pitifully.

'Understand what!'

'Consequences. Everything has consequences!'

But Jo had heard enough of Lawrence's mawkish self-pity. 'No, you did this to yourself. You! You've got no one else to blame but yourself. I don't even feel sorry for you. You deserve what happened to you.' She turned and began striding toward the door.

'I didn't deserve this!' Lawrence bellowed, as the Japanese tourist moved in for a close-up. Slumping back against the bar, Lawrence turned a dishevelled profile toward the camera lens. 'I really don't deserve this!'

Frustrated and angry, Jo marched down King Street toward Covent Garden. Despite a light drizzle and the late hour, the streets around the Piazza were still bustling. Tourists filled the pavements while drinkers watched the street performers from the balcony of the *Punch & Judy* pub.

Jo spent several minutes wandering aimlessly around the covered market, chain smoking one cigarette after another, until she finally found herself back at the old courtyard in front of St Paul's Church. Here she stood watching a street acrobat juggling knives under the church's imposing portico. Furiously tapping the back of her hand, Jo watched the spinning blades with a detached curiosity. It was a calming technique she'd adopted many years before, to help her manage her stress. But now she found she did it almost subconsciously, any time she felt overwhelmed.

Take control. Choose how you want to feel. Don't submit to your own negative feelings. Even this familiar mantra, repeated over in her head, did little to calm her raging mind.

As the juggler lit a fistful of flaming torches, Jo shivered and decided it was time she headed back to the station.

Gazing absentmindedly into the windows along the way, Jo suddenly ground to a halt outside a small bespoke bookshop in James Street. As the rain fell in earnest, Jo stood transfixed by the sight of a thin paperback novel at the centre of a busy window display extolling the works of several contemporary female writers. On the cover of the novel, a young girl ran barefoot through a flowery meadow.

A shiver ran down Jo's spine as she recalled the numb shock she'd experienced when presented with this very same edition during the first year of her English literature degree course. A book, her entire class, was meant to analyse and discuss. Jo remembered the creeping terror that had swept over her, as she had sat staring down at the photo of the young girl in the summer dress. It wasn't Jo's photo on the cover; but it was meant to be. It was supposed to be Jo's bare feet running through the long grass, Jo's excited exuberance. Because, in essence, it was a novel about her.

Jo remembered the impassioned voice of the lecturer fading into muffled silence as the dull thrum of panic had throbbed in her eardrums. '... a piece of outstanding beauty, expressing all the visceral intensity of childbirth and the psychological fear and disappointment of motherhood....'

She recalled her own the tears and the concerned glances from the other students. Her embarrassment and confusion. The emotional breakdown that had followed and the shame of her ill-conceived cry for help with the sleeping pills. She remembered her father's ashen face at the end of the hospital bed and her own depression during the long months of therapy. The insecurity she'd felt after switching her major and resuming her classes at university. But most of all she recalled the resentment she'd felt toward her mother and the disappointment she had felt for herself.

And now as she stood in a rain drenched London side street, staring at a photo of a young girl in a summer meadow. Jo felt it all again.

***

Mid-seventies news footage: A local news reporter stands on a blustery beach front. Pulling a strand of hair from her face, she addresses the camera directly. 'Police today confirmed that the body discovered here yesterday evening by a member of the public was that of the novelist Rachel Graham.'

The report cuts to footage of an air ambulance flying over the beach, followed by a wide-angle shot of two policemen walking through the sand dunes. 'This follows yesterday's search of the area around St Leonards-on-Sea, after the discovery of the novelist's car in a local carpark and the report a person seen going into the water.'

The scene cuts to a shot of an empty carpark. 'There have also been unconfirmed reports the writer's six-year-old daughter was also discovered with the vehicle.'

The shot returns to the weather-beaten reporter. 'An inquest into Ms Graham's death is due to be opened tomorrow morning at East Sussex Coroner's Court, but police say that for the moment the death is not being treated as suspicious, as it now appears the author may have taken her own life following a long battle with depression.' A sharp gust of wind buffets the reporter, but she quickly resumes her address to the camera. 'The tragedy is even more poignant considering the author's last and most accomplished novel *My Child* was a semi-autobiographical account of a woman who contemplates suicide while suffering the effects of postnatal depression. The family of Ms Graham has yet to make a public statement.'

7. Electronic Disturbances

Mild psychokinetic occurrences - lights flickering or turning themselves off and on again. A television flipping channels by itself. The screen on your computer blacking out for no reason, or your radio experiencing long periods of static. Even your child's electronic toy moving on its own can be an indication that something is surely wrong and often points to a haunting.

Other phenomena can include lamps, torches, electric clocks, and video games. In fact, any kind of electrically powered device can be affected. But unlike most other reported phenomena; this one is almost always witnessed during a haunting.

***

I stare down the aisle of racking. Hundreds of containers full of foam chip trays or paper cups or whatever the hell this company ships around the country. Behind me the warehouse gaffa is reciting the usual gumpth about strange noises and disappearing, reappearing stock. It's all routine stuff. I've heard it a million times before. I haven't even bothered to look at the dial on my E.M.F. detector.

As the gaffa falls silent, I can't recall half of what he's just said. 'What?'

He takes a step closer, contributing my lack of interest to bad hearing. 'I said, no one comes down this end of the warehouse anymore. Especially at night. That's where it happened. Crate fell from there and landed on Len right here. Bang!' He claps his hands together for graphic effect. 'Killed instantly, poor sod. Never had much luck did old Len. Crushed by two hundred weight of plastic spoons. There's nothing as funny as life is there.' The gaffa glances over at me. 'So what do you think?'

'What do you mean? What do I think? I think you need to have a word with your health and safety guy.'

If he realises, I'm taking the piss, he doesn't show it. Probably thinks I'm just an oddball.

'What I mean is. Do you think there's any chance of you know?'

'You know?'

'You know; that there might be something down here?'

'Well, there's usually something in these old places,' I tell him in an indifferent tone. 'And it's usually rats.'

'No, what I mean is. Do you think there's any chance old Len is? Well, putting in a bit of overtime?'

'What? Do I think your dead colleague is still working the night shift down here? Moving boxes of plastic spoons from one rack to the other?' I turn and slip the E.M.F. back into my jacket. 'There's nothing here.' I mutter as I walk away.

'Where're you going?' the gaffa calls after me. 'You've hardly looked around.' He sounds annoyed and I can't blame him.

'I said there's nothing there?'

'How can you be so sure?'

'Because there's never anything bloody there!'

I open a cardboard box and begin stacking the MiniDiscs inside. Enough is enough. I can't keep doing this. So much wasted time and effort. I want to smash my arm across the bench, scatter the discs across the floor. But my inner demons won't allow it. So instead, I angrily tidy them away, in order of date and time.

Unplugging the MiniDisc player from the laptop, I pop the cradle. A disc springs out.

The last recording from the pub cellar. The night Kalman paid me a visit. I stare at it in my hand.

No! Not this time.

I toss it into the box with the others.

I fry a sausage together with some eggs in a pan and eat them in front of the TV. I flip through the channels, but nothing catches my attention. Losing interest, my gaze strays back to the box of MiniDiscs on my worktop.

No. I'd just be torturing myself again.

But then...

I reconnect the MiniDisc player to the computer and open the sound analysis program. The usual colourful spectrogram appears on the screen as the audio transfers over. There's only a few minutes. Already disheartened, I highlight the section just before Kalman appeared in the cellar.

Over the sound of static and my own footsteps; a faint murmur. Almost lost in the ambient noise. I increase the volume and adjust the filters but I can't make it any clearer. Just before Elvis kicks in, I stop the recording, rewind it to the start and play it again. I cup my hands over my headphones, pushing the cushioning hard against my head to eliminate as much external noise as I can. There could be something there, but it's too vague.

A ghost in the machine.

'Fuck it!' I slump back in my chair. It's been three hours and I'm no closer to deciphering the sound than I was to begin with. If only I had a higher resolution. Or more to work on. If only the recorder had been running while I'd been asleep.

Now there's a thought!

Searching through the computer files, I open another folder in the audio program. The recording from the previous Friday night. The night I dreamt of the policeman.

As soon as the new waveform appears on screen, I drag the cursor over the large spike in the middle and push play. Hearing my own startled cry, I roll the marker back to just before the spike. I push play again.

There it is. Barely a whisper, but it's definitely there. The words that woke me from my dream.

'*Hear me!*'

'It's a message. I'm sure of it. I was this close to giving up.'

Sharman shuffles in his chair. 'Tony, we've been here before. You know what happens when you get fixated on something.'

'But this is different. It's there. This time I'm sure.'

'You thought you were sure the last time? And the time before that.' With that he sits back and folds his arms. It's far from the reaction I had hoped for. But I wait him out. 'It's easy to hear what you want to hear,' he says, breaking the deadlock. 'Plus we both know a person's perception can be altered and influenced through fear or illness or lack of sleep.'

Fuck no! I'm not having any of that. I shake my head, my earlier excitement long gone. Now I'm just angry. 'But you heard the tapes. You heard her voice.'

We've been through this before, Tony. There was no voice on those tapes.' His tone is stern; resistant. He didn't believe me then and he doesn't believe me now.

'If you'd only listen to this new recording.'

'Tony, this obsession of yours is not healthy.'

'No, I have control now. I know what I'm doing.'

He takes off his glasses and rubs his eyes. I've lost him.

'I'm telling you it's just like last time.'

He sighs and shakes his head. 'That's what I'm afraid of.'

There's another pile of bills waiting for me in the mailbox.

Leo's door opens. 'I've got a box for you,' he tells me in a weary tone. 'It came today.'

Inside his studio, there's a sealed parcel on the floor, covered in the usual courier labels. 'More work,' I tell him.

'More work is always good,' Leo says, while rubbing a handful of wet paintbrushes with a tea towel. The sound of a running tap, echos from his utility room. A small transistor radio is playing on his workbench. They're discussing the upcoming war, which seems inevitable now.

'Finished for the day?'

He nods towards a large easel in the middle of the studio. Glancing at the canvas, I'm surprised to see my own face staring back at me. 'I thought you gave up on this one?' I chuckle.

'I never give up on anything that's worth saving.'

We exchange an awkward glance as he drops the brushes into a jar on his workbench.

'I still think you made me look like a ghost.'

'Have you seen yourself in the mirror lately?'

'I try not to.'

'You still not sleeping?' I give him a shrug and he shakes his head. 'I saw someone watching your flat today.'

'Yeah, who was that then?'

'I don't know, big man, big jacket.'

I roll my eyes, as that could mean any number of people. But I tell him I'll sort it out.

'Maybe you should get out of here,' he tells me bluntly. 'Start afresh, somewhere new. It's not so hard.'

I have to smile. In his own way; he must be really worried about me.

'Sometimes it's good to forget the past,' he says ruefully.

I glance again at the haunted face on the canvas. 'If only.'

Christ, my' head's splitting. I've been over the recordings so many times I can't think straight. Sometimes I hear the words, other times it's just ambient noise. I don't know anymore. I can't see a way through.

I rip the lid off the olanzapine and scoop a couple of tablets into my palm.

Just enough to numb the chaos—

Unless?

I stare at the pills in my hand.

Numb the chaos?

I toss them into the sink and run the tap.

My heart is thumbing. I need to focus. To think straight. I need to see the truth.

Yanking open the bathroom cabinet, I rip through the shelves, grabbing wildly at the bottles.

I bin the olanzapine and the sertraline, but swig a mouthful of Panadol Syrup.

Well, you can't go completely cold turkey can you?

Throwing a tea bag into a mug, I flip the kettle on. I've got the shivers; cold sweats. My whole body feels like it's falling apart. The latest package from the agency is still sitting on the kitchenette counter. Can't bring myself to look at another set of saucepans right now.

Maybe I've got this all wrong? Maybe if I just took something to—

The intercom buzzes.

Christ almighty! I nearly jump out of my skin.

My hand hovers over the handset a moment before I pick it up. A face appears on the tiny monitor screen. I'm stunned, to say the least. 'Hello?' she leans towards the intercom panel. 'Hello?'

I slam the handset back into its cradle. I repeat the action as the buzzer sounds again. My hand is shaking.

Through the floor, I hear the dull echo of another studio getting buzzed. Then the rattle of the old lift.

Christ!

'How did you find me?' I growl over the security chain.

She tells me she found my business address in the Yellow Pages, which makes sense I suppose.

'I just wanted to say sorry.'

'For what exactly? Sorry your father destroyed my life, or sorry you thought it would be nice to pop by and remind me of the fact.'

Kalman looks embarrassed, which, of course, she should. 'You've got it wrong. I honestly wanted your help.'

'My help?'

'With the haunting, in your old house.'

'The haunting?' I can't believe she's still trying this shit on with me.

'Because it's true. Everything I told you about the family.'

She's laying it on thick now. If I didn't know better, I could actually believe her.

'I really had no idea who you were when I called you. I was given you card by...' she trails off.

'Yeah, by who?'

'Well, I got it from...' She dries up, at a loss for a convincing answer.

'Yeah, I thought as much.' I'm still holding her gaze as I close the door on her.

'It's not what you think.' she bleats as the latch clicks into place. For a moment, she remains outside. As if she's expecting the door to reopen.

Fat chance.

The gentle pitch of the train carriage is rocking me to sleep.

Well, almost.

I open my eyes. Someone just whispered my name.

At the far end of the carriage, a tramp is muttering to himself. Grunting, a stream of incoherent obscenities. Stretching his legs, he slumps back into his seat. It's the height of the rush hour and he's got half the carriage to himself. At the other end, a huddle of teenage girls are yapping and laughing over the persistent train noise. No one is looking my way. Staring around the carriage, I can feel my anxiety rising. I'm sure I just heard my name.

Reaching for my meds, I remember I've binned the lot. Christ, my minds all over the place.

At the next station, two black women get on and head for the empty half of the carriage before spotting the tramp and turning back on themselves in disgust. Sitting down opposite me, they start yakking on about nonsense. Talking over each other. Their voices, loud and piercing. 'You don't want to make them longer like a drag queen's. Just make them fuller. You get me.'

'I'm going to be honest with her, you know, like, we're supposed to be best friends and everything. But she's like totally a bitch and all.'

'I must have been drunk or high or something because I've totally mushed up my armpits!'

'What you staring at?' One of the women is glaring at me. 'I said, what are you staring at?'

Glancing away, I curl into myself, as she 'sucks' her teeth contemptuously.

'Yeah, you look away, you pervert!' she snarls, as several other passengers look up from their newspapers.

At the next station, I get up and head for the doors. The woman's glare follows me off the carriage. It's not my stop, but I can't bear her disdain any longer. Darting across the platform, I touch the wall tiles with my fingertips. She's still staring at me through the window as the train pulls away. I return her glare until my nerve gives out.

'Tony.'

I jump at the sound of my name. Spinning sharply, I gaze down the platform, searching for a familiar face. But nothing. Turning my ear to the crowd, I can't make out any individual voices, only a low mumble and a distant echo. Like wind blowing through the branches of an ash tree. I glance over at the information board. The dot matrix is blinking abnormally.

This can't be happening.

A gust of warm air bellows from the tunnel mouth as the train roars into the station.

Staring down the platform, something catches my eye. A young girl, close to the edge.

Tracey?

I lean forward, trying to get a better look, my fingertips barely touching the wall. But I lose the figure as the crowd shuffles forward at the sound of the approaching train. As more people flood onto the platform, my anxiety tips over into panic.

Damn!

My heart leaps as I move away from the wall and slip into the crowd.

As the train speeds through the station, I glimpse her again. Close to the edge. A young girl in a tatty nightdress. She turns, just as I lose sight of her behind a fat man dragging a rolling suitcase.

'Tracey!' Pushing through the crowd, I reach the fat man with the suitcase. Unable to see around him, I'm gripped with a sudden premonition of Tracey on the platform edge, falling backwards into the path of the train.

Panicking, I lurch forward, trying to reach around the man, grasping for Tracey's outstretched hand. But there's nothing there and I stumble into nothingness. My hand grapples with empty space as I topple into the void. Staring hopelessly at the rail tracks, I realise I'm about to die in the most horrific way possible.

I feel a tug on my collar and I'm yanked backwards. The fat man's suitcase knocks against a carriage as he pulls me clear of the moving train.

I feel numb. I can hardly move. The fat man says something to me, but I can only nod in mute acknowledgement. As the train comes to a halt, the crowd surges toward the opening doors. I get one last glance from the fat man before he turns away.

Left alone, my legs give way as my stomach churns. Stumbling back across the platform, I make it just in time to hurl my guts against the wall. The vomit splatters off the tiles, covering my Hush Puppies.

Clawing the tiles with my fingernails, I glance back down the platform. To the place, I last saw Tracey.

It's empty, of course. But in my mind's eye, I can still see her. On the edge of the platform. Reaching for me. Pleading. The same image from my dreams. But this time, she wasn't screaming for help.

She was beckoning me to join her.

I throw up again.

I tip over the pedal bin. Ripping the cap off the olanzapine, I empty the last of its contents into my hand. It's barely enough. I gulp the pills with a mouthful of water.

I'm speeding through the trees, my heart racing. I can feel the wind against my face, the exhilaration of speed. The euphoria of freedom. Tracey's behind me on her bike, laughing and whooping. We race each other into the woods.

Later, we climb through the broken railway fence and play hide and seek amongst the signal boxes and equipment sheds.

As evening creeps in, we lay together in the long grass watching the trains on the viaduct. It's getting dark and the sun has dropped behind the trees. In the autumn twilight she turns to me, her mouth twisting into a distorted snarl, as her lifeless eyes stare back at me accusingly—

I wake screaming. Another memory twisted and warped into a grotesque vision of madness. Soon there'll be nothing left.

Nothing but nightmares.

Opening a casement window, I step out onto the fire escape. The steel grating creaks underfoot as I light a cigarette and stare out into the night.

In the distance a solitary train glides through the darkness. A thin chain of lights appearing and disappearing behind a line of dark rooftops.

My head is throbbing. Twisting my neck, my gaze falls upon the parking bays below.

On the path behind the bin store, a figure appears faintly in the shadow. I watch it a moment unsure whether it realises I have seen it.

A fox howls in a nearby street.

I glance away, barely a moment. When I look back, the figure is gone, reclaimed by the darkness.

Closing the casement window, I stare back through the glass. The path remains in shadow.

I wait, but nothing moves.

I pull the print from the developing solution and hold it up against the safelight.

Bare cellar walls. A random floating orb.

Fuck it! I toss it down in frustration.

Not enough!

It doesn't take long to go through the same procedure again. But this time I subject the paper to a double exposure. It's old school but effective. I hold the new print up. It's the same picture as before, but with the addition of a ghostly white mist in the middle.

Hanging the alteration on the drying line, I take a moment to admire my own handy-work. Along with all the usual feelings of embarrassment and self-loathing. I allow myself the luxury of feeling something extra.

A little pride.

The bar's half-empty. Johnny's setting his equipment up on the low stage. Jerry gives me the stink eye the moment I walk in. But I don't give him time to start on me before I slap the print down on the bar.

'What's this?' he asks, eyeing the A4 envelope with immediate distrust.

'The start of your new marketing campaign.'

He opens the envelope and pulls out the photograph. 'Fuck me!' he exclaims. 'When did you take this?'

'Last night,' I tell him. 'Yeah, let's say last night.'

He whistles and slaps the photo with the back of his hand. 'Will you certify this as real?'

'It is real,' I tell him. Like there's any doubt.

A big mischievous grin appears across his big stupid face. 'I won't forget this.' He wags a knowing finger in my direction before spinning around. 'Hey Johnny, drinks on the house.'

Johnny glances around at the near empty bar. 'Last of the big spenders!' he laughs.

Down in the cellar, I stare into the darkness. Upstairs, Johnny has just begun his routine.

(You're the) Devil in Disguise.

You could say that Johnny; you could say that.

I'm startled awake by the camcorder ejecting its tape. Stretching, I check the time. It's nearly morning and for a moment I consider not replacing the cassette. But just knowing the camcorder is standing idle is already making me anxious. Reaching for a new tape, I notice there's already a date written on the label:

Jan/03

Kalman's DV tape. I stare at it in my hand.

The video from the old house.

I must be mad.

I shove it into the camcorder and push play.

***

Contemporary camcorder footage: The image is a chaotic blur of frantic movement. Behind the camera, the operator can be heard mumbling and cursing as he attempts to work the camcorder. In the background, a dull banging echoes over the sound of muffled moaning.

The shot cuts to a frail teenage girl frantically thrashing on her bed as her mother attempts to subdue her. The frame jumps and blurs as the camcorder attempts to capture both the mother's anguish and the young girl's distress.

The teenager is muttering maniacally in her delirium. Most of her words are indiscernible. Apart from one name, which cuts through the gibberish. 'Tony!'

'Tony, who's Tony?' the mother asks.

'Tony's my little soldier,' the girl replies in a brief moment of lucidity.

8. Inexplicable Movement

Objects moving on their own or with no visible reason can be a clear sign of paranormal activity in your home. Pictures or photographs flying off walls. Books thrown through the air by an invisible force. Cupboards flying open, doors slamming shut, furniture sliding across the floor.

Any unexplained movements in your environment can be an easy way to identify a haunting. But psychokinetic phenomena can also be far more subtle. Plates slipping across the dinner table. Items rolling out of touch just as you reach for them or objects gently vibrating on a shelf. These can also be signs that spirits from the other side are trying to attract your attention.

***

She could smell the salt sea air and feel the wet sand between her toes. Far out to sea, dark clouds hung on the horizon and she could feel the ominous presence of an oncoming storm. She watched as mewling seagulls rode the choppy air currants over the crashing waves, their tiny bodies fighting valiantly against the strong winds. Sensing someone's gaze upon her, she glanced over her shoulder, the sharp sea breeze thrashing the loose ends of her hair across her face.

In the distance, a young child stood on a tall dune, her mouth open in an anguished scream. Her desperate cries snatched away by the howling gale.

Ignoring the tiny figure, she turned instead toward the open sea. Striding forward, the cold water was soon lapping around her ankles. Forcing herself forward, the waves quickly rose above her waist. But instead of pushing against her and frustrating her advance, they seemed to open and embrace her, drawing her in, until finally she disappeared...

Jo woke with a jolt. Disorientated and startled, she sat staring into the darkness, her mind reeling. Unable to settle, she got out of bed and wandered over to the window. The dream had left a dull, empty ache inside her that refused to fade. Trying to distract herself, she lit a cigarette as she watched the passing cars in the street below. Even at four in the morning, Belsize Park was alive, if only barely.

Jo had never been a morning person. She found it cold and grey and unwelcoming. It was also when she felt at her lowest. When she was most susceptible to her own dark broodings and self-loathing. To counter these emotions, she now kept a notebook by her bed. Here she would record all her pessimistic thoughts. Then, by simply closing the book, she would leave them all behind on the nightstand.

But tonight, as Jo brought pen to paper, she found herself unable to focus her mind. Instead, her thoughts kept turning back to the same nagging question that had haunted her all her adolescent life.

Why her mother had done what she had?

Even her own moment of weakness at university had left Jo with no clearer insight into her mother's reasoning. While her own clumsy attempt had been a mistaken, foolish cry for help. For Jo, her mother's suicide had always been an unfathomable, irrational and deliberate act of selfish egotism. It was unfair of her; she knew. But there it was.

Jo slapped the notebook closed. It was no good she had to clear her mind. Pulling back the bedcovers, she decided to take Bruno for a walk.

He was sitting in a white people carrier outside Jo's block. It was a work vehicle he used whenever he was on call. He was staring grimly down at the steering wheel, his face pale and vacant. His clothes looked crumpled and his whole body wavered as if he was trying to muster enough strength to leave the vehicle and make the brief trip up to his apartment.

It was several moments before Greg even realised Jo was there.

The morning news anchors were discussing the enthronement of the new Archbishop of Canterbury, while the sound of Bruno munching his breakfast echoed from the kitchen. Greg took a large gulp of coffee as Jo settled herself on the sofa beside him. 'Tough night,' she enquired delicately.

At first, Greg merely nodded, but he soon succumbed to the urge to unburden himself a little. 'One of our charges tried to hang herself in the safe accommodation we'd just placed her in,' he said in a low monotone. 'No one saw it coming. I got a call from tonight's EDT, who didn't feel she could deal with it on her own. She's only been in the job a few months.'

'That sounds terrible. Is she okay, the child that is?'

'We called an ambulance and they'll keep her in tonight. She'll get reassessed later today and probably end up in a secure unit...' Greg trailed off, not wanting to burden Jo with too many details, but the desire to talk was still there. 'I don't know what more I could have done.'

Watching Greg, Jo noticed a change in his usual manner. There was actual anger there. Mixed with all the familiar frustration and fatigue. A definite seething fury. Jo liked Greg. She'd always found him pleasant company. But ever since his divorce, he had changed. He'd become more argumentative, more volatile. Just weeks before, he had called an emergency meeting of the residents' committee to complain about the sudden hike in the building's maintenance fees. He'd been unable to drum up any sufficient support to challenge the amount and, as a result, had become quite bitter toward the other tenants over the matter. The entire episode had left Jo with the distinct impression, Greg was now struggling on his single salary.

Greg worked as a team leader for the local council, organising and managing a large team of social workers. Forced to take on extra hours, the increased workload had clearly taken a toil on both his health and mental wellbeing.

'So how come you're up so early?' Greg asked, in an obvious attempted to redirect the conversation.

'I've been awake most of the night,' Jo admitted with a shrug.

'Sign of a guilty conscious.'

'What is?' Jo asked defensively.

'Not being able to sleep.'

Jo couldn't tell if Greg was joking or not. His weary tone was making everything he said sound increasingly sarcastic. 'You may be right,' Jo said tersely.

'Still worried about the show?'

'Yes, there's a lot going on at the moment. But nothing I need to bore you about, I'm sure.'

'To be honest, I'd welcome the distraction.' Greg assured her, but Jo tactfully let the matter go. Instead, they sat in silence, sipping their coffee and watching the television.

The news report had moved on to more local issues. Greg sighed as a photograph of the missing teenager, Ashley Hooper, appeared on screen. It was the same photograph the media had been using since her initial disappearance the year before. Ashley in her sixth form uniform. Her pretty face framed by two vibrant strands of pink hair. The fact she hadn't been wearing her uniform on the day she'd disappeared seemed of little concern to the news channel. After all; a missing schoolgirl held far more emotional impact than a missing teenager.

'Didn't you say she was once a client of yours?'

Greg turned a questioning glance toward Jo. Although he'd been watching the television, his mind had drifted elsewhere.

'Ashley Hooper?' Jo prompted.

'Oh yes; but that was before the disappearance.'

The news report cut to the previous day's press conference, as Ashley's father made a fresh appeal for her return. 'Right now; all I think about is Ashley. She's my world. I love her so much. It's so hard.' Rob Hooper's voice broke as he forced back the tears. 'Ashley, please come home. It doesn't matter what has gone on before. I love you so much. I just want you to come home.' At that point he broke down, prompting a stern-looking police woman to continue the appeal on his behalf.

'She and her dad had been going through a really tough patch,' Greg continued sadly. 'They'd just lost her mother and neither of them was taking it all that well. Ashley started missing school, and Rob had no idea how to deal with the situation. He was a total wreak himself. He got overprotective with Ashley, which led to all sorts of arguments between them.'

'So she could have run away then?'

'That's what everyone thought at first. Most teenagers leave home because of some kind of domestic disagreement.'

'Wouldn't she have said something? Or at least; let some-one know she was okay.'

Greg huffed. 'Most don't. It's their way of punishing the parents, but they usually get in touch again. Once they've had time to think things over.'

'But it's been too long now?'

Greg glanced back at the news report with detached resignation. 'Considering the amount of attention the case has had; I'd have to say yes. To be honest, I'm surprised they're still trying. God knows how he finds the strength to keep going.' On the TV, Ashley's father was being led from the conference room in tears.

Back on the sofa, Greg was also finding it hard to contain his emotions. 'And how do you do it?' Jo asked. 'Your job, I mean. How do *you* find the strength to go on?'

Greg rolled his eyes. 'I keep thinking of leaving. In fact, I think about it every day. I come home so drained. I can't do anything productive, or anything for myself. If I'm not running around after Hanna, I just sit there staring into space. I feel so numb. Honestly, I feel like crying sometimes. It all seems so pointless...' He seemed on the verge of breaking, but caught himself. 'I'm sorry,' he said, running his hand across his face. 'I'm overtired. It's been a long night. I must be holding you up. You've probably got a lot to do.' He pulled himself to his feet.

'Well, about that,' Jo said. 'There is something I'd like to ask your advice about.'

'Really?'

'But not now. How about tomorrow evening, I was going to watch a video? If you're not doing anything; maybe we could watch it together. We could have a chat afterwards. We could order a pizza.'

'Sounds great.' Greg said, smiling for the first time that morning.

Gillian took long, truculent drag on her cigarette. 'Milgallon was in that house for weeks.' She blew a dense coil of smoke across the interior of the Mercedes Vito. 'He must have compiled loads of stuff.'

'Well, if he did, he never gave it to the magazine.' Jo said brusquely, while waving Gillian's cigarette fumes away from her face.

Despite having been over this issue several times already, Gillian was not letting up. 'And what about your father? I know if someone had died following one of my features, I'd want to cover my arse. There must have been internal correspondence or company memos.'

This was feeling increasingly like an interrogation. Across the cabin, Malcolm Rice, the director of *The Max Schaffer Experience*, was keeping himself well out of the conversation, while Jasmine was pretending to read an email on her phone. 'Is all this really necessary?' Jo asked, as the people carrier pulled up outside the Mishal's house.

'If I think it's necessary, then yes, it's necessary. We need that material. Remember, you came to me. You wanted this job.'

'I do want this job.'

Gillian shot Jo an accusing glance. 'That's what you said last time and look what happened then.'

'That's not fair. I was dealing with a lot then,' Jo retorted defensively.

Gillian gave a derisory snort. 'You're always dealing with a lot my dear.' She pulled open the side door with a hefty tug. 'That's your problem.'

'I'm a big fan of the show, you know.'

'That's great.'

'I love all that night vision stuff. Are you going to be doing any of that here?'

'Well, we'll be a little stuck for space, but who knows?' Malcolm said brusquely, hoping his curt tone alone might be enough to dissuade Belo from any further interruptions and allow him to complete his location survey in relative peace.

'I've got a night vision setting on my camcorder,' Belo said, ignoring Malcolm's apparent indifference. 'If you need extra coverage.'

'That's great; I'll bear that in mind. Now if you don't mind, I've got things to do.'

But Belo wasn't about to be dismissed so easily. 'Will you be shooting the outside of the house today?' he asked, while casually gazing down at Malcolm's clipboard.

'No, we'll leave that until the day of the filming.'

'Great!' Belo clapped his hands together. 'Gives me the chance to finish the cladding. Run the whole thing over with a fresh lick of paint.'

'There's really no need,' Malcolm protested weakly.

'Well, not for you.'

Malcolm shot Belo a puzzled glance 'Wait what?'

'Well, I'm still looking to sell the place, after all. I thought if I finished the shiplap and maybe stick up a sign.'

Malcolm's face was a picture of sheer incredulity. 'Wait, you're trying to sell your house on our reality television show?'

'You have to admit, it would be great exposure.'

Malcolm intensified his stare. 'Our *paranormal* reality show?'

'What? You think it will put people off?'

'Well, maybe the fact you're claiming the house is haunted might.'

Undeterred Belo shrugged. 'Well, I was thinking, maybe instead of a séance you could finish the show with an exorcism or something? You know, show it's all been fumigated and all that.'

'I've got things to do,' Malcolm said, pivoting sharply away from Belo.

'You think about what I said, though?' Belo called after him, as Malcolm hurried past Jo in the hallway and disappeared upstairs.

Keen to avoid a similar entanglement Jo quickly deflected Belo's attention. 'I think Qamra was looking for you in the lounge.' she fibbed, while slipping nimbly out through the patio doors.

Finding a quiet space on the patio, Jo tugged the cellophane wrapping off a fresh packet of Silk Cut. Glancing back through the patio doors, she was relieved to see Gillian was still sitting with Qamra in the lounge. If Gillian had known Jo had been heading outside for a smoke, she'd have been hot on her heels. And right now, Jo needed a little space between herself and the whole Dark Dimension crew.

From the moment they had arrived, it had been clear Qamra had been having second thoughts. Having only agreed to the show under pressure from her husband. The presence of a full location survey team roaming her home had prompted an abrupt change of heart.

Overwrought and distracted, Qamra kept pacing the room and muttering to herself in Arabic. When she did switch to English, her delivery was less articulate and more laboured. 'But how this help, Lila?' Qamra had pleaded. 'I just want someone to tell me what is wrong with Lila.' But Qamra's objections and concerns had quickly paled when confronted by the linguistic machinations of Pam Martin.

Introduced to the Mishals as their location liaison, Pam was clearly a member of Gillian's legal team. If Gillian had been an aficionado of the fine art of manipulation, then Pam had been its dark master. For the past hour, the Mishals had been presented with a long succession of insurance documents and nondisclosure agreements, while Pam had bamboozled the couple with a persistent stream of legal jargon and technical psychobabble. To the point where neither Mishal knew what they were signing their names to.

As far as money was concerned, they'd been told there would be a nominal stipend payment. A ridiculously small amount in Jo's opinion considering the amount of upheaval involved. But there would be other benefits Gillian had reassured them. Various expenses would be taken care of. For a start, the location vans would have to be parked on the grass verge in front of the house, which could result in a lot of re-landscaping. The floorboards in the hallway would have to be secured and the electrical sockets refitted. The list had gone on, to Belo's obvious delight. In fact, Belo had been so eager to get any renovation work done to his property, he had practically given Gillian carte blanche to do anything she wanted in the house; short of firing Lila off the roof from a cannon.

Which brought Jo back to Lila. Throughout the entire process, the teenager seemed to be a peripheral concern to the Dark Dimension team. Of course, Gillian had offered all the usual assurances about the girl's welfare. That her health and mental wellbeing were to be the show's paramount concern. All the while Lila had sat silently on the sofa, scowling disdainfully through copious layers of black eyeliner. Her normal dusky makeup, starkly enhanced by a shroud of pale foundation.

In response to the teenager's sulky demeanour, Belo had attempted to tease the child over her gloomy appearance. When this had been met with stoney indifference, he had tried to tickle the sullen girl in an affectionate manner. Grumbling loudly, Lia had wriggled free of his grasp, retreating grumpily to another corner of the room. Where she'd remained, huddled in an armchair, her knees drawn up under her chin, chewing her nails and pretending to listen to her portable CD player. Despite the girls' apparent disinterest, there'd been no doubt in Jo's mind that Lila had been actively following everything being said. An assumption confirmed during Qamra's final exchange with Pam. 'But what does this mean, *exactly?*' Qamra had asked in exasperation.

'It's basically stating the investigation and the séance are *for entertainment purposes only.*' Pam had said, painfully over-articulating each word, having wrongly assumed Qamra's confusion was due in part to a poor understanding of the English language.

'I understand term,' Qamra had snapped back. 'I just don't understand what you mean by it?'

Pam had twisted her neck indignantly. 'You can appreciate we always strive for accuracy in our programming. But due to the format of the show; sometimes, certain occurrences have to be augmented to make them more engaging for the viewing public. You have to remember at the end of the day, this is only an experiment and no results can be guaranteed. And let's not forget this show is primarily entertainment.'

'I still don't understand any of this. What do you think?' Qamra had turned toward Jo. It had been clear from her expression that she still considered Jo as somehow separate from the rest of the television crew.

'I think it means that events may appear different in the televised show, to how they may have appeared here on the night.' Jo had said. 'I believe it's pretty standard practice on reality shows.'

'We prefer the term *unscripted*,' Pam had corrected Jo sternly. 'Because the term *real* can leave us open to certain legal complications.'

'But it *is* real!'

Lila's interruption had taken everyone by surprise. 'No one is saying it's not, dear,' Pam had retorted in a less than sympathetic tone.

'You don't believe me. Any of you!'

'It's not a matter of us believing you or not.'

'As long as it's entertaining,' Lila had snarled contemptuously.

'Lila, stop making scene. This is not helping anything!'

Ignoring her mother, Lila had leapt from her seat. 'So what's the point of me even being here, then? It's not like I've got any say in any of this!' With that, she had stomped from the room, slamming the door behind her. A firm glare from Qamra had dissuaded Belo from chasing after her. Curtailing any further family arguments, while the house was full of strangers.

The last matter discussed had been the thorny question of Roy Norris, which Gillian had been quick to brush aside. 'Although he may well provide some valuable insight into the haunting, I'm afraid we can't allow him to be present during the actual séance, as Max finds having another psychic present during an investigation extremely distracting.' Qamra had been about to object but Gillian had cut across her. 'Plus I have to remind you that you have agreed not to allow any other psychics, spiritualists or paranormal investigators into this house until our filming has concluded.' Both the Mishals had appeared surprised by this stipulation; but neither had been willing to question it. After a little more cajoling, a filming date had been confirmed for the night of the anniversary. At which point, Jo had left them to it.

Now outside, Jo took an irritated drag on her cigarette. Leaning back against a partially constructed plastic swing set on the patio, her gaze drifted out toward the end of the garden.

It was then she noticed the huddled figure.

Lila sat hunched on an old metal swing, partially hidden behind an overgrown rose trellises. As Jo walked toward the child, she could see the teenager nervously picking at a cluster of short cuts and scabs on her forearm. Hearing Jo's footsteps, Lila hastily pulled her sleeve over her hand and clenched the cuff closed. 'So have you got more things you want me to be aware of?' she sneered, as Jo took the free seat beside her.

'No, just wanted to have a little chat. See how you're doing.' Jo said cooly, keeping her own tone light.

'Would that be an *unscripted* chat?'

Ignoring Lila's curt sarcasm, Jo smiled amicably. 'No, I just wondered how you felt about all this.'

Avoiding Jo's gaze, Lila glared at the ground. 'They've already offered me a counsellor.'

'But you don't want to speak to her.'

'They're not interested in helping me, not really,' Lila said with a petulant snarl. 'They're just worried I'll have a mental breakdown or something and end up suing them.'

'I'm sure they just want to make sure you're okay.'

'I'm not mad you know,' Lila snapped, turning to face Jo for the first time. The swing's rusty metal chains creaking under her weight.

'No one is saying you are.'

'And I'm not a lier either.'

Jo turned to face Lila directly. 'Lila, I'm not trying to catch you out here.'

'No, you're only interested in making your TV show.'

'You don't have to do it if you don't want.'

Lila gave an insolent shrug. Despite her churlishness there was still something oddly compelling about the girl's conflicting mix of fragility and profundity. 'Are you worried about what your classmates will say when they see the show?' Jo asked. 'Your mum says you've been having some trouble.'

'Because I hit that girl. She called me a sand nigger.'

Lila's body tensed as she waited for Jo's response. Which, when it came it was far less critical than she had expected. 'Well, then she probably deserved it.'

Lila huffed. 'Well, you're the only one that thinks so.'

There it was, the first real sign Lila was letting her defences down. Encouraged by the girl's softening attitude, Jo pressed on. 'What about your friends from your old school? Do you ever see them?'

Lila grimaced dismissively.

'What about a boyfriend?'

The glare she received left Jo with little doubt; this was another topic best left alone.

As a tense silence fell between them, Jo pulled her cigarettes from her pocket. This action didn't go unnoticed by Lila. After a cautious glance over her shoulder, Jo flipped the lid of the packet. Tugging a cigarette free, Lila quickly hid it in her jacket.

As Lila resumed her original withdrawn position, it appeared as if their conversation had come to a natural conclusion. But the gesture with the cigarette had apparently brokered Jo an iota of trust. 'They didn't even bother asking me,' Lila said. 'They just moved here.'

'So you don't get to see all your old friends then?'

'Who would want to come here?' Lila nodded back toward the house. 'I don't even want to be here. No one does. All they do is argue and shout at each other. Everything is horrible. I hate it.' The more Lila spoke the more Jo realised how little there was of Qamra's native intonation present in her speech. If anything, she'd picked up some of Belo's thick London accent.

'Well, maybe when they sell the house, things will get better.'

Scowling, Lila dug her heel into the soil beneath the swing. 'It won't make any difference.' She fell silent a moment before adding, 'I'm not myself, you know. I never have been. It's just worse here.'

Jo could sense Lila's frustration, as she waited pensively for Jo's response. Unable to think of a suitable reply, Jo placed her hand gently on Lila's shoulder. Although bulking slightly from her touch, Lila didn't pull away.

Over on the patio, Malcolm appeared from the house and waved at Jo. Standing, Jo placed the open cigarette packet on the seat she had just vacated. 'For later.'

Lila gave an imperceptible nod, which Jo took to be a thank you.

'So what do you think? Gillian asked at the door of the people carrier.

'The girl's really troubled,' Jo said, while rubbing the last trace of rust residue from the pleats of her tan Burberry coat.

Gillian glanced back at the house as the sound of raised voices echoed down the drive. 'Problem is she's the centre of our program.' She turned toward Malcolm. 'Do you think it'll be an issue during filming?'

'I don't see why,' Malcolm shrugged. 'You know how these things usually pan out. The chances are, very little will actually happen on the night. It's only during Max's bit that there might be an issue.'

'I'll have another chat with Eileen,' Gillian said. 'See what she thinks?' Eileen was an associate psychoanalyst for Dark Dimension. 'Other than that, do you think there's enough there to be going on with?'

'More than enough. It should make a great show.' Malcom said, as a slammed door brought the latest Mishal family argument to an abrupt conclusion.

'Do you really think you'll find something then?'

Jo had aimed the question at Malcolm but Gillian provided the reply. 'Oh, we always find *something*,' she said mischievously, as she pulled her phone from her jacket pocket.

With no further explanation forthcoming, Jo turned to Malcolm for further clarification. 'Put it this way,' he chuckled, 'We've never been to a house that wasn't haunted.' Gillian glanced up from her Nokia just long enough to give Malcolm a mischievous wink.

'So what happens after all this is over? Jo asked, unsatisfied with the pair's flippant banter. 'Did you really mean what you said back there?'

'About what?'

'That you would provide counselling for the family.'

'To a point yes.' Gillian's tone sounded anything but sincere. 'Believe me, they'll get what they want from the show.'

'Maybe they just want help.'

Gillian shoved her phone back into her jacket with an exasperated sigh. 'Let's get something straight here,' she said, locking eyes with Jo. 'You came to us with this story. It was your idea to put these people on the television. Not *mine!*'

'But that was before...'

'Before what! Before you got to know them. Jo, for the last time, these people are not your friends and that girl in there is not one of those broken people you seem to collect.'

Jo stiffened at the insinuation. 'That's not fair—'

'Look,' Gillian said sternly. 'I've done a lot of these things and believe me there are only two possibilities for what is going on in there. Either those people are lying or they're *mistaken.*' Gillian's harsh inference on the word '*mistaken,*' implying there had been far worse expletives she could have chosen. 'Either way, it doesn't make a lot of difference to us. As far as the show goes, it's all real. We take everything as gospel and we give the public what they expect to see. A haunted house.'

'And then we just wash our hands of it afterwards.' Jo snapped, her expression hardening.

With the confrontation now in a deadlock; Malcolm felt compelled to break the mood with a little levity. 'There is, of course a third possibility you know,' he suggested, as both women threw him a surly glance. 'It could all be real and we're all on the verge of making television history.'

Dismissing Malcolm's witticism with a derisory snort, Gillian clambered inside the people-carrier, leaving Jo fuming on the pavement.

'Hello Jo, I've brought popcorn,' Hanna announced brightly, while holding the aforementioned bag up for Jo to inspect.

Greg's expression was apologetic as he followed his daughter in through the door. 'I've got Hanna again this weekend,' he explained. 'Last minute change of plans.'

'Not a problem.' Jo flashed Greg a diplomatic smile as Hanna ran over to Bruno and begun chasing the dog around the lounge.

Greg gave a sheepish shrug. 'I hope the film is age appropriate.'

Stepping back in dramatic fashion and displaying a robust vigour not normally associated with a man of his advanced age, a stoically handsome actor threw himself valiantly against a locked bedroom door. Bursting through a cascade of balsa-wood splitters, he gasped in horror. Suspended over a burning bed (on visible wires), a wild-eyed woman with billowing hair rose into the air. As superimposed flames flickered around her, she rolled her eyes and screamed, 'You can't kill me! I've grown too powerful!'

'Is this a comedy?' Hanna asked indignantly, while stuffing another handful of popcorn into her mouth.

'No, it's supposed to be a scary,' Jo admitted soberly.

Clutching Mr Sunshine, her favourite plush unicorn toy, Hanna slumped back into the sofa. 'It's silly.'

Jo couldn't deny that. The film was truly awful. Not that she hadn't been forewarned. When Belo had lent her his VHS copy of *Hell House: The Babcock Haunting*, he'd apologised for not having it on DVD. 'Not that it would improve the quality much.' he had quipped. Now Jo knew what he had meant. In the film, the stoic actor was now battling against powerful paranormal forces, which appeared to be little more than a wind machine, dry ice and pure enthusiasm on his part.

'Very silly,' Hanna repeated.

'Well, most ghost stories are,' Jo countered mischievously, trying to match the child's dour tone.

'Because ghosts aren't real,' Hanna concluded with a decisive nod.

'What makes you so sure?' Jo asked, unable to resist teasing the austere child a little.

Deep furrows appeared across Hanna's forehead as she pondered Jo's question. 'Because, if ghosts were real, you'd see good ghosts all the time wouldn't you? People you wanted to see, like their grandparents, or Princess Diana, or your mother.'

'My mother?'

Hanna's casual reference took Jo by surprise. Normally, when people mentioned her mother, it was always with some inevitable awkwardness. It was odd to hear her referenced with so little subtlety. Not that Hanna was aware of the effect her statement had made on Jo. 'If ghosts were real, you would see your mother wouldn't you? She would be here with you now—'

'Hanna that's quite enough!' Greg snapped, as he entered the lounge carrying a stack of delivery pizzas.

Hanna glanced over at her father, confused by his stern tone. 'I thought you would miss her?' she said, turning back to Jo.

Jo tried her best to sound blasé. 'Yes, I miss her. But I never really got to know her when she was alive.'

'So what do you miss then?'

Greg was about to reprimand Hanna further but a quick glance from Jo dissuaded him. 'I suppose I miss the time we didn't have together.'

Hanna pondered this notion for a few seconds. 'So it would be nice if she came to visit you as a ghost then,' she concluded, impressed with her own insight.

'Well, maybe she can't, because she's gone somewhere else.'

'Like Heaven?'

'Yes, like Heaven.'

Hanna gave the idea a little more thought. 'But people that don't want to be ghosts get to stay, while people that do, don't. Doesn't seem fair.'

Jo tried to construct an answer that would satisfy an audacious seven-year-old. 'Well, maybe Heaven's so nice. No one wants to leave it once they get there.'

'Not even to see their family?'

'No, not even to see their family.'

'Still doesn't seem fair.' Hanna shrugged.

'No, it doesn't,' Jo agreed, but by now Hanna had become distracted by a freshly opened pizza box. Greg mouthed the word 'sorry' over Hanna's head as he passed Jo her pizza. Which Jo dismissed with a polite smile.

Greg flipped open *Haunted London*, the book Lawrence had given Jo. 'Leaves little to the imagination,' he declared, staring down at a large crime scene photograph of Chris Babcock lying in a pool of blood. Behind Greg, Hanna was sleeping soundly on the sofa with a blanket over her. 'Isn't it the anniversary or something?' Greg asked, flipping the page over to the image of two covered bodies lying at the base of an imposing viaduct.

'In a couple of weeks.' Jo threw a dismissive gesture over the slew of photocopies scattered across her dining table. 'I've been trying to find something that hasn't been reprinted a thousand times already. But it's hopeless. Other than Milgallon's book there's hardly any other first-hand accounts of the hauntings.'

'What about your father? Doesn't he have anything you could use?'

'Dad shelved everything to do with the Babcock's long before I started there.'

'But I thought you'd always...'

'Worked there. No, I tried a few other things first; fashion design, life coaching, business management, before I settled on a communications degree.'

'So publishing wasn't your first choice. I would have thought, with your father and all?'

Jo huffed. 'Dad never encouraged me to be part of the business. I think he would have been far happier if I'd done just about anything else.'

'Well, you had plenty of opportunity.'

Ignoring Greg's sly swipe, Jo took a sip of wine. Since his recent separation and financial problems, Greg had become increasingly resentful over people who he, in his opinion, had 'had it easy'. An inference he'd begun to level, with annoying regularity, at Jo. Especially since he had learnt, via the residents' association, that Jo's flat was actually owned by her father. What he would make of the fact that her car lease was also being met by her dad didn't bear thinking about.

'So you're certain *this* is the same house?' Greg asked, plucking a photograph from a pile on the table.

'Absolutely; I've checked the records,' Jo said, buoyed by the change of subject. 'They renamed the street in the seventies. None of the other residents objected. In fact, I should think they'd have welcomed it, considering all the negative attention it had been receiving. The council just patched the house up and allocated it to new occupants.' Jo unfolded a photocopy, while Greg topped up their wine glasses. 'An elderly couple bought it from the council in the eighties and lived there uneventfully for the next twenty years. The Mishals purchased the property after the couple went into a nursing home. It was in a pretty sad state of disrepair by then.'

'And when the hauntings begun again the new owners contacted you. Because your magazine had published the original articles.' Jo took another sip of wine as she waited for Greg to ask the inevitable question. 'And you believe them?'

'I don't know what I believe anymore,' Jo admitted. 'I mean I never really took any of this supernatural stuff seriously before.' Greg hid a wry smile behind his wineglass as he recalled the numerous healing crystals he'd seen scattered around Jo's flat. 'That's what I wanted to ask you about,' Jo continued. 'Have you ever come across anything like this before?'

'You mean the whole demonic possession thing, not directly, but I know some colleagues that have. It's more common than you may think.'

'Hauntings?'

'Mental health issues.'

Smiling, Jo waved a good-humoured finger at Greg. 'I knew you'd say that.'

Greg shrugged. 'I don't think you can see it any other way. Unless, of course you want to concede that ghosts are real.'

'Yes, I know, but it's still hard for me to rationalise everything.'

'You mean the fact you could well be taking advantage of someone with an obvious mental health condition?'

'Not exactly, but thank you for pointing that out.'

'But it's true isn't it?' Greg picked up a loose production schedule from the table before dropping it back down again. 'You're lumping a spiritualist on these people, when you should be directing them toward a certified psychotherapist.'

Even though Jo had suspected this would be Greg's response, she couldn't help but feel defensive over her own involvement in the matter. 'Well, some would say a spiritualist provides the same sort of service as a psychologist.'

But Greg had heard this argument before. 'And they can also cause a lot of harm, too. Don't think this is all just harmless gobbledegook,' he said, waving his wineglass over the table. 'Even today; many Middle Eastern and African cultures still view mental illness as a direct punishment from God or the result of some form of possession by an evil spirit. The victims of these so-called possessions are vilified by their friends and family on the mere say-so of some unqualified faith healer or witch doctor. The sheer magnitude of shame and fear associated with these allegations forces the victim into complete silence, so the real scale of these abuses is never known. We had a case; a few years ago. A young girl was accused of possession by a local faith healer. And under the pretence of some kind of mystical treatment, he set about regularly molesting the child in her own home, while the parents sat dutifully praying in the next room. Believe me, these people are doing actual harm to some very vulnerable people. Most of whom are already suffering the effects of some form of trauma.'

'Trauma?' Jo lent toward Greg.

Spurred by Jo's unexpected attentiveness, Greg elaborated. 'You can associate most reports of spirit possession with some kind of exposure to trauma.'

'Such as?'

'Such as the guilt of a sexual assault or the anguish of having caused someone's death. The victim tries to divert the blame or the shame they're feeling away from themselves. They may not even know they've done this. In a lot of cases, they may actually believe what is happening to them is real.'

As Greg had been talking, Jo had been sifting through her research papers. 'Here,' she said, spinning an open book toward Greg. 'Patrick Milgallon doesn't dwell too much on the aftermath of his investigation. But he does claim the tragedy was all down to the intervention of a Christen Society.'

'Maybe. But they'd only have been building off a premise this guy Milgallon had already established. One delusion, feeding the next.' Over on the sofa, Hanna muttered something in her sleep and Greg fell silent. 'She has bad dreams,' he said dolefully before adding, 'Sorry about earlier. She can be quite forthright. Her councillor says it's her way of dealing with the divorce.'

'That's okay, I was just the same at her age.'

'Yeah, she's probably more messed up than she lets on.' Greg caught a vague glint in Jo's eye. 'I didn't mean that's why you were similar.'

Laughing, Jo dismissed Greg's concern. 'I imagine I was worse,' she said with a sad smile. 'To be honest, I don't know how my father put up with me.'

'It's difficult for children to deal with this sort of thing.' Greg said, glancing over at his daughter. 'They don't even know how to deal with their own problems; never mind all their parents' crap as well. We think we're doing the best for them. But who knows what damage we're really doing to them?'

'Like letting them stay up late to watch scary movies.'

Greg waved a playful finger at Jo. 'Oh no, that was entirely *your* doing.' As Jo laughed, Hanna begun making restless noises on the sofa. 'I should get her into her own bed,' Greg conceded with a reluctant sigh. Draining his glass, he got up and went over to wake Hanna.

'Are we going?' Hanna asked sleepily, rubbing her eyes with the heel of her hand.

'Yes, we're off.'

With half-closed eyes, Hanna got up and strode over to Jo. 'Good night Jo; Thank you for a very nice evening,' she said formally, before grabbing Greg's hand and leading him toward the door.

'Thanks again. It was lovely,' Greg called back over his shoulder as Hanna led him across the hallway toward the stairwell. As Jo waved them goodnight at the door, Bruno appeared briefly from the kitchen to watch the commotion before turning back to his bed with a disgruntled snort.

Jo had just closed the dishwasher when she heard a light tap on her apartment door. Puzzled by the knock, she glanced across the lounge and spotted a fluffy white unicorn laying by the sofa. Scooping up the soft toy, she pulled the door open. 'How could you forget Mr Sunshine?' she laughed.

'I wasn't aware I had.'

Jo was stunned into silence. Tony Vail was standing in the hallway clutching a sad bunch of tulips. If it had been possible, he looked even more tired and haggard than usual. 'I take it you were expecting someone else,' he said glibly, glancing down at the plush toy in Jo's hand.

'Well, just about anybody else, to be perfectly honest,' Jo admitted cooly, as Tony shuffled awkwardly on the spot.

'And you brought me flowers?' she added coyly, for want of anything better to say.

'It's what people do isn't it?'

Jo eyed the limp flowers in Tony's hand and the half-peeled garage price label still clinging to the plastic wrap. 'You don't have a lot of interaction with normal people do you?'

'Not if I can help it.'

Cradling her coffee mug in both hands, Jo peered nervously across the lounge at Tony.

'I used to think it was pity,' he said, glancing up from his own mug.

'What was?'

'That look you have in your eyes now.'

Jo attempted an apologetic gesture, but Tony waved it away. 'It's the same look I get whenever people realise who I am. I used to think it was pity, but now I know it's fear.'

'Fear?' Jo caught herself glancing toward the front door. Despite his placid demeanour, Tony's presence in her flat had provoked an unsettling sense of vulnerability within her.

Tony's eyes followed Jo's gaze toward the hallway, but fell short of the door. Falling instead upon a crumpled cardboard box by the coat stand, inscribed with the words:

JAMIES CRAP

'Fear of what I represent,' he said casually, turning back to face Jo. 'You see, I'm tangible proof that evil exists. That bad things happen. That look is their defence. It separates them from me.'

'And you from them.'

Tony tipped his head as if to say, '*I'll give you that one.*' 'But then you would know just as much about that as I would; wouldn't you Jo Kalman?'

Jo bristled at Tony's insinuation. 'This isn't about me,' she retorted.

'It never is.'

Sensing he'd annoyed her with his last comment and not wishing to antagonise her any further Tony gave Jo a half-smile. 'So what's the show about?'

'The show?'

'In the cellar you said you were working for a television company.'

'Oh yes, the company's called Dark Dimension. They specialise in paranormal investigation shows—'

Tony huffed. 'Yeah, I know the format. A bunch of overexcited halfwits equipped with camcorders and dodgy ghost-detecting devices lock themselves in a haunted house for the night. And by the morning, they've all either spoken to, seen or stumbled across some form of paranormal activity. Then they all go home happy and despite this apparent plethora of fresh evidence they never return to the building again.'

As Tony had been talking, Jo had been methodically tapping the back of her hand with her finger. Noticing Tony's interest, she dropped her hand to her side. 'I think that about sums it up,' Jo conceded grumpily.

'You know a real paranormal investigation takes place over several weeks or even months,' Tony continued. 'You won't find anything charging around in the dark, jumping at shadows. These shows aren't evidence-driven. They rely purely on the say-so of their cast and crew. It's about as far from actual scientific research as you can get.'

'So what brings you here then?' Jo asked sternly.

'I watched the tape you left me.'

'It couldn't have been easy for you.'

Tony looked surprised by the sincerity of Jo's tone. 'None of this is easy for me,' he whispered.

Encouraged by Tony's response, Jo continued. 'I understand how difficult all this must be for you. Considering everything you went through—' But this time she'd overreached herself.

'Everything I went through! How would you know what I went through? Reaching across the sofa, Tony retrieved the *Hell House* slip case from under a cushion. 'I'd say you haven't got a clue what I've been through.' He tossed the case aside contemptuously. 'If I do this for you; it'll have nothing to do with your TV show.'

'That's all I'm asking for,' Jo agreed genially. 'Just take a look, that's all.'

Surprised by how quickly she had conceded, Tony threw her a suspicious glance. 'Why? What's in this for you?'

'I just want to do something for the family.'

'Like exploiting them on a television show.'

Aware Tony was attempting to goad her, Jo ignored the comment. 'Look do you think you can help them or not?' she asked, with as little animosity as she could muster.

'Well, I don't think I could do much more damage, considering who else they've already let in that house.'

It took a second for Jo to realise who Tony was referring to. 'Do you mean the clairvoyant?'

'Roy Norris.'

Jo's brow furrowed. 'You know him then?'

'Yeah, I know all about Mr Norris.'

The hostile tone of Tony's voice prompted Jo to clarify her allegiances. 'He's no longer involved with the family.'

'Oh, I shouldn't think that will matter much to him.'

'Well, what else do you want us to do?'

Tony shrugged. 'I'll tell you that once I know how much damage he's already done.'

***

Contemporary camcorder footage: A slim teenager with a delicate olive complexion sits on a chair in the middle of a candlelit room, her hands tightly clenched in her lap.

The camera struggles to focus in the low light, as large man mutters incoherently behind the frightened teenager. Repeating his mantra, the man lowers his palms down onto the girl's shoulders. Gradually they move up the sides of her slender neck, caressing the skin until finally he is holding her head in both his hands.

The young girl looks close to tears.

9. A Sense of Coldness

If you're experiencing strange or unexpected cold spots in your home, or extreme fluctuations of temperature, you may be experiencing paranormal activity. It's thought a spirit will draw heat out of the environment (as well as any other available source, including people) in order to utilise enough energy to manifest.

Any significant variance in temperature, commonly accepted to be a difference of plus or minus three degrees, is a classic sign of a haunting.

***

'What was that?' I yell.

Kalman glances in her rear-view mirror. 'A pot hole, I think.'

'You think? Maybe you hit someone?'

'It was a hole in the road.'

She sounds too flippant, like she doesn't really know.

'Stop the car.'

'Are you serious?'

'Stop the car!'

She hits the brakes and I jump from the Mini, forcing another car to swerve around me. Dropping to one knee I peer under the Mini. There's nothing there.

'They could have rolled away,' I tell Kalman feebly, as I drop back into my seat. I want to double back and check for casualties along the roadside, but she's not having it. So, instead, I throw a strop. 'Slower,' I mumble as we start off again.

Kalman throws me a sideways glance. My bizarre behaviour must be making her nervous. 'It comes and goes,' I tell her, while popping the lid of my sertraline bottle. 'The more anxious I feel, the worse it gets and the worst it gets the more anxious I feel.'

'You're worried about today?'

Damn right, sweetheart. I can already feel the cold sweat on back of my neck. I acknowledge her concern with a half-smile and try to act like a normal person for the rest of the journey. Which is easier said than done. As we turn into Magnolia Close, my heart leaps. With my emotions thrown in all directions, I can't decide if I'm feeling anxious or afraid. Then I see the house. And I feel excited. Not crazy excited. Just excited. I can't stop staring at it. There's a tatty builder's van on the drive with a magnetic sign on the side:

B. N. MARSHAL BUILDING CONTRACTORS

Behind the van, an overfilled yellow skip blocks the path. Pulling up the handbrake, Kalman slips off her seat belt. 'Well, we're here,' she says with an uneasy smile.

I get out of the car and stare around the cul-de-sac. When I used to live here, every house looked identical. They all had the same windows, the same fences, the same dull paint jobs. Now everything is a chaotic mess of random alterations. No two houses look the same. There's no longer a coherent whole, just a muddled jumble of coexistence. And the old house is no different.

The windows are new, and there's a large extension where the old garage used to be. The roof tiles are a different colour and there's a rusty satellite dish strapped to the wall. But enough remains of the old building to force a chill down my spine.

I pull my equipment bags from the boot. Fighting the urge to inspect the bummer for any obvious damage, I round the front of the car. I can't let my mind distract me from what I'm about to do.

'Tony, are you sure you want to do this?' Kalman must have just read my expression.

I've never been less sure about anything in my life, but I tell her I'm okay.

As we reach the doorstep, my stomach twists as the door opens.

I'm introduced to the new owners and we shake hands in the hallway. The mother looks exactly like you'd expect. Fraught and tied. The husband just looks tense. They're less

Arabic than I was expecting and the mother's not wearing a head covering. I glance up the stairwell. A mopey teenager glares at me from under a black hoodie while nervously chewing a fingernail. 'That's our daughter Lila,' the mother says. I give the girl a nod, but I get nothing back.

The sprawling clutter in the lounge immediately sets my teeth on edge. There's packing boxes everywhere and the whole place smells of fresh paint. As we're shown around, Kalman chats to the parents, putting them at ease. The mother's diction is smoother than it was in the video, probably because she's less stressed. While the husband is all about the accent. South London to the bone. Considers himself a bit of ladies' man, if his banter with Kalman is anything to go by.

'So that's your van out front,' I ask, while Kalman is talking to the mother.

'Yeah, what of it?'

'It's just there's a different name on the side.'

He shrugs. 'It's my company name. People trust an English name more.'

'But you're English, aren't you?' I'm just stating a fact, but he takes it as an accusation.

'Yeah, I was born here,' he snaps. 'And I've worked hard all my life in this country. I provide, no one can say a bad word against me—'

I raise my hands in mock surrender. 'Just making conversation. Trying to get some background.' I've obviously hit a raw nerve here. 'Just talking here,' I add with a dry smile.

He fixes me with a harsh glare. 'Well, let's talk about why you're here then,' he growls irritably.

Now I get it. He's worried I'm here to disprove his claims. That I'm going to get him kicked off the show or something.

I get a sharp *'What did you say to him?'* scowl from Kalman as we follow both parents through into the new kitchen extension.

The extension smells of delicate Middle Eastern spices and there are several bowls of nibbles laying out on a large kitchen island. They've knocked the old kitchen through and extended it into the new extension, creating a new expansive kitchen space. The old French doors are gone, replaced by a wall of modern bi-folding patio doors. Turning on the spot, I try to trace the old layout in my mind.

That's where our old sink was, the back door there. And somewhere here, where I'm standing now is where my father bled to death. Somewhere under this new slate flooring, his blood trickled through the floorboards and soaked into the dirt.

Who knows, maybe it's still there.

Somewhere a memory stirs. The sound of a fierce argument echos around my head like a prowling creature yearning to break free. I feel again the cold lino under my bare feet, the goosebumps under my pyjamas.

A strangled gasp; a rasping groan.

'Tony.'

'You did this, you did this to us.'

'Tony?'

'Yes, what?'

Kalman is squeezing my arm. She tilts her head to hide her concern from the others.

182

Across the room, the mother's deep hazel eyes search for mine. 'You feel it, don't you? You feel uncomfortable here.'

More than you know, luv. More than you know.

'So you're not part of the television show then?' The husband asks suspiciously. 'I thought we couldn't have any....' He searches for the right word; '*investigators* in the house?'

He's still got his back up from our earlier altercation. 'This is different,' Kalman intervenes on my behalf. 'This is a kind of pre-filming investigation. So the TV team will know what to look for. Saves a lot of time.'

'Makes sense,' he admits, but from the dumb look on his face, Kalman could have spun him any old yarn and he would have fallen for it. But the mother's not so sure.

'So are you part of television show or not?'

Her intense gaze forces me to react. 'No, I'm not,' I admit.

I get a hard glare from Kalman. My hand is trembling and I'm probably coming across as a bit shifty. The mother glances between Kalman and myself. 'I don't understand; so why are you here again?'

'Because Miss Kalman here thinks I can help your daughter.'

The mother takes barely a moment to digest this information. 'And can you?' There's genuine desperation behind her words.

'Maybe?'

'Maybe?' the husband chips in.

'I mean, there are no guarantees with this sort of thing.' I'm surprised how reassuring my voice sounds. 'But one thing

I can definitely tell you; this TV company of yours is not interested in finding any actual solutions to your problems here. They're not looking for any real proof. Because they're not actually expecting to find any.'

The husband's posture stiffens, but the mother looks more receptive.

'And you are I suppose?' the husband asks with a sceptical sneer. 'So how is this any different?' he waves his hand over my equipment bag.

'Well, for a start, I actually know what I'm doing and I won't be relying on a load of old secondhand hearsay.' I nod toward a pile of brand new ghost books stacked on the sideboard. Ignoring a warning glance from Kalman, I push on. 'I'll be looking for actual scientific evidence. Whatever this TV crew stumbles across, they're going to declare it proof of paranormal activity no matter what. If a bat farts in your loft, they're gonna say it's the direct result of spiritual interference. What I do is actual scientific research. I'm a qualified paranormal and, more importantly for you, a *parapsychological* investigator.'

The husband shrugs. 'And the difference is?'

'Parapsychology is not just the study of the paranormal. It's also the study of all other psychic phenomena, such as telepathy, psychokinesis and near-death experiences.'

'What like mind reading?' He pulls a dumb face.

'Well, yes.'

'And what's that got to do with us?'

'Well, let me put it this way: you believe a paranormal entity haunts your home, yes.'

'Well, yeah.' He doesn't sound that sure, but nods anyway.

'See right there? That's a popular misconception. You have to realise you're not being haunted. If there is something here, it's not trying to scare you. The fear you're now experiencing is being generated purely from your side.'

'For good reason,' he interrupts, but I continue anyway.

'If there is an entity in this house and it is attempting to communicate, then it's trying to use your daughter as a form of psychological conduit.' He looks puzzled. 'It's communicating directly with her subconscious.'

'Her mind?' The mother moves closer.

'Whatever's going on in this house? You won't find the answer by chasing around in the dark, jumping at any random sound you hear.' The husband doesn't look convinced, so I focus my efforts on the mother. 'Believe me, what your daughter is experiencing is very real. We just have to establish what's causing it. Before too much damage is done.'

'And why should we take your word for any of this?' the husband grunts. Although I'm no longer addressing him directly.

'Because I know what I'm talking about.'

'Yeah, and what makes you such the authority then?'

'Because I've been here before.' Both the Mishal's exchange glances and I can see Kalman bristling. Realising my slip, I hastily rephrase my statement. 'I mean, I've been through a similar experience when I was younger.'

The husband's still looking sceptical, but the mother's expression has softened. Holding my gaze, she moves closer, staring deep into my eyes. 'It messed me up for a long time,' I admit. It's funny to be saying this out loud to some stranger. But there's something oddly compelling about this woman's desperation. 'I wouldn't want your daughter to go through the same thing.'

Both parents look intrigued, but neither press me any further, which is a relief, because I think I've just reached the limit of my honesty. Across the room, Kalman is giving me the old puppy eyes, which I ignore. The husband's still not convinced, but at least his tone is less resistant. 'So how long will this all take?'

I'm tempted to say, *'for as long as it takes'*, but I know he won't go for that, so I give a noncommittal shrug. 'One or two nights; maybe more if we find something.'

He doesn't like the sound of that. 'I don't know,' he shakes his head. 'Maybe we should leave it to the other lot.'

But the mother is quick to intercede in my favour. 'You heard him,' she snaps. 'They're not interested in Lila, not really. I don't know why you even want them in house. It's not good for Lila.'

'Oh, don't start this again!' he bemoans, throwing his arms into the air.

Turning away from her husband, the mother looks me straight in the eye. 'Do you really think you can help my daughter?' she asks.

'Maybe.' From the look in her eyes, I can tell she desperately wants to believe me.

'And you know what you're looking for?'

'Not completely, but I definitely know what it isn't.' I fix my gaze on the husband. 'It isn't entertainment.'

It takes a few seconds for the penny to drop. 'Are you saying I'm exploiting my family?' He steps forward, his temper flaring.

'Well, aren't you!'

We all turn toward the voice. The daughter's standing in the doorway. She's still got her hoodie up, but it can't hide the surly expression on her face. Finding himself under fire from all sides, the husband snaps. 'Lila, go back upstairs. This doesn't concern you.'

'Oh, I thought it did, considering it's me you're all talking about!'

'Lila, don't start!' the mother pleads.

'Or what? You'll drag some other weirdo off the street to gorp at me. How many times do we have to go through this before you believe me?'

'Lila darling, we do believe you. This is why we're doing this. To help you.'

'Then why don't you ask me what I want? Why don't you listen to me?' The girl's visibly shaking.

'Oh Lila.' The mother makes a move toward her daughter, but the girl brushes her off.

'Oh, do what you want!' she screams. 'You always do anyway! It's not like I've got any say in any of this!'

'Lila!' the mother exclaims.

'Just fuck off! Why don't you all just fuck off!'

Turning on her heels, the girl disappears up the stairs. Stomping on each step as she goes. There's a brief silence as everyone waits for the inevitable door-slam, which follows a few moments later. Shaking his head, the husband throws me a doleful glance. 'Yeah, now you tell me how anybody can communicate with that.'

I get halfway up the stairs and freeze.

Muttered, groaning and swearing from Tracey's room. The sound pierces my soul. I'd forgotten the sounds he made there in. The repulsive muddled slurring. And Tracey's silence beneath his drunken groans.

I grip the bannister, unwilling to remember more, but unable to stem the flow of memories. My legs feel like lead, and I have to force myself up the final few steps. As the husband directs us across the landing toward the girl's bedroom, Kalman's hand brushes my shoulder. The door opens.

The room inside looks more like a squatters pad than a young girl's bedroom. There's a few personal items scattered across the bed. A hairdryer; make-up box; pile of CDs; but that's about it. The walls are bare plaster and there's a thin rug on the floor, attempting to hide the rough floorboards. I feel relieved, apart from its size and shape. There's nothing here to remind me of the past. Only the echo of my own distorted memories. 'We haven't got around to finishing Lila's room just yet,' the husband says in a dismissive tone. 'We made a start; then things got on top of us.'

The girl is sitting crossed-legged on the bed, following my every movement with a suspicious glare. She's acting like she doesn't care, but it's taken a twenty-minute chat with Kalman to get me this far. She watches me closely as I get the full tour of the room. I don't return her gaze until we're about to leave.

A momentary glance, but it's enough to realise she's sizing me up, trying to work out my angle.

Well, we'll get to that soon enough.

The E.M.F. bleeps as the light on the dial flashes. 'You have a cold spot here.'

'That'll be the fridge, then?' The twat chuckles from behind his camcorder.

'Belo!' his wife snaps wearily. 'Just give it a rest.'

Behind the view-screen, I can see the husband rolling his eyes. Well, at least someone is having fun.

Moving the E.M.F. over the same area, I get a repeat reading. It would have to be the same section of floor where my father bled out. 'It's always like that in here,' the mother tells me from across the kitchen. 'We've tried everything but nothing heats it.'

My heart is racing and my head's all over the place, but I try to keep my mind on what I'm doing. 'Have you noticed any other sudden changes of temperature, or unusual noises, objects appearing out of nowhere?'

'Well, I keep finding a stack of final reminders on the doormat.' The husband turns his stupid grin around the room, but no one's interested in his feeble attempts at humour.

I cast the mother a questioning glance as she shuffles uncomfortably. 'No, nothing,' she says sheepishly.

'What about the stuff you found in Lila's room?' the husband ventures from behind his camcorder.

'That's nothing!'

Smarting from his wife's harsh rebuke, he turns instead to the light fittings. 'Well, the bulbs keep blowing for no reason.'

Casting a wry glance at the erratic wiring hanging from the ceiling, I opt for a different approach. 'What about things going missing?'

'Like what?'

'Like keys or personal items, disappearing, then reappearing again?'

'Would be hard to tell,' he huffs, glancing around at the chaotic jumble of decorating equipment scattered about the house. 'But we keep all the spare keys and stuff in here.' He pulls open a draw in the kitchen cabinet. I'm immediately irritated by the tangled mass of odds and sods inside. 'But I've seen the shadow,' he adds hastily, having misread the grimace on my face.

'The shadow?'

'Yeah, a man's shadow.'

The mother mutters something under her breath. Clearly another matter he would do well to drop.

'Where's this?' I ask the husband.

'Upstairs on the landing.'

'But it's the dreams that are worst?' The mother interjects, veering the conversation back toward her daughter.

'And when did they start?'

'She's had them ever since...' she trails off.

'Ever since we moved here,' the husband concludes on her behalf.

I glance between them. They're as bad as each other. If they are making this up, they really should get their stories straight.

'Plus, she's more moody and angry, the husband adds with a churlish shrug. 'Not to mention the other thing.'

'What other thing?'

'She keeps,' he searches for the right phrase, 'Shutting down. Like she doesn't know what's going on around her.'

The mother steps forward. 'Why? Why Lila? Why her?'

'It's not just her, is it? You all claim to have experienced something in this house? Your daughter is probably more susceptible. Children usually are. Animals as well. Has your dog displayed any odd behaviour?'

'He's been very unsettled since the move,' the mother admits. 'Restless; nervous like.'

'And your youngest child?'

The mother shakes her head staunchly, but there's uncertainty on her face.

'No, she's okay,' the husband states firmly, but he sounds way too dismissive.

I keep my focus on the mother. 'Well?'

She lets out a deep sigh. 'She says she sees things.'

'What things?'

'Dark figures. She says men are watching her sleep. But I think she's only copying Lila. Repeating what she says. You know how children copy each other. But then there's....' Her hand hoovers over a draw in the kitchen cabinet. Making her mind up, she pulls it open and takes out a loose pile of drawing paper. 'These are Kyra's,' she says in a frail voice.

'Before we came here, all she ever drew were princesses and unicorns.'

Taking the pile from her, I glance through the colourful drawings. Images of people being tortured and dismembered, drawn in thick red and black crayon. Severed limps laying discarded on the ground. A dark figure holding a large kitchen knife dripping with viscous blood. The mother looks close to tears. 'When I asked why she draw this, she said; it just came into her head.'

'What's this?' The husband snatches the drawings from my hand. Flipping through the pages, he looks genuinely shocked by the images. I guess it's the first time he's seen them. 'What does this all mean?' He stammers.

'It means you have a very serious problem here?'

Sitting on the edge of her bed, the daughter puffs nervously on a cigarette. She's putting on a good show, but I can tell she's new to this game.

'What's that for?' she sneers.

'It's for recording what goes on in your room tonight,' I tell her, twisting the camcorder into position.

'That'll be nice for you then!' she smirks. But I ignore her sarcasm.

'Aren't you worried I'll tell your parents?'

'About what?'

'About you smoking in your bedroom.'

She looks relieved but still throws up a strop. 'They don't care! They don't care what I do.'

Ignoring her outburst, I continue to angle the camcorder on the tripod. It's the fifth time I've adjusted it and I'm already getting the funny looks.

Watching her through the viewfinder, she takes a surly drag on the cigarette. But the defiant act is all for my benefit, as she's constantly listening out for footsteps on the stairs. Downstairs Kalman is still talking to the parents. I've asked her to buy me some time with the girl. But it won't be long before someone comes sticking their nose around the door.

I zoom in on the girl's face. It's all about the dark lipstick and eyeliner. Proto-Goth. Parents are probably still reeling her in, but it won't be long before she goes full Siouxsie Sioux. It's all defensive of course. A painted façade to hide behind.

I figure enough time has passed since her last tantrum. 'So that's what it's all about then?'

'You think I'm making it all up don't you?' she snaps. 'You think I'm lying? Well, I'm not! I have bruises!'

'Maybe you fell,' I insure my voice sounds suitably sceptical. I want to see how far she's prepared to go with this thing.

'Why would I bother?'

Good question.

'People do all sorts of things for attention.'

A mischievous sneer appears on her face. 'Well, you'd know more about that than me.'

What the hell does that mean? For a second, I'm thrown. I follow her gaze downward. The cuff of my shirt has come undone, exposing the many scars on my forearm. Her mouth twists into a cruel smile. 'I guess you fell.' She holds my eye with an insolent glare.

Fuck! How did this happen? How did I end up on the back foot here?

Tugging the cuff back down I make with the '*nothing happened here*' attitude. As silence falls between us, she sucks petulantly on her cigarette. Despite the bravado, she still looks like a kid trying to pass herself off as an adult. Peering over the viewfinder, I attempt to regain the upper hand by holding her gaze.

'What?' She couldn't have made the word sound more trenchant if she tried.

I keep my tone casual. 'I was just wondering about something you said during one of your nightmares.'

She shrugs. 'I say a lot of things. I don't remember.'

'Yeah, but this wasn't in any of those books downstairs. In fact, it isn't anywhere. I'm wandering how you knew it.'

There it is again, a calculating glint in her eye. 'Like I said I don't remember,' she sneers.

'Well, okay then.' I tap the camcorder. 'We're all ready to go.'

'So how come you know then?' she asks as I unroll the monitor cable out toward the landing.

Well, what do you know? She's sharper than she looks.

'You'd be surprised what I know about this place,' I tell her, flashing her an insincere smile.

Her eyes become tight little slits as she watches me out the door.

The television is playing softly across the lounge. A White House press secretary keeps repeating the threat that if the

United Nations doesn't disarm Saddam Hussein immediately, then the USA and their allies will be forced to intervene. It's the same clip they've been replaying all day. Doesn't stop the husband from brooding over it every time it comes on, though. He's been scowling at the TV all evening. Only looking up, to shoot me the occasional scathing glance.

I sit back in my chair. I've linked the camera directly to the laptop, so there's no need for a monitor. On the screen, the daughter is laying on her bed, aggressively flicking through a tatty teenage magazine. Reaching the end, she sulkily tosses it aside. Turning over on the bed, she flips the camera the middle finger.

'Charming.'

'You have to forgive her,' the mother squirms. 'She's been through so much. I try my best, but...' She obviously feels her daughter's insolence reflects badly on the family. 'I don't know what to do. She swears and smokes. She fights and argues all the time. It's like I don't know her anymore.' Her voice is tired and frail. She looks close to tears.' Across the room Kalman nods her head compassionately. The mother seems relieved to have found someone sympathetic to talk to. 'I always hoped, after we got to this county; things would be better.'

'It must have been tough for you,' Kalman says in a sensitive tone.

The mother pulls an embittered face. 'I used to pray she was too young to remember. But now, sometimes I can see it in her. It's the fear. It stays inside you.' She turns to face Kalman full-on. 'During the war, we lived our lives in fear, every day, every night. Even when we were in our own home. We were always scared.' Her body shudders as more recollections came back to her. 'You would wake at night to sound of tanks, explosions, and soldiers shooting outside. One day I was in market with Lila, we got caught in missile attack. We found shelter in garage.

'When we came out, the marketplace was full of dead bodies. I saw people who had lost their arms and legs. I was so shocked I could not stop crying. Lila was only three years old.' She turns back to the image of her daughter on the screen. 'All she has ever known is fear.'

Swearing in Arabic the husband leaps to his feet. 'What's wrong with these people?' He grunts, gesturing angrily at the television. His sudden switch back to English presumably for our benefit.

Kalman gives him an obligatory pity glance. 'Don't worry I'm sure it won't come to military action.' Her tone sounds almost condescending.

'And why not?' Why shouldn't they invade? Hussain is a monster; he deserves to be punished for what he's done.'

'But surely there are other ways,' Kalman objects meekly as he pulls a contemptuous face.

'Other ways! What if your neighbour starved, beat and raped his own children? What would you do then? Have a quiet word with him!' He throws a derisive hand into the air. 'Force is the only thing these people understand. They should attack and they should attack now! They should be made to pay for what they've done to our people!'

'*Our* people! Oh, for God's sake,' the mother screeches. 'What would you know of *our* people? You have never even been there!' She turns back to Kalman. 'The great revolutionary there; he knows nothing of our country? He was born here. His parents came here in fifties as economic immigrants. He does not know what it is like to be a victim of war; to be refugee. He has never known real persecution. To live every day in fear.'

She's venting a lot of suppressed anger here, but thankfully it's all heading in dozy bollock's direction. 'I know Hussain is an animal and he needs to be removed!' he retaliates, but his wife isn't backing down.

'At whatever the cost, no matter how many innocent people are killed in process.'

'If that's what it takes.'

'If that's what it takes' she repeats in a mocking tone. 'Listen to him. As if we don't have enough pain in our lives already.' Repulsed, she waves her hand at the television. 'Just turn that thing off! I've had enough talk of murder.'

The husband puffs out his chest, as if he's about to object, but instead compliantly punches the off button on the remote. Satisfied, the mother slumps back into the sofa, folding her arms defiantly. Left hanging, the husband turns, looking for somewhere to direct his anger. 'And what about you?' he snarls. 'What have you discovered?'

'Nothing yet,' I admit.

He throws his hands into the air in frustration. 'So what we're just going to sit here all night then?'

Yeah, well, I'm not all that thrilled about it either mate.

The daughter's sleeping soundly on the live feed, while out in the kitchen the Mishals are talking softly in Arabic. Over on the sofa, Kalman's flicking through *100 Real Life Ghost Stories*; a book she's taken from the pile on the sideboard. She's been tapping the back of her hand again. Between her pinky and ring finger. Standard EFT. Emotional Freedom Technique. Trying to release pent-up anxiety by tapping energy meridians. Dropping the book onto her lap, she stretches and arches her back, attempting to twist the tiredness from her aching muscles. She yawns and looks embarrassed. 'To many late nights,' she says wearily.

'Welcome to my world.'

She gives me a pleasant smile as she wraps her cardigan around herself. 'It's got very cold in here.'

'Central heating's probably packed in.' I cast a sardonic glance toward the husband.

Still smiling, Kalman turns back to her book.

'You shouldn't do that. Prejudices your opinion.' She glances up, intrigued by my statement. 'If you read a house is haunted by... I don't know; by a grey lady. Your subconscious goes looking for exactly that. Anything that might resemble a grey lady. Because you've already told your mind what you're looking for, it tries to oblige you.'

'You mean if you're told the sound of a child's voice haunts a room? Your mind will try to interpret any sound it hears as that.'

'Exactly.' I'm trying to sound relaxed, but as usual when I'm talking with Kalman I can't get the edge out of my voice. She must be getting used to me now, as she flashes me another appeasing smile and lets my harshness slip. 'It's best to go into these things not knowing what you're looking for.'

'But you do know what you're looking for. At least here.'

'Do I?'

'Why? Don't you think these hauntings are connected then?'

'We're not even sure if this is a genuine haunting yet.'

She gives me a long, studious look. 'You think she's making it up?'

I respond with an uncommitted shrug. As usual, all my pretences seem pathetically inadequate under her inquisitive gaze.

'But something made you come back,' Kalman continues in a soft voice. 'Something on that videotape made you want to return; after all these years?

Even though I'm attempting to avoid her gaze, I can't but help notice the light bulb over her head is flickering and not just figuratively. The husband's spotted it as well. He's now prodding a loose light fitting in the kitchen.

'I've avoided thinking about this house all my life,' I tell Kalman in a low tone. 'And now I'm here again. Things are coming back to me, images, sounds. I think they're actual memories I'd forgotten.'

'Is that why you never came back? You were afraid of what you would find here.' She's staring hard at me now, trying to decipher the myriad of emotions that must be raging across my face right now. And in return I notice her uncertainty.

She's thinking that bringing me here may not have been the best idea.

A loud crack echoes from the kitchen as the house plunges into darkness. Somewhere in the dark I can hear the husband cursing like a sailor.

I can smell the alcohol on his breath, the hard skin on the palm. His unshaven chin scratching against my cheek.

'Tony boy!'

I wake with a start as my elbow slips from the arm of the chair. I'm momentarily startled, but the room is quiet.

Strange dreams. A classic indicator of a haunted house.

I check the clock.

03:23

The laptop has fallen into standby mode. Reaching over, I tap the keyboard. The night-mode shot of the girl's bedroom reappears on the screen. It's the same image I've been looking at all night, the daughter sleeping soundly in her bed.

Across the lounge, the standing lamp is still on. Looks like the husband's botch job on the fuse box is holding.

I run my hand over my face. The unsettling sensations provoked by my dream are still whirling around my brain. The smell of candles, burnt toast cooked over an open gas flame, the aroma of paraffin and cigarettes.

'Tony boy!'

A shiver runs down my spine. It all feels too real.

With a shaky hand, I light a cigarette. Well, no one said I couldn't.

Kalman and the mother are both sleeping on the sofa. Kalman's book is still laying open on her lap. The mother shuffles and mumbles something in her sleep. Her prat of a husband has gone upstairs to the comfort of his own bed.

My entire body feels heavy and exhausted. There's a dull ache coursing through my whole being. The sheer effort of containing all my worst compulsive impulses for an entire evening has left me feeling anxious and edgy. Plus Kalman watching me like a hawk the whole time doesn't help much. She's not said anything yet, but I can feel her eyes on me every time I have to triple check a piece of equipment. Reaching for my meds, I give the bottle a shake. Just a couple left. Sighing, I shove them back inside my jacket.

A thin column of light glides across the room, as a car makes a slow u-turn in the cul-de-sac outside. For a moment it falls upon Kalman's face, provoking a vague aching sensation within me, but the feeling is only fleeting and I lose it almost immediately.

Slumping back in the armchair, I take a long pull on the cigarette. Savouring the taste of the nicotine in my dry throat. The pale smoke twists silently in the wan glow of the computer screen. Turning the cigarette around, I hover the tip over my bare forearm. Not that I'm thinking of burning right now. I just need to know I can if I want to.

The bulb in the standing lamp blows with a soft ping.

Electronic disturbances? Another classic sign.

I check the laptop. It's switched to battery mode, but I'm still getting an image from upstairs.

A floorboard creaks overhead.

Unusual sounds?

This place is really taking its cues from *The Bumper Book of Haunted Houses*. What's next a headless monk?

I check the live feed again. There's no movement in the girl's bedroom, just a motionless lump under the duvet.

Another creak. Twisting in my seat, I glimpse a movement in the hallway. A vague shape in the darkness.

Suddenly I feel apprehensive; scared. Anywhere else, any other time, I would feel excited. Eager to investigate the movement. But not here, not in this house.

Telling myself it's probably just the husband skulking about in the dark with a screwdriver, I pinch out the cigarette and move toward the lounge door. Taking a deep breath, I step into the hallway.

Nothing.

I glance up the staircase. There's only blackness on the landing. Turning away, something catches my eye. A shadow moving in the kitchen.

I freeze on the spot, as an echo of an argument whispers in my ear.

Forcing myself forward, the memory builds with each faltering step. The argument transforming into a violent fight.

A strangled gasp, a rasping groan.

I step into the kitchen and stop dead.

I see him out of the corner of my eye. A dark outline against the pale moonlight. I recognise him immediately. The figure that terrorised me as a child. The figure that has haunted me all my life.

My blood runs cold as my body convulses. I want to turn and run, but I can't move my feet. Unable to stop myself I turn to face the shadow.

Relief courses through me as I recognise my own bedraggled reflection in the patio doors. Wrenching out a hoarse sigh, I turn back toward the hallway. And nearly shit myself.

The daughter is standing in the darkness, her eyes wide and vacant. 'Jesus' I yell; and I mean; *Yell!*

Startled from her daze, the girl shrieks as I stumble back into a stack of packing cases.

'Lila!' The mother rushes to her daughter's side. The girl's surprise has transformed into panic.' It's okay, you've been sleepwalking, everything's okay.' There are tears on the girl's cheeks and she's shaking violently. Everyone is shouting over each other, even the bloody dog's going potty around our feet.

My heart is beating so hard I can hardly breathe. Kalman is by my side now. 'She just came out of nowhere,' I gasp between ragged breaths.

Brandishing a baseball bat and wearing only his boxer shorts the husband bursts through the doorway. 'What the bloody hell is going on?' he yells in blurry-eyed confusion.

Yeah, you and me both, pal.

The girl sways as her mother leads her into the lounge where they both sink down onto the sofa. The girl catches my eye as I slump into the chair opposite.

Was she just trying to gauge my reaction? I glance over at the laptop. The image from the bedroom hasn't changed. Just a puffy lump in the duvet. How did I miss her getting out of bed? I glare numbly at the girl until the mother takes her by the arm. 'Come on Lila dear, let's get you back up to bed.'

I watch them both as they head for the hallway, with the husband dragging on behind. I glance back at the image on the laptop. At the suspicious lump in the duvet, that's looking increasingly like a pillow. Reaching into my jacket, I pull out my meds and spill the last of the sertraline into my palm.

Fuck it! I swallow them down in one gulp.

Kalman takes the seat next to me. She smiles, but her eyes look troubled. 'I think maybe we should call it a night,' she says.

And for once; she'll get no arguments from me.

The first rays of dawn roll silently across the dashboard. Houses speed past the window in a muddled blur. My mind's a chaotic jumble of fragmented thoughts and images. I don't even know where to look for answers anymore. Or if I even want to.

Kalman keeps her eyes on the road, occasionally glancing in my direction. I try to focus on the shimmering beams as they slip across the dash. The passing tree branches splintering and distorting their pristine shape. This is all too disturbing. There's no pattern to the movement, no perceivable order. It's all just chaos. Glancing out the window, I recognise the street we're in. 'Stop the car!' Twisting violently in my seat, a sudden panic overtakes me. Kalman slams on the brakes as I stumble from the Mini. 'He could be under a bush,' I yell as Kalman gets out of the car.

'Who could be?' she says, her voice sounding terse and weary. She's clearly had enough of all this.

'The man you ran over yesterday.' My voice is wavering. Even to me, this sounds insane. 'He could have rolled under a bush by the side of the road. That's why we didn't see him.' I stare at her, pleading for any kind of reassurance. But it's not there. Neither is the confusion or the annoyance I saw on her face yesterday. Now all I see is pity.

'Tony, we didn't hit anyone yesterday. There's no one there.'

But I can't deal with her sympathy, not on top of everything else. 'There's no one there?' I wail as a tidal wave of emotion floods over me. 'I can't deal with any of this anymore. It's just too much.'

She looks at me, and for once I feel she understands. Finally, someone understands. I cry as she wraps her arms around me. Right there in the middle of the road.

The first time anyone has hugged me in years.

***

Mid-seventies television footage: Various establishing shots of a normal working-class family going about their everyday activities. The mother prepares breakfast, as the husband changes a plug at the kitchen table. A teenage girl and her younger brother play on a metal swing in the garden. It's all supposed to appear spontaneous and natural, but clearly these activities have been arranged for the benefit of the camera. A voiceover narrates over the images. The tone is formal and clipped.

'It could be any house, in any street. The family that live here could be any family. But this is the Babcock family home. And it has recently become one of the most famous houses in Britain. The reason; this house is haunted. It's been two months now since this alleged paranormal activity has turned this otherwise normal North London family into national celebrities.'

The scene cuts to an over-the-shoulder shot of the reporter sitting opposite the family as they squeeze together on their sofa. The mother pulls nervously at her hair, while her young son clings to her side. The reporter tilts his microphone toward the father. 'Chris, it must be quite difficult adjusting to all the attention your family has been getting.'

The father is wearing a bright, wide-collared shirt with matching kipper tie. His answer is stilted and toneless. 'Yeah, it is. Especially at first, but you kind of get used to it.'

'And how do you feel about being a celebrity?'

The father appears amused by the idea. 'Yeah it's alright.'

The reporter turns to the mother. 'And how are the children handling this new found fame?'

The mother is far more nervous than her husband. 'It's been difficult for them,' she stammers. 'We worry for them, in case you know it's affecting them somehow.'

'Some suggest the children themselves are in someway responsible for these occurrences.'

The mother bristles at the suggestion. 'Why would they want to do that? I mean it's not their fault is it? They didn't ask for all this to happen did they?' The mother looks aghast. 'People don't understand. They don't know what it's like living in his house.' She holds her youngest child tighter in her grasp. 'You don't know what to do for the best.'

The shot switches to a brief insert of the reporter nodding sympathetically. 'Are you worried for the children?'

'I'm always worried. I worry when they leave the house. But I worry more when they're in the house. There's a terrible evil inside this house that clings to you. Makes you feel you will never be free of it.'

The image changes to a shot of both children sitting together. 'We don't play in the house anymore,' the older girl says. 'We have to play outside. Mother doesn't like us going too far. She likes to know where we are.'

'So you're trapped here then?'

'Yes, I suppose we are.' She nods as if this notion has only just occurred to her. 'I suppose we're all trapped in this house.'

10. A Feeling of Being Watched

You may sense another presence when you are alone in the house, or even the sensation of being gently touched. Like a slight brush of the cheek or a light tap on the shoulder. You may also feel someone or something is watching you.

These are not uncommon sensations. But they could well have a paranormal source if the feeling occurs consistently in one particular area of your home. Or at a certain time of day. This is also the most common sensation associated with those who already believe their home to be haunted and can be particularly disturbing for people with strong intuition or heightened senses who may feel this sensation on a continuous basis.

***

The seven o'clock news bulletin had only just begun when Frank emerged from the old Edwardian town house. Even for this early hour he seemed more hunched and languid than usual, as he shuffled across the driveway toward his beloved

Mercedes Benz. Switching off the radio, Jo watched with a heavy heart as her father sluggishly lowered himself behind the wheel of the vintage motorcar.

Waiting until the Mercedes had completely disappeared down the steep hill toward Heath Road, Jo unclipped her safety belt.

Steeping out of her Mini, Jo felt herself swoon, due, no doubt, to her having just skipped breakfast again. She had to be careful. She could already recognise a familiar pattern emerging. Constantly fatigued and irritable, she had already begun experiencing sharp abdominal pains. As if on cue her stomach cramped as she crossed the road, reminding Jo she'd not only missed breakfast but yet another period. A familiar occurrence when Jo was feeling partiality stressed.

Taking a moment to steady herself by the front gate, Jo's gaze fell upon the scraggy flowerbeds running along the pathway. The front garden desperately needed attention. As did the pointing around the front porch and the paint on the window frames. Jo chided herself for not noticing before how dilapidated the old house had become. Gazing across the vibrant red brick façade, her gaze settled upon the round, blue English Heritage plaque inlaid between the bay windows.

RACHEL GRAHAM
1941 - 1977
Poet and Novelist
lived here
1972 - 1977

Staring up at the prominent roundel, Jo realised how indifferent she'd become to its presence over the years. How she hardly even noticed it anymore. Struck by an unexpected jolt of melancholy, Jo dung into her bag for her old house keys.

Inside, the hallway still smelt of the father and a subtle aroma of fresh coffee and toast wafted from the kitchen. Overcome by a sudden guilty paralysis, Jo froze by the front door. If her father returned now, she could still concoct some excuse for her visit, but the next transgression would be far harder to justify. Hurrying down the hallway, Jo opened the door to her father's study.

The packed room looked exactly as she remembered: a large wooden desk by the tall bay window, a battered Apple PowerBook on the desktop, a large metal filing cabinet and a wall of rickety shelving units.

Unable to find anything of interest on the shelves, Jo turned toward the metal filing cabinet. Opening the top draw she began sorting through the card files inside.

If her father should return now, she would have no excuse. This was a blatant betrayal of trust.

After several minutes of fruitless searching, it occurred to Jo that she was probably looking in the wrong place. Berating herself, she moved the desk chair to one side to reveal a large Samuel Withers safe nestling beside the desk. Like the prominent roundel outside, she'd almost forgotten it was there, its familiarity having rendered it practically invisible. She gave the orate handle a sharp twist.

Locked.

Half-expecting this, Jo turned back to her father's desk and retrieved a dented toffee tin from the top draw. Inside were several loose keys, including one with a red tassel fob which Jo knew belonged to the safe. Slipping the keyhole cover to one side, she inserted the key into the lock. Despite its age, the key turned easily and the door swung open. Inside the safe, Jo found a pile of old document boxes. Lifting the lid off the top box, Jo discovered several card folders tied together with string. The top folder marked:

Babcock Transcripts 74

Gillian had been right. Her father had kept every legal document and correspondence he, Lawrence and Patrick Milgallon had made to each other concerning the Babcock features. Along with the documents, there were also stacks of original photographs and type sheets inside the folders. Shifting through the documents, Jo found several papers she thought might be useful and thrust them into her handbag. She was about to return the remaining files to the safe when something caught her eye. Hidden behind an old document box at the bottom of the safe was a wide metal ledge.

Overcome with curiosity, Jo removed the box to reveal the ledge was actually a small inner compartment built into the base of the safe. Gripping its small ring handle, the door swung open with an audible squeak. Inside Jo found a stack of dogeared envelopes and folded documents. Reaching for an envelope, Jo felt a sharp twang of conscience.

Surely, this was a transgression too far. These were obviously the most personal and important documents belonging to her father. But as she withdrew her hand, Jo spotted something unexpected. A thick padded envelope at the bottom of the compartment, its edges decorated in an ornate Pre-Raphaelite design. With her curiosity piqued, Jo slid the envelope out from under the other documents.

The envelope was unsealed and she flipped it open. Inside she found three reels of Super 8 movie film. Jo's heart skipped a beat at the discovery. In sharp contrast to her earlier caution, Jo pushed the whole envelope straight into her handbag and tugged the zipper closed. Closing the compartment, she carefully returned all the contents to the safe and the key to the toffee tin. Returning the room to its original state, she quickly headed for the front door.

Moments later, she was steering the Mini Cooper away from the house she had once called home.

Clearing a space, Jo tipped the contents of the padded envelope out across her dining table. Along with the three Super 8 reels, two photo sleeves slipped from the envelope. Which, judging by the illustrations on the cover dated back to the nineteen seventies. There were no labels on the film reels, but in Jo's mind, they could only be one thing. Milgallon's Babcock footage. Flicking out the white leader from the first reel, Jo unwound a short section of filmstrip and held it up to the light.

It was an image of herself.

Thrown by this unexpected revelation, Jo pulled the strip out further, allowing the loose film to drop and coil on the tabletop. A closer inspection confirmed the film was definitely a home movie from her own childhood, no doubt shot by her father. Mystified, Jo re-spooled the reel and repeated the procedure with the other two films. As with the first reel, both were home movies from her childhood. One a birthday party and the other a trip to the beach. Perplexed, Jo turned her attention toward the photo sleeves.

The first sleeve contained a pristine set of 6×8 Kodachrome photos of her mother in a hospital bed, cradling a newborn baby. Her mother's face looked puffy and swollen and there were dark bags under her eyes. She appeared exhausted and frail, yet radiant and proud. Despite her sallow complexion, she looked beautiful.

As a lump formed in Jo's throat, she flipped open the second sleeve. It also contained a full set of family photographs, taken several years later. Her mother sitting relaxed on a blanket on a dune. Her father arranging pebbles on the wet sand, while her younger self ran barefoot in the surf.

Jo flipped to the last print and found herself transfixed.

Her mother standing by the seashore; the wind blowing through their hair, her arms draped around Jo's tiny shoulders. The image felt natural and unposed. Her mother seemed to embrace Jo with genuine tenderness. Both mother and daughter gazing out to an unseen horizon. There was a sweet unity and contented ease about the scene. Mixed with an undefinable sense of longing.

It was jarring to see her mother like this. Jo was familiar with images of her mother. But they were always media portraits of Rachel Graham the author and poet. Not Racheal Graham, the wife and mother. Growing up, there had been no photos of Jo's mother in the house. Jo had always assumed this had been an attempt by her father to shelter Jo from the reality of her mother's death. To distance her from the event. It had never occurred to Jo that maybe her father had done this to lessen his own pain. To distance himself from his own pain. This had been the woman he'd loved. The family he had lost. These photographs would forever be a reminder of everything denied to him.

Looking at this last photograph, Jo, too, felt her father's loss. And not only for her father but also for her mother. All the emotional turmoil was there on her mother's face. The creeping realisation something wasn't right. The stoic resolve in the face of the inevitable. For Jo it was all capsulated in this single photograph. Had her mother also realised her frailties in that moment, staring out to sea, with Jo in her arms? Had she known that only sadness and recriminations lay ahead? Had Jo's father seen it, too? Or had he recognised it later, in this photograph? Is this why he'd kept it hidden?

Overwhelmed by emotion, Jo envisaged that moment on the beach and the sensation of her mother's arms around her. The smell of brine. The cool breeze against her cheeks. She could see her father taking the photograph and pictured his expression slowly changing from proud sentimentality to resigned melancholy. As a tear rolled down her check, Jo traced her mother's image with her fingertip. But the photo remained a photo. Her touch had no effect on it. It remained simply a likeness trapped on a piece of card.

Qamra double-checked the catch on the window. 'There you go, everything secure,' she said buoyantly, more to ease her own concerns, then any currently displayed by Kyra, who was contentedly playing on her bed with her Barbie doll. 'I've had a look and there isn't anybody outside the window.'

Kyra gave her mother an indifferent glance. 'I know there isn't. Because now he's inside.'

Shocked, Qamra turned toward her daughter. 'Why do you say that?' she stammered. 'Kyra, have you seen someone in the house?'

Kyra shrugged her tiny shoulders. 'No, he's only here when we're not looking,' she said pertly as she cheerfully brushed Barbie's hair.

This was all Belo's fault. They should have left this house months ago. She had a cousin in Birmingham, they could have gone there. But Belo wouldn't hear of it. Too far to go, he had said. Too far! She had fled from Iraq. The least he could do was take a trip up the sodding M6!

Qamra slammed shut the lid of the laundry hamper. Snatching up the washing basket, she headed toward the landing. They would just have to sell the house at a loss and be done with it. The sooner they got out here the better. If Belo thought, he could just dictate to her, then—

Qamra stopped dead in her tracks. She could feel a presence close by. An icy shiver ran up her spin as the air turned cold. Without having to look, she knew someone was there, standing silently behind her. Gripping the rim of the washing basket, she slowly turned to face the presence.

Nothing.

Qamra's relief was palpable. The landing was empty. It was just her nerves. An earlier argument with Lila and Kyra's talk of strange men had left her feeling edgy. Drawing a deep breath, she was about to move away when...

Tap, tap, tap.

The sound of heavy rapping, somewhere close. Like fingers tapping against a windowpane. Qamra turned toward the spare room. The door was partially open. Surely it was just a bird outside the window or the dog? 'Is that you Rafeeq?' Qamra called through the half-open door. But the room remained still.

Qamra was on the verge of calling downstairs for Belo, but the thought of his inevitable condescension only made her more resilient. This was silly. She couldn't be held captive by every little sound in her own home. Keeping this thought in mind, she crept closer to the door.

Since the move the spare room had been used for little more than storing packing boxes, furniture and decorating equipment. With no curtain on the window, a broad shaft of moonlight cut across the room, casting sharp contorted shadows across the walls. Creeping between the covered objects, another noise caught Qamra's ear. A light scratching. Still clutching her washing basket, Qamra edged forward, her ears straining for the slightest sound. Maybe it was mice, or even worse; rats. 'Rafeeq are you in here?' she whispered. Please, let it be the dog, she thought. And nothing more rodent like.

The edge of a dust-sheet fluttered in the gloom. Maybe it was Rafeeq underneath? Sleeping in the darkness. Qamra took a tentative step closer.

Whoosh! The dust sheet sprung to life, soaring upward in the moonlight. Qamra leapt backwards, throwing the washing basket up into the air, a howl of utter terror emanating from her very core. As the sheet fluttered before her, a farcical wail reverberated around the room.

'ooooOOOOOoooo.'

Frozen in a state of absolute horror, Qamra stood gaping at the absurd manifestation as it bore down on her. It was almost upon her, when, like an illusionist, revealing himself at the end of an elaborate performance. The persona of the ghost fell away to reveal Bello smirking from ear to ear.

There was one, maybe two seconds of moderate calm before Qamra, in a state of utter dismay, unleashed an unmitigated torrent of abuse toward her husband. Screaming a string of vile obscenities in every language imaginable, she snatched the empty washing basket from the ground and swung it at Bello. 'What fucking wrong with you!' she yelled, lashing out at him with the plastic basket, tears welling in her eyes.

'What?' Belo pleaded, as he attempted to defend himself against the onslaught.

'You stupid bastard!' Qamra gasped as she rushed from the room. 'You stupid, stupid bastard!'

'Oh, come on Qam!' Belo called from the doorway, genuinely dismayed. 'It was only a joke!'

Across the landing, Rafeeq ambled from Lila's bedroom, glaring disparagingly at his master.

'Don't you start,' Belo grumbled irritably.

Jacob was standing outside Gillian's office, playing Brick Breaker on his Blackberry. 'Is Gillian about?' Jo asked.

Jacob tilted his head back toward the frosted glass partition. 'She's in a meeting with legal. Is it important?'

'I just wanted to run over some camcorder footage with her.'

Glancing up from his game, Jacob caught Jo massaging her temple. 'Still nursing one from last night,' he quipped mischievously.

'No, nothing like that. I just didn't get much sleep last night.'

Jo's defensive answer prompted a knowing wink from Jacob before he turned back to his phone. Over Jacob's shoulder, Jo could see several figures moving behind the frosted glass. Judging by the raised voices, the meeting was getting a little heated. 'It can wait,' Jo said with a dismissive shrug. 'I'll catch her after lunch.'

Jo popped two paracetamol into her mouth and swallowed them down with a gulp of flavoured water. Her head was throbbing and her stomach felt queasy. Her complexion in the lavatory mirror looked as bad as she felt.

Corralled into attending the weekly team drink by Gillian, Jo had on reflection rather enjoyed the previous evening, which had been spent talking, smoking pot and drinking ridiculously expensive wine in a succession of trendy Soho wine-bars. Gillian particularly had been on excellent form, laughing and joking in a manner that had taken Jo back to their earlier days together at uni.

A little too much, in fact.

Unsettled by the thought, Jo twisted her neck and caught the glass-eyed gaze of the hideous stuffed antelope's head hanging over the washbasins. Bloody awful thing! The whole facetious nature of the Dark Dimension offices were really beginning to annoy her. (Was there really any need for an artificial hedge in the break room?) There seemed to be no order or structure to anything. Although Jo understood the perceived wisdom in this. Everyone was part of a collective. She couldn't help but feel frustrated by it all. In fact, everything about the place was frustrating her at the moment. It was well over a week now and Jo was still unsure what her actual job role was; with most of her tasks still being assigned to her arbitrarily by Gillian. The whole situation had become increasingly infuriating and all of Gillian's glib reassurances were doing little to reassure her. Lurching forward, a sudden retching sensation cut short any further deliberation. Turning sharply Jo barely made it into a cubicle before she threw up.

Roy Norris shuffled anxiously in his chair, as he fought the urge to run his chunky fingers through his curly hair. 'I create a serene at-atmosphere and wait for a c-c-contact. It's a feeling I get. It takes over me, c-controls my actions—'

The image juddered as the videotape jumped into fast forward mode. 'There's a great sense of evil in that house,' Roy continued as the tape resumed normal speed. 'It caused Ruth B-b-babcock to lose her mind and to kill her family. I still feel its presence when I'm in c-con-tact with Tracey.'

'So you claim you're in contact with the dead?' Jo asked from off-camera.

'We're all in con-tact with the dead in someway,' Roy smiled. 'Whether it's in our prayers or in our dreams. Or through the feelings we get when we remember someone that has p-passed over. The dead are always speaking to us.' The large man's countenance lightened as he continued to elaborate on a subject he obviously felt passionate about. 'They stay with us; for as long as we need them. Or for as long as they need us—'

The image froze, held for a couple of seconds, before speeding backwards, as Carl, the video technician spotted Gillian at the door of the editing booth and began queuing the tape up for her appraisal.

Gillian entered the booth with a sour look on her face. 'Gillian, there you are.' Jo swung around in her chair. 'We think we've found something we could use.' Having spent most of the morning waiting impatiently for Gillian, Jo was now eager for Gillian to review the tape she had shot the pervious day at Roy's house.

Ignoring Jo's remarks, Gillian tapped Carl on the shoulder. 'Carl, could you give us a few minutes?' Tugging a cigarette from a crumpled packet of Marlboro Lights, she waited for

Carl to leave the tiny booth. 'We can't use it,' she said the moment the door closed.

'Well, I know we'll have to re-film it, but there's stuff here—'

'No, I mean we can't use *him*.' Gillian nodded toward Roy's frozen image on the monitor.

Jo looked stunned. It had been Gillian's idea to interview Roy on camera and now she was just dismissing her efforts without even viewing them first. 'But you haven't seen it yet. It gets better.'

'I just received his background check.' Gillian pulled a folded paper from her back pocket and handed it to Jo. 'He's on the list.'

'The list?'

'Christ, Jo! What do you think? The New Year's fucking honours list! The man's a registered sex offender. Apparently, it's not just paranormal spirits he likes to feel.'

Stunned, Jo unfolded the sheet. 'How did you get this?' she asked.

Gillian flashed Jo a patronising smile as she lit the cigarette. 'Take a guess. Half the people we deal with on these shows are certifiable loony-tunes. We run the odd unofficial check now and again to make sure we're not leaving ourselves open to anything *unpleasant*.'

Irritated by Gillian's abrasive attitude, Jo's gaze fell upon a sentence within the report. 'It says here the caution's nearly spent. So by the time the show airs, it'll no longer be on record.'

'Are you kidding me?' Gillian scoffed. 'If any of this got out; could you imagine? TV company puts disturbed child in a room with pedofile and turns out the lights.'

'So all this has all been for nothing, then?' Jo groaned, gesturing toward the video monitor.

Gripping her cigarette between her lips, Gillian dropped her hands onto Jo's shoulders. 'Well, it was worth a try. There might have been something we could've used.'

Jo twisted her neck appreciatively as Gillian began kneading her shoulders in a show of camaraderie. It wasn't quite an apology for having wasted her time, but at least it was a gesture of sorts.

'Was there any?' Gillian asked.

'Was there any what?'

'Anything we could use with Norris?'

Distracted by the shoulder rub. It took a moment for Jo to get her thoughts in order. 'No, not really. Nothing we didn't already know. In fact, it took a lot just to get him to speak on camera. I think he only did it, because he thought it might grant him more access to the family.'

'Yeah, well, now we know why.' Gillian's fingers snaked around Jo's neck. 'It's a shame, though. We could have used it.'

'Why? What's wrong?'

'Legal has just advised us not to use any of the Lila Mishal camcorder footage. They think it may leave us open to accusations of exploitation.'

'Does that mean we can't use her either?'

'We can still use her in the show, state she's likely the focus of the haunting. But they want us to avoid all the wobbly head possession stuff! So it's down to you now.'

'Me?'

'We're going to need more content to fill the gap.' Gillian's hands slid over Jo's collarbone. Her fingertips caressing the exposed skin around the base of Jo's throat. 'So, do you have anything for me?'

'Anything?' Jo stammered.

'The background from the magazine. Any luck yet?'

Jo's gaze fell toward the card file sticking out of her handbag. 'No nothing yet, but I'm still working on it.'

'I'm sure you are,' Gillian said, her voice taking on a more inviting tone. 'I remember how resourceful you used to be. And how grateful I used to be for it...'

Jo turned to face Gillian. 'Gillie I...' but her words swiftly faltered as Jacob appeared in the doorway.

'Oh, I'm sorry,' Jacob mumbled as Jo twisted in her seat away from Gillian's touch. 'Just wanted to let you know we're ready for you in 'The Forum'...'

'I'll be along in a moment.' Gillian flashed him a withering glare before calmly retrieving Roy's charge sheet and stuffing it back into her pocket. 'You will let me know when you have something for me won't you,' Gillian purred cooly, as she turned toward the door, her hand gently trailing across Jo's shoulder. 'I'd hate for this to become an issue between us.'

Back at her desk, Jo grabbed the paracetamol packet from her handbag. Struggling with the cap on her water bottle, she slammed it down.

Over in the 'Forum' Gillian had just begun her meeting. Jo's stomach twitched as she caught Jacob glancing back in her direction. Snatching at a packet of tissues, she began mopping up the spilt water splattered across her desktop.

Fuck Gillian! Why did she always do this to her? She should have known by now. Gillian would never change.

Throughout university; emotionally fragile and in need of validation, Jo had been easy prey for Gillian's flattery and influence. At the start, Jo idolised Gillian; for her self-assurance, her confidence, her sheer force of will. She'd been everything Jo had aspired to be. For a while, they'd been inseparable and the nature of their relationship had become the topic of much speculation amongst their fellow students. Although not a sexual relationship, their friendship had none-the-less grown into something quite intimate. At least for Jo.

In hindsight, it had been clear Gillian had been carefully crafting their friendship. Controlling it through subtle manipulation. Showering Jo with compliments one moment, then dressing her down in front of others, the next. This continual shifting between adulation and rejection had left Jo conflicted and confused. Which; of course, had been the whole point. After every calculated rebuff, Jo had been even more egger to reassert her allegiance to her new friend, to buy herself back into Gillian's good graces.

On some level, Jo had always known Gillian had been using her, playing on her insecurities. But she'd also known that without Gillian's support and encouragement she would never have completed her degree course. She had needed Gillian's strength, her reassurance. But she also knew that without her own help, Gillian wouldn't be where she was today. In fact, Gillian owed everything she had to Jo.

Everyone is due at least one major melt down at university and Gillian's had occurred at the most inopportune moment imaginable.

In their last term, each student had been required to create a specialised multimedia project on a subject of their own choosing. Gillian had chosen *The History of Advertising and its Importance in Modern Business*, while Jo had opted for *The Freedom of Speech and its Impact on the Media*. These final projects had meant to highlight a student's personal strengths and weaknesses. While Gillian's major strength had been her ability to motivate and direct other people, her lacerating style had made her few friends over the course. With her classmates less able or less willing to sacrifice their own time and efforts for Gillian's benefit, Gillian had begun to struggle.

Jo, of course, had remained staunchly loyal to her friend. Even when just days before their final dissertations were due for submittal, Jo had received a panicked call from Gillian. Dropping everything, she had headed straight over to Gillian's flat. When Jo had arrived, Gillian had been a total mess. And so had her dissertation. Gillian's eyes had been red and teary. A nervous rash which had appeared on her neck earlier in the year had now transformed into a large, angry blotch. All the bravado and self-assurance which had propelled Gillian throughout her course had deserted her at the worst possible moment.

After calming her down Jo had convinced Gillian that together they could salvage something from the situation. While Gillian had paced the room, anxiously smoking cigarette after cigarette and furiously clawing at her neck, Jo had set to work. By late evening, she'd been able to cobble together a coherent ten thousand word submission for Gillian.

With all the work done, Gillian had become a different person. Cocky, buoyant and confident again, laughing off her earlier meltdown, with relaxed aplomb. But the stream of Gillian's gratitude had only run so deep. With the deadline only hours away and Jo's own project in desperate need of attention, Gillian had turned an indifferent eye to her friend's dilemma. 'Oh, I'm sure you'll manage,' she had said with a dismissive shrug. Deflated and demoralised, Jo had thrown together a final submission for herself, scrapping through with a third.

With her own degree secured, Gillian had landed herself a senior position at Dark Dimension. When she had tried to recruit Jo several months later, Jo had been too resentful to even contemplate the offer. She'd gone instead, to the one place she had felt secure. To her father.

This recollection drew Jo's attention back to the card file in her bag and to the sole reason Gillian had brought her onboard now. She could have easily by-passed Jo to get to the Mishal family, but what Gillian really needed was Jo's unprecedented access to her father's records. And then what?

Fuck it!

Jo snatched up her bag. She had to get some fresh air.

As Jo strode through the reception area, a frosty voice called after her. 'What!' Jo snapped, turning toward the receptionist.

'There's someone here to see you,' the girl said in a haughty tone, nodding toward the Tuxedo sofa and the anxious teenager sitting upon it.

'Lila?'

'It wasn't my fault. I didn't mean to do it.'

Not wanting to conduct her conversation within prying earshot of the snooty receptionist, Jo lead Lila out of the reception area and down toward the Victoria Embankment Gardens, where she bought the girl a can of Fanta from a kiosk. Although clearly agitated and distressed, it was only after they had both taken a seat by the water gate that Lila attempted any kind of coherent explanation.

'It wasn't my fault.'

'What wasn't?'

'It's what's in my head. I can't help it.'

Even allowing for the pale foundation and dark eye shadow, Lila looked tired and gaunt.

'Do you mean the dreams you've been having?' Jo asked.

Lila shook her head. 'I hear voices in my head. When there's nobody in the house, I hear them talking, muttering, telling me things.' Lila begun tugging on a hemp bracelet tied around her wrist. Jo had seen similar bracelets on other teenagers. You made a wish when you put it on. When the bracelet finally broke and fell apart, your wish would come true.

'I'm afraid to sleep. I see horrible things.'

'Lila, they're only dreams.'

'I have bruises and cuts. Sometimes I don't even remember what I've done, where I've been. Sometimes I look at myself in the mirror and it's like I'm not looking at me anymore.'

'Lila, I'm sure that...'

'I've killed people.'

'Sorry what?'

'In my dreams. Men and women and children. I'm stabbing them, cutting them up, but the pieces won't die. They keep moving, so I have to keep stabbing them...'

'You know none of that is real though don't you?'

'But it is!' Lila snapped, her face flushing.

'No, I don't mean the dreams aren't real. I mean what's happening in the dreams isn't real. You may just have a vivid imagination. You've been under a lot of stress recently—'

'It's not that! It's always been there; in my head. For as long as I can remember. Mother thinks I'm evil. Sometimes I think she hates me. But it's not my fault, I can't help it. I don't think she wants me in the house anymore.' Lila's manner had become extremely animated, rocking back and forth, while twisting the Fanta can around in her hands. 'What if I can't go back? What if I can't go home?'

'Lila, why wouldn't you be able to go home?'

As Lila's rocking became more agitated, her eyes seemed to lose focus. Worried Lila might be slipping into another of her strange 'staring spells', Jo took the teenager gently by the shoulders and turned her around to face her. 'Lila, why can't you go home?'

It took a second for Lila to respond. 'It was an accident. She was playing with her doll. I got angry and broke it.'

'You mean Kyra?'

'I didn't mean it, but she wouldn't stop screaming. She wouldn't shut up! I couldn't think straight.'

Jo's tone hardened. 'Lila, what did you do?'

'I hit her. I kept hitting her. I couldn't help myself. She was crying but I kept hitting her.'

'Is she alright?'

Lila shrugged 'I don't know. I can't remember. I think so. I had to leave. I didn't know where else to go.'

'Lila, I'm going to have to call your mother.'

Jo had expected Lila to resist the suggestion, but to her surprise, she merely nodded compliantly. Pulling her Black-berry from her pocket, Jo dialled the Mishal's number. Qamra answered almost immediately. 'Lila?'

'No, it's Jo Kalman, but it's okay Lila's with me.'

The relief from Qamra's end of the line was palpable, as a rapid stream of questions came flooding over the phone. 'Is she alright? Where are you? What's she doing there?'

'Yes, yes, she's fine, she's just worried about Kyra.'

Qamra explained Kyra was okay and had only been shaken by the incident. Relieved, Jo held the phone toward Lila. 'You mother wants to speak to you.'

Lila took the phone from Jo's hand. 'Mum, I'm so sorry,' she cried. 'I'm so, so sorry. I didn't mean to do it.'

Lila kept snivelling and nodding as she listened to her mother, occasionally wiping her wet face with her sleeve. Until finally, Qamra had vented all her worry and pent-up frustration at her teenage daughter.

'Do you want me to take you home?' Jo asked, as Lila handed back the phone.

The girl gave a frail nod as she fought back the tears.

'Lila where the hell have you been?' Belo barked the moment Lila appeared in the kitchen behind Jo.

'Belo, I'll deal with this!' Lila tensed, as Qamra strode toward her. 'Well,' Qamra raged. 'What the hell do you think you were doing? We've been sick with worry. How could you do that to us?'

Lila jerked backwards as Qamra attempted to place her hands on her daughter's face. 'To you! What about me?'

'What about you?' Qamra countered. 'Look what you did to Kyra. You could've really hurt her. What were you thinking?'

Over at the kitchen island, Kyra was sitting on a high stool, cradling her broken Barbie doll. A large bruised swelled on the child's temple and there was a shallow nick across her chin. Behind her, on the patio, construction had resumed on the new swing set. Presumably to pacify the distressed child.

'It was an accident she was yelling at me!' Lila said.

'She's five-years old Lila. She's just child!'

'It's not my fault! I can't help it.' Lila was trembling. 'You always take Ky's side. You never think about me. I'm sick and you're not helping me!'

'That's not true. We're doing everything we can.'

'No, you're not!' Lila screamed. 'You don't care about me, you don't care what happens to me. I hate it here, I hate you, I hate myself. I wish I was dead! I wish you had left me to die with dad.'

The slap Lila received from her mother sent the teenager reeling backwards. Even Belo looked shaken by its ferocity. But not as shocked as Lila. Clutching her cheek, she glared in absolute fury at her mother. 'I hate you. I wish you would die as well.'

Spinning on her heels, Lila ran toward the garden. Snatching the broken doll from Kyra's hands, she threw it against the wall as she stomped past, sending the child into a fresh spasm of hysteria. Torn between storming after Lila, pacifying Kyra or comforting Qamra. Belo chose the latter. Only to be distracted by a loud banging from outside, as Lila begun unleashing her frustration on Kyra's new swing set. Cursing loudly, Belo rushed past the still howling Kyra to stop Lila from destroying his recent handiwork.

By Jo's side, Qamra's whole body was trembling.

Qamra's hands were still shaking as they clasped the sides of her coffee mug. Out on the patio Belo was attempting to repair the damage to the new play-set under both Kyra's critical gaze and Lila's contemptuous scowling. 'I don't know her anymore.' Qamra said, glancing out through the patio doors at her teenage daughter. 'It's like she's no longer my child. She steals; from shops, from her school friends. She hides things in her bedroom but we find them. We confront her, but she denies everything. She lies all the time.' Having finally built up enough courage to address Lila's earlier accusation, Qamra turned toward Jo. 'It's not like she said.'

'I'm sure she didn't mean it...' Jo begun before Qamra cut her off.

'No, she meant it. I just didn't think she remembered.'

Jo had been expecting some kind of denial from Qamra, but the woman's sudden openness surprised her. As she waited for Qamra to continue, Jo took a mouthful of coffee. It left a dull metallic taste in her mouth.

'It was terrible then, you've no why of knowing how bad it was,' Qamra begun, her tone almost hollow.

'So, is that how Lila's father died in the war?'

Qamra shook her head. 'The war was terrible. But what came after was worse. We are Assyrians. We came to this country to escape persecution. We are minority in Iraq. The government does not recognise our language, religion or culture. To them we are nothing. They don't even see us as people. After Americans withdrew, our county descended into civil war and Revolutionary Guard used unrest to ethnically cleanse our country. So many had died. They thought, who would notice few more?'

As her words dried on her lips, Qamra took a quick sip of coffee. 'My people were subjected to abuse, kidnappings and torture. Assyrian churches and businesses were targeted. Assyrians were abducted or killed because they held official or professional positions. Civil servants, religious leaders. My father was dentist. One day they attacked his surgery. A dentist surgery! Because he was successful Assyrian!

'Yonan, my husband, Lila's father, lost his job at transport authority and could not find another. I was still studying to become interpreter and we had a young child. We were left with no money. We had to accept help from my father. Yonan had always been a proud and stubborn man and he resented even the little help my father gave us. But with no job and no money of our own he had no choice. He grew resentful and started to drink and the more he drank the more angry he became.'

Qamra shuffled on her stool. 'He no longer cared about anything. He got into arguments with our neighbours and local officials. I begged him to stop, not to draw attention to ourselves, but he wouldn't listen.'

Falling silent, Qamra took a moment before she spoke again. 'Then one night soldiers came to our home; claiming to be searching for fugitive. They smashed furniture and ransacked house. They destroyed our utensils, so we couldn't wash or cook anymore. When Yonan objected, a soldier pulled out gun and hit him across head with it. I think he might have shot him on the spot if I hadn't begged him to be merciful. The soldier released Yonan, only so he could load our valuables onto their truck. They said they still suspected him of collusion and that they would be watching us. It was then my father decided we should leave.

'It meant making dangerous journey across desert at night arranged by professional smuggler. It cost my father all money he had. But we had no choice. Many Assyrians had already fled, but still Saddam's militia hunted them down. They burnt camps, bombed convoys. They killed our people even as we run from them. So our journey had to be arranged in strict secrecy. It was decided we would all leave together, myself, Yonan, Lila and my parents, in smuggler's taxi.

'But few days before we were due to leave Yonan was injured in explosion. They had bombed our church. Many had been killed. My father too was hurt; but not as bad as Yonan. He was coughing blood and bleeding from his ears.'

Qamra begun nervously tugging on the cuff of her cardigan. 'We tended to him as best we could, but we had no proper medicines, only what my father had left in his surgery. Yonan was badly injured. He couldn't travel. His chest had been crushed. In the end the smuggler refused to take him. Said he would never survive trip.'

Qamra's gaze strayed out through the patio doors, as if she was gazing at an unfamiliar landscape. 'In our minds, it was decided. The decision had been taken from us. We told ourselves we had no other choice. But truth was we had already decided to leave him behind. No one had said anything, but we had all known it, including Yonan. At first, we told him we would send for him later once we were safe. But it was obvious he would need intensive hospital treatment if he was going to survive. Plus he no longer had any money or any means of getting any. He knew if we left him, he would be dead within days.

'By then, he had developed fever from his injuries and had become delirious, raving and cursing us all. My father injected him with something. He said it was to help the pain, but it was really meant to sedate him, so we could leave. Yonan knew. He pleaded and begged us to take him. But what could we do? He was injured. This was our only chance to escape. So we left him.'

Staring down at the worktop, Qamra forced herself to continue. 'We had to travel several days before we reached border. No one spoke of Yonan. It was like he was already dead. Except for Lila, she kept asking when daddy was joining us. She had seen him bleeding in my father's house. He had tried to make her feel guilty about leaving him behind. Hoped if she pleaded on his behalf, it would sway our minds...'

Qamra wiped away a tear with the sleeve of her cardigan. 'When we reached border, we parked in desert during night. We had to wait for a friendly boarder officer to come on duty next morning. The driver took our passports and left the taxi. He told us to remain silent and not to leave vehicle. We were all so scared, we didn't even dare leave taxi to go to toilet. We just sat there, waiting. My parents kept praying for our successful escape. It was freezing. Lila was shivering in my arms. We didn't even know if smuggler would even come back.

'But he did come back. He was; for want of better word; an honest man. He told us he make deal with boarder officer. And we would be waved through. We crossed the border an hour later. We were lucky our driver kept his word. Many were not so lucky.'

Qamra looked close to tears, her voice barely a whisper. 'I didn't think Lila remembered any of that. We've always told her that her father had died that night in church; in the explosion. What must she think of me?'

Emotionally overwhelmed, Jo glanced away from Qamra, only to meet Lila's cold, accusing glare from the patio.

Returning to the house, Lila announced that she and Kyra were taking Rafeeq for a walk. As Belo objected, Lila snarled angrily at her stepfather, 'Nobody's asking you!'

'Don't speak to me like that!'

'Or what! What you going to do about it?'

'Oh God, just let her go, Bello!' Qamra exclaimed from across the kitchen.

Belo threw his hands in the air. 'Just don't be long,' he counted lamely, but Lila was already stomping down the hallway, pushing past Jo by the downstairs toilet.

Qamra turned toward the sink, fighting to regain some of her composure. After a moment; she filled a glass with water and passed it to Jo. 'Feeling better?'

'Yes, I'm fine,' Jo replied awkwardly. 'I just felt really sick there for a moment.'

'It's the house,' Qamra said dismissively. 'It does that to you. I've been feeling unwell ever since we moved in. In fact, I haven't felt this bad since I was pregnant with Kyra. This house it makes you sick.'

Jo shivered as another possibility occurred to her.

'We don't have to do this. We could leave it for another night.' Standing in the Mishal's hallway, Jo was about to leave to pick up Tony for that night's vigil.

236

'No, I want an end to this,' Qamra said, wrapping her cardigan across her chest. 'I want to know what is happening to my daughter.'

But Jo's resolution was not so firm. 'Qamra, considering everything maybe this is no longer the right course of action...'

'No, I have to know. I have to know if it's *him*. If he's come.'

'Him? You mean Mr Nox?' Qamra shook her head jerkily. 'Qamra, I don't thi—'

'I'm not mad!' Qamra snapped. 'I know what *he* is and why *he* is here. I know because I've seen him before.'

'In the house?'

'In desert, in Iraq, when we were fleeing.' Qamra's face twisted into an eerily knowing grimace. Her eyes, wide with a strange distant intensity. 'It was during night, we were waiting in taxi. My parents were sleeping. I thought Lila was asleep as well until she points out window and says, 'Look mummy. It's a man.'

'I looked where she was pointing. A figure stood on the horizon in the twilight. I was petrified boarder guard had discovered us. But the figure never moved. He just stood there motionless. I had heard stories about figures appearing in desert. Travellers would say how they had seen phantoms and shadows moving in the darkness. Heard voices and screams in desert at night. *The Dark Men*. Soldiers would see them after a battle. Standing on the outskirts of army camps, motionless on the horizon with their back's to the camp. The soldiers believed they were the souls of men they had killed.

'That night, I stared at figure for so long. Scared to take my eyes off him. But then smuggler returned, he knocked on window and I screamed I was so scared. When I looked back, the figure was gone. The horizon was empty.'

'Qamra, it could have been many things...'

'I know what it was! It was a lost spirit. Left on Earth to remind us of the evil we have done in our lives. It was there that night because of what we had done to Yonan. And I believe it is here again now.' Qamra lent closer to Jo. 'Because our sins follow us, no matter where we go?'

Overhead, a lush purple twilight tinted the sky with vibrant swirls of sumptuous colour. Below, in the Forest Park Playground, Lila and Kyra sat calmly on the swings, chatting and laughing, while Rafeeq lay peacefully at their feet.

Behind the park fence, a line of orange street lamps flickered into life as Lila pulled a packet of cigarettes from her jacket. While the younger sister watched intently, Lila tugged a cigarette from the packet and lit it. The flickering flame briefly illuminating her face in the evening twilight.

As late evening gradually faded into night, the two girls continued to chat and rock on their swings, unaware they were being watched.

Encouraged by the encroaching darkness and the girl's inattentiveness, a bulky figure moved closer to the edge of the playground. Feeling the evening chill, the figure pulled the collar of his donkey jacket up around his neck.

***

Contemporary video recording: A high-angle shot from a police interview room surveillance camera.

Two men sit across from each other, over a wide Formica table. The man closest to the camera is wearing a police uniform. The other is a large man with unruly hair and thick glasses. Wringing his hands, he sits hunched in his chair.

The interviewing officer reaches over and pats an SLR camera, which is sitting on the table next to a twin cassette recorder. 'Roy, you know we're going to get this film developed don't you? So why don't you tell us now what we're going to find on it when we do?'

'I've done n-n-nothing wrong.' Roy mumbles as he struggles with a pronounced stammer.

'Well, several of the parents at the lido might disagree with you.'

Lost for an answer, Roy shakes his head in a child-like manner. 'I've done n-n-nothing wrong.'

A knock echoes off-camera and a door opens. 'Sir, the suspect's mother is outside.'

The interviewing officer nods his head. 'Okay, we'll leave it there for the moment. Interview suspended at eighteen fifty-two and I shall stop the tape.' The officer switches off the recorder and gathers up his paperwork.

Across the table Roy is shaking his head vehemently. 'I've done n-n-nothing wrong. I've done n-n-nothing wrong.'

11. Night Terrors

Waking to the sensation of dread and fear, or an overall feeling of oppression. Being startled awake from a deep sleep by the feeling of a heavy weight on your chest, like someone is holding you down on the bed. A sensation sometimes referred to as 'Phantom Mania'.

Or waking to a feeling of absolute terror between the hours of 3 and 5 a.m. A time regularly cited as being 'The Witching Hour', or the 'Dead Hour'. The time supposedly when the veil between the living and the spiritual is at its thinnest.

***

'Are you here for him upstairs?' Leo's voice echoes up the stairwell. From the sound of it, he's cornered Kalman in the lobby.

'Tony? Yes, I've just buzzed him.'

I've taken the stairs, as someone's left the lift gate open on the ground floor.

'You have evocative face,' Leo continues.

'Evocative?'

'Is right word yes, expressive; striking?'

'Well, yes. Thank you.' I can hear the uncertainty in Kalman's voice. And I don't blame her. If you don't know him that well, Leo's directness can be quite unnerving.

'I would like to paint it someday.'

Kalman chuckles. 'I bet you say that to all the girls.'

She's making a joke, but Leo misses the intended humour. 'No, only those that interest me.'

'And want exactly interests you about my face?'

She's no doubt expecting the usual slew of cheap flattery from the old man. But as I round the stairwell, I can see genuine sincerity on the old man's rugged features. 'There's deep emotion there,' he says. 'A smile illuminates a face for only a moment. But deep emotion marks it forever.' He takes a long, lingering look at Kalman. 'The deeper the emotion, the more evocative the face.' He gives her a kindly smile.

'You ready?'

Kalman jumps at the sound of my voice behind her. Directing her away from Leo, I open the lobby door. 'I see you again I think,' Leo says as he watches us leave.

'Don't let him sweet talk you,' I tell Kalman as we head for her car. 'You should see the painting he did of me. Made me look like a corpse.' I catch the concerned look on her face but it's not the result of my poor joke. 'What's up?'

'It's Lila,' she tells me.

'Let me get this straight. You want to hypnotise Lila.' The husband scowls sceptically.

Thankfully, the mother's tone is a little more receptive. 'When you say light hypnotic state...'

'It's nothing heavy,' I tell her, ignoring the husband. 'She won't go into a trance or anything like that. She'll just be in a metal state, in which she can relax and speak freely. You'll both be there the whole time.'

'Damn right we will,' the husband snaps. Whatever's been going on with the girl, it's got everybody on edge. 'Didn't we try this already? You know with the séance.'

'That was spiritualism. This is science.' I'm not sure he knows the difference, so I try a different angle. 'People fall into light trances all the time. You can be in one yourself and not even realise. Daydreaming is a kind of light trance. Like driving your car down a familiar route and missing your turning because your mind's been on something else? It happens all the time. But while in this state, your mind is free to wander—'

'And you're qualified to do this?' he butts in.

I take a deep breath. I'm getting riled now. 'I've studied remedial psychotherapy and hypnosis under Dr Sharman at the University of Cambridge. I also have a degree in sociology. And I'm a damn sight more qualified than some of the jokers you've had traipsing around here lately.'

Rearing up, he's about to go off on one when the mother intervenes. 'And this is different how?' she asks.

'Because in most researched poltergeist cases the phenomenon usually turns out to be more *psychological* than paranormal.' I place a lot of emphasis on the word *psychological*.

She still looks confused; but lights are flickering behind the husband's eyes. 'Are you saying you think she's a bit? You know...?' He taps his temple with a fingertip.

'He's not saying that at all,' Kalman interjects. 'He's just saying there may be reasons behind all this; that even Lila may not be aware of.'

Nicely put.

'Plus we could spend all week watching monitors and still not discover anything that will help us,' I add for good measure.

'I don't know,' the mother says, turning to Kalman. 'What do you think?' She's looking for guidance. She's well out of her depth here.

Kalman flashes me a glance before addressing the mother. 'I don't think it would do any harm,' she says in a soothing tone. 'And he does know what he's doing.'

Wow, a leap of faith from Kalman there, but neither parent look convinced.

'Plus it might tell us if Lila is suffering from any kind of suppressed trauma,' she adds.

The husband's got his worried face on now. 'Hang on. I thought we all agreed it was a ghost.'

Waving at him to be quiet, the mother turns to me.' You really think it might help?' There's a genuine desperation behind her words.

'The mind comprises many levels of awareness and activity,' I tell her. 'Sometimes it's more difficult to recall some memories and sensations than others. Remember, she claims she can't recall any of these events after they happen. This technique might help unlock these lost memories.'

The husband steps forward. 'No, I don't think so,' he says in a firm voice. 'She's already been through enough.' He might have made his mind up, but the mother's still wavering.

'Maybe we should ask Lila,' Kalman suggests. But the husband's not having it.

'No, I said no.'

'But if they can help Lila...' the mother bleats.

'No, *I* know what's best for this family. And I say no.'

There you go, that's it then.

'Well, okay, not a problem. Whatever you think is best,' Kalman concedes with a conciliatory smile. 'Guess we'll just have to wait and see what happens on the night, then.'

'What do you mean?' the husband asks, distrustful of Kalman's sudden switch.

Kalman pretends to act surprised by the question. 'Well, whatever it is, I'm sure it'll come out during the show,' she says with a dismissive shrug. 'I just thought it might be good to know what we're dealing with before it's revealed on live TV.'

The mother's gone as white as a sheet. 'What do you mean?' the husband stammers.

'Well, they'll probably do the same thing during the séance. It's the highlight of the show. They always end on it. And they use the same technique as we're talking about here. They put everyone in a light trance just before the start.'

That's not what they do, but judging by the husband's worried expression, I'd say he's fallen for it. The mother too. 'No, I can't have people know,' she mutters, shaking her head. 'I can't. It was one thing with haunting, but not this...' Wrapping her arms around herself, she strides towards the kitchen, with the husband hot on her heels.

'That was a bit sly,' I whisper to Kalman, but she looks far from happy with her own chicanery.

'If this does turn out to be some kind of post-traumatic psychosis,' she says ruefully. 'Then I'm going to get them to pull the show.'

Huffing, I give her a doubtful glance. She's about to reaffirm her point when I suddenly sway backwards. Kalman grabs my arm. 'Are you okay?'

It's a withdraw symptom from the antidepressants. But I'm not about to tell her that. 'I'm fine. I just felt a little dizzy there.' Puzzled, Kalman glances down at my jacket pocket, where I usually keep my medication. 'I'm off the meds,' I tell her sourly. 'Trying to keep a clear head.'

Truth is, until I can source something stronger, I'm scraping by on little more than ibuprofen and nicotine. Concerned, Kalman leans forward. 'Tony, I think maybe...' she trails off as the husband reappears from the kitchen. From the look on his face, he's taken the bait.

'Okay but only if Lila agrees,' he tells us gruffly.

Kalman nods towards the door, and I follow her out onto the landing. She glances back over her shoulder. 'Are you really sure about all this?' she asks in a low voice.

245

'You're the one talked them into it,' I point out. But my flippancy does little to reassure her. Back in the girl's bedroom, the husband is still in deep conversation with his stepdaughter. The girl is scowling at him fiercely. 'It's gonna be fine,' I tell Kalman. 'People do this all the time.' My hands are shaking and I have to cross my arms to disguise the trembling.

'And you? Do you do this all the time?'

She's got me there. 'Well, it's been awhile I admit.'

She looks less than impressed by this revelation.

'It'll be okay,' I tell, with a tight smile, 'Trust me.'

I explain the procedure again for the benefit of the girl. She's perched on the edge of her bed, with a blanket draped over her shoulders. Kalman's sitting across the room, at the girl's dressing table, while the parents are hovering over my shoulder. The husband's got his bloody camcorder out again. But thankfully he's staying well out of the way. We've switched all the lights off except her sister's night light. Pink ponies dance across the bare plaster walls, over fluffy translucent clouds. 'Okay Lila, I want you to know this is a normal procedure used in many relaxation therapies. And this level of hypnosis is not dangerous in any way.' She stares back at me blankly. 'Don't worry, while you're in the trance; you won't do anything you don't want to do.' The girl makes a humphing sound like, '*you can take that for granted.*'

Well, at least she's listening.

'Plus we'll have your parents and a neutral observer in the room.' Kalman bristles at being called a neutral observer. Her finger is tapping furiously against the back of her hand.

I start the procedure as the girl shuffles on the bed. 'Imagine you're in your favourite place. The place you feel most comfortable, the most secure.' She huffs, but she's not fighting against it. 'Imagine you're with friends. The people you feel most comfortable with. The people or person who makes you feel the most safe.'

Her breathing's steady, her muscles relaxed. I'll give it to her. She is actually committing to this. Maybe too much; maybe this is all for show. Hopefully, once she slips under, she'll let her defences down. 'You can feel your eyelids getting heavy. Let them fall as you allow yourself to slip deeper into a calm, peaceful trance….'

She's finally under. Her eyes have closed, and her breathing has slowed to a relaxed rate. This is better than I had hoped. I glance over at the parents. The mother seems a little calmer. Fuck knows what the husband's thinking behind his camcorder. But he's not said a word in ages, which is a welcome change. We start off easy, letting her relax in the trance.

'Lila, I'm going to ask you a few questions. Is that okay?' She nods her head sleepily. 'Do you remember the nightmares you've been having since you moved into this house?' The girl shifts a little. 'Lila, *do* you remember these dreams?'

She shakes her head. She remembers alright, but she's fighting the urge to talk about them.

'It's okay Lila, nothing in these dreams can hurt you now. They're only dreams. If you tell me about them. Maybe I can help make them go away.' She tilts her head to one side. Her eyes are darting back and forth behind her eyelids. 'Can you tell me what is happening in these dreams?' She mutters something, some kind of a lullaby. It's hard to make out.

'What's happening?' the mother asks.

'I'm not sure but I think she's regressing to an earlier period of her life.' I'm trying to sound relaxed, but the mother is picking up on my anxiety.

'Should she be doing that?'

'It's fine, she isn't in any harm,' I contend, if only to reassure myself. I turn back to the girl. 'Lila, I would like you to tell me about what happens in your dreams.'

'I'm afraid to.'

'What are you afraid of?'

Her thin body twists on the bed. 'Him!'

'Him? Who is *Him* Lila?' I'm trying to keep my voice neutral, but it's difficult.

'My father.'

I resist the urge to look over my shoulder at the husband. But the mother is looking anxious now.

'How old are you now?'

'I don't know.'

'Where are you? Are you inside or outside?'

'Inside.'

'Is your father there with you now?'

'No.'

Well, that's a relief.

'Are you with anybody else?'

'My brother.'

I glance over at the mother, who shakes her head in bewilderment. I turn back to the girl.

'What are you doing?'

'We're playing our game.'

'What kind of game?'

'It's a secret game.'

'Can you tell me about this secret game?' She turns her head, staring off at something unseen. Humming that bloody tune again. 'Lila! Can you tell me about the game?' She's ignoring me, or maybe just not responding to her name. So I try something else. 'Your little soldier.' She stops humming. 'You said in one of your dreams 'your little soldier'. Do you remember that Lila?' My voice falters, as crooked half-smile appears on the girl's face.

'She said that before,' the husband pipes in. 'She said Tony was her 'little soldier'. That was Tracey Babcock's brother, right?'

Ignoring the husband, I lean towards the girl. 'Lila who is your little soldier?' Her head rolls backward; she's coming out of the trance. 'Tell me!' As I take hold of her shoulders, I sense some uncomfortable shuffling behind me. My face and neck feel clammy. I'm sure they can see I'm sweating. 'Lila, who is your little soldier?' The girl's eyes spring open, and she stares directly at me.

'*My little soldier is brave and strong. My little soldier marches on.*' There's a cruel malice to her voice now, like she's taunting me.

'Stop it!' I growl.

'Tony, what is it?' Kalman asks as I leap from my chair.

'My little soldier is going to war,' the girl continues, her voice rising in tone. *'My little soldier hears the cannon's roar.'*

'Stop it!'

'That's enough' the mother cries, pushing herself between me and her daughter. 'Leave her alone. Wake her up!'

'My little soldier has nothing to fear. My little soldier, I'll keep you near.' The mother's shaking her daughter, trying to wake her up. Groaning mournfully, the girl's eyes roll back into her head. This is utter mayhem. Everything you shouldn't do. 'Tony!' Jolting forward, the girl cries out, the word raw and rasping. Her arm stretching out toward me.

No, it's not possible.

Digging into my pockets, I fumble with the E.M.F. and it drops to the floor. I can't think straight. The room is spinning. I stare numbly back at the girl's anguished face. At the same, anguished expression that has tormented me all my life. Haunted all my nightmares. All I can do is stare, as the child struggles and claws at her mother. Then she screams. A deep guttural roar, emanating from her very core. 'What did you do to her?' the husband yells, over the agonised wailing. Staggering backwards, I trip over my own feet. Kalman grabs my arm. Then everything stops. The girl slumps in her mother's arms and everyone falls silent. No one moves.

After a moment, the girl lifts her head, gazing around at the shocked faces staring back at her. 'Mum,' she cries as the mother squeezes her in her arms. 'What happened? What's going on?'

No, no, I'm not having that. I'm overtaken by a sudden rage. Pulling away from Kalman, I stomp toward the bed, jutting my finger at the child. 'You do not do that!' I snarl.

'Oh no you don't!' The husband throws himself between me and the girl.

'Who told you?' I yell over his shoulder. 'Who told you!' Who told you what to say?'

As I push forward, the girl instinctively cowers behind her mother. 'I don't know what I said,' she pleads.

'Bollocks! Was it Norris? Did he tell you what to say?' The husband's got a firm grip on me.

'Nobody told me, it's just there!'

'You're lying!' My legs buckle as the husband hauls me back across the room.

'I'm not,' the girl screeches. 'It's not my fault!' Snatching at her own hair, she twists in her mother's arms.

'Tony, leave her alone. She doesn't know what she said,' Kalman entreats on the girl's behalf.

'The fuck she doesn't! She can't know it. It was a secret. It was a secret!'

Out on the landing, my legs give way completely and I collapse to the floor. I'm too stunned to cry out. Kalman crouches by my side as the husband looms over me. But my wretched condition has defused a lot of his aggression. 'So what does it mean then, 'My little soldier?' he asks gruffly.

'Tony, is that something you recognise?' Kalman asks, wrapping her hand around mine as my fingers clench the wooden spindles of the banister.

'My little soldier,' the husband repeats. Like everyone else, he's in shock and jabbering for the sake of it. 'My little soldier?'

'Stop saying that!' I shuffle my legs over the top step of the staircase, pulling myself into a seated position. 'It doesn't mean anything.'

'It's not in any of my books.'

'I told you it means nothing!'

'I've read 'em all. It's not in any of them.' He turns to Kalman, but she has even less idea what's going on.

'Tony—?'

'It's nothing,' I cut her off. 'She couldn't know it. No one knows it!'

'Well, you knew it,' the husband says. 'You knew what she was talking about?' He turns toward Kalman. 'So if no one knows it, how come he does?'

'Tony?' Kalman squeezes my hand. 'Is it something your sister used to say?'

I have no time to answer. 'What's *his* sister got to do with it?' the husband interrupts.

Jesus, the man is dense.

'Tony, what's going on?' Kalman asks, as I push myself up onto my feet and stumble down the staircase.

Ripping open the front door, I burst out into the night. The girls's plaintive wailing still ringing in my ears.

Silence.

The cool breeze feels fresh against my face. I can smell the damp leaves on the path. The tall ash trees, swathed in moonlight. Their branches silhouetted against the clear night sky.

I stare over the broken parapet at the black void below. It would be so easy to step over the rusty scaffold. To launch myself into nothingness. The ground below is a dark, tangled mass of overgrown bramble. They probably wouldn't find the body for days.

'Tony.'

I turn at the sound of my name. It's Kalman standing on the cycle path that now runs over the viaduct. Behind her, the husband lingers nervously in the shadows.

I have to give it to her, though. It didn't take her long to find me. Considering I didn't even know I was heading here myself. Had it been the same for my mother? Had she too, found her way here by utter chance? Or had she known all along this would be her final destination?

Kalman steps forward, her eyes flickering between me and the broken parapet.

Don't worry love, I'm not there just yet.

By the time she reaches my side, I feel almost relaxed. She waits for me to speak.

'We used to come here to play,' I tell her, 'Down there in the park. Me and Tracey. It was the only place we ever felt free.' A lump forms in my throat. As Kalman leans closer, I have to resist the urge to look directly at her, in case the words dry in my mouth. 'I've been searching so long. I don't know what's real anymore....' Choking on my words, a tear rolls down my cheek.

Kalman places her hand on my shoulder. 'Come on,' she says. 'Let's get you home.'

***

Early-eighties Cine film footage: A teenage boy sits slumped in an armchair. His eyes are closed and he appears to be in a light hypnotic state. The camera angle is static. Placed at a discreet distance from the subject.

Off-camera, we hear a sympathetic male voice with a delicate West Country accent. 'Where are you now?'

Still within his trancelike state, the boy tilts his head to the side. 'I'm with my sister. We're in the glade. It's summer.'

'Is this place close to your home?'

'Yes.' The contented look on the boy's face disappears. There's a slight pause as the unseen speaker contemplates this sudden change in the boy's demeanour.

'Tony, I want you to leave this place.'

'No, I don't want to. I want to stay here.'

'I want you to go home now, Tony. Is that okay?'

The boy squirms in his chair. 'No, I don't want to. I want to stay here with Tracey. I want to stay here.'

Faced with the boy's increased distress, the speaker changes tact. 'Okay Tony, you don't have to leave if you don't want to. You can stay exactly where you are. For as long as you like.'

As the boy calms, a tight smile appears on his face.

12. Physical Injuries

Physical Injuries appearing overnight for no obvious reason. You may awaken to find scratches or minor bruises, like fingermarks on your body, as if something has touched or gripped you during the night. These injuries can be caused independently or as a result of having experienced other paranormal phenomenon, for instance, sleepwalking or violent sleep disorders.

***

Jo rapped her knuckles against the bathroom door. 'Tony, are you okay?'

No answer.

She knocked again with more urgency. She was getting worried now. Tony had hardly said a word during their tense journey back to his studio. He had sat slouched in the passenger seat, staring blankly out of the window. On arriving home, he had headed straight for the bathroom, leaving Jo standing awkwardly in the lounge. 'Tony, open the door!' Jo twisted the handle with increased force. Still, it still wouldn't budge. She threw a glance behind her. There was just enough space. 'Tony, I'm coming in.' Bracing herself against the hallway wall, she slammed her foot against the bathroom door. It broke open.

Tony was bent over the sink, blood splatters covering the basin. Jo grabbed the razor blade from his hand, which he gave up without objection. Wavering on his feet, Tony sank down onto the toilet seat. Attempting to get a grip of the situation, Jo turned his forearms toward her. Both were a mess of jagged nicks and scratches, but none appeared to be life-threatening. Turning the double-edged razor around in her hand, it was blunt and dull. 'Just as well I switched to electric,' Tony muttered feebly.

But Jo was in no mood for jokes. 'What the hell are you playing at?' she fumed, her anxiety giving way to anger. 'So what now? Do I call an ambulance?'

Overwhelmed by fatigue, Tony slumped back against the cistern and shook his head. 'Maybe just a decent physiatrist.'

'Which cupboard?' Jo yanked open another cabinet door.

'In the middle, right-hand side,' came the irritable reply from the bathroom. Reaching inside the cabinet, Jo's fingers grasped a battered shoebox. Hoping it contained some kind of medical supplies, she yanked it open only to discover, not bandages, but an odd assortment of random knickknacks: a neon plastic bracelet, a knitted scarf, a Tamagotchi keyring and hand-drawn greetings card. Sifting through the items, Jo glimpsed the adolescent face of Tracey Babcock. It was a torn page from *Broken Spirits*. Underneath were several other images of Tracey, all torn from different magazines and books. With glum comprehension, Jo realised she had inadvertently stumbled across a memory box for Tony's dead sister. These ripped pages were probably the only images Tony had of her. Scavenged from the very media that had helped to destroy her. Feeling an odd disquiet, Jo pushed the frayed pages back into the box and closed the cabinet.

Apart from the persistent drip from a leaky bath tap, they sat in awkward silence as Jo bandaged Tony's bleeding wrists. The medical kit Jo had finally found in the kitchenette had been remarkably well-stocked and it hadn't taken long to clean and dress the shallow cuts. A little light pressure had stopped the bleeding almost immediately. Tony had clearly known what he'd been doing. All the cuts had been just shallow enough to avoid hitting any major arteries. Jo hadn't commented on the many older scars on Tony's forearms. 'Hold that,' she said firmly. As Tony obediently placed his finger on the end of the bandage, she secured the end with a piece of medical tape. Leaning back, Jo assessed her own handwork. She'd bandaged both wrists cleanly and smartly. Probably a little over the top considering the amount of damage done. But they had both needed the time it had taken to get their heads straight. Although Tony still looked discernibly less concerned by the whole incident than Jo did.

Opening the mirrored cabinet above the sink, Jo began searching through its contents. Immediately, she recognised several prescription antidepressants among a slew of other unlabelled pill bottles. As she removed a small packet of

Disprin from the cabinet, Tony shook his head. 'I don't need anything.'

'They're for me, if it's all the same to you,' Jo said curtly.

'Well, I've got something better than that.'

'How is all this so normal for you?' Jo's hand trembled around her whisky glass, as the whole emotional rollercoaster of the last few hours finally overtook her.

Tony half-smiled. 'Practice.' Sipping from his own glass, he slumped back in his chair. He too looked exhausted and could barely keep his eyes open.

'Why do you do it?' Jo asked, glancing over at his bandaged wrists.

For a moment, it seemed Tony had ignored her question. Then he shrugged. 'I've always done it. Ever since I was a kid. It helps me cope.'

'Well, if you don't mind me saying, you don't seem to be coping all that well.'

Snorting derisively, Tony ran his fingers back through his tangled hair. 'Yeah, well, who knows? One day I might get lucky and do the job properly.'

'You shouldn't joke about it,' Jo retorted tersely. 'It isn't funny.'

'What would it matter, anyway? What would my death matter to anyone?'

'It would matter to me!'

Tony shot her an inquisitive glance.

'What if you had died tonight?' Jo continued, her voice wavering. 'Then what? Did you even think how that would affect me? What I would do?' Huffing dismissively, Tony's head fell back against the chair. 'Well, of course not. People like you never do,' Jo berated him. 'You're all just selfish and weak!'

'Maybe it's not me you're really mad at.'

'Well, who then!'

He gave her a momentary glance, as if to say, '*You know who.*'

'Oh, you mean my mother,' Jo snarled, infuriated by both Tony's brashness and his acute insinuation. 'It always comes back to my bloody mother!' Gulping her whiskey, she got up and stomped toward the kitchenette. Her hand trembled as she grabbed the whisky bottle. 'Do you know what it's been like? Being '*her daughter*'. '*The Child* that killed her mother.' Jo's fingers tightened around the bottle as her anger turned to bitter remorse. 'It's haunted me all my life. That I'm the reason she isn't here anymore. I think that's all my father sees when he looks at me. I'm like a ghost that follows him round. A constant reminder of what he's lost. No wonder he can't bear to be near me.'

It was an odd sensation. Now she was talking. Jo felt no reticence in her words, no mental barrier holding her back. It was as if, even in his current half-comatose state, she had found a congruent audience in Tony Vail. But still she couldn't turn and face him, not while her emotions were so raw. 'Did you know I was there when it happened?' she continued, her voice stilted and hollow. 'That morning; she drove us both down to the coast. Parked the car in a visitor carpark. She even bought a ticket from the machine and put it in the window. Then she walked down to the beach and straight on into the sea. Left me sitting in the back seat. Like she'd forgotten I was even there.'

Jo wavered a moment before continuing. 'They said she'd been suffering from some kind of breakdown following months of depression. I guess she just snapped. Of course, I didn't know what was happening. I just remember sitting there, waiting for her to return. I must have been there for hours. I can't even remember if she kissed me goodbye or not.' Jo sighed. 'She didn't even leave a note, this amazing, innovational author and she couldn't even be bothered to write a note.' Jo took a sip of whisky. 'Now all she's remembered for is the manner of her death and a novel she wrote about a woman's inability to love her own child....' Jo's mouth twisted into a joyless smile. 'I guess in a way that was her note.' Jo made a soft humping sound in her throat; as if this realisation had only just dawned on her. She glanced over to see what effect her words were having upon Tony.

But Tony was asleep.

The music ended. They were still arguing in the next room. 'I work hard for this family. I provide!' Her stepfather's voice echoed through the bedroom wall. 'When the bills need to be paid. Who has to pay them, me that's who. Not you! Not your daughter. Me!'

Your daughter. It was always *your* daughter when he was angry. *My* daughter when he introduced her to strangers or Amirti when he wanted to be affectionate. But his affection only lasted so long.

'She doesn't show me any respect. I deserve to be shown respect!'

Lila flipped open the Discman and changed the CD.

He didn't deserve any respect.

She pushed play.

Not after what he had done.

The nightmares had eased after the first hour. After which he had fallen into a deep sleep. Still fully dressed, Tony had curled himself into a ball on the edge of the bed. Unwilling to leave him alone, Jo had taken it upon herself to watch over him for the night. But after an hour of anxious pacing, she too succumbed to fatigue. Vowing to rest her eyes for only a moment, and mindful not to wake him, she had lain down next to Tony on the bed.

No sooner had she lowered her head upon the adjacent pillow, than Tony's eyes had flickered open. At first startled by the sight of someone laying next to him, his expression had relaxed into a contented half-smile as he had fallen back to sleep.

Lila awoke to silence. The house was finally quiet. As the Discman whirled to a standstill, Lila considered pushing play again, but she was far too tired. She liked to listen to music at night. It helped her to sleep, gave her something to occupy her mind. Somewhere to escape to. Some nights she would sit for hours on her bed, her knees clenched against her chest, gently rocking back and forth, lost in the rhythm of the music, gradually retreating into herself.

She'd been dreaming. A latent image still lingered in her memory. But no sooner had she identified it than it flickered and died. It was getting harder to hold on to any precise thoughts these days. They all seemed to just escape her grasp the moment she perceived them. The tablets the doctor had prescribed weren't helping any, but the thought of dealing with everything without them only filled her with dread. Tugging the headphones off her head, Lila turned over on the pillow.

Across the room, on the folding camp bed, Kyra was fast asleep. In any other circumstance, Lila would have resented the idea of sharing a bedroom with her younger sister. But recently, she'd found Kyra's presence oddly comforting. She always seemed so peaceful, so content. For a moment Lila recalled attacking the young child, but like so many other memories, the thought faded the instant she tried to inspect it, leaving only a blank space in its wake. Like the fight at school with the girl who had called her a 'sandnigger'. Or when she had discovered a brand new boxed Discman in her schoolbag. When just hours before, she had been admiring a similar player in a shop display and wishing she had owned one. Or the time she had woken with fresh scratches across her arms and neck. Lila shuddered. Some things were best left forgotten.

She turned over again, resigning herself to sleep. But no sooner had she closed her eyes, then she realised she could hear an odd noise echoing from outside. A distant low creaking. Recognising the sound, Lila pulled back her bedcovers and moved over to the open window.

Crisp moonlight bathed the garden with a chilly luminance. Illuminating the open areas while plunging the periphery into dark silhouette. Between the inky shadows, nothing moved. Apart from one seat on the old metal swing. Which swayed back and forth. As if someone had just vacated it.

Leandro loaded the last of the large canvas into the back of the van. Inserting a foam rubber strip between each one, he strapped them all in place with a thick piece of rope. The smaller pieces he would lay flat on the floor between more rubber strips. Front-to-front and back-to-back fashion, to prevent damage to the painted surfaces. Leandro preferred the foam rubber. It was less expensive than bubble wrap and much more reusable. Plus, its spongy suspension offered better protection for the artwork.

With measured diligence, he began piling the smaller paintings into the van. He'd included several portraits, although they rarely sold at art sales. His abstract work was far more popular. But Leandro preferred his portrait work. These he found more rewarding. Picking the next canvas from the sack barrow, Leandro froze mid-movement as he caught sight of the portrait in his hand.

No, not this one. This painting was not for public display. Somehow it had got mixed in with the others. While most of his portraits were private commissions, retirement portraits, weddings, anniversaries. Dreary work done purely for the money. Occasionally a face would come his way, that would transfix him. Inspire him. Afford him a break from the mundane. These paintings weren't just idolised images but a glimpse into a person's very essence. These portraits he painted for this own satisfaction. His own need. Such faces challenged his abilities as a painter. Challenged his own perceptions. Stirred his emotions.

Leandro gazed sullenly down at the portrait in his hands. At the captivating image of a young girl with two distinctive pink streaks framing her face. Her gaze, penetrating yet elusive. Her smile, sensuous and mischievous.

That smile had gone now. Her eyes would never sparkle again with such vibrance. That hidden passion he had glimpsed within her would never reappear. But it wasn't entirely lost. That fervent spirit would continue to exist here in this painting.

In that way, he had captured something of her.

Concerned her voice might carry across the studio, Jo moved further away from the bedroom. Hoping to mask her call, she had already switched on GMTV. 'Yes, I'm trying to reach Dr Eric Sharman in the Parapsychology Unit,' she mumbled over the sound of heavy American artillery rolling over the Iraq border. Still clutching Sharman's dog-eared business card in her hand, she moved impatiently toward the window. Outside on the iron fire escape, a fat pigeon sat preening its feathers in the morning sunshine. While in the far distance, a National Rail train moved silently between the rooftops on the East London Line. Directly below, in the loading bay, Tony's artist friend was loading a stack of canvasses into a battered transit van, while over a hedge a grubby yellow bin lorry was slowly making its way—

'Hello, Psychology Department.'

'Oh, hello, yes hello, I'm trying to reach Dr Eric Sharman in the Parapsychology Unit.' A restless shuffling from the bedroom made Jo lower her voice further. 'Yes, my name is Jo Kalman. I'm ringing on behalf of Tony Vail. Yes, Vail, V-A-I-L. Please, it's very important the doctor call me back as soon as he gets this message.'

Jo repeated her telephone number and ended the call just as Tony appeared from the bedroom. Dishevelled and blurry eyed, he looked even more crumpled than usual. 'You're still here?' He said, sounding more groggy than surprised.

'I thought I should just in case—'

'In case what? I found a razor that wasn't blunt,' he quipped gruffly.

'I just thought I should stay to make sure you were okay.' Even to her own ear, her reasoning sounded a little clumsy. But Jo's apparent discomfort didn't appear to register with Tony, who merely shrugged off her concern as he shuffled toward the kitchenette. 'And you're welcome,' Jo grumbled sarkily behind his back.

'Were you on the phone?' Tony asked as he flipped the kettle on.

'I was just letting work know I wouldn't be in today,' Jo replied with an awkward smile.

Tony seemed to accept this explanation without question. And didn't even notice as Jo slipped Sharman's business card into her back pocket. He'd also failed to notice his wallet laying open on the tabletop. 'What time is it?' he asked, moving away from the kitchenette.

'About ten, I think.'

'A bit late to be calling in isn't it?'

'Well, I've been busy with other things,' she said as he disappeared into the bathroom.

Jo had just enough time to retrieve Sharman's card from her pocket and slip it back into Tony's wallet and the wallet back into his jacket before Tony's head reappeared around the side of the bathroom door. 'Did you clean in here?'

'Like I said I've been busy,' Jo said a tad breathlessly. Pulling a shrug face, Tony disappeared back inside the bathroom 'And again you're welcome,' Jo muttered sullenly.

The hydraulic arm shuddered as it reached the top of its arc, tipping the contents of the wheelie bin into the gaping hopper below. With a sudden release of pressure, the arm juddered back down again. As the bin hit the ground, a waiting refuse worker yanked it free from the arm and dragged it back toward a large communal bin store behind a converted block of studios. Dumping the wheelie bin by the entrance, the large man glanced cautiously over his shoulder before disappearing inside the bin store. Ignoring several closer bins, the man moved quickly through the store, stopping by a battered wheelie bin, stencilled with the words:

STUDIO 9

Flipping the lid, he lent inside. Rifling through the bins contents, he immediately found something of interest. Stuffing a clutch of torn photographic prints down the front of his dungarees, Roy hurriedly buttoned up his donkey jacket. Flipping the bin closed, he tugged it out of the bin store and up the short driveway toward the waiting rubbish truck.

'Stop looking at me like that.'

'Like what?'

'Like the moment you take your eyes off me, I'm gonna leap out that window.'

'Well, considering what you put me through last night. I'd say I have every right to look concerned.'

'If I really wanted to do it. I would've used one of these.' Tony pulled a large professional chef's knife from a well-stocked block on the kitchenette counter. 'A perk of my job,' he explained in response to Jo's curious expression. 'My day job that is.' He nodded toward a large photographic backdrop in the middle of the studio, on which stood a shiny chrome chair, encircled by several freestanding lamps.

'So this is what you do; when you're not searching for ghosts?' Jo said as she moved over toward the chair.

'Well, it pays the bills, Tony replied, following Jo across the studio. 'And gives me something else to focus on, if you forgive the pun.'

Tony had been attempting to keep the mood light, but Jo could detect an uneasy tension behind his casual manner. 'So who sits in the chair?' she asked in an upbeat tone, keen to dispel the brooding atmosphere.

'No one sits in the chair. The chair *is* the subject.'

'The chair?' Jo smiled, unsure if Tony was pulling her leg.

'I specialise in inanimate objects. You know, for catalogues and brochures.' Moving a large gold reflector to one side, he revealed a tall white plinth, on which rested an electric kettle.

'A kettle?' Jo laughed.

Despite himself, Tony chuckled. 'Don't knock it. Shiny objects are my forte. You have to get the angle just right. Otherwise, you catch the reflection of the camera or the surrounding room. I do other household items as well. Last month I did a magazine cover shot of the new Game Boy Advance.'

'And this pays?'

'Enough to get by on. Plus, I enjoy it. And it's a lot easier than shooting bouncing babies in shopping centres.'

Encouraged by the subtle change in Tony's mood, ran her finger over the back of the chair. 'So do you get to keep the stuff afterwards?'

'Hell no,' Tony laughed. 'I get the odd freebee, like that knife set. But generally it all goes back. That chair alone is worth two grand. A courier brought it here last week. Once I'm done with it, he'll be back to collect it.'

'In that poky little lift?'

'There's a larger goods lift around the back of the building for deliveries.'

'Must be an interesting place to live.'

Despite the drama of the pervious night, Tony's studio had made an immediate and favourable impression on Jo. Although modern and stylistic, the converted warehouse still retained many of its original features. Black framed photographs adorned bare brick walls, while wide arched casement windows ran the entire length of the studio. Ostensibly open-plan Tony's studio had been divided into two distinct spaces, a spacious photographic studio and adjoining living space. The lounge area contained a comfortable leather sofa, sanded wooden flooring and a widescreen TV. Although cluttered, the whole place was immaculately tidy and well organised.

'We get quite the assortment around here.' Tony said, returning the reflector to its original position. 'Hoxton's renowned for its artist community. In this block alone we have several artists, a couple of graphic and textile designers. There's even a holistic architect in the basement. It's a right mix bag of oddballs.'

'You must feel right at home then,' Jo said playfully, as Tony precisely realigned the reflector.

Thrown by her comment, Tony turned awkwardly back toward the kitchenette. 'Are you hungry?'

'I could eat,' Jo admitted. In fact, she was starving. She'd hadn't eaten anything since the pervious evening.

'I've not got much in but I could rustle up a stir-fry.'

'If you don't mind. That would be great.'

Pulling a bag of vegetables from the fridge, Tony begun washing them individually under the tap, before drying each one separately with its own paper towel. 'How do you stand it?' Jo asked in a delicate voice, as she watched him meticulously preparing each item of food. 'In the cellar, I mean?'

Tony shrugged. 'I don't like it, but I can live with it. Cleanliness doesn't really bother me. It's order I struggle with.' He shuffled awkwardly before continuing. 'You may not have noticed, but I have a bit of a condition.' Avoiding Jo's eye, he smiled self-consciously. 'I get stuck in these rigid thought patterns. I check, arrange, repeat things over until I feel secure. Having things arranged a certain way helps me cope, gives me a sense of control. Otherwise, I can get overwhelmed by everything.'

'It must be difficult,' Jo said with genuine sympathy.

Tony gave a weak chuckle. 'It's exhausting, to be honest. But some days are better than others. I can usually deal with it. But it's hard. For me and also for people around me...' catching her eye, he lapsed into silence.

Noticing Tony's discomfort, Jo smiled and casually turned toward a line of framed photographic prints hanging along the back wall of the studio. 'These are nice?' she said. 'I think I recognise some of them.'

Each print displayed some kind of paranormal image. Vague, spectral children, or wraithlike figures hovering over the shoulders of sombre Victorians. 'That's what you might call my rouges gallery,' Tony said in a relieved tone, glad of the change of subject. 'They're my personal favourites. I did the enlargements myself, in my darkroom, over there.' He pointed a half-chopped pepper toward a doorway on the far side of the studio.

'You still have a darkroom?' Jo sounded surprised. 'I thought all that stuff was pretty much redundant now.'

'I still prefer the process,' Tony said as he resumed chopping the pepper. 'It takes longer and is more technical, but I like the feel of it. The smell of the developer, the texture of the paper. Even the colour of the bulb. Makes it all feel more *real*.'

Jo moved closer to examine one of the framed prints. An atmospheric print of a ghostly white figure floating down a dark panelled staircase in an eerie Jacobean mansion. 'So, how do you know? If it's a fake or not?'

'That's easy enough. They're all fakes.' Jo glanced back at Tony, surprised by the frank revelation. 'Some paranormal photos are optical illusions,' Tony explained. 'Some are tricks of the light or a damaged negative. But most are, as you say; just out-and-out fakes.'

'So why....?'

'Why do I hang them on the wall? Because I admire the craftsmanship. Those photographs were all done long before modern techniques made it easy. It took real dedication to produce those illusions. They're real artworks of the imagination. Plus, they remind me how easy it is to get fooled.' Prompted by Jo's interest, Tony continued. 'You show someone a printed readout of an erroneous temperature reading and they couldn't care less. But show them a blurry image of a phantom child and suddenly you've got their attention.'

Sensing her prolonged gaze was making Tony uneasy, Jo turned back toward the print on the wall. 'There's a thousand ways to deceive someone,' Tony continued. 'But with the paranormal, half your work is already done for you. People only hire a paranormal investigator because they already believe they have a ghost in the house. They only want confirmation of something they already believe to be true. That's why there's so many crooks in this game. It's way too easy to just tell someone what they want to hear.'

'And what about you? Do you ever tell people what they want to hear?' Jo had attempted to sound nonchalant, but her question had provoked a sudden silence from the kitchenette. Fighting the urge to glance over her shoulder, Jo kept her gaze on the framed print, hoping to make her enquiry seem less pertinent.

'You don't help anyone by lying to them,' Tony finally said, as the sound of chopping resumed.

'Roy Norris says it offers people hope and reassurance.'

'I bet he also said that while pocketing a fistful of sweaty bank notes.'

Ignoring the fact Tony also took payments for his investigations, Jo moved along the wall to the next print. 'So what is it with you and him?' she asked.

'There's nothing between me and him.'

'But you do know him?'

'You run into a lot of the same people in this game.'

'But you think he's somehow responsible for all this, don't you?' The sound of chopping stopped again. 'That he's been feeding the family information.'

Silence.

Jo huffed. She was getting nowhere, talking across the studio like this. She turned back toward the kitchenette. 'But how would he know what to say? How would he know what you know?' Tony's head was bowed, the chef's knife hovering over the chopping board. He appeared to have lost all focus on his task. 'Tony?' Jo tapped him on the shoulder.

Jerking violently, Tony spun around, the knife flaying wildly in his hand. 'Jesus! Christ, don't do that!' he yelled, slamming back against the counter, scattering the chopped vegetables behind him. 'I could have stabbed you!

'Tony, you wouldn't have stabbed me,' Jo exclaimed, her tone both startled and dismissive, in equal measure.

'But I could have!' Tony insisted, his voice riddled with panic, the knife still quivering in his hand.

'Tony, you've cut yourself.'

Tony glanced down at a sizeable nick on his free palm. 'Damn!' Shocked, he dropped the knife into the sink. As Jo tore off a sheet of kitchen roll, Tony pushed her aside. Snatching up a dishcloth, he began frantically scrubbing the knife. The blood from the cut mingling with the running water. With every failed attempt to clean the blade, he became increasingly frantic.

'Tony, it's okay,' Jo said, the dry kitchen roll still clenched in her hand.

'It's not. It's not okay! I have to clean it. I have to do this!'

'You don't have to do it right now.'

'I have to. I have to get it back into the block!' Yanking the knife from the water, he dropped it onto a tea towel. Holding his bleeding hand away from the counter, he dabbed the blade dry with the towel. Finally, he thrust the knife back into the wooden block. With an exasperated sigh, he slumped back against the counter, his muscles still twitching. Unable to ignore her concern, his eyes flickered toward Jo. 'I must seem like a headcase to you.' He said, his voice faltering.

'It's okay, honestly.' Jo assured him shakily.

Tony chuckled nervously. 'Most of the time; I can control it. I have coping mechanisms—' Embarrassed, he tried to turn away from Jo, but couldn't decide which direction to face. 'Sometimes it all becomes too much,' he said after a moment of indecision. 'I can't free myself.' He banged the side of his temple with the heel of his injured hand. 'Sometimes it just gets too much and I panic. My mother had the same thing. The same fucking thing!'

'Yes, I know,' Jo said in a tone she hoped sounded sympathetic.

'Oh yes, of course you know!' Tony snapped in a sudden fit of anger. 'I keep forgetting you already know everything about me and my family. In fact, you're quite the expert aren't you!' Recoiling away from Jo, Tony knocked back against the kitchenette cabinet. Immediately, his gaze sought the knife block, desperately reassuring himself the blade was still secure in its slot. 'I think you should go,' he said.

'Tony, there's no need....'

'I think you should go.' He repeated, his tone harsher, more insistent.

'Okay, no problem.' Not wanting to push it any further, Jo collected her coat and handbag from the sofa. 'I'll call you later,' she said from the hallway. 'See how you're doing?'

Tony managed a taut nod as she let herself out.

Qamra burst into Lila's room. 'Did you put this on Kyra's bed?' she yelled, thrusting a brand-new Barbie Doll in Lila's face.

'No!' Lila snarled back defensively.

274

'Lila, I've warned you about this before!'

'I said I didn't!'

Qamra lurched forward. 'Don't lie to me. Things don't just appear out of nowhere!'

'I said I didn't!' Lila shrugged churlishly, turning away from her mother.

'Don't turn your back on me!' Qamra yanked the teenager forcibly around by her shoulder! 'I want to know where you got this from? Did you steal it?'

Although shocked by the ferocity of her mother's accusations, Lila refused to back down. 'I said I didn't put it there!'

Qamra looked fit to burst, but the appearance of a bawling Kyra in the doorway curtailed any further outburst. 'See what you're doing,' she snapped, pointing at the distraught child. 'I can't take any more of this!' Storming from the room, she thrust the Barbie into the outstretched hands of her youngest daughter. 'You're all driving me mad!'

Roy spread the torn photo fragments out across his kitchen table. As he paired the original prints with their altered darkroom counterparts, a look of dogged satisfaction appeared on his clammy face. Fixing each print with Sellotape, he placed them all into a large black lever file labelled:

BABCOCK

Closing the file, Roy carried it through to his bedroom and placed it on a bookshelf, alongside another thick lever file:

MISHAL

Taking this file from the shelf, Roy flipped it open. Inside was a clutch of 4 x 6 photographs. Lila Mishal standing at a bus stop; Lila and her sister, in a park; A people carrier parked outside the Mishal's house. Jo Kalman speaking to another woman on the driveway.

Choosing a photo from the file. Roy moved over toward a large stylised IKEA print of Times Square hanging on the wall. Pushing the print into the picture's silver frame, he took a step back to survey it in its new location.

Lila Mishal posing awkwardly for her school yearbook photograph.

Alongside the image, another photo, already wedged into the frame.

A smiling schoolgirl with two distinctive pink streaks framing her face.

'Belo! Belo!'

Belo woke in a daze. He could feel Qamra clawing at his shoulder. 'What is it, what!'

'There's someone in house,' Qamra hissed.

'What?' Belo turned over in the bed.

'He was in doorway.' Qamra pointed across the bedroom. 'It was man. I saw him on landing.'

'There's no one there,' Belo mumbled dismissively, turning away.

Qamra gripped her husband's arm. Her nails digging into his skin. 'Belo do something!'

In a fit of indignation Belo threw back the bedcover. 'Alright already!' Reaching under the bed, he gripped the handle of his emergency baseball bat. 'Stay there,' he growled.

As he crept out onto the landing, Lila appeared from her bedroom, rubbing the sleep from her eyes. 'What's going on?' she asked wearily.

'Nothing go back to bed,' Belo snapped. Lila eyed the baseball bat in Belo's hand but remained where she was. She watched as her stepfather cautiously stuck his head into the spare room and then the bathroom before tiptoeing downstairs.

After a quick sweep of the lounge, Belo turned toward the kitchen.

Empty.

On an impulse, he tried the patio door.

Click.

Belo's heart skipped a beat. The door was unlocked. Searching his memory, he tried to recall whether he had checked the door, the pervious evening. Unable to convince himself either way, he pulled the door shut and twisted the locking lever.

'Well?'

Belo jumped at the sound of Qamra's voice behind him. He turned to find both Qamra and Lila creeping into the kitchen. 'There's no one here,' he told them decisively.

'And door?'

'It's locked.'

Qamra's relief was swiftly replaced with incongruity. 'But I saw him. He was watching us through doorway.'

Under different circumstances, Belo may well have seized upon this admission, to corroborate his own assertions of the dark presence in the house. But instead, he tersely shrugged off the whole incident and ushered everyone back to their beds.

After some unsettled thrashing, Qamra had eventually drifted back to sleep, while Belo spent the rest of the night thinking about the lock on the patio door.

'Daddy says the war is stupid and financially motivated. That the Americans are worried Opick will switch from dollars to euros.'

'Well, that might be true.'

'So why do it then?'

'Well, that's a good question. Maybe people just do silly things sometimes.'

'Like your TV show.'

'My show?' Jo gave Hanna a puzzled look.

'You said that was silly, yet you're still doing it.'

'Well, that's different.'

'That's just what adults always say when they know they're wrong.'

'You spend way too much time with adults.'

'I like unicorns as well.'

'Well, that's okay then.' Jo chuckled as Hanna took a long, studious sip from the giant Coke cup she was still carrying from the cinema.

Following a last-minute shift change, Greg had found himself without a babysitter and Jo had offered to take Hanna for the evening. Still feeling guilty about not joining them on the demonstration, Jo had also offered to take Hanna to the cinema as an extra treat. After checking the listing the only child-friendly movie available had been a science-fiction reinterpretation of *Treasure Island*. For a Disney animation it had been far darker in tone than Jo had been expecting, but Hanna had thoroughly enjoyed it. The offer of the cinema trip had also meant Jo had been released from the obligation of having to engage the precocious child in conversation for an entire evening. A situation Hanna was now actively attempting to rectify.

'Which dead people would you like to meet?'

Again, Hanna's eclectic pool of thought took Jo by surprise. Even if the subject was less surprising. Ever since she had first learnt of her involvement in a paranormal reality show, the topic had been a constant source of fascination to Hanna.

'What a question? Ah well, I don't know...'

'Jesus Christ?'

'Well, yes, I suppose that would be interesting.'

'Do you speak Aramaic?' Hanna asked, her precise articulation of the word betraying her own delight at her correct pronunciation.

'Aramaic?'

'Miss Sanderson said Jesus spoke Aramaic, so unless you spoke the same language, it wouldn't be all that helpful to meet him.'

'I suppose not.'

'If you're going to meet a ghost, you've got to pick one that speaks your own language.'

Jo nodded her head wearily as they scaled the steps toward their apartment block. Jo liked Hanna well enough, but was rapidly tiring of the child's relentless queries and observations, and was already looking forward to handing her back to her father. But the evening had not been without its benefits. At least Jo would feel less guilty the next time she asked Greg to walk Bruno for her.

Pushing the entry code into the keypad, Jo held the foyer door open for Hanna. 'Do you think ghosts see other ghosts?' Hanna asked as they walked toward the stairwell. 'What if two ghosts are haunting the same house? Would they haunt each other?'

'Well, that's another good question.'

'Daddy says I ask too many questions. He says it annoys people.'

'He may have a point.'

Turning the corner onto Jo's floor, Hanna squealed as she walked straight into the heavyset figure of Roy Norris. 'You have to stop this!' Roy barked over the head of the startled child. His face was red and sweaty. 'You have to stop this, b-before it goes too far!'

Instinctively, Jo reached down for Hanna's shoulders. 'Hanna, go to the door,' she said firmly. But Hanna remained where she was, pushing back against Jo's legs. Her eyes fixed on the menacing presence of Roy. 'I said go to the door!' Jo harried the child toward her apartment door. 'How did you get in here?' she asked Roy, her gaze still trailing after Hanna.

Roy ignored the question. 'They w-won't let me in the house and they don't a-answer my calls. You have to speak to them, persuade them to see me.'

'There's nothing I can do,' Jo protested as she shuffled sidewards along the wall. 'You can't come to my home like this.' Turning sharply she began striding toward Hanna. Only to be pulled back by a fierce grip on her arm.

'She told me this isn't right.'

'What! Who told you?' Somewhere in her bag Jo had a rape alarm, along with a lot of other crap, through which she was now franticly rummaging.

'Jo,' Hanna called from across the landing.

'Just stay there Hanna,' Jo said sharply.

'Tracey, told me,' Roy said. 'Her voice is weak, but I can still hear her. She knows something t-terrible is going to happen.'

'Jo!' Hanna's voice sounded increasingly concerned.

'Tracey? Tracey Babcock told you?' Jo's mind was racing.

'I can still hear her.'

'Tracey Babcock is dead!' Jo tugged her arm free from Roy's grasp and turned toward her apartment.

'Dead, but not gone,' Roy called after her, his tone painfully sincere.

Gripping her door keys, Jo froze by the door. Once unlocked, Roy could easily push his way into her flat, trapping them all inside. At least out in the hallway; she had some control of the situation. Clutching her keys in her fist, Jo spun toward Roy. 'This is over. Do you hear me? All this crap! There's no money in it for you anymore. So just forget it.'

Whether faced with Jo's unexpected retaliation or the uncertainty of his own actions, Roy's tone became more pleading. 'What would you give to speak to someone you have lost? For a chance to forgive them, or to b-b-be forgiven. Wouldn't you want that more than anything?' For a moment, Jo seemed almost swayed by Roy's words. But this proved to be short-lived. Bolstered by Jo's apparent deference, Roy overstepped himself. 'Your m-mother says you should be careful.' It was the same tone he'd used on the widow Dolly. The same sympathetic tilt of the head. The same patronising mannerism.

'No!' Jo roared, the rage bursting from her. 'You do not do that! You do not!' Faced with Jo's unexpected hostility, Roy recoiled backwards. Straightening her back, Jo fixed Roy with a steely glare. 'Don't ever come here again,' she said, her voice cracking under the sheer weight of authority, now demanded from it.

Placing herself firmly between Hanna and Roy, Jo lifted her door key. Angling her body toward the door, she pushed the key into the lock and twisted it. The door clicked open. Shepherding Hanna in through the thin gap, she quickly slipped in behind her. As the door slammed behind her, Jo glimpsed Roy standing motionless in the hallway. 'She d-deserves to be heard,' he growled through the door, as Jo slapped the safety catch on.

'How did he even get into the building?' Twisting a clenched fist into his palm, Greg resumed his frustrated pacing of Jo's lounge. 'I'm gonna have to bring this up at the next residents' meeting. The fact he could just walk into our home like that.'

'Greg, it's okay,' Jo said soothingly, reaching across the coffee table for the TV remote. 'He just spooked us that's all.' The game show Hanna had been watching had just finished, replaced by news footage of a Royal Navy submarine firing Tomahawk missiles at Baghdad. Figuring the child had endured enough trauma for one evening, Jo swiftly flipped the channel. Not that Hanna appeared in any way distressed by the earlier incident in the hallway. Instead, she seemed more concerned with her father's uncharacteristic behaviour.

'But it's not bloody okay is it!' Greg fumed. 'I was just here. I was just upstairs!'

'Greg, I said it's fine, claim down.' The anxiety in Jo's voice finally made Greg take stock of his actions.

'Yes, sorry,' he said ruefully. 'It's the fact he could walk in here like that.' Turning away from Hanna, he lowered his voice. '*Anything* could have happened! I should at least put some flyers in the foyer. Say there was a suspicious man in the building.'

'You don't have to,' Jo assured him. 'I'm sure he won't come back.'

Greg didn't look convinced. 'Well, I still don't like the idea of leaving you alone tonight. I should stay over.' Greg's face flushed as he nodded toward Hanna. 'I mean *we* should stay over.'

'That's really not necessary. But if I need you; I can always bang on the ceiling with a broom-handle.' Jo doggedly held his gaze until finally he deferred to her suggestion with a polite inclination of the head. 'It's nice to know you're there if I need you,' she added amiably.

'I'm always here if you need me. You know that...' A loud ping sounded from Greg's jacket, just as their eyes locked. Making an apologetic expression, Greg pulled the mobile from his pocket. Flipping open the phone, his face dropped and he let out a long, anguished sigh.

***

Contemporary news footage: A local news reporter addresses the camera directly from the side of a high road bridge overlooking a railway line. 'Police searching for the missing teenager Ashley Hooper have today confirmed the discovery of a body.'

The shot changes to an image of a young girl in her school uniform. 'The seventeen-year-old from North London was last seen in the Pine Hill area on the tenth of June last year.'

The shot changes again to show a group of crime scene officers, clad in white overalls gathered on the side of a steep slopping embankment. 'According to a police spokesperson a body was recovered from a disused railway pillbox late last night. We understand Miss Hooper's family has been informed of the discovery, although a formal identification has yet to take place.' The shot returns to the reporter. 'Police have yet to determine whether the teenager's death would be treated as suspicious.'

13. Unexplainable Feelings

Consider any signs of physical illness or sensations of feeling unwell; especially those that appear to have no clear medical explanation. It's not unknown for people to experience the sudden onset of unusual illnesses or odd ailments that defy explanation while living in a location that is known to paranormally active.

Less obvious signs of sickness may also be experienced, including fatigue, dizziness, nausea, stress and a general malaise, with little or no relief for that person until they have left the suspected area.

Generally, when the individual is free of the location, the symptoms will either decrease or vanish completely.

***

'I thought you might like this.' Kalman hands me an old photograph. It's a photo of Tracey. It's the same photo they used in Milgallon's book. But this is an original print. I flip it over. There's a publisher's date stamp on the back.

'Where did you find this?' I ask, as a lump forms in my throat.

'It was in an old file, back at the office.'

Kalman's face flushes. So I doubt that's the full story. But I'm grateful, nonetheless.

Gesturing that she should come in, I turn toward the lounge. Opening the cabinet, I root out the old shoebox. Across the studio, Kalman is watching me closely. 'It's where I keep what I have left of her,' I tell her.

She nods her head and smiles. 'I understand you lost all your family photos in the fire.'

'Yeah, there isn't much left,' I mumble, as I slide the photo into the box. For a moment, I consider showing her the other contents, but decide against it. Instead, I offer to make her a cup of tea at the kitchenette.

She doesn't say a word as I pour hot water over a couple of tea bags. I can still see she's still thinking about the shoebox and everything it represents. 'I hope I'm not interrupting you.' She glances over at the pile of Minidiscs on my work-bench.

'No, just listening to my recordings.'

'Music?'

'Audio recordings from The Station House. I wanted to check if I missed anything.'

She gives the pile another glance. 'And had you?'

Ignoring the question, I pull the milk from the fridge. I can feel her eyes on me as I slurp it into the mugs. I've been up all night. I must look terrible. Sensing my discomfort, she searches for a diversion. 'So what's in here?' She asks, reaching for two portfolio cases resting against the sofa.

'My work.'

'Can I?'

I give her a *'help yourself'* shrug, as she places the cases on the breakfast bar. I sip my tea as she flips through the first case. Which doesn't take long, as once you've seen one photograph of a kettle, you've seen them all. She tries to hide her disappointment. 'So what's in the other case? More of the same?'

'No, that's my other work.'

Her mood lifts. 'Ghost haunting?'

I ignore the impulse to correct the terminology, as she unzips the second case. 'I warn you now, not to get your expectations too high.'

'I'm sure they're not that bad; Oh!' Her face drops as she beholds even more insipid imagery.

'Not what you were expecting is it?'

'I don't know what I was expecting,' she says, but a fleeting glance toward the framed prints on the wall betrays her true exceptions.

'I told you, all that lot are fakes. This is what actual paranormal investigation looks like.' I tap the portfolio with my finger. 'Unusual dust deposits, weird insect trails and moisture damage.'

As she stares down at the uninspiring photos, the obvious question forms in her mind. 'So is this...?'

'All I've got to show for all my years of research?' I huff despondently. 'Well, how do you think I feel?'

There's no disguising her disillusionment as she stares down at the folder. It's clear from her expression she doesn't know whether to admire my perseverance or pity my naivety. Flipping the pages sullenly, she glances back over the pages. 'Tony, can I ask you a question?'

'Like you've ever needed permission before.'

'Why do you do it? Search for ghosts I mean.'

'I assume you already have your own opinion,' I tell her in an evasive tone. But she's not fazed by my stroppy manner.

'Is it to vindicate your sister somehow? Prove she didn't make it all up. That what happened to your family was real.'

'It was real,' I snap.

She rephrases her statement. 'Was actually caused by a poltergeist. And not something else.'

'I take it there's a reason behind all this sudden interest in my sister.' I'm being arsey now, but she's still persevering in the face of my increasing irritation. Kalman takes a moment to refashion her next question.

'Tony, how well do you know Roy Norris?'

There it is.

'What's he said to you?' She flinches at my sudden rancour. 'Well!'

She looks uncertain. 'He was at my flat last night.'

'He was what!'

'He was waiting in the lobby of the building.'

She sounds way too dismissive, as if she's playing the whole thing down.

'And what did he want?' I attempt to push the edge from my voice, but she's still unsettled.

'He says something terrible is going to happen.'

'To who?'

'He didn't say. Only that something terrible was going to happen.'

I give an angry chuckle. 'And I can guess where he got this information from.'

Her expression turns more sympathetic. 'He says it's your sister, Tracey.'

'The fucker,' I slam my fist against the countertop.

Not wanting to scare Kalman into silence, I force back my anger. 'What else did he say?'

'Nothing else. Just that he could still hear her. That she's been trying to get a message to somebody, either you or the Mishals. I'm not sure which, he was rambling a lot.'

'Yeah, that's all he fucking does.'

Despite my best efforts, Kalman can clearly read my emotions now. 'Tony, is this how you know him? Has he been telling you the same thing?'

'Yeah well, not for much longer,' I declare, striding around the end of the breakfast bar.

'You know what he's saying isn't true don't you?'

But I'm not listening anymore. I check my watch. We've still got time. 'Okay, I need a lift.' She stares at me with a look of sheer incredulity. 'I don't have a car,' I tell her, pulling a mug face.

She shakes her head. 'Am I going to regret this?'

'Probably.'

Kalman checks her watch. 'I don't think he's going to show.' Her tone implies she would be quite happy if that remained the case.

From the sound of it, the service in the hall has already begun. But I'm not about to give up just yet. 'He'll show.'

'What makes you so sure?'

I give her a wink. 'I'm psychic.'

Shaking her head, she glances back at her watch. For a moment I think maybe she's right, maybe he won't show, but then I spot him, lumbering down the road like a shambolic orangutan. I nudge Kalman as Norris shuffles through the doors of the old mission building. 'That's us then,' I declare as I head across the road.

At the door, Kalman stops to read the sign outside:

Spiritualist Church and Healing Centre
Divine service this evening: 7:00pm

Sloping in behind a group of latecomers, we hang back in the foyer. Trying to look inconspicuous, Kalman picks up a flyer and pretends to read it. Inside the hall, the congregation's singing some God-awful hymn. It sounds annoyingly modern and inclusive. I sneak a peek through the glass partition.

Norris is making his way around the side of the congregation. He apologises to a couple of sour-faced biddies, before taking a seat on a raised platform up front. As the hymn stops, one of the biddies rises to her feet. She reads out a list of names and asks everyone to focus their minds and to send healing thoughts to these people. She then recites some pseudo prayer. Everyone mutters alone, including Norris who is clenching his fat hands together in his lap.

Kalman moves closer to get a clearer view into the hall. Her perfume smells of jasmine and cedar-wood. It reminds me of a meadow field in the summer.

The old biddy turns and introduces Norris to the congregation. As he stands, he nervously folds his glasses into his pocket. He takes a moment to explain what is about to happen before settling into a convincing trancelike state. Tapping Kalman on the arm, I push the partition door open. Before she can object, I'm striding into the hall. Left with no alternative, she hurries after me.

There's about forty people parishioners seated on plastic chairs in a semicircular formation, four or five rows deep. Most are mums or pensioners, but there's a few younger faces scattered about. One old scrote in the back looks suspiciously like a dozing vagrant. But it's not a bad turnout.

We drop into a couple of free seats at the back, in the same row as the tramp. Up at the front, Norris has begun his routine. Throwing about a series of general references that could apply to any of this bunch. He keeps touching on all the old favourites. I'm getting a message from 'Mom', 'Dad', 'Granddad'. It's the usual gumpth, tailoring each of his messages to fit the subject, making the punters do all the work. But the crowd is lapping it up. I glance around the hall. This is rich pickings for him. An entire room of vulnerability and grief.

Squinting at the audience, Norris singles out one old girl from the congregation. 'Your husband suffered a long time before he passed,' he says in a sickly sympathetic tone. The old girl nods her head.

I wonder which of the two perennials he's going to plum for. Cancer or heart disease?

'I feel a pain here,' he says, tapping his chest.

'That would be his heart,' the old dear declares. 'My Jim died of a heart attack.'

Norris nods solemnly. Heart disease it is then.

A younger woman in the next chair clasps the old woman's hand in hers. Probably her daughter.

Norris warbles on a bit, reeling out a litany of aliments and grievances which you would associate with heart disease. He finishes with some generic obversions about the old girl herself. 'And of course you have someone special with you today.' The daughter squeezes her mum's hand. He's good at this, I'll give him that.

He's heading into the home straight now. He mentions a special piece of jewellery the husband claims to have given her. Trying to hit on an explicit detail which will complete the illusion of specificity and legitimise his reading. But all he's getting is a blank stare. Norris recites a list of non-specific jewellery items. A necklace, a clasp, a bracelet... As nothing registers, he has to fall back on his fail-safe.

'A ring?'

'My wedding ring?' the old dear ventures.

'That's it, your wedding ring. He says it was the happiest day of his life.'

Fuck me, I can't listen to too much more of this.

'He says you shouldn't be sad when you think of him because—'

'He's watching over you,' Kalman mutters, as Norris repeats the same phrase to the old dear. It appears she's already seen this show. And from her expression I can tell she's enjoying it even less this time around.

Norris lifts his hand in the air, closing his eyes tight. 'Hold on.... I'm getting another message from someone who's just crossed over.'

Leaping to my feet, I stride forward, dragging my plastic chair with me. After a moment of indecision, Kalman opts to stay where she is.

'Is there someone here tonight that has recently lost someone dear to them?' Norris asks the audience in a sceptical tone. Although judging by the average age of the congregation, that question is already a forgone conclusion. Some doddering old sod in an aisle seat raises his arm, which I promptly push back down again as I pass.

'I believe this ones for me.' I dump my chair down in front of the raised platform.

Norris opens his eyes at the sound of my voice. Rooting in his pocket, he pulls on his glasses. The shock on his face is undeniable. I drop into the chair before he breaks for the emergency exit. 'I gather you have something to tell me.'

'I'm afraid it doesn't work like that,' one of the sour-faced biddies chimes in.

'Oh, I'm sure he'll make an exception for me,' I keep my gaze fixed firmly on Norris, 'As Roy here seems to be running a spiritual answering service for me these days.' Crossing my arms, I sit back in my chair, waiting to hear what he's got to say for himself. But now I'm here in person he doesn't seem all that eager to talk.

'Tell me!'

Norris jumps at my raised voice, but holds himself in check. He gives the biddies a quick '*it's okay*' gesture before turning back to me. Closing his eyes, he tries to return to his earlier trance-like state, but he's having a hard time with it.

His eyes snap open as a chair leg scapes against the floor. Relieved I'm still in my seat, he resumes his pretend trance. 'And you can knock that crap on the head,' I bark, as he starts again with the whole '*I'm crossing over*' bollocks. 'Just cut to the chase.'

Ignoring me, he continues on with the theatrics for the benefit of the congregation. After another minute, he gets to wherever he thinks he needs to be. 'I can hear her now,' he says wistfully. 'It's faint, but she says you're not to worry about her anymore.' There's a mumble from the congregation. 'She says she looked after you b-before and she wants to look after you again.' He runs his tongue around the inside of his dry mouth. 'She's worried about you, Tony. Worried what will happen if you keep on.'

'Keep on with what?' I snap, but he ignores my interruption.

'You're holding her b-b-back.' His stammer's getting worse. He thumps his thigh with the side of his fist to force the word out. 'You have to let her g-go. She wants you to live your life, a ha-happy life. B-b-but you have to let her go. For her sake.' Struggling with the message, he stamps his foot and jerks his head to the side. 'You ha-ha-have to stop this Tony, f-for me.' His face contorts as his voice raises in pitch to a painful falsetto. 'You must stop!'

'Stop what?'

Norris forces his voice back down into his normal register, but it doesn't sound any less distressed. 'Searching.' His eyes fix on mine. 'There's a shadow following you, Tony. You know this. You must stop searching.'

'And if I don't?'

'Then you k-k-know what w-w-will happen.'

My fingers curl into tight fists. 'What?'

'What always happens. She will die again.'

He slumps back as if released from his connection. I spring to my feet, sending the plastic chair toppling over. Grabbing the chair by its legs, I hoist it up over my shoulder, ready to strike. But Norris doesn't flinch. He stands firm, staring at me through those thick milk bottle glasses of his. Oddly defiant.

I balk as Kalman touches my arm. But it's enough to break my rage. Now I'm more confused than angry. I stare numbly around at the congregation. Dropping the chair back down, I glare at Norris. 'That's not Tracey.'

'You have to be-believe me,' Norris pleads.

'No, I don't believe you. Because you're lying. And do you know how I know? Because Tracey would never tell me to give up! Never!'

'It's her voice.'

'No, it isn't!,' I yell. 'Because she would speak to me.' My voice is breaking. '*Only to me!*' I'm crying now. My whole body is trembling. 'Only to me.'

'Tony, don't listen to this.' Holding Kalman's gaze, my anger fades. Not completely; but enough to allow her to steer me toward the exit.

Norris steps off the platform. 'M-m-make him listen,' he calls out to Kalman, as we disappear through the door. 'It'll happen again! You know it will happen again!'

'Tony, wait!' Tugging at my jacket, Kalman pulls me to a standstill. My whole body is shaking, there's too much emotion cursing through me. 'What did he mean? She will die again?'

I don't need this now. I shake my head. 'It means nothing. The man's fucking mad!' Suddenly I want to go back into the hall and confront Norris again. Guessing my intention, Kalman blocks my way. I shrug her away, infuriated by her intervention. 'Just leave me alone, won't you?'

She looks hurt and confused. 'Tony, I'm only trying to help—'

I push her hands away. 'Who? Just who are you trying to help?' She looks stunned. 'What is it with you, anyway? Is this some kind of guilt thing? Is that it? Feel responsible for what your family did to me, do you?'

She doesn't deserve this right now. But she's getting it all the same.

'Yeah, I know your sort. I bet as a child, you only played with your broken dollies because you felt sorry for them.'

She's searching for something to say, but she can't contend with the sheer blizzard of vitriol I'm now hurling at her. I lean in toward her. 'I don't need your pity. And I don't need you to fix me. I just need you to leave me alone!'

With that, I turn on my heel and walk away.

Down on the platform a familiar voice echoes over the hubbub. It's the loon in the fedora hat from the other night. Still inflicting the world to his gaudy fashion sense and abysmal singing.

'I Ain't Got Nobody and Nobody Cares for Me'.

You said it, pal.

I've been walking for hours. My body's tied and my mind's numb. I struggle up the steps to my studio. The lift would be easier but I can't face its clunky histrionics.

At the top of the stairwell, I stop dead. My studio door is open. The doorframe, a splintered mess of fractured pieces. Moving cautiously across the hall, I tap the door with the toe of my shoe. It swings open. There's no movement inside. Looks like whoever's responsible has come and gone already. But I'm not convinced.

Now I've got two choices. Walk away, or see what the damage is.

Of course I choose the wrong option.

The moment I step through the door a sharp blow to the small of my back sends me toppling. I know what's coming next before I've even hit the floor. As I curl into a ball, a steel toecap finds my stomach.

Now this will go one of two ways. Either they're here to talk and they're just making their introductions or the discussion's already over. In which case, I'm not getting off this floor without considerable medical assistance. Clasping my belly, I brace for the next blow.

Nothing.

I open an eye, squinting upwards. Two big lumps standing over me. Both in hooded sweaters and black leather jackets. The debt collectors from the other day. So far so good. At least I know why they're here. But the hoodies covering their faces are a bad sign, so is the large kitchen knife glinting in the hallway light. *My* kitchen knife. God knows how hard I'm gonna have to scrub that when all this is over.

Crouching, the knife guy plants his knee in my balls. Whimpering, I twist on the floor. I want them to know I hurt easily, so hopefully they won't see me as a challenge. The blade touches my cheek.

Then I get me the whole last chance bullshit.

Jesus, the relief courses through me. If they're still asking for cash, I've still got half a chance of getting off this floor in one piece. As if he's just read my mind, the second oaf delivers a sharp kick to my kidneys. Writhing on the floor, I bellow in agony. And this time I'm not putting on an act.

Knife Guy tells me they'll be back to settle the debt in a few days and drops the blade, point first into the wood flooring, just inches from my face.

Grumbling loudly, they haul a couple of large black holdalls down the stairwell.

I give it a minute before pushing myself up onto my knees. Even in the half-light, it's clear they've cleaned me out. They've even had my Zenhausier and lenses. The fuckers!

Probably sell them down the pub for fuck all! They've left the metal chair, though; Fucking Philistines. I have to laugh, but it comes out as a twisted groan.

Hauling myself off the ground, I stagger over to the kitchenette. Between the pain in my kidneys and my stomach, I don't know which way to bend. By sheer good luck, they haven't found the whisky in the pantry cabinet and I pour myself a glass with a shaky hand. The whisky stings my mouth. My gums are bleeding and I don't even recall getting hit in the face.

Well, at least the worst is over.

'Having a rough night?'

Spinning around, a sharp spasm rips through my abdomen.

Some woman is standing in the doorway with an amused look on her face. Short cropped hair, designer jacket, unmistakable air of self-confidence. I can tell straight out she's here on business. 'If you're from the bank. You're about twenty minutes too late,' I tell her glibly. 'There's some small change in the bowl, but that's about it.'

She glances down at the telephone table. 'You sure about that?' she quips.

'You're fucking kidding me!' I'm genuinely amazed. 'Those fuckers!' I drop onto a breakfast stool with a groan.

'May I?' She gestures toward the interior of the flat.

'The doors open,' I tell her, nodding sardonically at the remains of the front door.

I attempt to pour myself another whisky, but my hands are shaking too much. To my surprise, she takes the bottle from my hand. After topping up my glass, she pours herself one.

299

Fuck me, she's got some front! But at least she's not beating me over the head with the bottle. 'Help yourself,' I tell her with a sarcastic shrug, as she raises her glass in a small, ironic salute.

She takes a sip of whisky and reaches inside her jacket. 'Gillian Bishop; Dark Dimension.'

I snort with derision as she pushes a business card across the breakfast bar. 'Oh now my day's fucking complete.'

'I hope I'm not catching you at an inopportune moment.'

Piss-taking bitch. But I have to give it to her, she is funny.

'As it happens, I was just entertaining a few friends...'

'Yes, I saw them leaving; with half your studio in tow.'

Now she's not so amusing. 'Shame you didn't have a camera crew with you. You could have made yourself a quick buck.'

She repays my comment with a mocking smirk.

'So, how did you find me?' I ask.

'I got a call from Belo Mishal.'

'Oh, the chairman of my fan club.'

'He told me all about his celebrity visitor.'

'I bet he did.'

Fixing her eyes on me, she takes another sip of whisky before turning her attention toward the breakfast bar. 'What's this?' she asks, pulling a portfolio case toward her.

'That's what a real paranormal investigation looks like.'

'Kettles?'

'The other folder,' I snap, dragging the second portfolio across the counter.

Smirking at my annoyance, she opens the second folder. 'Makes the first one look exciting doesn't it?' she quips drolly.

I may have just had the crap beaten out of me. But I'm not about to take any shit from this stuck-up piece of work. 'Just because I haven't found it yet, doesn't mean it isn't there...'

'Or maybe it just means you've been looking in the wrong place.'

Yeah, now I get it. 'So let me guess, by the *wrong place* you mean the Mishal house? And you're here to warn me off?'

'Quite the opposite.'

I give her a suspicious scowl. 'What *do* you want?'

She takes her time before giving me an answer. 'I want to know why you waited so long.'

'Waited?'

'Before going back to that house. To your old home. You're a paranormal investigator, or so you say. Yet you don't investigate the one place where you know for certain paranormal activity has occurred.'

I stare silently down at my whisky glass.

'That is unless of course you know different.'

'That house *was* haunted!' I can feel the muscles in my jaw tightening.

'Was haunted, or is still haunted?'

'I don't think I have anything further to say to you.'

Undaunted by my harsh retort, she flashes me a mirthless smile. 'You know they could prosecute you for what you did to that little girl.'

'Let em!' I snap. 'I've been through worse.' I give her the full '*as you can see*' gesture.

'They've got a good case against you for aggravated assault,' she continues in the same flat tone. 'Plus another for intent to deceive through false representation.'

'And let me guess; you could make it all go away.'

'Let's just say we could help each other out of a bind here.'

I can't help but laugh. 'So let me get this straight. If I do it on my own, it's criminal deception, but if I do it for you, it's what? A bit of harmless entertainment? Well, we already tried it once and it was less than a resounding success. I'm sure Mr Mishal told you as much.'

'That was a mistake,' she says. 'Miss Kalman wasn't acting on our behalf when she approached you to conduct your investigation.'

'Which is a point in her favour I guess.'

'You don't think much of our company do you?'

'Maybe I don't like the way you misrepresent the truth.'

'Evidently.' She holds up a test strip for the ghost mock-up I made for Jerry.

'Well, I think this meeting is over!' Plucking the strip from her hand, I toss it back into the portfolio case. 'Now, if you don't mind I've got the Japanese Yakuza popping around later to extract my gold fillings with a crowbar. So if you could see yourself out.'

I extend my hand toward the gapping hole in the wall where my front door used to be, but she remains where she is. Draining the last of her whisky, she places the glass back on the breakfast bar. 'Don't you want to know?' she asks in a flat tone.

'Know what?'

'Whether it really is your sister inside that little girl's head?'

Cow thinks she's being clever. I hold her gaze. 'Right now; the only head I'm concerned about is my own. And how I can avoid it being used for football practice?'

I catch a sly glint in her eye. 'Like I said, we might be able to help you there.'

I grunt sceptically. 'Not unless you've got a stack load of cash in your tightarse.'

'Well,' she smiles, 'as it happens...'

'This is not a good idea.'

'Why?'

'Don't pretend I have to tell you.'

'Well, you're always telling me I bottle everything up. That I should express my feelings more!'

'But this is not the answer.' Sharman's patience is wearing thin.

'I have to do something! I have to know.'

As I throw up a sulk, his tone softens. 'Maybe the answers you're looking for are not in that house.'

'And where are they then?'

'You know where they are.'

I throw up my hands and slump back in my chair. Sometimes I really hate this man.

'You're going to have to talk about it, eventually,' he tells me.

I shake my head. 'Why do we keep going back to this?' My frustration is building again, but he's not letting up.

'Because it's the only way we're ever make any real progress. How else can we understand what has brought you to this?'

'I can't. You know I can't!'

'Why?'

'Because you won't understand.'

He leans forward. 'Try me.'

Sitting back, I cross my arms over my chest. Standard defensive manoeuvre.

He stares at me a moment, then closes his notepad. 'Well, then; if you're not prepared to talk to me, I don't see any point in our continuing with these sessions.'

That hits me like a brick. 'No, I need this. I need to talk to you.' The mere idea of stopping these sessions has sent me into a sudden panic.

He slips his pen inside his jacket. He really means it this time. He's had enough.

'Tony, in all the time I've been treating you, you've never once addressed directly what happened to you as a child. You've never given me a straight answer or any real insight into your feelings. Why do you keep calling on me if you don't want me to help you?'

Tears well in my eyes. I try to hold them in, but I can't.

'Because you're all I have left.'

***

Mid-eighties video camera footage: The shot sweeps across an abandoned factory at night, alighting on a small group of high-spirited teenagers as they congregate around an older man. 'Dr Sharman, over here,' a voice calls from behind the camera.

The man looks over and smiles. The feeling within the group is relaxed, almost carefree. One teenager is taking photographs, while others are taking notes. Every time the camera settles on a youthful face, it's greeted with a silly grin or mischievous expression. One teenage boy seems particularly endeared to Dr Sharman. They laugh and joke together as they adjust a small portable cassette recorder.

As they work, a teenage girl moves over and drapes her arm over the young man's shoulder. He clasps her forearm and they exchange a lingering glance. Realising they're being filmed, the young couple turn away in unison, laughing and waving the camera away.

The image flickers and cuts to black.

14. Emotional Disorientation

The presence of a ghost can have a detrimental effect on your mood and mental wellbeing.

If you find yourself experiencing dark depressing feelings, or a creeping sense of grief, sadness or foreboding in a specific room or area inside the house. Or if you find yourself having continual dark thoughts which is unlike you or someone else in the house is experiencing a prolonged and distinct personality change, this can also be a sign that you or they are being possessed or influenced by a spirit. It's not uncommon for people who are normally happy and carefree to become depressed, distracted, and introverted during prolonged exposure to a spectre.

These feelings can rapidly escalate into a genuine fear for your own safety and the safety of others around you.

***

'Hi Dad, I'm at the house. Just popped by to see how you're doing. I'll wait for you inside, okay see you soon.' Gripped by a sudden urgency, Jo pushed the end call button. Despite having just created a convincing cover for herself, if her father's Mercedes appeared in the drive now, she would have no alternative but to wait for him on the doorstep. Her chance to return the papers and envelope to the safe would be gone. Hopping from her Mini, Jo hurried across the street toward her old home. Inside, the hallway felt cold and dour. The central heating had yet to come on and the air smelt musty and stale. Despite the house being in total darkness, Jo still felt compelled to call out. 'Hi only me.'

Silence.

Expecting headlights to glide across the stained glass door panels at any moment, Jo quickly slipped down the hallway and into her father's study. With increasing agitation, she retrieved the safe key from the desk and opened the safe. Removing all the document boxes, she opened the inner compartment.

Click.

Jo froze at the sound of the front door latch closing. Guilt struck, Jo waited with mounting resignation for her father to appear at the study door.

But there was no movement in the hallway.

Maybe he had gone straight into the lounge, or upstairs? Could she still replace everything to the safe before making her presence known? But then how could she explain her presence in the study? Jo could feel cold sweat forming on the back of her neck. With shaky hands, she rapidly stuffed everything back into the safe and returned the key to the desk draw. Breathlessly, she chanced a peek out the study door.

Nothing.

Jo glanced over at the coat stand. The hook on which her father would have hung his jacket was vacant. Mystified, she tiptoed down the hallway and opened the front door.

The driveway was empty.

Perplexed, Jo turned back to the hallway. Maybe Maria, her father's housekeeper, had let herself in? But surely Jo would have seen her in the hallway. Plus Maria only worked in the mornings.

Still, she was certain she had heard the latch.

Suddenly, Jo didn't want to wait for her father inside the house anymore. She wanted to sit outside in her car and wait there. But that was foolish. She should just turn on the heating. Fill the kettle and wait in the kitchen, like any normal person.

Forcing herself to relax, Jo wandered into the kitchen and opened a jar of coffee. Searching for milk, she opened the fridge. It was nearly empty. With sudden comprehension, Jo realised why the house felt so vacant. With his business struggling, her father, of course, would be spending all of his time at his office. Attempting to hold things together there.

Now the guilt felt too much. Checking her watch, Jo slipped out of the house and marched over to her car. At this time in the evening; she could easily make Neasden in twenty minutes. Not wanting to pass her father on route, Jo called Frank's mobile again. But as before, it went straight to answerphone.

Maybe he just didn't want to talk to her?

Well, if that was the case. It was all the more reason to see him. They couldn't keep on like this.

A quick glance up at the soot stained windows of Kalman Publishing was enough to confirm Jo's earlier presumption. A light still burnt in her father's office.

As Jo's gaze lingered over the old building, it was hard to ignore how tatty the old place had become. The once innovative nineteen thirties Art Déco structure, reduced now to little more than a grimy eyesore on the side of the North Circular Road. Even as her father fought staunchly to save it; it seemed the building had already resigned itself to its inevitable fate.

In the main foyer, the internal security alarm was still disarmed, further confirming the presence of someone inside the building. Leaving the lights switched off, Jo made her way through the deserted offices. The glow from the duel carriageway outside the windows, providing ample enough light to see by, but in the half-gloom the cramped work spaces felt even more repressive than usual.

The building's original partitioning still divided each of the larger office spaces into smaller compartments. The oppressive maze of thick wooden panels and wire mesh embedded glass, designed to lessen the sound of noisy typewriters and copying machines, was now, by modern standards hideously antiquated. In fact, the entire building needed complete remodelling. To Jo's recollection, little had changed here over the past thirty years. Apart from a few newish Packard Bell computers and some horrid nineties style telephones, everything looked exactly as it had always done. The creaky old filing cabinets, the desks, the chairs, the faded lime green wall paint. Even the few framed magazine covers decorating the office walls were all dated from the early eighties.

Jo opened the door to the small anteroom adjoining her father's office, which had once been the office of Joan Friedman, Frank's elderly secretary. But since Joan's retirement, it had become a dumping ground for remaindered books and unsold magazine returns. A stark metaphor for his company's ailing fortunes, which Frank had to pass through every morning before he started work.

Across the room, the door to Frank's office was half-open. Not wanting to startle her father, Jo tapped on the doorframe. 'Hi, only me.' She pushed open the door. To her surprise, the office was empty. The shaded desk lamp was casting a tight pool of light over the desktop, but the chair behind the desk was empty. She took a step toward the desk.

Then she saw him, slumped on the floor, his face a deathly shade of white.

Qamra woke. The room was dark. Turning over she reached across the bed. Belo's side was empty. She waited in the darkness, listening for any familiar sound from the landing or the toilet. But there was only silence. Climbing out of bed, she wandered out onto the landing. Checking Lila's bedroom, both girls were sleeping soundly in their beds.

Still barefoot, Qamra crept downstairs. Expecting to find Belo asleep in front of the television, she was surprised to find the room empty. Pulling back the lounge curtain, Qamra glanced outside. Belo's van was still parked on the driveway. Feeling a sudden unease, she turned back toward the lounge, searching the shadows for an explanation for Belo's absence.

Over in the kitchen, Rafeeq was sitting by the patio doors, staring out at the darkness. Qamra had grown used to the dog's recent erratic behaviour, but this sudden fixation with the night seemed particularly disturbing. Keeping her eyes trained on the dark glass, Qamra crept toward the sliding doors.

A dark figure stood on the patio.

Although partly hidden by shadow, behind a stack of new fence panels, Qamra could clearly see Belo's profile in the pale moonlight. He was clutching his baseball bat to his chest, slowly twisting the handle in his clenched fist. From his tense posture, he looked poised for something to happen. As if he was laying in wait for someone to appear in the garden. As she watched her husband in silence, Qamra sensed another presence behind her. She turned her head.

Kyra was gazing at her intently from across the kitchen. 'I can't sleep,' the child said wearily.

Qamra stared back at the child, her own expression oddly inert and impassive. Tiptoeing over to the Kyra, Qamra took the child silently by the hand and lead her back upstairs, where she climbed into the camp bed alongside her daughter. Within a few minutes, Kyra was fast asleep. It would be another hour before Qamra heard Belo creeping up the stairs. He lingered by Lila's door a moment before returning to his own bedroom.

A pale shadow moved across the cubicle curtain separating her father's bed from the rest of the recovery ward. Jo had yet to catch sight of the silent visitor in the next bay, but occasionally she would catch a vague movement through the polyester curtain whenever the visitor tended to the patient in the next bed.

Jo's gaze returned to the occupant of her own bay. Like the silent visitor next-door, he too resembled little more than a pale shadow. Framed against the hospital pillow, his face had lost all its colour. His forehead felt clammy and cold to the touch. He didn't even resemble her father anymore. His eyes appeared sunken, while his cheeks seemed to have lost all their fullness. It was as if his entire face had collapsed in on itself.

Jo took her father's hand in hers, mindful not to dislodge the thin cannula taped to his skin. Squeezing his fingers, she felt a numbing sense of reality sink in. Repulsed by the idea of her father might spend his last moments in this dull, depressing room, Jo felt a heavy weight forming in her chest. Surely he deserved better than this?

The sound of footsteps broke her malaise.

'Joanna.'

'Ray?'

Ray Melnick stepped into the bay with a sympathetic look on his face. 'How's he doing?' he asked in a gentle tone after they had hugged.

'It's definitely a heart attack,' Jo said as Ray moved toward the bedside. 'Ray, he's not waking up. It looks like it could be a coma.'

Ray let out a long protracted sigh. As her father's oldest friend and colleague, his remorse seemed genuinely heartfelt. Jo had been, in two minds, about calling Ray. But now he was here. She was glad she had. Despite his drawn and sullen expression, there was something inherently comforting about Ray's earnest disposition.

'The doctor said it's not unusual for patients with diabetes to remain unconsciousness after resuscitation. That he could remain like this for hours or even days.' Jo's voice wavered as she struggled to maintain her calm facade.

A benevolent smile appeared on Ray's face. 'How are *you* doing?' he asked, taking a chair next to Jo and placing his hand over hers.

'I've been here since they brought him in,' Jo said, deftly side-stepping the question. 'When I found him at his desk, I thought he was dead.'

Ray gave Jo's hand a tender squeeze. 'But he's still with us. And that's down to you. If you hadn't been there; who knows what might have happened?'

'He shouldn't have been on his own. I should never have left him.'

'Joanna, you have your own life. This probably would've happened. If you had been there or not.'

In her fragile state of mind, Jo instantly latched upon Ray's seemingly innocuous comment. 'Why has he been ill?'

'I mean, he's no longer a young man. When you get to our age, things tend to break. Especially when you push yourself too hard.'

But Ray's well-meant words were doing little to reassure Jo. 'So he has been unwell?' She turned her mind back to the last time she'd seen her father. The day she had walked out on him. But she was unable to conjure a clear image. 'How did he look? The last time you saw him.'

'The last time I saw him was at Shabbat. He looked tired, but he always looks tired—'

'Wait, what? You saw him at your synagogue?'

'Last Saturday. We were due to meet next week for a financial review—'

'Sorry, are you saying he's been going to the synagogue?'

'Yes, not as often as he should. But hey...'

'Since when?'

Ray finally registered Jo's confusion. 'Oh, he didn't tell you.'

Jo shook her head, bewildered. 'How long has he been going?'

'Maybe a year now. Can you imagine, he returns to his Jewish faith after a lapse of nearly thirty-five years?'

Sitting back in her chair, Jo stared at her father. Not only had his physical appearance changed. But now his actual character seemed unrecognisable. 'He never told you he was coming back?'

'Not at all. He just appeared one day and sat down next to me. I tell you no one was more surprised than I was and I've known him for over forty years.'

'What made him return?'

'I don't know.' Ray admitted. 'But your father has always had a complicated relationship with his faith.'

Jo still couldn't make any sense of it. She'd never considered either of her parents to have been particularly religious. There'd been nothing overtly Jewish or Catholic about their home. Her father had never kept kosher or any of the festivals. They had celebrated Christmas, but they had never gone to church. Jo had never been baptised, or had ever attended Sunday school. Growing up, it had never even occurred to her that her parents had been from different religious backgrounds. It had simply never been an issue.

Ray could see this contradiction on Jo's face as she studied her father in the bed. 'Jewishness is an irreversible status,' he told her. 'It's not defined by how you choose to live your life. Even if you ignore it, it's still there.'

'But why now?'

'Old age can do that to you.'

Was that it? Had her father suspected his coming illness, had he feared the ravages of encroaching age, had he sensed the inevitable?

'I'd like to believe he was looking for something,' Ray said. 'Something he felt he'd been missing.' In response to Jo's puzzled glance, he shrugged affably. 'You see. Your father gave up a lot to be with your mother. It was a big issue with his family.'

'I knew there was some kind of falling out,' Jo admitted, although she knew very little of the actual circumstances.

'But they loved each other, and they didn't care,' Ray continued. 'But it caused a huge rift. To be honest, as a faith we're not known for our tolerance toward interfaith marriages, but this was particularly bad.'

'So they threw him out.'

Ray gave a mock look of horror. 'No, he walked away. Turned his back on everything. So he could be with your mother.'

'So you think he's been looking for some kind of redemption?'

Ray made a dismissive motion with his hand. 'It's not that straightforward. You haven't been brought up in the Jewish faith, so it may be a little harder for you to understand.'

Jo turned to face Ray, her expression saying *'try me'*.

Ray made a conciliatory gesture. 'You see, to someone of the Jewish faith, the person you marry becomes a part of who you are. It's not something you do casually or without great consideration. You make that person a part of your identity, and they become a part of yours. To us, our partners fill a void in our very being. So marriage, like Jewishness itself, isn't something you do, it's something you are.'

'So if you don't marry another Jew?'

'Then a part of you will remain a void, forever.'

Greg pushed the end call button on his mobile. It had been an effort to keep his voice from sounding strained. Jo's father was ill and she had asked him to walk Bruno for her. It wasn't a problem. It would give him something to do. The flat always felt so empty when Hanna returned to her mother's. That's

316

when it hit him the hardest. Greg ran his hand over his face, smearing the tears across his cheeks.

No, this wouldn't do.

Tilting the rear view mirror, he appraised his own reflection. His bloodshot eyes glaring back at him reprovingly. It was all getting too much. It was getting harder to hide his emotions from Hanna. To put on a brave face, for her sake. Hanna had barely begun skipping up the drive to her mother's new home before the tears had sprung from his eyes. He was falling to pieces. Constantly snapping at Hanna. Finding reasons to be argumentative. He'd become opinionated and belligerent at work. He was turning into someone he didn't recognise. Greg twisted the mirror back into positioned. He couldn't bear to look at himself any longer, in case he glimpsed the real reason for his tears.

The discovery of Ashley's body had rekindled so many suppressed emotions. They now threatened to overwhelm him. Rob Hopper had asked for Greg personally and Greg had felt duty-bound to accept. But it was hard. Hard to ignore the guilt. He'd let Rob down before.

He had let Ashley down.

He had let himself down.

It had been a bad time. The divorce had hit Greg hard. It had left him feeling diminished, small, angry. He had felt lost. Even a teenager's smile had been appreciated. Longed for even. He had looked forward to seeing her. Spending time with her. She had become an obsession; possibly. Who knew anymore? But there was no getting around the truth. She had trusted him. Rob had trusted him.

There was no crueller emotion than guilt.

A wax lined paper cup dropped from the dispenser with a noisy rattle followed by a squirt of insipid brown liquid, that did little to strengthen Jo's flagging spirit. Jo wanted to cry. To bellow and release all her frustration. But she could barely hold herself straight anymore.

Across the waiting room, a rolling news channel was repeating a report on the British Army's assault on Basra. Tall buildings tumbled to the ground in flames, as excited news analysts presided over large tactual maps.

Somewhere in the ICU a woman was crying, a hollow, pitiful wail. However distressing, Jo couldn't help but wish the cry had come from her father, just so she could hear his voice again. Ray's revelations had left Jo dumbfounded. 'I think he only comes for the food and the conversation,' Ray had said; in order to lessen the significance of his revelation. But no matter how delicately he had framed it, Ray's disclosure had made Jo realise just how little she really knew her father. The distance that had always existed between them had never felt so vast.

The revelation had also called into question her own belief in God. Jo had never attended church. Or felt the need to do so. She wasn't sure if she even believed in the concept of an afterlife. Neither of her parents had ever pushed any religious education or instruction upon her. Her mother, in fact, had been virulently against all forms of organised religion and her father had always remained diplomatically quiet on the subject. Which made Frank's attempt to re-embrace his old faith even more perplexing.

Across the room, the earlier images of death and devastation were rolling around again. As Jo watched the same news footage of distraught parents digging through the rouble of a pulverised school, another round of plaintive wails echoed from the ICU. Reaching for a crumpled packet of Silk Cut from her bag, Jo immediately tossed them back again. She didn't want to step outside, not even for a minute. She needed to be there when her father woke up.

Jo was about to return to her father's bedside when Ray appeared by her side. For a instant Jo's hopes flickered, but Ray dispelled her expectations with a gentle shake of his head. 'He's still sleeping,' he said. 'The nurse is changing his gown, so I thought I would give them some privacy.'

Jo excepted the situation with a gloomy sigh. 'I would offer you a coffee but...' she held up the cup of insipid brown liquid for Ray to inspect.

'I think I'll pass,' Ray concurred. They stood in silence for a moment before Ray said. 'You know in someways; this might be a good thing. Maybe this will finally convince him to take things easy. Take up a hobby; fishing maybe?'

Jo huffed, amused by Ray's suggestion. 'He won't do that. You know how stubborn he is.'

'I think that's a family trait.' Ray smiled, planting his palm upon her shoulder. 'You should go home. Get something to eat, sleep a little.'

'No, I'm going to stay. At least until I know he's going to be alright.'

Ray turned her gently by the shoulders to face him. 'You said it yourself. It could be hours or even days before he wakes. You need to think about yourself. Your father wouldn't want you to make yourself sick over all this.'

Jo was indeed tired, tireder than she'd ever felt. All the occurrences of the last few days had left her drained and disorientated. Ray could see she was wavering. 'Go on. I'm here with him now. I'll call you if anything changes.'

Jo reluctantly nodded. 'They say you should talk to him as much as you can. It's good for them. About anything. Normal day-to-day stuff—'

'Joanna, don't worry. Go home, get some sleep.'

'I'll be back in a couple of hours.'

'Take as long as you need. I'll be here when you get back.'

Jo kissed her father before she left. His face still looked gaunt and pale. But at least someone had pulled back the cubicle curtain. The dawning sunlight shone in through the open blinds, across the empty bed in the next bay.

With the volume on her Discman turned as high as it could go, Lila stood on the edge of the platform, staring vacuously at an advertising poster on the bowed wall opposite.

BECOME WHAT YOU WANT TO BE
London Southbank University

The poster's inscription, printed in a large bold font over a multitude of less prominent job titles: Lawyer; Civil Engineer; Business Analyst; Publicist; the list went on and on. The poster looked new but its edges were already peeling.

All around her, disgruntled commuters squirmed and twisted like irritated eels in a barrel. It was the height of the morning rush hour. And as usual; all the trains were running with delays. When the next train finally crawled into the station, it, like all its predecessors, was already packed to the gills. Impatient and frustrated, Lila thrust herself into the already congested carriage. As more people pushed in behind her, she became lodged within a mass of writhing human bodies.

Several times the doors attempted to close behind her, only to spring open again with a angry clunk. A murmur of disgruntled annoyance resonated through the carriage as the driver made an ill-temper appeal over the tannoy for passengers to stand clear of the closing doors. Finally, the doors slammed shut for good and the train lumbered out of the station.

Attempting to remove her puffer jacket in the stifling heat, Lila became lodged between a large bald man gripping a briefcase and a woman carrying a bulky rucksack. Unable to brace herself against an unexpected judder, Lila toppled face first against the sweaty shirt-front of the bald business man. Embarrassed, the man twisted away and pretended it had never happened. Deep inside, Lila could feel herself screaming. She hated this journey and she hated her new school. Right now, she hated everything about her life.

Rubbing her scarf across her face, Lila pushed further toward the middle of the carriage. From here she had a

321

clear view down the entire length of the train. By watching the train's snaking movements through the interconnecting doors, she could at least predict the sudden lurching movements of her own carriage, and hopefully avoid another tumble.

As the train slammed into the next station, Lila spotted a free seat by the emergency door. Pushing through the carriage, she roughly jostled herself onto the small ledge before anyone else could claim it.

Blanking the scowls of her fellow passengers, Lila set about making the space her own. Folding her jacket on her lap, she leant back against the window, securing her headphones over her ears. With Eminem ranting and raging at full velocity Lila recoiled into her own little world.

As her expression glazed over, Lila no longer felt the proximity of the other passengers packed around her or even the presence of Roy Norris standing immediately behind her, watching her intently through the glass partitions separating his carriage from hers.

Jo was halfway up the stairwell when she met Greg, coming down in the opposite direction. 'How's your father?' Greg asked, pulling up beside her.

'He's still unconscious, but stable,' Jo said resignedly.

Greg gave a sympathetic nod, glancing down at the plastic bag in Jo's hand. 'It's some food from my father's favourite deli,' she told him. 'I figured he'll be hungry when he wakes up.'

Greg knew very little about neurological conditions, but was fairly sure a stacked salt beef sandwich would be about the last thing any recovering coma patient would be advised to eat. But he could see what it meant to Jo.

'So, where are you off to?' Jo asked in a more upbeat tone.

Greg wavered a moment before telling her. 'They've reassigned me to Rob Hooper after the discovery of Ashley's body. He asked for me especially. I'm just heading over there now.'

The news knocked Jo back again. 'It feels like everything is going wrong at the moment, doesn't it?'

'I'll be back later,' Greg reassured her as he recommenced his descent down the stairwell. 'So if you need anything, just give me a buzz okay?'

'If you could take Bruno around the block again, that would be great. If you've got time, that is.'

Assuring her it would be no problem, Greg disappeared out through the building's foyer.

Throwing her coat on the sofa, Jo fought the urge to drop in a heap beside it. Instead, she shuffled over to the kitchen and made herself a mug of coffee. Emptying a pouch of dog food into a bowl, she watched idly as Bruno greedily gobbled it up. She felt exhausted. All her muscles ached. She made herself some toast and Marmite, but felt unable to eat it. Pushing the plate away, her gaze fell upon the tatty cardboard box by the coat stand.

Jo had been meaning to call Jamie for weeks now. But each time she'd been poised to call, she had lost her nerve. She hated this weakness in herself. Even now; even as the injured party, she'd begun doubting herself again. Questioning her own motivations for making the call. Her reasons for holding onto what remained of his stuff. This was typical of her. It had been his affair that had ended their relationship and yet here she was, looking for faults in herself.

But hadn't that been their relationship all along?

She'd been immediately attracted to Jamie Burns when they'd first met. He'd been charming and funny. A soft-spoken, well-educated, amiable extrovert. He had been supportive of her. Well, to begin with, anyway. But that had changed with time. She hadn't seen it at first. The change had been that slight. Gradually his encouragement had transformed into snide criticism, his attentiveness into unreasonable demands. His charm had morphed into subtle manipulation, his kindness hinged on her conforming to his expectations. He'd become critical about what she choose to wear. Making jokes at her expense.

If ever she complained about his behaviour, he would deny everything. Twist things around. Implying she was being unreasonable. Or even worse, that she was crazy, that she was the one imagining things. Seeing things that were not real. Over time; she'd come to believe this version of herself. Sensitive to her own failings. It wasn't hard to believe she was at fault again. That she'd been too demanding, too unreasonable in her expectations.

Too weak.

Under pressure from Jamie, she'd question her own judgment. Her own perceptions. Her own reality. Under Jamie's criticism, she had lost her own identity.

His affair had changed all that. It had cut through her confusion like a blade. Her life had been thrown into disarray, but at least it had finally shown Jamie for what he was. If it hadn't been for that; well, maybe...

Jo shook that notion away. She was tired. Her mind was all over the place. Checking her watch, she stretched. She could just catch a couple of hours' sleep before returning to the hospital.

As she stood, her gaze fell upon her handbag on the kitchen counter. Reaching in, she retrieved the pregnancy test she'd just purchased from the chemist and placed it on the counter.

Yes, everything was going wrong.

Belo spotted him in the wing mirror, lurking by the school gates, trying to look inconspicuous. Shabby donkey jacket, filthy dungarees and a shifty disposition. He would've been hard to miss. Normally, Belo wouldn't have bothered picking Lila up from school. But after they had received a call from Gillian Bishop regarding Roy Norris' criminal record, Qamra had insisted.

Just as well she had.

Spotting something in the crowd, Roy began moving purposefully against the flow of students. Leaning out the window, Belo saw what he already suspected. Lila had just appeared from the main entrance.

Belo was out of his van and across the road in seconds. 'What the hell are you doing!' he yelled as he got within striking distance of Roy.

Startled by Belo's sudden appearance, Roy shuffled backwards. 'You d-d-don't understand, your d-d-daughter is in danger,' he stammered, blinking nervously, under Belo's threatening glare.

'Damn right she is!' Belo thundered, 'From you!'

Most of the waiting parents had now turned in their direction, while several students were already edging away. As Roy turned toward Lila, Belo pushed him further away from the stunned teenager. 'No, you don't!' With each word, Belo thumped his finger harder against Roy's chest. 'I know all about you now. You fucking nonce!'

Under pressure, Roy snapped and let off a flailing punch. To both men's surprise, it connected with force against Belo's jaw, sending Belo tumbling to the pavement. An audible ripple of shock reverberated around the startled onlookers. As a flustered teacher ran from the building, punching the buttons on her mobile phone, Roy glared down at Belo. 'You're going to regret this,' he growled as he turned on his heel and ran.

'Hi Dad, it's me. I'm back. I've brought you something to eat. It's here on the side. I got that matzoh ball soup from Reuben's that you like. You can have it later when you're feeling better.

'By the way, they all wish you well, everyone at the deli. They hope to see you on your feet again real soon. Maybe in a day or two, when you're feeling a little better, I'll smuggle you in some of their apple cake. I'm fussing, I know, but that's just me, isn't it? I guess it wouldn't be the same if I wasn't frustrating the hell out of you in some way. Guess I've always done that, haven't I.

'Even as a child, following you about bugging you all the time, trying to get your attention. I just saw so little of you. So when you were there. I just wanted you all to myself. But you were always busy or had work to do. I used to hate it when you disappeared into your study.

'Then Mum died, and you seemed to take another step away from me. You were there for me, of course. But maybe not in the way I needed you to be. In some ways, you were just as distant as mother had been.

'I know now it must have been tough for you. Everyone tells me how much I remind them of her. It can't have been easy living with someone that constantly reminds you of someone you've lost. I guess that's why we couldn't get along. You see too much of Mum in me.

'You know I've always thought you secretly resented me, just for being here, when she wasn't. I always assumed you blamed me in for her death. That if it hadn't been for me, she might still be alive.

'I was so angry at her. And I had nowhere to unleash that anger, but at you. But I know now that was just how Mum was. It wasn't her fault, not really. She was just incapable of loving me. Which is not the same as not wanting to love me. It wasn't her fault. It was just how she was. And I suppose I'm not much better, when I've never been able to tell you how much I love you. And I do love you very much. In fact, I've only ever wanted you to be proud of me. I want things to be better between us. I want us to be a family again. But the first thing we need to do is get you better. Don't forget your soup, it's there on the side for you, for when you wake up.

'I'll go now. Let you sleep. It's getting late. I'll see you in the morning.

'Goodnight Dad.'

Frank died a few hours later, without regaining consciousness.

***

Seventies silent 8mm home movie footage: A beguiling woman playfully waves away the camera. Laughing she turns her back, as the cameraman persists with the close-up.

The grainy image flickers and skips as the shot changes to a smiling middle-aged man sitting on a beach. His bare feet are stuck in the wet sand, his trouser legs rolled to his knees. A young child clambers onto his lap, scrabbling for a foothold and delighting in her father's attention.

The shot changes again; the young girl squeals with delight, as she's swung between her father's legs.

The image changes once more. It's later in the day. The sun is low in the sky. The woman is standing alone, close to the water's edge. A gust of wind catches her hair. She's appears to be unaware she is being filmed, her gaze fixed on the horizon. The young girl appears from the bottom of the frame, running toward her mother—

The film reel judders to an end.

15. Mysterious Images

Strange and ghostly images seen in photographs and video film. Mysterious images that appear at first glance to be nothing more than a smudge on the print or a random light flare. Possibly even a scratch on the lens or a damaged negative.

Sometimes these images may resemble a barely perceivable figure hovering in the background or a strange floating orb dancing around the screen. Although easily dismissed as simply double exposures or reflected light sources on a camera lens, these strange enigmatic images could well be evidence that a paranormal entity is trying to make its presence known.

***

A large Grip Truck is parked in front of the house. The skip and the builder's van are gone, replaced with a giant pop-up gazebo on the driveway. Several neighbours have gathered in the street to watch the unfolding spectacle. In my day, they used to cross the road to avoid our house. Now they want to have their photo taken in front of it.

'Well, we're here,' the dickhead with a prat hairdo tells me with a perfunctory smile. Dressed like a hip barber, the guy calls himself Jacob. I'm still getting over the fact it was him on my doorstep today and not Kalman. There's no reason it should have been her, of course. But I would have liked the continuity.

As I watch the production crew unloading the truck, I'm gripped by a sudden urge to turn and run. To leap from the people carrier and never look back. But I fight the impulse. Clasping the handle, I take a deep breath and pull back the sliding door.

As we enter the house, a grubby teenager in a Resident Evil T-shirt barely knowledges my existence as we pass in the hallway. Behind him, other crew members are busy with their allocated jobs. No one knows who I am. Or if they do, they don't care. They've all got work to do.

In the lounge, they've rearranged the furniture and cleared all the clutter away. It could almost pass for a normal family home. If it wasn't for the clutch of bustling production crew buzzing around. The Jacob guy points across the room. 'This is Malcolm Rice. He's directing the show tonight.'

Malcolm Rice extends a welcoming hand and a smile. 'So you're the famous Tony Vail then,' he says in a tone which is surprisingly warm. He's holding a ragged shooting script, which, from the look of it, has already seen several alterations made to it. 'You'll have to bear with us,' he tells me. 'They only sprang you on us this morning. And to be frank you're really butt-fucking my entire schedule, but we all have to bow to the decrees of the ice queen, don't we!'

Fuck it, it's going to be hard to dislike this guy.

He shuffles the pages of his shooting script. 'Must be strange being back.' I assume he means after all these years. And not to the fact I was already here with Kalman. 'Don't worry,' he continues, mistaking my quietness for nerves. 'We won't be asking too much of you. Just a couple of quick interviews with Posey. One before the lockdown and one after. But she'll do most of the talking. We should be able to coast you through it.' As he babbles on, I glance over his shoulder toward the kitchen extension.

'Looking for Jo?'

I turn around, startled by Bishop's sudden appearance by my side. She offers me neither her hand nor a pleasant smile in greeting.

'Don't tell me you've sacked her.'

'I should have. But no; she's had a bereavement in the family.'

'Her family?'

'Her father.'

She watches me to gauge my reaction. 'Sorry to hear that,' I tell her, keeping my tone neutral.

She seems surprised as if she expected a different response. 'So, how are you two getting along?'

For a moment I think she means myself and Kalman, but she's referring to me and Malcolm what's-his-name.

'We're only just getting started,' Malcolm tells her. 'I was hoping we could have a quick chat about how best to incorporate Tony here into the live show.'

Bishop waves away any logistical concerns. 'I'd like him in as much as we can, including the lockdown.'

'*Including* the lockdown?'

Ignoring Malcolm's bemusement, Bishop turns to me. 'Tony, how would you feel about being part of the investigation?'

'I take it by investigation you mean the part of the show where you all traipse around in the dark screaming at every little noise you hear, then fine.'

Malcolm smiles, but Bishop is standing by the format. 'The lockdowns make good television and they set the scene nicely for the séance,' she tells me in a measured tone.

'Oh yeah, the séance,' I huff.

'Don't worry you'll just have to sit there. Max will do all the hard bits.'

'Hang on a second. You never said I'd have to be part of the séance.'

She casts me a prickly glance. 'Why? What are you worried about?'

I shrug as she holds my gaze. 'Falling asleep in the middle of it.'

Bishop flashes me a mirthless smile, but I get a chuckle out of Malcolm.

'So where do you want to start?' Malcolm asks. His tone dispelling any pretence that he might actually be in charge of this shoot.

'Maybe we could film a little stepping back into the house segment.'

'We're live in less than four hours,' Malcolm objects, but from his tone I can tell he's already given up trying to fight the decision.

'Well, you'd better get started then.'

'Okay fine.' Huffing, Malcolm folds his shooting script away.

'But I've already been back.'

Bishop turns, surprised by my statement, 'What?'

'I've been back twice already.'

'Oh, we're not going to mention that. We'll just play it like it's the first time you've been back in thirty years. Posey escorting you around, that sort of thing.'

'So, I haven't been here five minutes and you're already making stuff up?'

'We're not making anything up,' Bishop tells me dryly. 'We're just allowing ourselves scope to illustrate the narrative.' I try to hold her glare, but she's way better at this than I am. 'Oh and this, of course, is Max.' I turn to find myself facing the star of this side-show; Maxwell Schaffer.

'Tony, I've been *so* looking forward to meeting you.' Schaffer extends a large hand. He's far taller than he looks on television, with a burly build. He looks more like a smartly dressed builder than a spiritual medium. An impression emphasised by his vice-like grip. He's wearing a dark jacket over a black polo neck, with a large spiritual medallion hanging garishly between the lapels. He stares directly into my eyes. I've seen this shtick before. He's trying to mesmerise me with the sheer magnitude of his presence. 'So what's it feel like being back?'

'Unpleasant,' I tell him truthfully.

Nodding sympathetically, he draws a sharp breath. Gripping my hand tighter, his whole body shudders, as if he's just come in his pants. 'There's such a dark aura around you,' he says wistfully.

'Yeah, I get that a lot,' I tell him in a deadpan tone.

With his hand still clasped around mine, he leans closer. 'I'm picking up a genuine sadness from you and regret. You're unsure if you're doing the right thing by being here.'

Well, you got that much right.

'I feel this is the end of a very long journey for you.' He clamps another hand over the top of mine. 'But we'll finish this together.'

I throw up in the bathroom. No one knows. I've locked the door.

I step through into the kitchen extension. I'm still feeling nauseous and probably look it, too. The Mishals are all huddled around the kitchen island. There's just the three of them. I imagine they've packed the youngest sprog off for the duration of the shoot. They're all smartly dressed for the cameras. They've even got 'misery guts' out of her hoodie. The mother's sitting hunched on a stool, wringing a tatty tissue around in her hands. She looks even more wretched than usual. She's muttering in Arabic, but falls silent the moment she spots me.

It isn't long before the husband's bowling over. 'Never thought I'd see you here again,' he smirks.

'Well, somebody's got to look out for the wellbeing of your family,' I retort harshly.

He's up in my face in an instant and it takes a couple of passing crew members to talk him down. 'Hey if you boys can't play nicely together, I'll stick you in separate playpens.' Bishop bellows from across lounge as we're both directed to different ends of the kitchen.

It was just posturing, but the whole incident has left me feeling sick. I grab a glass from the draining board and stick it under the tap. Across the room, a runner calls the Mishals into the lounge. Filling the glass, I gulp a mouthful of water. As I turn from the sink, the mother is standing by my side. From her glazed expression, I'd say, someone's cracked open the sedatives early.

'I'm sorry about all that,' I mumble, thinking she's annoyed by my altercation with her husband.

Ignoring my comment, she leans closer. 'You shouldn't be here,' she says in a strained, muted monotone.

'Well, they didn't leave me much choice.'

She holds my gaze with the same numb scowl until the runner reappears and leads her away.

Lighting a cigarette, I slouch back against a stack of new fence panels on the patio. In the kitchen extension, Bishop's arguing with some bloke with a goatee. He keeps shaking his head and throwing his hands in the air. Grabbing a ghost book from the side, she pushes it under his nose. Pointing at a photo page. They glance up in unison as they realise I'm watching them through the glass.

Seems my fame precedes me.

I'm sitting in the kitchen in a folding chair while a teenager with excessive face piercings dubs powder on my forehead. I feel dumb and inert. My face feels clammy and I'm sweating so much, no amount of powder is likely to cover it up. But I let it happen.

Throughout the house, there's the sound of focused activity. Lots of purposeful chatter and bustle. I check my Motorola. Still no messages from Kalman. Not that I'm expecting any. I'm not even sure if she knows I'm doing the show. Tucking the phone away, I catch sight of the space by the hallway door. I try to ignore it. But the more I do; the more I'm drawn toward it.

Hysterical voices. A slap, a roar of anger. A knife cutting through flesh. My mother's tortured scream—

'Hi, I'm Jazmin. Can I get you a coffee?'

'What?' I'm too startled to say anything else.

'Can I get you a coffee?'

Another teenager; this one's clutching a clipboard to her chest.

'No.'

'A tea?'

'No.'

'A cold drink?'

I can't just keep saying *no*, so I simply stare at her instead. She returns my gaze with the same inane expression until she finally gets the message. 'Would you like me to leave you alone?' she asks chirpily. 'Okay then.' She turns and leaves in exactly the same annoyingly upbeat manner she arrived in. I glance back at the doorway. The memory has faded, leaving only the busy chatter of the production crew and the sound of my own racing heart.

'Tony.'

'Yeah.'

'Could we do it one more time, please, but this time could you look...' Malcolm searches for the right words. 'In awe of your surroundings,' he finally suggests. We've done my entrance into this fucking house three times already and frankly, I've had enough. 'This time; could you bear in mind, you're returning to the house which represents so much personal tragedy for you?'

'Yes, thank you, I am aware of the history.'

Malcolm shuffles and looks suitably contrite, so I give it another go for his sake. This time I crank the whole wide-eyed shock and awe to the max, as I survey the Mishal's bland choice of wallpaper and generic NEXT photo prints. Malcolm's not impressed. 'We'll go with the first take,' he tells the crew gruffly.

'I don't know, a lot of this stuff doesn't really tally with the original haunting,' Dan Philips - the guy with the goatee, flips the page of his production notes. 'There are a lot of inconsistencies here.'

'Well, it's what we're going with,' Bishop tells him abruptly.

'I thought we'd have some new material.'

'Well, we don't!' She snatches the file from Philips and flips the sheet. 'Here; Posey's drawn up a short list of names. Just pick one.'

Philips doesn't look convinced. 'It's going to be hard to tie any of these names to the original haunting...' He dries up as he spots me watching him.

'Well, that's a fair point,' Bishop concedes. 'Tony, your sister never identified Mr Nox, did she?' she says, while barely acknowledging my presence behind her.

'No?' I admit cautiously.

'See, so it's still open to interpretation then,' she tells Philips in an arrogant tone.

'Meaning you're free to make something up.'

Scowling, Bishop ignores my sarcasm. 'Meaning we have a little free rein as to his identity.' She forces an uncomfortable smile onto her smug face as she slaps the production notes back at Philips. 'Just speak to Posey and see what you can drum up.' As Philips hurries off, I attempt to catch Bishop with a contemptuous glare, but she returns my gaze, unmoved. 'Well, we have to give the viewers what they expect,' she says pointedly. 'And you should know all about that.'

Fuck it, she's not even pretending anymore.

Out in the gazebo; several neighbours are wandering around with cake tins. It's all pretence, of course, but I can't help feeling bitter. I don't remember anyone turning up with fruit cake in my day. I watch the idiots laugh and wallow in the spectacle. Max Schaffer's even signing autographs. 'So do you really think the house is haunted then?' one of the curtain twitchers asks. There's a tangible sense of relish to her voice.

'Of course it's haunted.' Schaffer tells her casually. 'Because every house is haunted.' A sly smile appears on his face as the old dear waits expectantly for him to explain. 'You see every place where people have lived and died is haunted. Everywhere holds some kind of ghost for somebody. Some echo of the past. Every time we enter a room or walk down a corridor, we are passing through someone else's memories, someone else's past. Memories linger everywhere. We keep them with us, because they're part of who we are. And sometimes after we leave, these memories remain.'

It's all straight out of the Max Schaffer playbook. Flouncy nonsense, dressed up with a lot of ambiguous bullshit, but the townsfolk are lapping it up.

The Jazmin girl appears by my side, sporting the same inane grin she's had on all evening. 'Tony, they're ready for you inside.'

Another one calling me Tony, without asking first.

Everything is making me edgy tonight. I resist the urge to check my phone again.

'Okay people, we're live in five, four, three, two....'

As Malcolm gives the 'on air' signal, Posey and Schaffer spring into life. 'Hello and welcome to a very special live spook-tacular edition of *The Max Schaffer Experience*.'

Fucking twats!

I grunt my way through an interview with Posey. Everyone's on edge because of the live format of the show. Especially Posey who keeps glancing nervously at her notes. Apparently she's also the show's resident historian, although she doesn't look old enough to remember who the prime minister was before Blair.

The entire exchange is just a setup for the viewers' benefit. To let them know who I am. Over on a floor monitor, I can see the usual assortment of grainy images appearing over our conversation. The family standing together in the living room, Milgallon conducting his experiments, Tracey gazing into the camera. Most of my responses are setup for me by Posey. 'It must be strange being back in the house after all these years; This must feel very familiar; It must have been scary living here back in the day....'

I just have to agree with her, or nod my head. I dodge anything more probing by saying, 'I don't remember', or by staring blankly back at her. Every time this happens, she glances anxiously over at Malcolm, who just gives her the 'keep going' gesture. She doesn't mention what I do now, or my name change, or that I'm also a paranormal investigator. She doesn't touch upon anything that doesn't relate to the original haunting. Behind the camera, half a dozen production crew watch on listlessly as they wait for this segment to end. Out in the kitchen, the husband's filming everything on his camcorder. He must think all his Christmases have come at once. Posey prattles on with more of her cobbled together nonsense, reaped from the pages of *The Junior Puffin Book of Ghosts and Ghouls*.

From the doorway; the daughter never takes her eyes off me.

'She was definitely the focus. I think it's quite clear.'

'The focus?' Posey feeds Schaffer another question like a mug, while he nods thoughtfully. They're both doing a piece to camera about the history of the house. They're breezing through it. It's clearly a fine-tuned routine the pair have honed.

'Yes, *the focus*. With a poltergeist haunting, there's always *a focus*. Where a ghost will continually appear at a certain time and place, oblivious to its currant surroundings. A Poltergeist will respond directly to its environment, or more precisely to a single person within that environment; usually a teenage girl; The focus. In this case the Babcock's daughter Tracey.'

I bristle every time someone mentions her name, but I'm able to keep a lid on it.

'And do you think we're witnessing a repeat phenomenon now?'

'Almost certainly. I can already sense a lingering shadow in this house. There's a lot of residual fear still here. You see, the occupants of the house may have changed over the years, but the poltergeist, Mr Nox, has remained its sole constant resident.'

'Wow,' Bishop declares sardonically as she steps up beside me. 'If you roll you eyes any harder, you'll do yourself a mischief.' A thin smile creases her face.

I have to chuckle despite my reticence. 'This is all a joke you know.'

She cocks her head. 'You know, you're very sceptical for someone who claims to believe in the paranormal.'

'Don't worry, I know the real thing when I see it.'

She holds my gaze, attempting to decipher my insinuation.

'Fuck's sake!'

It's Schaffer's voice, sounding very *un*-mystical.

They've just broken for an advert break and Schaffer is using the opportunity to voice some concerns. 'Jesus Malcolm! Can you do something about this? It's bad enough we have to do this shit live; without having to deal with all this bollocks as well!' Schaffer points to the husband who's just drifted into shot with his camcorder.

'Give me strength!' Bishop mutters under her breath 'Mr Mishal, would you mind waiting out front during taping in future?'

'Well, I'd like to—'

A sharp glance from Bishop cuts him off mid-sentences and he's read the riot act. Grumbling, he disappears out the door.

Back in the lounge, they're going live again. So it's all smiles for the camera.

Across in the gazebo, I catch the Jazmin girl staring at me. It's the usual thing. An awkward mix of prerequisite pity and morbid fascination. She's clearly intrigued by me, yet repelled at the same time. The instant I catch her eye she glances away. That's the usual response as well.

'We're ready for everyone inside,' the T-shirt guy calls from the front door.

Raised voices coming from the kitchen. The mother's just gone into one and Bishop's attempting to talk her down. The daughter's watching everything from across the room chewing her nails. 'What's up?' I ask Malcolm who's keeping himself well out of it.

'Issues with the family,' he tells me with a dismissive shrug.

'No, no, this is wrong!' the mother wails, while the husband hovers haplessly by her side. They're watching a pre-record-ed insert on a monitor with Bishop. Posey on location in a vast derelict building, which I recognise as an old Victorian workhouse situated several miles from here. A locale far more in keeping with the show's normal M.O.

'We're just taking an educated guess as to the identity of Mr Nox,' Bishop tells the Mother. 'Hopefully, the séance will confirm this for us later.'

I'm sure it will. I bet Schaffer's sitting inside the mini van right now rehearsing his lines.

'But it's wrong—' the mother objects, but Bishop cuts her off.

'It helps the public if we can give an identity to the ghost. It plays extremely well with the viewers...'

'But I know what it is. Why it's here! You must listen to me!' She's close to hysteria, tears rolling down her cheeks. Other crew members are turning in her direction. 'No, we can't do this, this is mistake!' The husband attempts to take her in his arms, but she squirms in his grip, attempting to break free. 'No, you have to stop!' she yells desperately.

'Okay, I think we need to take Mrs Mishal outside for a while.' Bishop snaps her fingers at Jasmine.

'Where should I take her?' Jasmine asks as she attempts to guide the struggling mother away from the husband's grip.

'Just fucking out of here!' Bishop snarls. Despite her cool exterior, the pressure of the live production is finally getting to her.

'Hey, you can't talk to us like that in our own home.' The husband releases his grip on the mother and points a finger at Bishop.

What do you know, he's got a backbone after all?

Unperturbed Bishop squires herself toward him. 'Well, before you have any second thoughts about the situation,' she tells him in an arrogant tone. 'May I remind you that you've signed a legal contract rendering you liable to considerable financial restitution, should you at any point, place us in the unfortunate position of having to cancel tonight's show.' The husband stops dead in his tracks. The mere mention of financial repercussions has been enough to render him mute. 'Now if you can take your wife outside; we going live again in a couple of minutes.' Turning away, she leaves him fuming in her wake, while the hapless Jasmine tries to corral his wife out toward the gazebo.

'Fucking bitch!' the husband mutters as he pushes past me in the hallway.

Well, that might be the only thing we'll ever agree on.

I spot Philips passing a clutch of A4 to Schaffer by the people carrier. Feeding the prat his lines for the séance, no doubt. Philips acts all shifty the moment he clocks me watching them, while Schaffer gives me a friendly wave.

Fucking tosspots!

Speckled beams of sunlight flicker through the matted branches of the looming woodland. The sky above the treetops, a rich canvas of purple and red.

Shifting on my seat, the old metal swing creaks under my weight as I rummage for my Moratoria.

No messages.

It's almost nine o'clock, there's little chance of anything now. Fuck it! Why is this so important to me? I shove the phone back into my jacket.

Glancing up, I glimpse a fleeting movement behind the old wire fence. A dark shape creeping against the murky overgrowth.

Squinting into the gloom, I wait for another movement.

'You're on my swing.'

Startled by her voice, I twist around in the swing. It's the daughter skulking in the twilight.

'Well, it was my swing once,' I tell her churlishly as I reach for my B&H.

'I thought you didn't remember any of it?' She plonks herself down on the free seat next to mine, thrusting her hands deep inside her puffer jacket.

'Well, some things stay with you?' I glance back toward the house. I'm surprised to see she's alone. The husband's been keeping her on a tight rein all evening.

'So what do you remember?' She stares sulkily at the cigarette in my hand.

'Just odd things, fleeting images.' Turning the packet toward her, I offer her one, which she quickly accepts.

'Do you still get the dreams?' she asks nervously, as she bums a light from my cigarette.

I nod my head sullenly. 'Most nights.'

For the first time, her eyes search for mine. 'Do you think they'll ever go away?' Her voice wavers with suppressed emotion.

'No,' I tell her frankly, hauling myself out of the swing. 'They're the gift that keeps giving.' Her pained expression tells me I've been too blunt. 'But I do remember this swing, though.' I tell her in a softer tone.' I used to sit here with my sister and watch the treetops over there. I find if you hold on to a few good memories, they help with all the bad.'

I hold her gaze a moment before breaking it off. Turning toward the house, I remember the movement behind the fence and I glance back at the dark woodland. The only movement now is the gentle sway of tree branches in the evening breeze.

Probably just my mind playing games again.

Dan Philips waves his E.M.F. around in a wide arc. Mugging it big time for the night vision camera. 'I'm getting something here,' he states surely, as he attempts to localise the reading.

Christ! Feels like we've been at this forever. We keep traipsing from one room to another, staring into the darkness. They've even thrown blackout sheets over the windows to darken the place further. As Philips moves to the back of the kitchen, we all trail after him. First the cameraman, then the sound guy, then the husband, Schaffer, Posey and me. Everyone else has been banished to the gazebo, in case they wander into shot.

'There!' Philips stops dead in his tracks, holding his hand in the air, like he's some kind of dark-ops commando or something. 'Can you smell that?' he asks.

Everyone falls silent, as we all sniff the air.

'Yeah, I can smell something, a sickly sort of smell,' Posey confirms what everyone else is sensing.

'Foul smells are often associated with poltergeist activity,' Schaffer declares in a serious tone.

I take a deeper breath. There's a foul stench alright.

'Bloody Ell!' the husband yells, his face a picture of utter disgust.

'Oh God! What is it?' Posey squeals as we all spin around.

'Dog's just shit itself!' The husband nods down towards the floor.

A mixed sense of relief and disappointment floods over the group, but Schaffer doesn't miss a beat. 'There is definitely some form of phenomena happening here,' he says knowingly. 'Even the dog is sensing it.'

Fuck me, he talks to the animals now.

'This is where the figure of Mr Nox was sighted on numerous occasions by the children,' Philips says in a hushed voice toward the camera. 'We're hoping he's in the mood to make another appearance tonight.' We all wait expectantly on the upstairs landing, but to little avail. Surprisingly, Philips's E.M.F. remains silent. 'Seems he's choosing not to make his presence known. Maybe he's irritated by our presence.'

Well, he's not the only one.

Philips decides on a different tack. 'Can you get our attention in some other way then?' he bellows. 'Come on, where are you, Mr Nox?' He's clearly decided that aggressively taunting the ghost would be a far better approach to the investigation. 'Come on, show yourself, you don't scare us!' But all the tormenting results in nothing.

Schaffer leans over to Posey. 'It appears Mr Nox is not up to communicating with us tonight.'

There's a fucking surprise.

'Oh crap! Something touched me!' Philips yelps, leaping across the landing. Posey shrieks and everyone jumps. The cameraman spins around, but has no idea which direction he's supposed to be pointing the camera.

After a few seconds of bedlam, Schaffer attempts to appease the angry entity. 'We don't mean you any harm. We only want to know if anyone is trying to communicate with someone in this house.'

Ignoring Schaffer, Philips continues barking random questions into the dark. 'Have you been here a long time?'

Nothing.

'Make the device beep to answer yes.'

Nothing.

'Did you die here?'

Beep.

A ripple of expectation pulsates around the landing.

'Are you male?'

The E.M.F. flashes and beeps again. 'There, did you see that? It's definitely male,' Philips declares. 'Are we speaking to Mr Nox?'

Beep.

'Do you recognise any people in our group?'

All eyes turn in my direction.

I wait for the inevitable.

Beeeeeeeeep!

I punch a loose fence panel on the patio. That doesn't do it for me. So I keep on punching it. Again and again.

When the anger passes, I turn to find the daughter staring at me, wide-eyed and flustered. The husband pushes past her. 'You'll fucking pay for that,' he barks, jabbing a finger at the broken panel.

'I'm always fucking paying for it!' I snarl back.

Bishop appears behind the husband. Crossing her arms, she stares at me like a disappointment school teacher scowling at a disobedient pupil. 'Finished!' she snipes.

Holding her gaze, I defiantly rub the pain from my grazed knuckles. With a pitiful shake of her head, she waves the husband and daughter back into the house.

'I know how he does it.' I call after her. 'It's his watch. It's disrupting the field. Every time he brings the sensor up close to his wrist, it causes the meter to light up like a Christmas tree.'

She turns in the doorway, fixing me with a piercing glare. 'If you're so convinced it's all a con, how come you're still here? You've got your money. Why didn't you just storm out the front door?' She leans forward, her eyes locked on mine. 'Just what do you think is going to happen here tonight?'

'History has a nasty habit of repeating itself,' I tell her in a sombre tone. I'm trying for enigmatic, but she's not buying it. Her gaze turns cold.

'Especially when it's the same people involved,' she tells me.

The husband's scowling at me from across the room while the daughter sulks on a beanbag in the corner. Posey has also joined us in the spare room while the rest of the crew prepares for the 'lock down' across the landing. 'So I guess this was once your bedroom,' she says in an almost breezy tone.

'Yeah, I suppose it was.' I try to sound blasé, although I'm all too aware of the fact.

'You don't remember?'

I shrug and lean back against the wall, rubbing my grazed knuckles.

'You must remember something?'

'To be honest, my memory of this place is constructed primarily from crime scene photographs.' She's not sure if I'm being sincere or not, but she gives me an awkward smile and tries to look sympathetic. 'I missed out on a family photo album when I was young. All I got was *The Bumper Book of British Ghosts*.'

'But you must remember something?' She's ignoring my sarcasm, so there must be a reason for all the interest.

Softening my attitude, I lean toward her in a confidential manner. 'Well, there is one thing. Just before we saw *him*...'

'Mr Nox?' she whispers, expectantly.

'Yeah, well, before we saw *him*, there was always this smell of....' I take a moment to conjure the right word. 'Burning; like from an old clay oven. Now whenever I smell something similar, it always provokes the same dark, unremitting dread I felt then.'

For a second I think I've laid it on too thick, but from her expression, I can tell she's swallowed it, hook, line and sinker.

T-shirt guy sticks his head around the door. 'Okay everyone we're ready to go again,' he chirps as Posey gives me a parting wave and disappears out onto the landing.

The husband gives me a knowing look. 'You just made that up,' he declares with a grumpy snarl.

Smirking, I give him a sardonic wink.

There's a large circular table in the middle of the girl's bedroom. It's draped with a William Morris tablecloth and dressed with tall white candles. None of which I suspect belongs to the Mishal family. The candles may not be entirely aesthetic I grant you. It's widely accepted that spirits are attracted to heat and light sources. But the OTT gothic candelabra in which they've been stuck reveals their true purpose here. Set dressing.

As is the swathe of teenage posters pinned across the wall. None of which were here last week; All Saints, Will Smith,

Madonna. Looks like someone raided the Woolworths poster bin.

The crew is already set up and waiting, as Malcolm claps his hands together. 'Okay people remember, if you have them, switch off your mobile phones. If you need to go to the bathroom; go now before we go live.'

We all squeeze around the table. It's so large there's hardly any space left in the room. I'm up against the wall between Posy and the husband. Posey gives me an uncomfortable smile, while the husband does his best to ignore my presence completely. Across the table, the daughter's wedged between Schaffer and Dan Philips.

Malcolm interprets everyone's uncertain glances. 'I know a lot of people like to do it, but there's no need to hold hands.'

Thank fuck for that. I exchange a relieved glance with the husband as we place our hands flat on the table. Bishop taps Schaffer's arm and leans over his shoulder. 'Did you get the new pages?'

'Yeah, no problem.'

I wonder which of the usual suspects they've gone for. My money's on the wicked Victorian workhouse owner.

Malcolm gives the signal and the cameramen take up their first positions. All the crew know the drill. They've all done this a million times before. Suddenly, I feel uncomfortable under all this scrutiny. Along with the mobile cameraman, there's a second camera on a tripod and a third on remote in the corner, which I assume is covering the whole room.

'Tony?' I glance over at Malcolm. 'Would you mind not doing that?' I'm rocking in my chair and drumming my fingers on the table. I must look a right headcase. As I pull myself together, I catch Malcolm exchanging a worried glance with Bishop. But she dismisses his concern with a quick shake of the head. Everyone's still on edge following the earlier incident with the mother. Word has it she's at a neighbour's house under sedation, but who knows anymore?

Schaffer clears his throat. 'I'm going to go into a temporary state, where I will suspension my personal consciousness, in order to allow myself to be used as a means of communication.' He lets this sink in a moment. 'Please be respectful of the spirits and to other guests around the table.' He may have cast a glance in my direction there, but it's hard to tell in the candlelight.

After a few more minutes of kerfuffle; we finally get down to business. Malcolm does the now familiar; going-live in five, four, three, two.... and we're off again.

I zone out through much of Schaffer's séance warm-up act. 'I'm going to ask the spirits to join the group.' He spreads his arms out theatrically. 'I summon the dead,' he declares for the benefit of the cameras. Several more minutes creep by as he continues to pad out his routine.

'I can feel a presence in the room.'

With the warm-up over, a sense of anxious excitement ripples around the table.

'Can you make yourself known to us?'

There's a faint rapping. Probably one of the production team lurking in the darkness. A few heads start to twitch.

353

Eyes peering into the blackness. Meanwhile Schaffer is harping on about how remarkable it is to get such a powerful presence so quickly. Which is a stroke of luck; considering the show's going out live. Glancing across the table, the daughter's looking increasingly unsettled. Even the husband looks less like his usual gormless self. There's an edgy nervousness about him.

'Can you smell that?' Philips pipes up. We all glance around the room except the husband who is checking under the tablecloth, as if he's half-expecting to see the bloody dog scuttle out. Across the table the daughter's looking less settled with every passing minute. The longer the séance continues the more she's recoiling into herself. Even in the candlelight I can see she's trembling.

'It smells like burning. Can you smell it too?' Posey asks. Philips nods eagerly, while I exchange a smug glance with the husband.

Without warning Schaffer jerks his head back as if he's receiving psychic contact. 'There's a certain energy trapped in this location. I can sense it now.' His voice has become an unnaturally deep, guttural rasp. Everyone is staring nervously at Schaffer, but I keep my eyes on the girl. She's rocking in her chair, muttering something under her breath, while flickering candlelight dances across her face. 'He's been trying to reach out to someone here,' Schaffer continues in the same harsh whisper. 'I can feel him drawing closer.'

Another bang and the whole table jolts. Posey lets out a startled gasp. It even shakes me up. I glance around the table.

I wonder who it was? My guess is Philips. He's looking way too pleased with himself.

'He's here,' Schaffer declares. 'The spirit is amongst us.'

From behind the camera, Malcolm is waving everyone down as he attempts to install a little calm back into the situation. Bishop's face has lit up. It's the first genuine smile she's cracked all evening. Probably relishing how well this crap will be playing with the viewers. Schaffer's eyes widen as his voice shifts in tone. 'There's darkness in this room. Like a man's shadow but it's much darker.'

Here we go.

Although I've been expecting him to pull something like this, I can't help but feel a sudden sensation of dread. And I'm not the only one. Across the table, the daughter's shaking her head and squirming in her seat.

This is all a mistake.

Schaffer groans. The low moan morphing into a deep, choking roar. Then nothing; he slumps back into his chair, staring blankly into the middle distance. It stuns everyone into silence. Heads are turning in all directions. I catch Posey glancing back behind the camera for guidance, but Malcolm's also at a loss. It's now Bishop waving everyone on, instructing them to keep going.

'Tony Boy.'

An icy chill runs through my body. Unable to stop myself. I turn toward the voice. The words are coming from Schaffer, but it's no longer his voice. 'Don't do this,' I mutter.

Even Schaffer's face seems to have changed, his pained expression transforming him into someone different. 'It's me.'

'No, it's not! It can't be!' I want to leap from my seat, but I'm transfixed by shock. Across the room, Malcolm is checking his notes, like he's missed something. 'What do you want from me?' I have to claw every word from my dry throat.

Schaffer's head tilts to one side. 'Forgiveness.'

It's like a kick in the gut. I can't breathe. 'Fuck that!' I snarl. 'I'd never forgive you. Never!' I can't think straight. My mind is spinning. This can't be real.

Across the table, Schaffer looks puzzled. 'No,' he slowly shakes his head. '*I* forgive *you*, Tony Boy.'

'*Me?*' I choke on the word.

'I forgive you, son, for what you did to us.'

It can't be him, it can't. Can it?

'Tony Boy.' He reaches his arm out across the table, his hand open, beckoning me to him. I try to struggle free of my chair, but I'm too tightly lodged between the husband and Posey. I can feel the panic overtaking me, as Schaffer's face changes. It's now a twisted mixture of despair and betrayal, the ends of his mouth twisting into a cruel sneer.

His outstretched hand contorts into an accusing finger as I slam back against the wall. 'You did this. You who did this to us!'

'Stop it!' the daughter screams, leaping from her seat, startling Schaffer from his trance. 'This isn't real! None of this is real. I can't do this anymore!'

The husband tries to stand but he's also trapped by the table.

'I sense some conflict between the spirits here....' Attempting to salvage something from this fiasco, Schaffer lifts his hand over toward the daughter, as if he's attempting to redirect the possession toward her instead. But she batters it away, annoyed at his interference. He recoils away as all her fear and panic erupts into a cascade of fury. Malcolm's the first to restrain her. Clamping his arms round her thin body he yanks her backwards. The husband's also out of his chair, forcing his way around the table toward his stepdaughter.

'It was just his game,' the girl screams as Malcolm hauls her away from the table. With her arms pinned to her sides, she jabs her head in my direction, her eyes pleading with me to back her up. 'Tell them you made it up! Tell them!' Tears are rolling down her cheeks. 'Tell them this isn't real!'

Everyone is jostling about, it's total mayhem. Over the melee, I hear Posey's strained voice. 'Do we still keep going?'

Panicking, I thrash at the toppled chair, attempting to free myself. Across the room the daughter twists in Malcolm's grasp. Her face, a terrifying depiction of desperation and horror. 'Tell them!' she shrieks. 'This isn't real!'

I'm on my feet now, stumbling toward the door. Everything is chaos. The mobile cameraman doesn't know who he should be following. Schaffer, me or the kid. He chooses me.

Bad move.

***

357

Mid-seventies television footage: A skittish middle-aged woman, nervously pulls at a long strand of blond hair.

'We hear people running up the stairs. Muffled conversations in other rooms. Doors open and close by themselves. We hear screaming in the night. It wakes you from your sleep.'

'And this happens all over the house?' a male reporter asks from off-camera.

The woman nods. 'Yes, although it's worst upstairs. That's where the children first saw him.'

'Saw who?'

'Mr Nox.'

The shot changes to an image of the mother preparing a young boy for bed. 'Mr Nox is the name the children have given their paranormal visiter,' the reporter states over the scene.

The shot changes once more. A teenage girl in her dressing gown is addressing the reporter directly. 'It's a feeling really, a feeling of dread, lurking in the darkness. It's like your ribcage is being crushed. Squeezing the joy out of you. Tony doesn't like to sleep alone anymore, so he sleeps in here with me.'

The shot widens to reveal the young boy next to her on the bed. The reporter moves his microphone toward the child. 'And do you feel better, sleeping in here with your sister?'

The young boy shakes his head reluctantly.

'It doesn't make much difference,' his sister declares, on behalf of her brother. 'Because it follows Tony wherever he goes.'

16. Scents and Smells

Unusual odours are commonly associated with hauntings, although they're often seen as part of a wider set of 'symptoms' related to a paranormal disturbance. These smells can range from anywhere between pleasant aromas like rose scents or perfumes to downright foul and repulsive odours such as rotting meat or putrid vegetables.

A sudden aroma or fragrance you cannot associate with anything in your home can be an indication of a 'ghostly presence'.

***

'Accompanying the departed on their final journey is one of the greatest acts of kindness you can ever do,' Ray had told Jo that morning, as he had picked her up from her apartment. And his words had stayed with her throughout the day.

There had been a brief service at Frank's synagogue. Some of her father's business associates had read a few eulogies, including Ray, who, despite stammering throughout, had delivered a eulogy that had been both comforting and heartfelt. There had been a few brief prayers by the graveside. And that had been it. Jo's father had been laid to rest.

All the mourners had expressed kind sentiments and compassionate words. Several flower arrangements and fruit baskets had arrived, including one from Frank's elderly sister in Austria who had been too frail to make the trip herself. Most of the congregation had been work associates of her father. Although Greg had taken the day off work, so he could attend. A gesture Jo had appreciated, considering he had hardly known her father.

Gillian had failed to make an appearance. But a bouquet had arrived from Dark Dimension, accompanied by a condolence card in Jasmine's florid handwriting. This had come as no surprise to Jo, as the live show was scheduled for later that evening. What had been a surprise, though? The unexpected appearance of Jamie Burns on the synagogue steps.

'Jo, I'm so sorry.' Jamie had taken her hand in his. Apart from the odd, strained phone call, Jo had barely had any contact with her ex-fiancé since their split three months before. 'I just wanted to express my sympathies. I was always very fond of your father.' Jamie had smiled in the same charming manner she had once found so attractive. 'Jo, I was wondering if I could speak to you later...'

'You're welcome to come back to the house,' Jo had said. 'You remember the address?'

'Yes, yes, of course.'

Throughout the drive to the cemetery, Jo had sat quietly, thinking how surreal the entire experience was. Seeing all of her father's colleagues gathered together had created a powerful impression of her father in her mind. His absence from the proceedings only compounding his presence on the occasion. This feeling of disjointed reality continued as Jo took Ray's arm at the graveside. 'Do you believe in heaven?' Jo asked, as she watched a small mound of earth gradually accumulate on the lid of her father's plain pine coffin.

'Well,' Ray smiled benevolently. 'The Tanakh doesn't dwell at any length on the afterlife and we don't spend a lot of time speculating on its details. But if you're asking whether *I* personally believe in heaven? Then I would have to say, maybe. I'd like to think there's something waiting for us.'

'And dad, what do you think he believed?'

'I don't know.' Ray admitted dolefully, 'He never said anything to me either way.' Sensing this may be an unsatisfactory answer he continued. 'But I guess in the end heaven means something different to all of us. Each might be unique to ourselves. I'm sure your father knew what his own personal heaven would be like.'

An image of her father sitting on a beach with his wife and young child flickered across Jo's mind. 'Yes, I'm sure he did,' she whispered.

As the mourners made their way back to their cars, Jo noticed a lone figure lingering at the edge of the cemetery. 'I owe you an apology,' Lawrence said as Jo drew up beside him.

'I think you do.'

'Well, I'm sorry, I shouldn't have done that to you.'

'So why did you?'

'Bitterness,' Lawrence admitted bluntly. 'Simple as that. I don't expect you to forgive, but I am sorry.'

Jo huffed. 'So that's it then? You're sorry.'

Lawrence licked his dry lips, his hand hovering over the pocket of his overcoat. For the first time since Jo knew him, Lawrence seemed genuinely lost for words. 'I thought I had put the past behind me.' He mumbled gruffly. 'And then when we met and it brought back so much anger. So many feelings I thought I'd buried.'

Not wanting to be subjected to yet another bout of Lawrence's waspish self-pity, Jo huffed. 'You could have salvaged your career. You had the choice.'

Lawrence sighed. 'If it had only been my career,' he said ruefully before abruptly dismissing the statement with a curt shrug. 'But the past is the past. It can't be undone.' He fixed Jo with a firm eye. 'No matter how much we might wish it.'

Annoyed by Lawrence's belligerence, Jo shook her head. 'You know I'm not the only one you should apologise to,' Jo said reprovingly.

Lawrence harrumphed as he caught Jo's insinuation. 'You know, you don't owe him anything.'

'Don't I?'

'Our mistakes are not yours too correct.'

Jo's shoulders slumped. 'Well, it's my mistake now.'

Lawrence turned toward Jo. 'Why, what happened?'

Wavering over how much she should tell him, Jo opted for the abridged version. 'I took him back to the house.'

Lawrence frowned. 'For the show?'

'No, I'm finished with the show. Well, I guess I have. After everything that's happened.'

'It didn't go well I take it.'

'You were right. I should have left it alone.'

Lawrence took a long studious look at Jo's stoney expression. 'But that's not what you're going to do?'

'I have to do something.'

Turning away, Lawrence's gaze fell upon the rows of stone memorials stretching out across the cemetery. 'Do you know why people believe in ghosts?' he said wistfully. 'Because they remove the finality from death. They offer promise. The prospect of an existence beyond this life. Maybe even a chance to atone for our mistakes in the afterlife. But in reality, ghosts are nothing more than manifestations of our own grief. Our own regrets. If we're haunted by anything in this life, then we're haunted by our own failings.'

Lawrence had declined Jo's offer to return to the house, claiming he had a ghost walk to conduct, although Jo had suspected he'd been eager to avoid the company of so many of her father's old publishing associates. Returning to the car, Jo found Ray talking with another mourner in the carpark. Reaching out, the woman gave Jo's hand a tender squeeze. 'You don't remember me do you?' she said, in response to Jo's quizzical smile. 'I'm Laura Milgallon. Patrick Milgallon's niece.'

Most of Frank's work colleagues had migrated straight toward the back patio, where they had remained, smoking cigars and talking business. While another group had gathered in the lounge to watch the capture of Basra by British troops on the evening news. A third closer group had settled themselves in the dining room, where they now sat drinking tea and chatting. 'It hasn't changed at all,' Laura said, glancing around the room. 'I half-expect your mother to come walking in at any moment.'

Jo's eyes followed Laura's gaze out through the French doors, toward the back patio. 'So you've been here before?' Jo asked, surprised by Laura's admission. Even allowing for the passing years, Jo still couldn't place Laura's face.

'I suppose you would've been too young to remember, but we used to play together,' Laura continued. 'Uncle Pat used to bring me with him sometimes when he came to see your father. I was a little older than you. We used to play hide and seek in the garden. Your mother used to make us those little fancy cakes with the icing on.'

'Angel cakes with the coloured sponge layers.' Jo was surprised by the vividness of her own recollection.

'I'm sorry Uncle Pat couldn't make the trip himself,' Laura smiled poignantly. 'But he never leaves the house now. He has Parkinson's the poor dear, and he's going a bit doolally in the head, but he was very sorry to hear about Frank's passing.'

'He lives with you then?'

'Yes, since mother died, it's been just the two of us.'

'And your surname is Milgallon as well?'

Laura smiled demurely. 'My mother never married. She kept her maiden name. Uncle Pat took us in when we had nowhere else to go. I've been with him ever since. Now mum's gone, he doesn't have anyone else.' Laura chuckled to herself. 'I suppose I don't either.'

Jo shook her head, bemused by Laura's ability to find humour in the strangest things. 'Well, it was nice of you to make the journey yourself. How did you know about the service?'

'From Joan.'

It took a second for Jo to realise Laura was referring to Joan Friedmann, Frank's elderly secretary. 'Mrs Friedmann? Well, that was good of her. How did she find you?'

Laura waved her hand dismissively. 'Oh, we're still in contact. Have been for years; with Joan and Ray and your father.'

'My father?'

Jo was really confused now. 'But I thought....' Laura stared back at Jo with a bemused look on her face, which forced Jo to explain her rather awkward assumption. 'I thought my father fell out with your uncle years ago, over that incident with the....' Jo hesitated as she searched for a polite way to address the subject of The Babcock Haunting. A topic, she suspected, held a lot of negative connotations for the Milgallon family. But to Jo's relief Laura appeared to hold no such reservations.

'All that Babcock business. No, not really. They never worked together after that, but they remained friends. In fact, your father was very good to us after Uncle Pat's little indiscretion.' Laura rolled her eyes and wobbled her head as Jo recalled Milgallon's embarrassing incident in the railway station toilet. 'Who told you they had fallen out?' Laura asked.

'Well, Lawrence Ashby.'

Laura rolled her eyes again. 'Ah well, that may be true of Lawrence Ashby. Uncle Pat never spoke to *him* again, that's for sure. But that was because of your mother. It had nothing to do—'

'Laura, here, have some quiche.' Ray thrust a plate of nibbles into Laura's hand. 'Sorry Laura, do you mind if I have a quick word with Joanne?' Before anyone could object, Ray took Jo deftly by the elbow and lead her out to the kitchen.

Ray waited until Maria had left the kitchen with a fresh tray of hors d'oeuvres before pulling a thin brown envelope from his jacket. 'I know this isn't the best time and place, but various financial considerations have made this a somewhat pressing matter.' Opening the envelope, Ray extracted two sheets of folded paper. 'It's regarding the business. You're going to receive legal confirmation of this in due time. But I wanted to speak to you about it first.'

Jo was in no mood to discuss the probable collapse and impending insolvency of her father's company right now. The day had been depressing enough. But the earnest expression on Ray's face told her she should at least hear him out.

'I've taken control of the business for the time being,' Ray said.

Jo nodded solemnly. Given the circumstances, it seemed the best course of action for all concerned. 'Yes, of course. What have you decided to do with it?'

'Well, that's really up to you now.' Ray unfolded the top paper and handed it to Jo. 'Because as it stands, it's still a family business. Your father was the majority shareholder and he controlled the board, such as it is. So, in essence he could nominate anyone he liked as his successor. You'll be hearing this officially from the board in a day or two. But I thought you should know in advance that your father nominated you as his successor.'

Jo looked back at Ray, stunned. 'When did he do this?'

'The dates there; but I believe the initiative has been in place ever since you were a child. I believe it was always your father's intention to pass the business on to you.'

Jo was almost struck speechless. 'He never said anything to me. I never even thought he even wanted me there.'

Ray shrugged evasively, while Jo composed herself. 'And there is also this.' He passed her the second piece of paper. 'As you know, your father was not the publisher of your mother's work. But he was the primary beneficiary of the royalties. Which, since your mother's death has been held in a trust fund for you. In the understanding that the funds be transferred to your name after your father's death.' Jo stared in disbelief at the figure printed on the paper. 'Which is now a considerable amount of money.'

Back in the dining room, Joan Friedmann had taken the seat next to Laura. The pair were flicking through a pile of old family photo albums which Maria had left out for the mourners. 'Look at this, dear,' Joan said, as Jo wandered in through the door. Joan tilted the album so Jo could see. It was a photo of Frank sitting on a sofa, wearing a lopsided paper crown, a young Jo kneeling by his feet. 'This must have been what? Christmas seventy-three? What were you then, dear, four?'

Jo glanced down at the small faded photograph. An excited young child in a pretty party dress kneeling amongst a pile of tinsel and ripped wrapping paper. 'Look at all your presents,' Laura said with good-humour, as Jo glared ruefully at the photo. Christmas seventy-three. Most of the country was in recession; but you wouldn't know it from the photo. As if she had just read Jo's mind, Joan smiled. 'Well, you know your father. He would have given you the moon if he could.'

Jamie had been moping around the house all afternoon, sipping wine and making occasional chit-chat with some of the other mourners. To Jo, he seemed preoccupied and tense. Which, in turn had made her feel anxious and uneasy. She'd already caught herself wondering what she'd done to upset him. A reaction she had immediately berated herself for.

The moment Jo left Laura's side, Jamie seized the opportunity to speak to her alone. Not wanting their conversation to be overheard, Jo directed him out into the garden. After a little awkward preamble, Jamie addressed the topic he'd been eager to discuss. 'Jo, I've made a terrible mistake.'

'With what? Jo pulled a packet of Silk Cut from her pocket.

'With us.'

'*Us?* What happened to Rosanne?'

Jamie shuffled on the spot. And to Jo's surprise, actually appeared to pout. 'We split up.'

'You mean she kicked you out?' Jo scoffed as she lit a cigarette. Even by Jamie's standards that had been short-lived. 'So what happened to the internet start-up?'

'Well, we've had a few setbacks, ideological conflicts, some financial issues...'

Huffing, Jo rolled her eyes. She'd lost track of the many schemes and half-baked ventures Jamie had embarked upon over the years. 'And what?'

Now Jamie looked surprised. 'It was a mistake I admit, but that doesn't mean we have to lose what we had together.'

If it hadn't been for the occasion, Jo would've roared with laughter. Typical Jamie. Utterly incapable of seeing anything from any other perspective than his own. 'You've got a nerve, you know that. This is my father's funeral...'

'Yes, but I thought...'

'What? That you'd have a better chance if I was feeling low!'

'Jo, you're overreacting. This is just like you.'

'*I'm* overreacting. You were sleeping with another woman behind my back!'

'Well, I wouldn't have had to if I'd been getting anything at home!' Jo was too stunned to reply. 'Yeah I know,' Jamie went on. 'You're gonna blame your medication, or your *issues*.' He even made the air quotes. But it was *your* attitude that pushed me into that affair. You can't blame me. It was the only way I had of expressing—'

'No, you don't,' Jo barked. 'Don't you fucking dare! This breakup was all your fault, your issues!'

'Jo, you're becoming hysterical.' Jamie said in a patronising tone, nodding back toward the house. 'Look you're embarrassing yourself in front of all these people.'

'Oh no! You don't get to do that anymore.' Jo's tone hardened. 'Jamie, I want you to leave now!'

'Come on Jo, you know you don't mean that.'

'I said get out!'

'Is everything okay here?'

Jamie turned a dismissive eye toward Greg. 'Nothing to do with you, mate,' he snapped.

'Jo, are you okay?'

'She's fine. She's just a little upset, that's all.'

Ignoring Jamie, Jo turned to face Greg. There were tears welling in her eyes. 'Greg, it's fine. Jamie was just leaving.'

'Jo...' Jamie objected.

'I said you were just leaving.' Jo's whole body was shaking.

'See this is what you do. You make everything about you.'

'Jamie, this is my father's funeral.'

'Like you ever cared for him.'

The slap from Jo forced Jamie back a step. Incensed by the blow, he lurched back at Jo, only to be blocked by Greg, who quickly stood between them. After a brief scuffle, Jamie threw his hands into the air in a consolatory yet condescending fashion. He took a step backward. Familiar with this kind of move, Greg braced himself for a fresh assault. Which failed to come. Glancing around, Jamie blenched under the scrutiny of the other mourners. 'See what happens when I make the effort,' he snarled, brushing past Greg and stomping back to the house.

Greg turned to Jo. 'Are you okay?'

But Jo looked anything but. Trembling uncontrollably, she lurched to the side and vomited.

There was a gentle rap on the bathroom door.

'Are you alright, dear?' Laura gave a kindly smile as Jo slipped the catch on the bathroom door and peered out. Over Laura's shoulder Greg was hovering on the landing, but a sharp prompt from Laura sent him shuffling back downstairs. 'Oh, you don't look well,' Laura said in a sympathetic tone. 'It must have all been too much for you today.'

Jo gave a meek smile. 'I'm feeling much better,' she reassured her. 'I'll be down in a few minutes.'

'Well, you take your time. There's no rush. I'll be downstairs if anyone needs anything.'

Laura had barely turned away when Jo called her back. 'Oh, Laura?'

'Yes, dear?'

'I've been meaning to ask you. Would it be alright if I came to see your uncle one day soon?'

'Oh,' Laura seemed both surprised and conflicted by Jo's unexpected suggestion. 'Well, he's not really up to visitors these days....'

'I wouldn't ask, but it is important.' Jo hoped her hangdog expression mixed with her already pallid complexion might help sway the issue in her favour. But Laura still looked unconvinced. 'It's just that; we were thinking of reprinting his work on The Babcock Haunting. And I was hoping to go over some details with him beforehand.'

'Republishing,' Laura's face lit up at the mere prospect. 'Oh, he will be pleased.' Laura's elated tone immediately made Jo regret her spur-of-the-moment ruse. But the unlikely pretence had apparently done the trick. With a knowing smile, Laura lent forward and tapped Jo's hand. 'I'll see what I can do.'

When Jo had reappeared downstairs, everyone had been very sympathetic and considerate, expressing the same opinion as Laura, that Jo had overtaxed herself during an extremely emotional day. The incident in the back garden, having been tactfully overlooked by all those that had witnessed it. But Jo's tied demeanour had signalled the end of the reception and gradually the mourners had dispersed. With the house now empty, Bruno had been allowed out of Jo's old bedroom and had immediately begun investigating his new surroundings.

In the back room, Greg and Ray were quietly sifting through a shoebox of loose photographs, which had been unearthed along with the old photo albums. Leaning across the large Edwardian dining table, Jo picked a tatty self-adhesive photo album from the pile. Its plastic page covers, curled and yellowed with age. Taking a seat next to Ray, she flipped it open. Inside was a succession of random family photographs, primarily of Jo as a child, on various occasions: birthday parties, Christmas grottos, trips to the zoo. On the rare occasion her father made an appearance, it was always with a detached sense of stilted obligation. Crouching awkwardly by her side or standing stiffly behind her, a hand officiously resting on her shoulder.

Unable to bear the painfully impersonal images any longer, Jo swapped the album for another from the pile. A battered leather-bound tome, the pages fastened with a chunky red cord. Its faded sepia photographs held in place by threadbare photo corners. Jo remembered being fascinated by this album as a child. Intrigued by the quaint, old-fashioned people inside, with their stiff, formal poses and expressionless faces. 'You know, I don't even know who half these people are,' Jo admitted, turning a page. 'I'm not even sure I was ever told their names.'

Ray glanced over at the album. 'When your father married your mother, a lot of ties were broken,' he said solemnly.

Across the table, Greg flipped over a small photograph he had just discovered in the shoebox. On the back was a handwritten inscription. 'Feivish Kalonymus im alter von sechs jahren?' he read out loud, before turning a quizzical glance first toward Jo and then Ray, who took the print from Greg's hand. It was a faded photo of Jo's father as a young boy in Germany.

'Frank's father changed the family surname to Kalman after he settled here in the thirties,' Ray explained.

'And Feivish became Frank,' Greg deduced.

'In those days, it was the excepted thing to do. It enabled you to interrogate more easily into your new life.' Passing the photograph over to Jo, Ray tapped his frail hand against his chest. 'But you always remained the same person inside.'

Staring at the photo, Jo attempted to decipher some subtle nuance from her father's prim, youthful expression. Had that been the reason he had returned to his old religion? Had he been hoping to find the person he had once been?

Across the table, Greg was also following his own line of thought. 'So Feivish became Frank and....' he fixed Ray with an inquisitive gaze.

After a moment's hesitation, Ray relented. 'Reuben.'

Greg nodded his approval. 'Nice name.'

Ray shrugged despondently. 'A good name is better than good oil,' he lamented. 'But we all make sacrifices in life.'

'You should go back to it.'

Ray dismissed this notion with a good humoured shrug. 'What do I care what people call me now? We all know in ourselves who we really are.'

Jo said goodnight to Greg and Ray on the doorstep and closed the door. Switching off the lights, she tiptoed upstairs. She had decided to stay over in the old house. It hadn't felt right to leave it empty, not yet anyway.

As she climbed into her old bed and switched off the light, the house fell silent. The only sound was Bruno, shuffling around in the dark, futilely searching for an acceptable place to sleep. Furiously sniffing at every unfamiliar scent. But to Jo, everything in the house smelt as it always had. A delicate mixture of evocative fragrances that transported her back to her childhood, to the home she had once known.

In that moment, a sad reality dawned upon her. As time went by, this house would smell less and less familiar. It would smell less of her father. His aftershave, his cigarettes, even his choice of fabric conditioner. All this would gradually fade until his presence here would disappear completely just as her mother's had. Sometime soon, someone would tow away his cherished car. His clothes and possessions would be boxed and given to charity. The house would be sold. The new owners would redecorate and exorcise the last lingering spirits of the past. Her mother's plaque would remain on the front of the house. But there would be no memorial to Jo's father. His only legacy would be a short footnote to the Babcock family tragedy.

And of course, Jo. She was his other legacy. A fact she continually forgot. Her father would live on through her; and her children. But this thought brought Jo little comfort as she lay staring into the darkness.

Jo knew someone was there even before she opened her eyes. From the moment she awoke, she had sensed a presence in the room. Holding her breath, she turned over on the pillow. A black shadow sat motionless in the armchair across the room. She could feel instinctively the featureless figure had been watching her as she had slept. With her heart racing, she reached for the bedside lamp.

Click.

The chair was empty.

Bruno, who had been fitfully sleeping by her feet, hopped down from the bed with a grumpy humph. Otherwise, the room remained still. Turning over in the bed Jo detected a faint scent. A delicate fragrance she immediately recognised.

Her father's tobacco. It smelt oddly fresh. But no sooner had Jo identified the smell than it had gone. Slumping back under the covers, Jo pulled the quilt up around her neck and prepared herself for another long night of disturbed slumber. But within moments, she felt herself drifting off to sleep again. Reaching for the bedside lamp, she glimpsed Bruno contentedly making a bed for himself on the empty bedroom chair.

Jagged lightning flashed against a veil of dark clouds. Wrapping her arms across her chest, Jo shivered. How anyone could find solace in such a place was beyond her. A place of convergence her mother had once called it. A place where all three elements met. The land, the sea and the air. But to Jo the shoreline felt cold, desolate and unwelcoming.

All day, thoughts of her mother had swamped Jo's mind. She couldn't help it. In Jo's mind, her mother and the sea were forever interwound. While most people envisioned a person's soul floating gracefully up towards the heavens. Jo had always imagined her mother's soul drifting silently through the dark depths of the ocean. If a building could hold an echo of an individual life within its walls. Surely a vast ocean would contain all the lost souls that had perished beneath its waves.

Jo shuddered. Turning away from the grey brooding horizon, she ran a critical eye over the rust-covered wrought iron pier and the dilapidated buildings lining the seafront.

Southend-on-Sea, like so many other English seaside resorts, had seen a dramatic decline in its popularity since the emergence of the cheap package holiday and was now little more than a pale shadow of its former self. The once attractive Victorian promenade reduced now to little more than a repetitive succession of tacky bars and seedy amusement arcades. The quaint Peter Pan's Playground and sunken gardens, long since demolished to make way for the sprawling corporate Adventure Island Pleasure Park. From which, now rung the hollow screams of the park's few drizzle-lashed patrons.

Southend was less than a two-hour drive from Hampstead, but Jo had opted to take the train instead. She had taken Bruno as company. To her relief, the little dog had proven to be a patient traveller. Sleeping peacefully in her lap, while Jo who had sat anxiously staring out the window attempting to make sense of the last few days.

This recollection prompted Jo to check her Blackberry again. She had left a message for Gillian; but had yet to receive a reply. Despite everything, Jo was still curious to learn how the live show had gone. She had set her own VCR to record the program, but without a satellite dish at her father's house she'd been unable to watch the show live.

Frustrated and annoyed, Jo slipped the Blackberry back into her coat.

The call Jo had received that morning from Laura Milgallon had been a surprise. Even more so, Laura's suggestion that she meet her uncle later that same day. 'Of course you don't have to, if you don't want to,' Laura had apologised. But to Laura's surprise Jo had promptly accepted the invitation, assuring Laura that she would welcome the distraction.

Laura had sounded relieved over the phone; as her uncle was having, as she had put it 'one of his good days'.

The first heavy rain was just hitting the pavement as Jo arrived at the Milgallons' address. Sheltering on the doorstep, Jo cast a reproving glance over the building's shabby frontage. The once opulent townhouse had long since lost its grandeur and was now divided into several smaller flats. All of which, according to Ray, were owned by a local housing association. Ray had also let slip that for many years now, Frank had been sending Milgallon the occasional residual cheque, even though his book had long since gone out of print. Once again, Jo regretted her invention of the republishing ruse. If the state of their home was anything to go by, the Milgallons could probably have used the extra money.

Laura opened the door with an enormous smile on her face. Extending her arms wide, she gave Jo an affectionate hug. 'How are you holding up, dear?' she asked, squeezing Jo's arms. Removing her nylon overall and declaring Bruno to be 'simply adorable,' Laura ushered Jo through a small grubby vestibule toward her own front door.

Once inside her own flat, Laura stopped by the first door in the hallway. Resting her hand on the door handle, she lent toward Jo. 'He knows who you are and he's very keen to speak with you,' she said in a delicate voice. 'He's been very insistent. In fact, he's been driving me up the wall all morning. But please be patient with him. He understands everything, but he can occasionally lose track of what he's saying. It can be very frustrating; *for everyone.*' Laura rolled her eyes in her usual comical fashion. But her good humour swiftly evaporated the moment she set foot through the door. 'Oh Uncle Pat,' she bewailed angrily, 'what have you done?'

In the centre of the room, Patrick Milgallon glared forlornly down at a scene of utter chaos. 'I needed to find my typescripts,' he muttered despairingly, as he surveyed a sprawling mass of scrunched typescripts and handwritten notepaper strewn across the floor.

'You needed to find nothing,' Laura chided her uncle harshly. Snatching a clutch of crumpled A4 from the old man's hands, she slammed them down on top of a ransacked metal cabinet next to his bed. 'Just look at this mess.'

Following Laura's exasperated gaze, Jo glanced around the cramped bedroom. Chock-full and cluttered, the once spacious lounge was now struggling to accommodate a lifetime's worth of random ephemera. Piles of old books and journals covered every available surface, while a bewildering array of curious artefacts and objet d'art packed every nook and cranny. Despite an obvious attempt to air the room by opening the tall bay window, the fuggy scent of cigarette ash still hung in the air.

As Laura continued to snatch scattered paperwork off the floor, Milgallon shuffled forward, extending a shaky hand toward Jo. 'So you're Frank and Rachel's daughter?' The old man fixed her with a milky gaze, his beseeching stare amplified disconcertingly by the thick lenses of his glasses. Clasping both her hands, he took her in.

Milgallon himself was now totally unrecognisable from the photograph on the back of *Broken Spirits*. Almost bald with sunken eyes, his face was a pale, haggard reflection of its former self. A pasty green tint to his skin made his complexion appear almost translucent. As he lent closer, Jo noticed a patch of white hair on his neck, which had escaped his razor blade, as well as a deep blade nick on his chin. While his trousers were a patchwork of grubby stains and creases, he had on a clean jumper and fresh shirt.

Exasperated, Laura threw a handful of papers down onto the cabinet. 'What did you do all this for?' she bemoaned.

'I was looking for my typescripts for Frank's daughter.'

'She's not interested in all that.'

'She'll need them for the reprints.'

Feeling a further stab of guilt, Jo made a mental note to speak to Ray about maintaining Milgallon's residual payments. At least for the time being, anyway.

'Let's get you back into your chair,' Laura grumbled, as she guided the old man over toward a high-backed armchair in the centre of the room. As he dropped into the chair, Laura tugged a heavy woollen rug across his lap, covering his grubby trousers. Presumably, she had expected her uncle to remain seated throughout Jo's visit.

Tentatively, Jo took a seat on the edge of Milgallon's bed, opposite his chair.

Stretching over an ornate occasional table, Milgallon pulled a thin book toward him. 'Here,' he said, tilting the cover toward Jo.

My Child by Rachel Graham.

'You look so like her,' Milgallon said with a weak smile. 'So talented, so beautiful.' He gestured for Jo to open the book as she took it from his trembling hand. On the inner title page, Jo recognised her mother's distinctive handwriting.

At Milgallon's insistence, she read aloud the inscription. 'To Patrick, may we both find what we're looking for.' The old man beamed proudly as a pang of sentiment struck Jo.

'Well, I'll let you two chat while I put on the kettle,' Laura said, taking Bruno's lead from Jo. 'And we'll see what we can find for this little fella in the kitchen.'

As Laura disappeared out the door, Milgallon reached back across the table and retrieved a half-smoked cigarette from a large Art Déco ashtray. Lodging it between his nicotine-stained fingers, he took a couple of rasping puffs, which immediately triggered a sudden fit of coughing. Holding his hand in the air, to restrain Jo from interfering. Milgallon let the fit subside, before slurping a mouthful of cold tea from a mug which had been standing alongside the ashtray. With one final retch, he cleared his throat. 'Noisy ghost!' he croaked.

'Pardon?' Milgallon's statement had been so abrupt it had caught Jo by surprise.

'Poltergeist is German for noisy ghost.' Milgallon settled back into his chair.

'Really?' Jo said politely.

'Yes, really! Milgallon continued enthusiastically. 'And did you know poltergeists have been reported for over two thousand years? Roman historian Titus Livius described small stones being mysteriously hurled at Roman soldiers.'

Cocking an inquisitive eyebrow, Jo attempted to appear attentive, while Milgallon rambled on for several long minutes.

Eventually, though, he arrived at the topic he had been eager to speak to her about. 'I've spent a lifetime researching the subject,' he said earnestly. 'It's been my whole life. Revealing the secrets of the paranormal. That's why I had to see you, to make you understand...' his words broke off as his bottom lip wavered.

Convinced Milgallon had lost his train of thought, Jo lent forward. 'Well, there was something I wanted to ask you about,' she said, reaching into her bag for her copy of *Broken Spirits*. An act which instantly resinated with Milgallon. His face lit up in reverential delight as Jo opened the book on her lap. 'I've read through your book and all your articles for the magazine. But there are some inconsistencies. I was hoping you could clear up for me.' Milgallon's continence clouded at the mere mention of the word '*inconsistencies*'. 'I've read in other books,' Jo went on, ignoring the old man's scowl. 'That in all major poltergeist disturbances there is normally a focal point to the disturbance.'

'Indeed,' said Milgallon. 'Where a ghost will appear oblivious to its surroundings. Appearing at a certain time or place. A poltergeist is more unpredictable. Responding to whatever is happening around them—'

'Or to be more precise around a single person, the focus,' Jo interrupted, hoping to curtail another rambling explanation from Milgallon. 'Usually an adolescent female enduring some kind of emotional turmoil, in this case Tracey Babcock.'

'That is correct,' Milgallon agreed gruffly.

'See what I don't understand is why?'

'Why what?'

'Why you never state the reason behind this emotional turmoil? There's nothing in your book or any the magazine articles. In fact, you never mention the mother's agoraphobia, or the father's drink issues. Or even the extent of children's medication addictions.'

Milgallon waved a dismissive hand in the air. 'I wasn't interested in all that tawdry stuff. I was more concerned with the actual haunting itself. My focus was on uncovering the mysteries of the spirit world.'

'But you do concede that something provoked this activity.'

'Of course!'

'And you know what it was don't you?'

'Of course I know. I'm not an idiot!' he snapped angrily, before immediately softening his tone. That's why I needed to see you.' He leant forward in his chair. 'To make you understand. It wasn't my fault.'

'What wasn't you fault dear?' Laura asked as she entered the lounge carrying a large tray ladened with teacups.

'It wasn't my fault.' Milgallon repeated more forcefully. The gruffness of his tone triggering another brief fit of coughing.

'What are you doing? You know you shouldn't be smoking so much?'

Waving Laura away, Milgallon gasped the stale air. 'What other joy do I have left?' he grumbled.

'Well, you still have me don't you?' Laura winked at Jo as she nudged the tray in amongst the piles of clutter covering the sideboard. Behind her, Milgallon snorted in disdain.

'Patrick, what wasn't your fault?' Jo asked, craning her neck around Laura, who was now occupying all the free space between Milgallon and herself.

'He's worried about his legacy, aren't you dear?' Laura said as she placed a fresh cup of tea on Milgallon's side table and affectionately tapped the back of his hand.

Ignoring his niece, Milgallon turned to Jo. 'They claimed I was a fool, that I had been gulled and conned. But the paranormal plane is very real. It's all around us. The spirits of the departed are everywhere. They're with us all the time. I've seen them myself, with my own eyes.'

'No, you haven't' Laura corrected him, with a flippant sneer.

Again Milgallon ignored his niece. 'I have seen the boney people.' He said, his bottom lip wavering in frustration.

'Uncle Pat enough of that talk.' Laura turned an apologetic glance toward Jo. 'He thinks he sees dead people. Just like in that film.' Laura shook her head despairingly.

'It's true,' Milgallon protested, annoyed by Laura's belittling attitude. 'I know!'

'Okay, now don't work yourself up into a state, dear,' Laura cooed scornfully. 'No one's doubting your word.'

'But what wasn't your fault?' Jo repeated, her sharp tone betraying her irritation at Laura's constant interruptions.

'What?'

'You said it wasn't your fault. What wasn't your fault?'

'The children, that wasn't my fault.'

'Yes, we know that,' Laura said dismissively.

'I could have done something, but I didn't. Your father understood...' The words dried in his mouth as his mind appeared to drift.

While Jo was prepared to wait for Milgallon to regain his line of thought, Laura was less patient. 'Understood what, dear?'

'Why we had to lie.'

As the sound of pounding rain echoed through the drawn tapestry curtains, Tracey Babcock's distorted grimace leered disconcertingly across the room.

After much cajoling, Milgallon had persuaded Laura to set up his old Super 8 projector. But she had drawn the line at erecting the cumbersome pull-up projector screen, opting to project the image directly onto the wall instead.

In the film Tracey Babcock's thin body twisted in a series of jerky movements, the camera lingering on every convulsion and spasm. Despite having seen Lila Mishal in an eerily similar situation, Jo found these older, grainier images vastly more disturbing in comparison. Even after so many years. Milgallon too appeared transfixed by the distressing imagery. 'At first, I wasn't sure,' he said wistfully. 'You can never be sure what's going on in a child's mind. Just a bunch of make-believe most of the time. But there was something about the girl. Something about how she looked at you. Something that made you want to believe....'

On the wall, Tracey Babcock peered directly out from the projection. 'It's like she's looking right through you,' Milgallon reflected, his manner becoming increasingly disconnected from his present surroundings. Even without Milgallon's observation Jo had already sensed an unnerving intensity about the teenager's gaze. Even in the earlier shots of her going about her normal everyday activities, she had exuded an unsettling detachment toward her environment.

'Lawrence Ashby insisted on a human interest angle,' Milgallon's tone had become a raw mixture of remorse and deference. 'A face the public could relate to. He also wanted photographs. But as you may know paranormal activity is notoriously difficult to capture on film. A spectral being won't just perform a trick for you whenever you set up a camera. It can't be bribed into giving a performance, plus we didn't have the time or the resources to run a film camera continually....'

'So you faked it.'

Milgallon bulked at Jo's suggestion. 'I faked nothing!' he snapped back.

But Jo was unswayed by the old man's indignation. 'So what would you call it then?'

Milgallon glared at Jo, his anguished expression exaggerated by the gleaming projector beam. Jo held his gaze until finally Milgallon conceded. 'Let's just say we had to recreate some of the incidents that occurred. But they did occur. Make no mistake about that. There was something in the house. Something very unnatural, but something very real.'

Jo lent forward on the bed, the old wooden frame creaking beneath her. 'Are you saying you actually saw paranormal occurrences with you own eyes?'

Training his rheumy gaze on Jo. Milgallon squinted through his thick-rimmed glasses. 'As clearly as I can see you now!' he said fervently. His earlier animosity seemingly forgotten.

Jo couldn't help but smile at Milgallon's ironic statement. 'So, is this real?' Jo asked, nodding toward the wall.

'To a degree.'

In the film, Tracey Babcock now appeared to be enduring some kind of catatonic trance. Her eyes rolling back into her head.

'So you're saying she recreated what had already happened to her?'

'Well, not to her...'

'Then who...?'

'You have to understand. Tracey had the power to persuade. It was easy to believe her. Tony was too withdrawn, too young. Readers would never have related to him. Not like a teenage girl—'

'Sorry what?' Jo interrupted. 'Are you saying Tony was the focus?'

Now the subject had been broached. Milgallon seemed eager to get everything off his chest. 'In a way, it was ideal. Tony never wanted to appear on camera. He hardly ever spoke. But they had a very close relationship, the brother and the sister. They were never separated. If they were, the boy would start performing and screaming. So we just conducted our research around the both of them. But all the paranormal activity was centred around Tony. Tracey only reinterpreted it for the camera. Ashby knew, your father knew....'

Jo glanced over at Laura, her rueful expression confirming that she too was aware of her uncle's subterfuge.

'It was always Tony,' Milgallon reflected dolefully. 'It was his fear that drew the spirit to them.'

'Of what?' Jo asked.

'Pardon?'

'Tony's fear of what?'

Milgallon's lip quivered as he looked away.

'Patrick. Why was there a poltergeist in that house? What were those children trying to tell you?'

Milgallon glanced over to his niece, who smiled reassuringly back at him. With a resigned sigh, he turned back to the Ciné film projection. 'It was quite obvious the father was abusing the children,' he said, his voice almost hollow with regret. 'But it wasn't a matter we felt the magazine should or could get involved with. Plus, by the time we realised the full extent of the abuse; well it was all too late. They were already celebrities, so I had no choice but to ignore the fact. I should have done something I suppose, but you know.'

'You had your career to think of.' Milgallon cast Jo a sharp glance, but let the comment go. Which was more than Jo was prepared to do. 'So you just let it happen?'

'What could I have done?' Milgallon protested. 'If I'd said anything, it would have meant the end of my research. The authorities would have got involved. They would have dismissed everything as just some tawdry social issue, some trivial fabrication by a frightened child.'

Laura shuffled in her chair as her uncle's anxiety increased.

'But there was a ghost in that house,' Milgallon insisted, his bottom lip trembling. 'There was!'

'Oh, there was an evil spirit in that house alright,' Jo snipped. 'And it was the children's fear and loathing that gave it form; Mr Nox! Their own father. You knew it was a cry for help and you did nothing.'

Milgallon jerked forward, energised by a sudden, violent spasm. 'No, it was a spirit. I know it was! It had to be.' Overcome with the weight of his actions, he slumped back with a heavy groan. 'I had to do it, for the sake of my research. It was wrong but I had to. Don't you think I know that? Don't you think I'm already being punished for that action? Look at me. Look what I've become. Am I not already serving my penitence?' Laura began tenderly stroking the back of Milgallon's hand as tears welled in his milky eyes. 'I can only hope they'll be more forgiving in the next life,' he muttered despairingly. 'How was I to know what would happen? How was I to know?'

Repulsed by the old man, Jo turned to the image on the wall. Tracey Babcock stared maniacally into the camera, while behind her, Tony sat rocking back and forth with his head in his hands.

'Don't think too badly of him,' Laura said, placing a fresh cup of tea in front of Jo. They had left Milgallon in his room. Despite his protestations it had been clear the meeting with Jo had left him exhausted and disoriented.

'It's all he has left. That book of his,' Laura said, taking the chair opposite Jo. 'He's very protective of it. All that stuff about the children. He would never have admitted to any of that a few years ago. But it's his age, poor dear,' Laura sighed despondently. 'Life, eh! All it does is take away.' She took a sip from her own teacup. 'And he's been so unsettled all week. Ever since that girl from the television company came to see him.'

'What girl?'

Leaning back in her chair, Laura plucked a slip of flowery notepaper from a kitchen memo board. 'Jasmine, somebody. Said she was a researcher for a production company. Apparently, they were doing a programme on the Babcocks. God knows how they found us.' Laura handed the slip to Jo. Sure enough it was Jasmine's handwritten contact details. 'She wanted to know all about the haunting. You know, who did uncle think Mr Nox was? What was the family like? What the children's nicknames were, that sort of thing. It was all pleasant enough until she asked if he thought it possible that Tracey could have faked it all.'

'She said that?'

'Yes, or something like that. But it really upset Uncle Pat. Now he's worried it will ruin his reputation, I ask you, as if anybody remembers who he is anymore. That's why he wanted to speak to you so urgently. He wanted to get the facts straight, for any reprints. So you would understand.'

'Like my father did.'

Laura gave Jo a sad smile. 'Your father did what he felt was best. Besides, they didn't really lie did they not really. So they distorted the facts a little. I mean where's the harm in that?'

With time on her hands, before her return train to London, Jo took Bruno for one last run along the promenade.

The storm clouds had finally blown over and to Jo's surprise, the sea breeze felt both refreshing and comforting against her cheeks. The salt air brought back a flood of childhood memories. The smell of seaweed, wet skin and sunscreen. Soaked dogs, cotton candy and doughnuts. The sensation of a soft towel being wrapped around her shoulders. For a moment, everything seemed almost peaceful.

Then her mobile rang.

***

Contemporary CCTV recording: A static shot from a traffic control camera, showing a pedestrian crossing.

As the lights change, a teenage girl, in an oversized puffer jacket, leads a stocky Labrador across the road. Listening to her headphones, the girl appears oblivious to her surroundings. On reaching the far side of the road, the pair continue toward the entrance of a local park.

Behind them, a heavyset man in a dark jacket appears at the crossing. He watches the pair pass through the park gates before hurrying after them. He momentarily hesitates by the gates, anxiously glancing over his shoulder, before following them into the park.

17. Abnormal Behaviour

If your pet continuously stares or fixates on something across the room, or barks and snarls repeatedly at an empty space. This could point to a paranormal presence. Dogs may refuse to enter a room they're normally happy to spend time in or cower for no apparent reason. Cats may react suddenly to something unseen, or appear to be 'watching' something move across the room.

Animals possess more heightened senses than humans and can detect any abrupt or disturbing changes in their environment, which researchers think can often be a clear indicator that something paranormal is present.

***

'I don't deserve this! This is not me. This is not who I was supposed to be. Can you understand that?'

Sharman remains silent. It's taken him this long to get me talking. He's not about to interrupt me now.

'But I guess I can't be anything different can I? Not now. It's like I've not changed. That I'm still trapped there, back in that house. If I close my eyes, it's like I never left.'

It's hard to find the right words. But I persevere.

'To me it's always winter. There's always darkness. And I'm always afraid.'

A picture forms in my mind.

'There would be a power cut and we'd all sit in the darkness listening to my father swearing and my mother muttering through her idiotic routines, driving herself crazy in the candlelight. With no heat or light, there was nothing else to do but go to bed and shiver. We had an old paraffin heater, but mother lived in constant fear of the fumes, so we never used it. We'd just huddle together under a blanket. Tracey used to draw pictures in a notebook and make up stories for me. To take me somewhere else in my mind. She would comfort me, wrap her arms around me. But the fear never went away.'

I swallow hard as my throat dries.

'It would always start with an argument downstairs. When he was very drunk, my mother would lock him out of their bedroom, make him sleep somewhere else. That's when he would find his way into my room. He would stand in the doorway, staring at me. Grunting and smelling of alcohol. Most nights he'd just collapse drunk onto the bed and pass out. Those were the better nights.

'But there were other nights when he would become *playful* with me. He'd never been what you might call a loving parent, unless he had a drink inside of him. Then it was a different story. Then he used to hug and tickle me. Pulling me onto his lap. I used to hate that more than when he used to slap me. At least you knew what to expect when you're being beaten. But I hated it when he used to touch me. He had a name for me then 'Tony Boy'. He only ever used it when he was drunk. Or when he wanted to be affectionate. 'Tony Boy', come to daddy. It still makes my skin crawl when I think about it. But I guess you already knew this didn't you? I suppose I display all the usual indicators. I bet you knew the moment I first walked into your office?'

Again, Sharman has nothing to say and for once I'm glad. I think if he interrupted me now I wouldn't be able to go on.

'Anyway, as I say it begun with the tickling and the cuddling, but that always led to him rubbing his cock against me. I knew I wanted him to stop, but what could I do? He had total control over me.

'The only thing that stopped him was Tracey. She would come into my room whenever he was there. She used to put herself between him and me. It was the only way she knew how to protect me. That's what she did for me. That's how she protected me. She would cry afterwards, as she held me in the dark. She would try not to, but she did. She would cry while he snored. And if you have to know the truth. I was grateful. Grateful that she did what she did. I was terrified of my father. I lived in total fear of him.

'On those nights he came into my bedroom, I would pray for her to appear. For her to save me. And she always did. She was the only thing I could rely on. The only thing I had.

'It was around this time that mother turned on us as well. She used to beat Tracey and yell at us at the slightest provocation. It was like living on a knife-edge. It wasn't really her fault. She was half-crazy herself by that point. The most enduring memory I have of my mother is one of her on a continuous loop. Repeating the same actions over and over again. Continually washing the dishes or checking the kitchen appliances one by one, making sure they were all securely switched off. She lived in constant fear of the world around her.

'Eventually her paranoia overtook her. The house became a virtual prison for all of us. We weren't allowed to go to a friend's house after school. We had to come straight home. No one could ever come to ours. The only real friends we had were each other. Me and Tracey, that's all we had. We had nobody else to turn to except ourselves. We created our own games and our own secret codes, like prisoners passing secrete messages to each over, living under the constant threat of father's violence and mother's insanity. Is it any wonder we became what we did?

I'm struck by a sudden thought, a feeling I've long suspected I've been harbouring all these years.

'But my father deserved to die. He really did.'

There I've said it and it feels so good to hear it out loud.

'And mother? I don't know what she deserved? I think in the end I hated her as much as I hated him. She had just abandoned us to him. I know what you're gonna say. That she was just as much a victim as we were. But fuck it! She was our mother! She should have done something! But Tracey didn't deserve any of it. She didn't deserve to die like she did. That was my fault. I was so scared. She was reaching out to me and

I did nothing! She'd done everything she could for me. And I did nothing. But the worst thing was. Secretly, I was glad. Glad it was her and not me. That's what I've had to live with all these years.'

I can taste the salt as the tears stream down my face.

'There, you wanted me to talk. Now you know. Now you've got what you've always wanted. So tell me; how are you going to help me? How are you going to make it all okay?'

I can't keep fighting this anymore. My defences fall away.

'Because I need help. I really do. I need for you to tell me what to do. Tell me it's going to be alright. I need you to do that for me.'

But there's no haughty reply. No thinly concealed condescension. No nothing.

Across the room, there's only silence and the empty shattered remains of my photographic studio.

'Tony, what the hell are you doing?'

'I know it's here.'

'What's here?' Jerry stares dumbfounded at the scattered debris strewn across the cellar floor.

'The answer; I know it's here.'

'Mate, you can't just turn up like this anymore. I thought you'd finished?' He looks uneasy. He's staring at the bruises on my face.

'Not yet, not until I know.' I toss another crate across the cellar. 'Everything's unplugged!'

'Of course it is. I haven't seen you in weeks.'

Grabbing an extension lead, I trail it across the floor. 'I need this plugged in. Don't you realise what I could have missed?'

'Trust me, pal, you ain't missed a thing.'

'You don't understand. This equipment should have been left on....'

'Listen fella, I've got the photo. That's enough. That's all I need. I'm not paying for anything else.'

'I don't care about the money. I just need answers.'

'And I just need you out of my cellar.'

He's getting irate. But fuck it, I'm not having it. 'No, no, no!' I tell him. 'I heard the voice right here. You know I heard it. It was a message; a message for me.'

'Mate, you said yourself it could have been radio interference.'

I shake my head. 'No, it was real.'

'I really don't think it was.'

Fuck me, he's changed his tune. I throw the lead down in frustration as it falls short of the power socket.

'I think it's best if you just leave.'

'I can't!' I tell him through gritted teeth.

'Well, you're gonna have to. And you can take the rest of your junk with you.'

'But I'm not finished!'

'Oh yes, you are, pal. You're all done here. It's over.'

Jerry makes a grab for my arm, but I shake him off. 'I know what I heard!'

'I don't think you do. I want you out of my cellar right now.' I can feel the fight draining from me. Jerry can see it too. His

397

tone softens. 'Mate, trust me, you've got to let it go. There's nothing down here.'

'But I heard the voice right here.'

'Yeah about that...'

I can't get into my studio. There's a news crew outside the block. Leo's giving them some strive, but they're not budging.

Christ! How bad could it have been? Instinctively, my hand reaches inside my jacket. But the pocket's empty. I've no meds left. Just some temazepam, but that's up in my studio.

Right on cue, a searing jolt rips through my skull. Reeling from the withdrawal, I slump back against the cycle barrier.

Down at my feet Scruff brushes against my leg.

Sorry pal, I can't be doing this today.

Grasping my head, I shuffle back into the alleyway.

Fuck it! What's happening? My mind's a blur. Everything's still spinning. Fragments of the live show keep coming back to me. Vague images of screaming and fighting and Schaffer's distorted face leering at me. My knuckles throb and my hand aches. Jesus! What have I done?

Reaching down to give Scruff a scratch, the little fucker snarls at me.

Well, that about sums it up.

I spot him walking home. I'd recognise that walk anywhere. But there's something different about his stance. He's slower, a little stooped. He must have had a long day.

A single Victorian wrought iron street lamp illuminates the cobbled side street. It's soothing. Almost calming. I like it here. It's a posh area. Respectable people.

He stops under the street lamp, rummaging for his door keys. 'Eric!'

He looks up startled, shocked by my sudden appearance. 'Tony? Is that you?' he shuffles back a step.

His face is still in shadow, but now I'm closer I can see him better. He's changed his glasses. They're not his usual pair. They're much thicker, with a fuller frame. His face looks rounder, too. In fact, his whole body looks different. Even accounting for his overcoat, he looks heavier and his hair is shorter. How could he have aged so much?

'I need to speak to you,' I tell him. 'I need your help.' He backs into the soft amber glow of the street lamp. 'Christ!'

There's a long scar cut across his cheek. A deep gauge, running from the temple, down through his jowl. Instinctively, his hand moves to cover the injury. 'You shouldn't be here. You know that.' Backing away he collides with the street lamp. Grabbing his shoulders, I turn him into the light.

He's an old man; a petrified old man. It's him, but it's not. Up close, the scar on his cheek looks even worse. And it's old; like the rest of his face. 'What the hell happened to you?' I ask.

He looks confused. 'You did.'

What?

'You did this. Don't you remember?'

I recall an image of a blade and a struggle. And screaming. There's always screaming. I see myself, but it's not me, not really. It's a different me. I loosen my grip on Sharman. Tripping on the cobblestones, he falls to the ground.

In an instant it all comes back to me, like I'm watching a film playing in my head. There's blood everywhere. Sharman is there. Like he is now. Cowering on the ground, his arm raised, shielding his face. But his face is different. Younger, but just as scared.

As my mind spins, I turn and run. Just as I did then; back when it wasn't really me.

It's late evening. The pavement's packed with grumpy commuters and meandering tourists. People sprawling everywhere, pushing in all directions. I get some lip as I bundle through, but I ignore it all and stumble on.

In Leicester Square, an old woman in a tatty Afghan coat, berates a young couple for kissing in the street. 'You can't hide your sins,' she harangues them. 'God sees everything.' I quickly move away before she turns her condemnation in my direction.

I turn onto Regent Street, walking fast, with my face down. I can feel the eyes of every person I pass turning to follow me. It's like a contagion, passing from one person to the next. I duck into a side street. I need a place to hide. Somewhere to get my head together. I find a small cafe and order a coffee. It's the only non-chain cafe in the area. It's an anomaly, like myself.

Ignoring the cautious glances from the counter assistant, I take a seat by the window. Hunched over the table, I watch the world filing past outside. Gripping my mug, I can feel the heat radiating through my palms.

Startled by a sudden roar, the hot liquid spills over my hand. Behind me, some old fucker claps his hands at the TV. On a small portable, above the counter, a giant statue of Saddam Hussein's topples to the ground, while a crazed mob batter it with flip-flops.

The world's gone crazy.

Turning away, I suck the back of my scotched hand, trying to ease the stinging. Another cry; but this one sounds more familiar, more personal. I glance back at the TV and I'm shocked to see my own face glaring back at me. A crazed man screaming at the camera. A melee of violent jerks and distorted actions.

It's a clip from *The Max Schaffer Experience*. My stomach churns as more pictures appear on the screen. Images from last night, interwoven with snapshots from my past.

I glance around the cafe. No one is looking in my direction but they all realise it's me. I can tell. I can even hear them whispering my name to each other.

In my mind, I relive the events of the previous night. The accusations, the struggle, the girl's tortured screams. I see myself fighting, lashing out, but the faces keep changing. Sometimes it's Schaffer, then it's Jerry, then Sharman with his face covered in blood.

I'm gripped by a sudden sense of panic as I stare at my hands, each a canvas of blotched bruising and scratches. I clench my fingers into tight fists. I can feel them tightening around her throat. I feel the anger I felt then. The anger

I've always felt. It all feels so long ago and yet it feels like yesterday. It feels like now. Like it only just happened. Oh God! I no longer know where the past ends and the present begins. All my memories have become blurred. Everything is happening at the same time. It's all still happening now, because it never ended then. The same pattern repeating itself endlessly. Like my mother continually checking the gas stove switches, trying to keep us safe, but only prolonging the misery. Grabbing my temples, I try to stop every memory I've ever had from spilling out over the formica tabletop.

I see myself being led by social workers to a waiting car. Tracey falling from the viaduct. My father's accusing glare and my mother's terrified hysteria.

I see the girl's face.

No, not again, not this! Not this madness forever. Over and over again. The past becoming the present, the present slipping back into the past. The endless accusations, the compounding of guilt. Time and time again. Like a ghost condemned to haunt the same time and place forever.

'You did this. You did this to us.'

I leap from my chair, slamming back against the wall. I'm caught in an endless loop, the worst parts of my life forever repeating themselves. It's never ending. It never will end, eternity repeating itself forever.

'Are you alright, pal?'

At first I think it's the policeman from my dreams, but it's a security guard from the night club up the road. He's wearing a black bomber jacket and there's a stupid little earpiece stuck in his ear. Probably nipped in for a quiet cuppa on his break.

As I stare around the cafe, a myriad of concerned faces stare back at me. Maybe I'm wrong, maybe it is a policeman. Maybe he's here for me. I can no longer trust anyone, not even myself.

The knucklehead steps forward, his hand outstretched, but I push him away. You're not taking me back, not again.

Visions of the psychiatric secure unit flash through my mind. The wipe-clean mattress, the security fences, the spy holes in the doors. The endless fucking analysis. I can't face it, not again.

I make a break for the doorway and escape into the back streets.

A gust of warm air buffets my face. I can smell the soot in my nostrils. Somewhere in the labyrinth below, a train howls like a wounded creature. Excreted passengers stand pliantly on the escalator, ascending toward the light. While I alone descend into the ground.

Suspicious eyes glance across the metal divide. But for once I don't recoil from their reproving stares. Instead, I hold my arms out, crucifixion style. For all the world to see.

Look at me. I'm here. My head tilts backward as the billowing air caresses my cheeks. Breathing deeply, I fill my lungs with the pollutant infused smog.

And all eyes turn away. Nobody wants anything to do with me. Just another crackpot on the tube. Another mad, broken soul that everybody looks straight through.

The real ghosts that walk among you.

On the platform there's the usual spattering of late night commuters, impatiently waiting for the next arrival.

I've never felt more alone.

Looking around, I remember Tracey perched on the platform edge. Falling backwards into the void, her hand stretched out, beckoning.

Moving away from the wall, a familiar cry echoes down the platform.

Bargain basement George Melly, giving the world another tune. I feel sorry for the norms tonight. They're getting more than their fair share of nut jobs on their journey home this evening.

I take another step forward, closer to the edge. Drifting over the growl of the approaching train, a familiar refrain.

Engelbert Humperdinck - 'Please Release Me!'

It's like he was expecting me.

***

Contemporary CCTV recording: A man in a crumpled army jacket stands in the middle of a near empty London Underground platform.

Dazed and confused, he stares vacantly at the train tracks. Several late night stragglers mill past, but no one is paying him any attention. The quality of the image is grainy and pixilated, taken from a fixed camera position used to monitor activity on the platform. At the top of the shot, headlights appear in the tunnel mouth. The man steps closer to the edge.

18. Disappearing Objects

Dubbed the 'Disappearing Object Phenomenon' or 'The Borrowers Phenomenon'. This is the unsettling experience of losing a regularly used item: such as a set of door keys, a mobile phone or a dog lead. Only for it to reappear again. Usually in the last place you remember leaving it.

Sometimes these items are not returned for days or even weeks. But when they do reappear, it's always to an obvious place. A place you couldn't have possibly missed or overlooked during your initial search.

***

Time was standing still at Old Street Underground Station. Or so it seemed. Departure time on the platform LED was still displaying 3min, as it had done for the past twenty-four minutes. The official word was; they'd lost electricity following an accident further up the track, but rumour had it; someone had jumped under a train.

Jo checked her watch again. It was ridiculous. She couldn't spend all evening waiting on a train, which might never arrive. Besides Bruno was growing heavy in her arms. Grabbing her bag, she headed to the surface to find a taxi.

'We thought she might go to you again—'

'It's bloody Norris! I know it is!' Belo yelled over his wife. 'I'll fucking kill him! That bastard! I knew it. The moment the dog turned up here alone, I bloody knew it.' Unable to contain his anger, Belo began furiously pacing the lounge.

Over on the sofa, Kyra was teetering between frightened tears and numb panic. 'Belo, please!' Qamra pleaded as she attempted to calm the bawling five-year-old. 'We don't know that!'

'Who else could it be? I caught him outside Lila's school, for fuck's sake!'

'For God's sake Belo stop shouting!' Qamra yelled, her own voice teetering on hysteria.

Ignoring Qamra, Belo turned to Jo. 'And the police won't do anything. They say we should just wait until she gets in contact. Wait, I ask you.' He threw his arms in the air. 'God knows what could happen by then? She does this on purpose you know!'

Thrown by Belo's sudden variance, Jo turned to Qamra for clarification. 'She's run away before,' Qamra said in a monotone. 'But she's always turns up a day or two later when she runs out of money, or places to stay.'

'I tell you it's Norris, it has to be.'

'But why would he?'

'Why would he?' Belo exclaimed, surprised by his wife's continued objections. 'Well, maybe because he's a bloody child molester! What more reason do you need?'

'But it doesn't make any sense,' Jo interjected, even though it meant placing herself in the uncomfortable position of defending Roy Norris. 'He was convicted for inappropriate behaviour around young children at a water park. This doesn't seem like something he would do. I mean, if he was going to take anyone...' Casting a fleeting glance toward Kyra, Jo left that thought unfinished.

'I'm telling you, it's him,' Belo stated firmly.

'And I suppose he stole van as well.' Qamra snapped.

'The van?' Once again, Jo found herself wrong-footed by the constantly shifting argument.

'On top of everything else, some toerag's pinched my bloody van,' Belo explained. 'I had to move it up the road for the filming. When I went back for it this morning, it was gone!'

'Forget van!' Qamra screamed across the room. 'Lila is missing.'

'And we know why that is. She's got no respect for this family!'

Qamra turned to Belo in a fury. 'No respect! You can talk! She has run away because of you! You and your bloody ghost! Well, I hope you've got what you wanted!' Snatching a shabby notebook from the sideboard, she turned to Jo. 'I found this in Lila's bedroom. And he knew all about it.' Jo barely glimpsed the book before Qamra spun around and threw it at Belo. Bouncing off his turned shoulder, it landed on the floor, opening on a stick cartoon of two children laying under the aches of a tall bridge. 'They found it under floorboards when they were decorating Lila's room.'

Jo lent over to retrieve the notebook. Between the drawings, there were thin spidery lines of childlike scrawl. Flicking through the pages, several familiar sentences immediately caught Jo's eye. 'So this is how she knew what to say?'

'It's all there,' Qamra raged. 'All that stuff about little soldiers, the nursery rhyme, everything!'

'I didn't know, not at first,' Belo objected. 'By the time I realised it had gone too far.'

'Yes, you'd already taken their money hadn't you!' Qamra threw her arms in the air in disgust. 'I don't even know what he expected to get from it. Who would buy haunted house anyway, I ask you!'

'I thought the publicity would be good. That we might get a book deal or something. That notebook alone must be worth something.'

'Well, let's see what it's worth now.' Snatching the book from Jo's hand, Qamra began furiously tearing at its tattered pages.

Leaping forward Belo tried to seize the remnants of the notebook from Qamra's grip. 'Are you crazy!'

'Am I crazy! Am *I* crazy! Yes, I'm crazy. Because you make me crazy. You make everyone crazy! You make that man crazy. That's why he attacked you!'

'He attacked everyone, not just me!'

'Sorry what?' Jo interrupted. 'Who attacked who?'

Qamra cast Jo a look of sheer incongruity. 'You don't know?'

'I don't know what?'

Scooping up a crumpled newspaper, Qamra slapped it into Jo's hands. 'Here, look. See what his greed has done!'

'I did it all for you and Kyra,' Belo protested. 'And for Lila.'

The mention of her daughter's name sent Qamra into a fresh spasm of anguish. Despite her initial attempts to bat him away, Bello wrapped his arms around her. 'If anything happens to her, I'll never forgive myself.' Qamra sobbed into Belo's shoulder, while Kyra blabbered hysterically on the sofa.

Little of which registered with Jo, as she stood staring down at the newspaper headline:

Celebrity psychic attacked on live TV

Underneath were several screen images from the live broadcast along with an archive photograph of Tony as a child.

Jo knew now why Tony hadn't been answering her calls.

Jo had left the Mishal's house, with her head spinning. Taking Tracey's notebook with her for safekeeping, she had spent the rest of the evening watching and then rewatching her recording of *The Max Schaffer Experience.* Watching in numb horror as the live séance had descended into a maelstrom of screaming and violence. The whole thing seemed like madness. The fact Tony had even agreed to appear in the show was bewildering.

Receiving no answer from Gillian's mobile, Jo had called the production office first thing the following morning, only to get the runaround from Jasmine, who had sounded uncharacteristically aversive over the phone. Annoyed, Jo had tried Tony's mobile again, only for that to go straight to answerphone again.

Exasperated, she had driven over to Tony's studio, only to discover a small TV news crew camped outside the building, chatting with a uniformed police officer by a panda car. Evidently, Jo had not been the only person interested in speaking to Tony that morning.

Reaching for her mobile, Jo called Tony's business line, but like his mobile it too went unanswered. If Tony was in the studio, then he wasn't picking up. If he was even there, that was? Considering all the unwelcome attention directed at his home, he would have probably found somewhere else to hideout. Knowing of only one likely location, Jo put the Mini into gear.

Apart from a few glum lunchtime patrons The Station House was deserted. With no one behind the bar, Jo seized her opportunity. Slipping through the kitchen, she pulled open the trapdoor in the larder floor. After a moment's hesitation, she descended the steep steps into the cellar. With her gaze focused solely on the murky gloom below, Jo totally failed to notice the appearance of a dark silhouette in the open trapdoor above her. Framed against the bright fluorescent kitchen light, the figure watched her silently as she disappeared into the darkness.

410

Despite the dim aura cast by Jo's pocket lighter, it was immediately evident the cellar was empty. Sheets of sodden newspaper still covered the floor, but all of Tony's equipment had gone. Giving the cellar one last sweeping glance, Jo turned back toward the staircase.

'*I see you!*'

Jo spun on her heels, her eyes probing the darkness, but no other sound broke the silence. Unsettled, she turned again toward the staircase.

'*I see you!*'

Jo's heart leapt as she thrust the flickering lighter flame toward the whisper. A dark corner of the cellar, stacked with broken bar furniture. Casting the light at the top of the staircase a forlorn glance, Jo took a step toward the dark corner, just as the faint whisper morphed into a low, guttural moan. Clutching the lighter tight in her grip, Jo edged forward.

Rounding the edge of the furniture stack, she saw it.

With one hand fiercely gripping the side of the cabinet, Jerry lent further into the dumbwaiter, the toe of his shoe barely touching the kitchen lino. For a moment, Jo considered hoicking Jerry's flaying leg up into the air, but there was a genuine possibility this would send him tumbling headfirst down the shaft. Not that he didn't deserve it. Deep within the shaft Jerry was still making a ridiculous moaning sound. Thoroughly engrossed in his task, he had yet to realise Jo had already left the cellar.

'I see you,' Jerry moaned down the shaft.

'And I see you!' Jo barked into Jerry's ear.

Cracking his head on the top of the hatch and still clutching a long card funnel, Jerry stumbled away from the shaft. 'Christ sake!' he gasped 'You scared the living shit out of me!'

'The bar's been losing money for months,' Jerry muttered sorely, as he pushed a large vodka and orange across the bar. Wincing, his hand quickly returned to his aching scalp. If he had been hoping to extract any further sympathy for Jo, then the action was entirely unnecessary, considering the current state of his face. Along with the bleeding scalp, Jerry was also sporting a vibrant purple cheek and split lip. Injuries he had yet to comment upon. 'I figured, if I played up the old ghost thing. It might bring in a few more punters. I thought with some actual proof. I could get on one of those ghost walk things. You know; bung the tour guide a few quid so he'll bring the tourists in for a last drink.'

Jo nodded knowingly. 'So you hired Tony.'

'Yeah, but...'

'He didn't find anything.'

'Paid him up front and he came back with zip! He was about to call it a day when....'

'Suddenly he heard voices.'

Jerry shrugged. 'I thought it might sway things in my favour a bit.'

'Does he know?' Jo asked, nodding toward the ridiculous cardboard cone, laying on the bar.

'Oh, I think he's worked it out,' Jerry said sardonically, rubbing his split lip.

'When was this?'

'Last night, he turned up all crazy like. I mean, more crazy than usual. I'd never seen him so bad. I used to hear him talking to himself down there some nights. But this time he was raving like a proper loon. He'd got it into his head it was all real. That *voices* were trying to tell him something. I thought if I told him the truth it might calm him down a bit.'

'And did it?'

'Let's just say he was less than impressed. In fact, he went right off the deep end. Refused to believe me, said the messages were real and I was trying to hide the truth from him.'

'So what happened then?'

'We had a little set-to. After which, he loaded his van and was gone. And I hope to God he never comes back. The guy's a total headcase, if you ask me.'

Jo shook her head at Jerry's deriding tone. 'So with Tony out of the picture, you thought you'd try it on with me instead.'

Jerry gave an indifferent shrug. 'Well, needs must and all that. I've been calling your production office, but no one's returning my calls. Don't suppose you'd fancy putting in a good word in for me, then?'

Jo gave him a *'you must be joking'* look as she hopped down from her barstool. Glancing down at the ludicrous card funnel, she couldn't help but feel a little disappointed. 'And all this time; he never even suspected it was you?'

Jerry smiled sympathetically. 'Well, you know what they say. If you look hard enough for something, you'll find it; whether it's there or not.'

Jo had almost reached the door when a sudden realisation struck her. Spinning on her heel, she turned back toward the bar. 'Did you say his van?'

'I not talk to press.'

'Hello, hi remember me?'

Leandro peered around the edge of the door. 'Ah yes, you are friend of him.' Engaging her most beguiling smile, Jo slipped into the foyer. 'I thought you were vermin,' Leandro said, casting a reproachful eye over Jo's shoulder.

'Sorry?'

'News people asking for him, but he's not in.'

'Yes, I know. I just rang his buzzer. I don't suppose you know where he is, do you?'

'No idea. Not seen him since yesterday. That's what I tell vermin.'

'You saw him yesterday?'

'He wanted to borrow van again. But I tell him I need it for exhibit today.'

'So he can drive then?'

Leandro chuckled. 'I should hope so. I don't think he pushes it everywhere.'

Jo lent forward. 'So do you often lend Tony your van?'

Leandro made a dismissive gesture. 'Now and again. When he has to move equipment. He gives me a few quid each time, for petrol. It's no problem.' With his interest waning, Leandro turned back toward his studio.

Not wanting Leandro to vanish on her just yet. Jo casually followed him in through the door of his studio. 'And you say you saw him yesterday?' she asked breezily.

Leandro lent toward Jo in a conspiratorial fashion, apparently unconcerned that she had just invited herself into his home. 'Yes, yes, he looked pretty bad, worse than normal. All that stuff on television. I felt sorry for him. But I needed van myself, for art fair in Leeds.'

'What did he do instead?'

'Who knows? He said he would sort something out.'

Concerned she was losing Leandro's interest again, Jo gestured toward a line of painted canvases stacked along the wall. 'Wow? These all look marvellous, may I?'

Leandro waved his arm, as if to say, '*Be my guest.*'

Initially intending to flatter the grumpy artist, Jo instead found herself immediately captivated by Leandro's work. 'They're all amazing,' she said honestly as she wandered from one painting to the next.

Leandro appeared less appreciative of his own creations. 'To you maybe, but to me...' He huffed harshly, before adding in a softer tone, 'But I love them all the same, like my children.' He gestured toward a stack of portraits close to his workbench, which had been separated from the others. 'But children don't always turn out like you hope.'

'Well, I think they're all fantastic.' Moving toward the workbench, one large portrait caught Jo's eye. 'Hey this is Tony,' she declared, picking the canvas from the stack.

'Yes, he sit for me.' Leandro nodded. 'I paint faces I like. Don't forget, I want to paint your face.

Ignoring Leandro's preoccupation with her own face, Jo studied the portrait of Tony. The depth of the image was haunting. 'What made you paint him like this?' she asked.

'It's how I see him. What I feel from him.'

'Well, it's clearly him. You've really caught his likeness.'

Leandro shrugged, implying, '*I try*'.

As she replaced the painting back with the other portraits, Jo spotted another face she recognised. An enigmatic image of a young girl, her face framed by two distinctive streaks of pink hair. As she picked the canvas up, Leandro noticed the look of recognition on Jo's face. 'It's so sad,' he said, walking up beside her. 'Such a sweet girl. I wanted to give it to her family as a gift, but I didn't know where to send it.'

In a flash Jo realised where she had seen the face before. 'It's the girl that disappeared, Ashley...?'

'Ashley, yes, so very sad.'

Jo looked down at the canvas again. Now she knew the identity of the young girl. The portrait took on an even greater poignancy. Ashley's eyes shone with such vibrance it was almost cruel to see her like this. 'She looks happy,' Jo whispered, her voice tinged with sadness.

'Yes, always.' Leandro nodded solemnly. 'That's what I thought when I saw her, so happy, so alive. I see her coming and going in the hallway. So I asked her to sit for me. It breaks my heart when I think of her now.'

It took a moment for Leandro's statement to fully register with Jo. 'Sorry did you say she sat for you *here*?' So this isn't from a photograph?'

'No, no, I never use photographs, she sit here for me.' He pointed toward an old wooden stool in the middle of the studio.

Jo turned to face Leandro full-on. 'Sorry, are you saying this girl was here in this building? In the hallway outside?'

'Of course. She was here for him upstairs.'

Rob Hooper had cried the moment he had set eyes on the painting. He had held it in his hands, tears rolling down his sallow cheeks. Only then had Greg cast Jo a conciliatory glance.

Leandro had been content for Jo to take the portrait to Ashley's father, especially after she had explained her connection with the family's social worker. She had even offered to provide him with some form of proof, but Leandro had waved away such necessities. 'You have a trustworthy face,' he had said, adding, 'Besides, who would want to steal portrait of dead girl?'

But it had taken a little more persuading for Greg to agree to the meeting. Even now, as they sat together in Rob's lounge, he still appeared to be harbouring some reservations about the meeting, despite Rob's apparent gratitude for the gift.

'You say she posed for this in his studio?' Rob said, as he propped the painting in a chair opposite so he could look at it while they were talking. Rob looked tired and pale. His hair needed a trim and grey stubble covered his chin.

'Yes, while she was waiting to pick up some items from the photographer's studio upstairs.'

'Oh, her courier job,' Rob nodded. 'I must call the artist and thank him.' Along with his business card, Leandro had included a short but heartfelt message with the painting, explaining how inspiring and beautiful he had found Ashley and how proud Rob should be of his daughter. Glancing again at the note brought fresh tears to Rob's eyes. Averting her eyes discreetly, Jo's gaze drifted out through the lounge doorway, toward the half-open door at the far end of the hallway. Behind which she could see a neatly made bed, a tidy dressing table and the edge of an Avril Lavigne poster.

'She had everything going for her,' Rob said mournfully, while gazing at the image of his dead daughter. 'She'd just passed her driving test and had got herself a good job with a promotions company. It was only a courier job, really. But they gave her a lot of responsibility right from the start. She used to deliver new products to agents and magazines. I think she liked the fact she got to see all this stuff before it got released. Made her feel special and all that.'

Jo suspected Rob would normally have been more reserved about discussing his daughter with a stranger, but the overwhelming emotion provoked by the portrait had left him emotional and open. 'How long had she been working for the promotions company?' Jo asked.

'Just a couple of months,' Rob smiled. 'She loved it. She was starting at the bottom. But she saw it as a challenge. That's what she was like. Determined, confident. She had everything going for her. It's just not fair...' Rob's voice broke as his shoulders slumped. Putting his coffee mug down, Greg placed his hand on Rob's shoulder. Rob looked close to a total breakdown. Jo wondered how many hours Greg had spent patiently consoling Rob like this. First, after the death of his wife and then his daughter. It felt so inadequate, but this simple gesture seemed to reassure and strengthen him. Steeling himself, Rob straightened his back and with a resilient intake of breath, he turned to Jo. 'I'm sorry, sometimes it all gets too much.'

Jo waved away Rob's concerns with a sympathetic smile. Catching Greg's eye, she realised he was about to suggest they leave Rob alone now. Having yet to raise the subject she had orchestrated this meeting for, Jo quickly glanced around for a possible in-road. 'So is this Ashley's?' she asked, picking up a thin book entitled *Love Horoscopes* from the cabinet next to her chair. Jo had purposely used the present tense when referring to Ashley, a tip Greg had suggested she use whenever she had to refer to the dead girl.

Despite his pain, Rob couldn't help but chuckle. 'Yes, that was one of hers. She loved all that astrology stuff. You know how young girls are. Matching star signs to find their perfect romantic match. Silly if you think about it.'

Ignoring Greg's cautious glare, Jo pushed on. 'And did she do anything else, you know like visit fortune tellers?'

'Well, not fortune tellers as such, but after her mum died, she started getting into all that psychic stuff. Her therapist said it was normal for her to want to keep some kind of connection with her mother. He assured me it would run its course in time. So I went along with it for her sake.'

'And did it? Run its course?'

'No, the opposite in fact. She got quite obsessed with it all. That's when I put an end to it. It wasn't right, especially that psychic reading stuff. She'd just lost her mother and these people were just exploiting her grief.'

'So she visited clairvoyants?'

Rob shrugged. 'One or two, I think.'

'Did any of them ever come here? To your home?'

'No chance I wouldn't allow it.'

Jo could feel Greg scowling at her from across the room.

'So what happened after you told her to stop seeing them?'

'Nothing she stopped. That was the end of it.'

'She didn't put up a fight about it?'

'No, I guess she realised how stupid it all was.'

Greg slapped his palms against his thighs. 'You know Rob I think we've taken up enough of your time,' he said, rising abruptly to his feet. 'I really think we should be going.'

Realising she had one last chance to get the confirmation she needed, Jo plunged her hand inside her handbag. 'Would you happen to know if Ashley ever attended a service here?' She quickly passed Rob a flyer for the spiritist church she had visited with Tony.

Bemused, Rob stared down at the leaflet, while Greg glared at Jo. 'You know I think she did mention this place,' Rob said, much to Jo's relief and Greg's bemusement. 'I think she wanted me to go with her, but I'd had enough by then. So I said no. I guess she might have gone by herself, but she never mentioned it to me if she had. Why? Is this important?'

'No, it isn't,' Greg insisted firmly, while glaring at Jo. 'It isn't important at all.'

'What the hell is going on?' Greg asked the moment they left Rob Hooper's flat.

'I don't know,' Jo admitted. 'I really don't know anymore.'

An empty pill bottle lay on the floor. She couldn't focus on the label. Even if they could; she wouldn't have known what they were. He had forced a handful into her mouth. Lila had guessed they'd been tranquillisers. Her head felt groggy and she kept losing consciousness. The sharp edge of the electrical tape covering her mouth was now cutting into the base of her nose. He had left the door slightly ajar. A narrow blade of light cut through the darkness. Somewhere behind the door she could hear him moving about, muttering to himself.

Lila twisted on the floor. As searing pins and needles coursed through her arms, she attempted to loosen the bindings around her wrists. But they were secured far too tightly to the metal pole. Probably a water pipe, judging by its clammy surface. The small room stank of turpentine and chemicals and above her she could hear the repetitive drip of a leaking tap.

Her heart skipped as a dark shadow moved behind the door, distorting the pristine shaft of light. Panic-stricken, she waited for the door to open. For the madness to begin again.

The door slammed shut, plunging the room into utter blackness. Overwhelmed by despair, Lila felt the tears streaming down her cheeks. She desperately wanted her mother. She missed her sister and wanted to be home again.

Even if it was that horrible house. As she drifted into unconsciousness, she prayed Rafeeq had found his way home safely.

Dodging the shrill woman on reception, Jo followed the signs to the Psychology Department. From there, she found her way to Dr Sharman's office. Arriving at the doctor's door, she discovered a university caretaker in the process of changing the lock. 'Not in luv,' the man said dismissively, as Jo asked for the doctor.

'Well, do you know where I can find him?'

Instead of answering her directly the man simply nodded over her shoulder. 'All yours Doc.' he said to the tall, imposing figure that had just appeared behind Jo.

'Thank you Gavin,' the man said politely, as the caretaker dropped a set of keys into his hand.

'Dr Sharman?' Jo asked as the caretaker disappeared down the corridor.

'Yes?' The doctor turned a dignified, yet indifferent glance toward Jo as he slipped the keys into his jacket pocket. Cooly confident, his whole demeanour would have been quite reassuring if it hadn't been for the disconcerting presence of a broad white scar running across one eye and deep into his cheek.

'I'm Jo Kalman. I tried to call you earlier.'

'I was out of the office,' the doctor replied gruffly.

'Yes, I know. In fact, every time I've rung, you're either out of the office, unavailable or lecturing.'

'Yes, well, there are procedures students are required to follow...'

422

'Dr Sharman, I'm not a student. I'm a friend of Tony Vail...'

'Vail!' A sudden look of unease creased Sharman's face.

'He is a patient of yours?' Jo asked, tentatively.

It took a moment for the doctor to regain his composure. 'No, Miss Kalman I'm no longer Mr Vail's doctor. In fact, until yesterday; I hadn't even seen the man in over fifteen years.'

Jo looked dumbfounded. 'But he told me you worked together here at the university.'

'Then he misled you.'

'Why would he do that?'

'I'm really not in the position to speculate,' the doctor said, gripping the door handle firmly. 'I suggest you ask him about that yourself. Now, if you don't mind. I have a lot to do.' Turning to enter his office, he flashed Jo a curt smile.

'Please Dr Sharman, a young girl has gone missing.'

Sharman froze in the doorway. As his shoulders fell, he turned to back toward Jo. 'You better come through,' he said in a low voice.

Although Dr Sharman's office was bright, modern and decorated in a pleasant aesthetically pleasing style, it still felt strangely officious and impersonal, much like its owner. The only anomaly to this finely crafted order being a ransacked filing cabinet behind the doctor's desk. The cabinet's displaced contents, now heaped in a series of haphazard piles across the office floor.

'What else has he said?' Sharman asked, gazing over his thick horn-rimmed glasses at Jo.

'Just that,' Jo said, shifting uneasily under Sharman's measured gaze. 'That you were his doctor and his friend and that he helped you with your research here at the university?' The whole while Jo had been telling her story, Sharman had tried to maintain a state of professional decorum, but his true emotions had revealed themselves gradually through the nervous tapping of his pen against his palm.

'Well, that explains yesterday evening,' Sharman said with an exasperated sigh, tossing the pen to one side. Having softened his initial tone, Jo could now detect a subtle West Country inflexion to the doctor's voice. Which was becoming more apparent the more he spoke.

'You said saw him yesterday?' Jo asked.

'Outside my home, he looked like he'd been in some kind of fight and was quite delusional.'

'He's stopped taking his medication.'

'That might account for it; and possible this.' Sharman gestured toward the damaged filing cabinet.

'You think Tony did this?'

'He always believed I was hiding something from him. It's possible that recent occurrences have reignited these paranoiac delusions.'

Sharman lent back in his chair, pondering his own hypothesis. Having already endured several lengthy silences from the doctor while recounting the circumstances of Lila's disappearance. Jo was in no mood to endure another. 'Do you think Schaffer's séance could have triggered all this?' she asked.

'It's so incredibly irresponsible.' Sharman declared his reserved reticence, giving way to annoyance. 'He should never have been put in that position. Not after the last time.'

'The last time?' Sharman's eye twitched as he realised what he'd let slip. 'You're not talking about his childhood are you?' Jo speculated correctly.

Sitting back in his chair, Sharman regard Jo closely for a moment. 'How close are you to Tony?' he finally asked.

'I'm probably the closest thing he's got to a friend right now,' Jo admitted, while Sharman continued to assess her from across his desk.

'There may be certain aspects about Tony's childhood that, if disclosed to you now, you might find distressing,' Sharman said gravely.

'I know about *all* the events of his childhood,' Jo emphasised, as the doctor cocked a sceptical eyebrow. 'Please, I just need to know what he's likely to do now. I really think he's liable to harm himself.'

'It's not him you should be worried about,' Sharman retorted sharply. But after a moment of consideration, his manner softened. 'If I was still treating him, I couldn't tell you any of this,' he said bluntly.

'I understand.'

'But in his currant state, he could be an actual danger to himself and possibly others.'

Jo nodded solemnly.

'Okay then.' Leaning forward, Sharman laced his fingers together. 'Well, as you're already aware of the circumstances of Tony's childhood, I won't go into any unnecessary details, suffice to say that during this time both he and his sister were the victims of continual sexual assaults by their father, as well as a prolonged period of psychological abuse from their mother. Because of these shared traumatic experiences, the two children formed a very powerful bond between themselves. A bond they both attributed to their own continued survival.

'That bond was broken when Tony's sister died. Suddenly lost and alone, Tony closed down completely. He withdrew from everything and everyone. He had already been displaying early prodromal symptoms, which after the tragedy escalated into full-blown psychotic behaviour. No one knew what to do with him. He was passed from one social care department to another. In the end, a program of sedative medication was considered the only viable solution for his condition. But this fragmented form of treatment and the overreliance on medication only exacerbated his existing condition. By the time he found his way to me, he'd been through the mill so much it was impossible to tell where his original psychological issues ended and any newly created psychosis began.' The doctor shifted his position in his chair. 'We began a new program of treatment and over time he responded to my therapy. It took a while but we made good progress. He responded well to my methods and we developed a kind of friendship. An element of trust grew between us. For the first time in years. He found someone else he could rely on, someone he could trust.'

Jo nodded again. This sounded more like the relationship Tony had described to her.

'But despite our progress he still struggled with a lot of unresolved trauma concerning his childhood. Even under hypnosis, his recollection of the past was patchy and confused. His own memories seemed to be a chaotic mix of truth and media invention. I'm not even sure if he could tell them apart. But with a more balanced use of antipsychotics and the right calming techniques, we found methods that helped him deal with his issues. By the time he turned nineteen, he was a different man. In fact, the change in him was remarkable. He was like a new person. He had finished his exams and had found a job. He'd enrolled in a photography evening class and had developed a keen interest in psychology. He even asked to join a social psychology course I was running at the university.'

'Social psychology?' Jo asked not wanting to interrupt the doctor's flow too much.

'It's the scientific study of how people's thoughts, feelings and behaviours are influenced by the actual, imagined or implied presence of others. We still run the course today, it's very popular. It examines individual behaviour in a communal context and involves a lot of social interaction between the students. I thought it might be good for Tony, so I allowed him to join. And at first it all seemed to go well. He was a talented student, he responded well to the course, he mixed well with the other students...' Sharman trailed off.

'Until?' Jo prompted.

'Until the EVP.'

Jo's eyebrows rose.

'Electronic voice phenomena.' Sharman elaborated. 'It was part of the course at the time. It was a module in which we explored the different effects of pareidolia on a group.'

Preempting Jo's inevitable question, Sharman went into more detail. 'Pareidolia is a psychological phenomenon in perception which causes people to see patterns in random objects. Like seeing faces in clouds, or patterns in tea leaves. The phenomenon also applies to sound. Our minds are constantly alert to the sound of specific noises. Like our own names, the cry of a child, an emergency alarm bell. So when we hear something that closely resembles those noises. We can make the false assumption we're actually hearing the sound we are listening out for.'

'Like when you're expecting a phone call and you keep thinking you can hear the phone ringing?'

'Precisely, when your mind is expecting to hear a specific sound, it's continually attempting to identify that sound from within a vast cacophony of other noises. Sometimes it can jump to conclusions and interpret a sound that isn't there. This happens more often in a heightened situation. So in order to intensify the phenomenon, I would take the students to a known haunted location. We would leave a reel-to-reel tape machine running while we wandered around asking questions or attempting to provoke any disembodied spirits that were supposed to be present. We would listen back to the recordings in the class at a later date.'

'Like a ghost box.'

Jo could see Sharman obvious irritation with the comparison, but he nodded gracefully in confirmation. 'Similar yes, but the point of our experiment wasn't to prove the existence of ghosts. But to demonstrate how different people interpret the same sound on the recording differently. Depending on their own individual belief in that sounds origin.'

'So everyone would hear something different on the tape, depending on their belief in ghosts?

Again, Sharman looked annoyed Jo had preempted him with her own conclusions. 'Yes, depending on their own physiologic make-up, one person would hear one thing, another person something different. And because of the heightened haunted house setting. These beliefs would be that more resolute.'

'Because some of the students would expect to hear a ghost.'

'Exactly, the exercise demonstrated the ability we all have to deceive ourselves. Our ability to perceive something which isn't there, simply because we expect it to be.'

A moment of silence fell between them as Sharman waited for Jo to raise the inevitable question.

'So what did Tony hear?'

Sharman sighed deeply. 'I made a mistake with Tony. A colossal mistake. I thought he had put his childhood experiences behind him. To be honest, I didn't even think he remembered much of it. Plus, I thought if I excluded him from the exercise it would undermine the progress he'd already made.'

'He heard voices on the tape didn't he?'

Sharman nodded. 'He became obsessed and begun making his own recordings. He would spend hours trawling through each one. Playing them over and over. He'd always shown early indications of OCD, but in just a matter of weeks his patten of behaviour became extreme. He convinced himself that he could hear voices speaking to him on the tapes. He couldn't be persuaded otherwise. The more you contradicted him, the more difficult and argumentative he became. That's the thing with pareidolia. Once you see a cloud as a rabbit. It's difficult to see it as anything else. It's the same with sounds. Once you've heard something one way. It's hard to perceive it as anything else.'

Jo shuffled anxiously. 'So that's why he left the university?'

'Not entirely...' Sharman trailed off again, unsure whether he should give Jo the full story. Making his mind up, he continued. 'There was an incident during the course. Somehow, Tony became convinced one of the other students was possessed by the spirit of his dead sister. Quite preposterous, of course, but there you go. The girl had also been receiving psychotherapy for mental health and behavioural problems. Partly because of her own condition she seemed to have been encouraging this delusion. Like I said, there was an incident, Tony became quite angry and violent. I had to intervene. Fortunately, the girl wasn't hurt too badly.' Sharman's hand wavered over the long scar on his cheek. Falling silent he bolstered himself to continue. 'It was all hushed up of course. The university couldn't afford any bad press and the board considered both teenagers had already been through enough in their lives. The family of the girl didn't press charges...'

Jo sat back in her chair, her head spinning. 'He attacked you and another student?'

'My own fault, really. I had ignored the fundamental rule of psychotherapy. That you never befriend your patients.' Sharman opened his hands toward Jo. 'But I felt sorry for him. I wanted to help him, give him a chance in live. I was still new to the profession. I wanted to see the positive in him.'

Jo couldn't help but notice the irony of Sharman's statement, considering the scientific topic he had just been describing. Sharman hadn't failed to notice it either and a sad ironic smile appeared on his face.

'What happened then?' Jo asked.

Sharman shrugged. 'After the incident, he ran away. They found him several days later in an old pillbox on some disused railway siding. Apparently, it had been a building where he had played with his sister as children. He'd suffered a complete mental collapse. They put into a secure unit and I never saw him again.'

'Until yesterday.'

Sharman bristled. 'Miss Kalman, please understand. Tony has endured things most people couldn't even comprehend. It has damaged him. Affected him in ways, even he's not fully aware of. You should be very careful if you intend to have any further contact with this man.'

Outside in the university carpark Jo checked her Blackberry. She had a voicemail from Roy Norris. Scrolling to the message, Jo pushed the play button.

Roy sounded agitated and panicked. Jo could hear him struggling to insert coins in a pay phone. 'Hello... Hello...Miss

Kalman. I s-s-s-saw what happened. He t-t-took her in the van; her father's van... Hello—'

***

Mid-nineties camcorder recording: A young girl plays with a small Labrador puppy on a sunlit lawn.

The child is excited, squealing at the puppy's playful antics. Although she is heavy-handedly tugging him about, the puppy remains playful and patient with the child. Exhausted, the girl drops to her knees and drapes her arms around the puppy's neck, squeezing him tight.

An abrupt transition replaces the pervious scene with a shaky image of a teenage girl in pyjamas sleepwalking in a dark moonlit garden. Muffled voices echo behind the camera, as the cameraman hurries to catch up with the girl, who is struggling through the garden's wild overgrowth.

A woman reaches the girl and spins her around by the shoulders. The girl stares blankly into the camera, her large white pupils glowing eerily in the green-hue of the camcorder's night-vision.

Somewhere off-camera a dog barks.

19. Visible Signs

Broken mirrors, vandalised photos, even unexplained fires can all be contributed to the work of a disenchanted soul. In all occurrences, it will be apparent the spirit is showing definite and directed anger toward you.

Considered direct messages by an entity toward you or your household, these acts will appear to be done in rage or with the explicit intention of frightening you. You may find graffiti or disturbing messages scrawled around your home, or strange trinkets and other ominous items left in places designed to startle you.

A disruptive entity may attempt to destroy any religious artefacts like crucifixes, bibles or rosaries that you may have in your home.

Thankfully, these kinds of occurrences are extremely rare. But if they do occur, it's practically a certainty you have a maleficent spirit present in your home.

***

Jo had been in two minds whether to play Roy's message to both parents or just Qamra. The idea Belo Mishal had abducted his own stepdaughter seemed quite preposterous. Yet, she'd been unable to dismiss the idea completely. But as chance would have it, when Jo had arrived at the Mishal house, Belo had been busy venting his anger on a new fence post at the far end of the garden. With the decision made for her, Jo swiftly sat Qamra down at the kitchen island and played her the message.

'It makes no sense,' Qamra said, taking the Blackberry from Jo and pushing the replay button. 'Why would he even say that?' Her hand trembled as she gripped the phone. Although Qamra seemed perplexed by the strange message, Jo couldn't help but notice she hadn't simply dismissed it, either.

'What's that!' Both women jumped as Belo appeared through the patio doors. Engrossed by the recording, both women had both failed to notice his return from the garden. 'I said what's that!'

'She got a message from Roy Norris,' Qamra said nervously, as Belo snatched the phone from his wife's hand. He replayed the message while both women watched him cautiously.

'This is all bollocks!' he declared fiercely as the recording finished. 'What the fuck does he think he's playing at? Call him back now!' He thrust the Blackberry at Jo.

'I've tried, but he made the call from a phone box. He doesn't own a mobile.'

'Of course he wouldn't,' Belo snorted. 'Seeing as he just hears the voices in his head!'

Upset by the sound of raised voices. Kyra appeared in the kitchen, her bottom lip quivering.

Faced with Bello's escalating fury, Jo held her ground. 'But why would he say he saw her in your van?'

'How the fuck would I know?' Belo snapped. 'The man's mad. He's just trying to deflect suspicion from himself. And he couldn't have seen her in my van could he? It was fucking stolen remember!'

'Oh, for God's sake stop shouting! You're upsetting Kyra,' Qamra gathered the mewling child into her arms.

'I'll shout if I fucking want to shout!' Belo raged. 'I'm the one being accused here!'

'No one is accusing anyone,' Jo objected sternly.

'Well, I think you are. I think you've already made up your minds.' Belo's whole body was quivering with rage. 'Is that what you think I am? What I'm capable of? How can you take that man's word for anything? He's nothing but a fucking liar!'

'Which makes him no better than you!' Belo drew his hand back sharply, as if to strike his wife. But Qamra barely flinched. 'Go on, I dare you,' she sneered. Faced with Qamra's defiance and the terrified look on Kyra's face, Belo turned away sheepishly. 'Yes, I thought as much,' Qamra chided him. 'Look at him now, the big man! You're pathetic. Lila's missing Belo! And what are you going to do about it?' But her anger quickly transformed into utter despair. 'Belo, *our* daughter is missing.'

'I'll tell you what I'm going to do.' Belo said decisively, grabbing his jacket. 'I'm going to see Norris right now!' He spun around to face Jo. 'You're giving me a lift.'

'What?' Jo said, dumbfounded by her sudden inclusion into Belo's plan.

'I've no van!' Belo growled.

Jo shook her head. 'No, I'll tell you what we're going to do. I'm taking this message to the police. See what they have to say.'

'I told you, they'll do nothing.' Belo counted. 'So he saw her getting into my van; so what! That's what they'll say and they'll do nothing!' But Jo was already heading for the door.

'No wait,' Belo called after Jo as she strode purposefully down the driveway, 'At least tell me where he lives.'

'I'm going to the police with this message,' Jo retorted, as she rooted furiously in her bag for her car keys. 'I'll let them sort it out.' With her attention distracted, Belo lurched forward and snatched the Blackberry from her hand. Outraged, Jo begun swiping at the phone as Belo wedged himself between her and the car door 'What the hell are you doing?' she yelled as Belo made a further grab for her car keys. With Belo wrenching at her fingers, Jo shrieked in pain. Stunned by her cry, Belo froze on the spot, shocked by his own actions.

Shamefaced, he held the Blackberry out toward Jo. As she snatched the device back; he brought his fingers together in a beseeching gesture. 'Please,' he pleaded, 'You don't understand. We're so in debt. I've been working around the clock, but I can't get on top of it.' He glanced over his shoulder, concerned his voice might carry back to the house. 'The bank is threatening to take the house,' he muttered despairingly. 'I don't even have enough money to finish the renovations. Qam doesn't know. When she finds out, it will destroy her. It'll destroy everything.' Belo edged closer to Jo. His tone, unnervingly intimate. To Jo's surprise, there were tears welling in his eyes. 'I've promised her so much. I promised to look after her. Her and Lila. I promised to give them a home. A proper home, somewhere where they would feel safe.'

'Well, you've done a great job there,' Jo snapped, but her tone contained very little real scorn.

'You're right. This is all my fault. When Lila found the notebook; I thought maybe I could use it somehow. You know, television or a magazine. You hear about this stuff. Lila was already having bad dreams. So I just encouraged her to throw in the stuff from the notebook. I told her if she did it, we'd get out of the house quicker. But I swear to God, I didn't think it would come to this. This is all my fault, I know. I let that man into our home. I let him into our lives. If anything happens to Lila, I'll never forgive myself.' He opened his hands toward Jo. 'Please. What would you do in my place?'

'Norris! Open this bloody door!' Belo yelled through the letterbox, while simultaneously banging his fist against the door. 'Lila! Lila, are you in there?'

Already regretting her decision to allow Belo to accompany her to Roy's home, Jo cast an anxious glance over her shoulder. They'd still not drawn any attention to themselves.

Which, considering the volume of Belo's banging, was a minor miracle in itself. 'I really don't think he's in,' Jo said pragmatically, hoping to calm Belo down a little.

'Or he's hiding somewhere inside,' Belo countered, as he tried to prise off one of the plywood boards from the lounge window. Recalling her first visit to the bungalow, Jo conceded how that might actually be a distinct possibility. Especially considering Belo's current volatility.

She had reasoned during their tense journey over that Belo may have been right. The police would see nothing suspicious about Lila being in her stepfather's van. If she wanted to clarify Roy's message, then she would have to confront him directly. And if that was the case, then she would rather have someone with her when she did. Although having that someone be Belo Mishal had probably been a bad move.

As Belo worked himself up into another angry frenzy, Jo pulled her Blackberry from her pocket. Spinning the trackwheel, she scrolled down to Roy's name and pushed the call button. Once again, Roy's landline echoed deep inside the bungalow. Punching the boarded window, Belo turned on his heel. 'I'm going around the back!' he declared gruffly, pushing past Jo and stomping around the side of the building. Leaving Jo with little option but to trail meekly after him.

A quick check confirmed the bungalow's backdoor was even more fortified than the front. With the kitchen window secured with another hefty plywood board. Apart from a thin gap at the very top. Scrambling on top of a grubby plastic dustbin, Belo gave a sudden jolt, as he peered through the exposed slat. 'Fuck me that's her jacket!'

'What where?'

'On the kitchen table.'

It took several seconds of clumsy kerfuffle for Jo to switch places with Belo. Sure enough, on the kitchen table, Jo could see a folded black puffer jacket. 'Well, it looks like hers,' she admitted. Although the interior of the bungalow was far too dark to say for sure.

'Of course it's her's,' Belo snapped. 'What would he be doing with a jacket like that? He's got her in there, I'm telling you.' Belo gave the back door handle another angry shake, but it still refused to budge. Frustrated, he began surveying the exterior of the bungalow.

The whole place felt like a fortress. Every window was securely boarded, apart from one small frosted pane with a plastic vent. Probably the bathroom and presumably left un-boarded to allow for ventilation. Dragging the dustbin over, Belo peered in through the vent. 'All I can see is the bathroom door,' he said despondently.

'We should call the police.' Jo said decisively.

'And what? Get told we have to fucking wait again. No chance. God knows what he's doing to her in there!'

'So what do you suggest we do then?'

'Hang on a second.' Leaping from the bin, Bello began searching the back garden. As Jo watched with baffled trep-idation, he dislodged a piece of broken paving slab from under a derelict rabbit hutch. Striding purposely back to the bathroom widow and before Jo thought had time to object, he launched the slab against the plastic vent.

The frosted glass cracked, but stayed intact. A second blow put paid to that. As the whole window shattered, a hail of broken glass flew across the bathroom.

Leaping back onto the dustbin, Belo cautiously unfastened the window catch. As the shattered frame swung open, he dropped back to the ground. 'Okay then,' he said, lacing his fingers together to form a cradle for Jo's foot.

'No chance!' Jo declared indignantly, as she realised just what Belo was implying. 'I'm not going in there!'

'You're the only one that will fit through.'

'Not in a million years!'

Twisting his hands back into a beseeching gesture, Belo's face contorted into an image of absolute wretchedness. 'Please,' he pleaded, his voice surprisingly brittle.

'Oh, for God's sake!' Exasperated Jo threw her hands into the air. 'I better not get stuck in there!' Steadying herself against a drainpipe, she stamped her foot into Belo's inter-locked hands.

With the small window located directly above a hideous Coral Pink bathtub and with nothing to grab onto inside, Jo immediately began to struggle. Frustrated by her slow progress through the tight aperture, Belo began pushing her from behind, impatiently heaving Jo away from the wall and further out into the open space above the bathtub. 'Okay, okay take it easy,' Jo yelled back through the window as she franticly grappled for a handhold. Grasping a long metal grab rail, she ungracefully pulled her legs free from the window frame, narrowly avoiding a headfirst plunge into the ugly pink tub.

'Are you okay?' Belo called from outside.

'Yeah, no thanks to you,' Jo barked back. Clambering from the bathtub, Jo glanced back at the broken paving slab in the basin. 'Well, there's another one for the collection,' she muttered ruefully as she recalled the tidy brick pile in the front lounge.

'So what's it look like?'

'What does what look like!' Jo growled. Apart from the broken slab and jagged glass shards in the bath basin, the bathroom looked extremely tidy. It also appeared to have been accessibility fitted for a disabled person. There were grab bars around the toilet and raised toilet seat. Spurred by a sudden stab of guilt and wishing to leave the room as quickly as possible, Jo reached for the door handle.

Lila may have been sleeping, but now she was awake. She could feel her body against the cold floor tiles and the sharp duct tape cutting into her wrists. Something had startled her back to consciousness. Her body tensed as she recalled the sound of breaking glass.

Holding her breath, Jo opened the bathroom door a crack and peered into the hallway. With no exterior light source, the interior of the bungalow was dauntingly dingy. Leaning out the door, Jo pricked her ears for the slightest sound.

'Lila!' Belo hollered through the open window, making Jo jump.

'For fuck's sake!' Jo growled, her heart thumping hard. 'Do you have to? Go around the back. I'll let you in there.' The moment Belo's face disappeared from the window, Jo slipped out of the bathroom and crept along the hallway, expecting at any moment to be confronted by an irate Roy Norris.

Apart from a thin shaft of light seeping through the narrow slat at the top of the window, the kitchen was in complete gloom. Casting a dejected eye over the drab eighties kitchen appliances, Jo picked the jacket from the table. It was definitely a coat designed for a teenage girl. The shoulder of one sleeve had been torn open, exposing the white padded lining. Cautiously reaching inside a front pocket Jo found a portable CD player and a plastic Travelcard wallet. Flipping open the wallet, she held it up to the thin shaft of light. Inside was a London Underground, Child Rate Photo ID card. Stuck to the card, a photo booth image of Lila Mishal, sitting hunched against a blue curtain background.

With her heart racing, the sudden bang on the back door made Jo leap from her skin. 'What's going on?' Belo hollered from outside. 'Open the door!'

Clutching Lila's jacket, Jo hurried over to the door. 'There's no key in the lock,' she declared, rattling the handle. Glancing around the kitchen, Jo immediately dismissed the idea of rooting blindly through the cabinets draws for a key. In her highly strung state, she wouldn't even know where to begin. 'I'll have to let you in the front.' As Belo griped angrily outside, Jo hurried from the kitchen. Tearing down the hallway, she flipped the catch on the front door.

Locked.

Like the back door, it too required a key to release the lock. Jo swore. She was now effectively locked inside the bungalow.

'I'm coming back out through the window,' she declared, as Belo arrived on the doorstep, her voice edging toward panic.

'No! You've got to let me in.' Belo yelled through the letterbox.

'I'm coming out!'

'Not until you've let me in!'

Jo gave an angry sigh. Without Belo's help she couldn't possibly make it back through the bathroom window. Muttering under her breath and hoping Roy wasn't in possession of the only key to the front door, Jo began rooting haplessly through the draws of a small storage unit in the hallway.

Almost immediately she stumbled across an enormous bunch of keys. Surprised by her good fortune, Jo snatched them up. On first glance, the bunch appeared to contain a full array of spare keys. Door locks, padlocks, meter boxes, all clumped together on a souvenir Wookey Hole keyring. With no keyhole inside, Jo shoved the keys out through the letterbox. 'Here, maybe there's something on this lot.'

Turning back to the hallway, Jo realised, for the first time, that Roy's bicycle was not in its usual place by the lounge door. 'His bike's not here,' she exclaimed with some relief. With the bike gone, the likelihood of Roy lurking somewhere in the bungalow had become significantly less likely. Just to make doubly sure, Jo stuck her head into the lounge. There was still no sign of the bike; or anything else amiss come to that. Everything looked exactly as it had on her pervious visits. Which would have been reassuring, if it wasn't for the fact Jo was still clutching Lila's torn jacket in her hands.

Lila had been sure she'd heard footsteps. But now the sound had stopped. She'd even thought she'd heard someone calling her name, but she was no longer sure. Her head felt so muggy it was hard to tell what was real anymore. The medication and the total darkness had left her feeling disoriented and muddled.

Jo stepped back into the hallway and sighed. Having come this far, she might as well see the whole thing through. There were now only two rooms inside the bungalow she hadn't seen the inside of. Steeling herself, Jo pushed open the closest door. The room was pitch black. Feeling round the wall inside the door, Jo found the light switch.

It was a bedroom of an elderly woman. Roy's mother.

Next to the door, a flannel dressing gown hung draped over the back of a metal walking frame. Over on the bed, the quaint Victorian bedcover had been neatly folded back, while a full box of tissues sat on the bedside cabinet. If it wasn't for the musty smell, it would be easy to believe the room was still in use.

Drawn toward an ornate dressing table close to the door, Jo picked a decorative hairbrush from the tabletop. The bristles were still clogged with fine white hair. Replacing the brush, Jo's gaze fell upon the large Duchess table mirror. Around the mirror, several faded photographs had been wedged into the frame. Leaning closer, Jo recognised the sensitive boyish face of Roy Norris in each of the photos.

One curled photograph had slipped from the frame. Jo picked it up. It was a discoloured image of a smiling Roy sitting on a tricycle. Written on the back in thin spidery handwriting:

Ro Ro, 4 years 6 months

Feeling she'd encroached enough on the dead woman's privacy, Jo placed the photograph back onto the tabletop and quickly left the room. Down the hallway, she could still hear Belo swearing and fumbling with the keys on the doorstep.

There was only one door left now. Which, by elimination had to be Roy's bedroom. Accepting the rationale that the sooner she checked this room, the sooner she could leave. Jo took a deep breath and clasped the handle.

There was movement outside the door. Lila felt her heart leap as someone turned the handle.

Empty.

Jo felt an odd mixture of relief and disappointment as she entered Roy's bedroom. Unlike the rest of the bungalow, this room alone appeared to claw itself into the new century. A large screen TV stood on a metal stand by the bed, alongside a new DVD recorder, a stacked tape deck and chunky CD player.

Gazing around the room, Jo was struck by a melancholic thought. Even now, with the full run of the house, Roy was still restricting himself to his own bedroom. All his personal stuff was here. The sole exception being his bicycle. Which was too bulky to fit anywhere else but the hallway.

Turning to leave, Jo noticed a tall shelving unit behind the door. Its shelves packed with a verity of card files and lever folders. Several of which had names or content descriptions written on their spines. One name immediately caught Jo's eye:

MISHAL

Jo pulled the file from the shelf.

Inside she found several crumpled letters addressed to the Mishals, including an overdue notice for Belo and a mail-order receipt addressed to Qamra. There were also various other medical and legal documents, which, if combined would make a fairly comprehensive dossier on the entire household. Information, especially useful for anyone in the business of conjuring such personal details seemingly out of thin air.

Casting her gaze over the other folders, Jo spotted another familiar name:

BABCOCK

Inside this file, Jo found a wad of old magazine articles and several damaged photo prints. Along with a stack of more recent photographs, including one of herself standing with Tony Vail outside the Mishal's house.

Slamming the folder shut, Jo jammed it under her arm, along with the Mishal file. Turning back toward the door, another photo caught Jo's attention.

With a shaky hand, Jo pulled the image free from the large IKEA print hanging over Roy's bed.

Lila Mishal posing in her school uniform.

It was an original copy, with the photographer's business stamp on the back. No doubt lifted on one of Roy's earlier visits to the Mishal home.

Alongside this image, there had been a second photograph, stuck inside the frame.

Ashley Hooper.

Unable to remain in the room any longer, Jo turned toward the hallway and ran directly into his arms.

A bright shaft of blinding light flooded the tiny room. Squinting, Lila twisted on the floor as her eyes fought the harsh glare. Between her own delirium and the dazzling light, it took a moment for her to recognise the bulky figure standing in the doorway. It was the man that had performed the séance at their house. The same man her stepfather had attacked outside her school.

Roy Norris.

Belo had called the police the moment he'd seen the photos in Jo's hand. By the time a patrol car had arrived, he had already ransacked most of the bungalow. But apart from the torn jacket, there had been no further trace of Lila inside the property.

As two uniformed police officers had entered the bungalow, Belo had been climbing the walls. Ranting incoherently in several languages at what he perceived to be the officer's total lack of urgency. But in a brief moment of clarity, he had managed to exonerate Jo completely from the break-in. 'I only called her afterwards,' he had declared emphatically.

'Once you had already broken into the property?'

'Yeah, she came afterwards.'

The officer had cast a sceptical glance between the narrow bathroom window and Belo's bulging midriff but had said no more about it.

With the officers appearing less interested in Belo's claims of abduction and more concerned with his unlawful entry into the property, Belo's frustration had grown. Jo had even played them the telephone message from Roy. But just as Belo had predicted, the fact Lila had been seen getting into her stepfather's van had not been deemed sufficient evidence of abduction. Enraged by their attitude, Belo had lashed out angrily at the officers, which had resulted in a formal caution. A subsequent name check, revealing his recent altercation with the owner of the bungalow had not improved the situation.

But the presence of Lila's torn jacket in the bungalow had been enough to prompt the officers to seek further calcification from their superiors. Belo had been detained while further enquires were made. Jo had been told she could leave once she had given the officers her details.

Outside, the indifference they had received during their initial arrival at the bungalow was now well and truly over. The sight of a police car outside Roy Norris's bungalow had brought out half the estate.

As she returned to her Mini, Jo scanned the gathered faces, but any hope of seeing Roy lurking amongst the onlookers was quickly dashed.

Wherever Roy Norris was right now, he sure as hell wasn't here.

Ladle - potato masher - cheese grater. One after another, Roy pulled a series of useless implements from the kitchenette draws, only to toss each one aside in frustration. Until finally he found something of use. A large knife block, pushed to the back of a deep pot draw. Roy grabbed a large carving knife from the block and ran back into the darkroom.

Crouching next to Lila, he attempted to cut the electrical tape binding her hands, but the blade kept missing its line. As his panic increased, Roy's efforts became more frantic. 'Please stop moving,' he pleaded. 'I'll cut you if you k-k-keep moving. Please, he'll be b-b-back at any m-m-momm...' The words dried in his mouth as he noticed Lila's had stopped struggling and was now staring wide-eyed over his shoulder. Roy turned to face the doorway.

Tony Vail stood, blocking the darkroom door. 'Take your hands off her!' He snarled, as Roy slowly rose to his feet.

Roy did his best to sound defiant despite his raging panic. 'I'm t-t-taking her out of here T-t-tony.'

Strangely, Tony seemed equally unsettled. Following Tony's taut gaze, Roy glanced down at the large craving knife in his hand. Realising his advantage, Roy thrust the knife out in front of him.

Frozen to the spot, Tony's eyes fixed on the blade, swaying nervously in Roy's unsteady fist. Clearly more fearful of the implement itself than the man wielding it.

Both men stood motionless, neither prepared to make the first move. Until finally, in a rush of panic, Tony lunged for Roy, sending both men careering into the darkroom bench.

Horror-stricken, Lila attempted to wriggle away from the wrestling men as a shower of photographic equipment clattered around her. As more equipment smashed to the floor, the two men threw each other around the tiny room, stumbling over themselves and the terrified teenager underfoot. Petrified and frantic, Lila attempted to crawl under the legs of the workbench, but was unable to twist herself into the tight space. Tripping over her protruding legs, both men crashed to the floor; groaning in agony.

Several long minutes passed before one body twisted on the ground.

Lila watched in horror as he hauled himself, hand over bloody hand across the shattered darkroom debris. With the teenager close to hysteria, he grabbed her ankles, pulling her toward him. Dragging himself on top of her, he let his full weight press against her slight body. Blood covered his hands and shirt front. Dark treacle like in the red safelight. He touched Lila's face, the blood from his fingertips mixing with the tears on her cheek. With her nose and throat clogged with tears and mucus, Lila struggled to breathe. 'No, no, no,' he muttered, attempting to soothe her tears. His blood stained hand brushing against her hair as she tried to pull away from him. 'I'm here; don't cry. I'm here,' he said, his voice becoming more childlike, as he drew his face closer to hers. Turning away, Lila caught sight of Roy Norris lying in a pool of blood. His spasmodic twitching sending her into a fresh spat of hysteria. 'No, stop it! Stop it!' Tony barked. 'Why are you crying? You need to stop crying. I'm right here for you. I'm your little soldier! Don't you remember, I'm your little soldier!' His bloody finger touched the tape stuck across her lips. Frozen with fear, Lila stared wide-eyed at Tony. Encouraged by this sudden stillness, he brought the blood covered knife up to her face, touching her cheek with the tip. 'I have to put this away now,' he said softly. 'Otherwise I might hurt someone with it.'

Jo had already rung Leandro's buzzer when she remembered he was attending an art festival in Leeds that weekend. Unwilling to disturb any of the other residents at two in the morning, she tried instead the goods lift around the back of the building. But a quick twist on the handle confirmed the metal shutter to be securely locked.

Stepping away from the loading bay, she could see a dim red glow in Tony's studio window. Intrigued, she decided to risk the steep climb up the iron fire-escape attached to the back of the block. Stepping around a large black bicycle in the loading bay, Jo tentatively began to scale the creaky stairwell.

It took less than a minute to reach the top gantry. Barely enough time for Jo to decide what she intended to do upon reaching Tony's window. Not that it mattered.

Someone had broken a small corner pane in one of the large casement windows, releasing the latch. Evidently, Jo had not been the first person to use the fire escape to gain access to Tony's studio that night. Gripped with a sudden sense of apprehension, she lent in through the open window.

The studio was dark and still. The light she had seen from the carpark, was emanating from Tony's darkroom, while shafts of pale moonlight cast long, distorted shadows across the wooden floor.

Could Tony have broken into his own studio to avoid having to use the front entrance? But then, why hadn't he just used the service left? Jo glanced down at her Blackberry. It would make perfect sense to call the police right now, but the prospect of having to explain her involvement in yet another dubious break-in held her back. Instead, she took a firm grip on her phone and stepped in through the window.

Staring anxiously into every pocket of darkness, Jo moved cautiously across the studio, until something knocked against her boot. She glanced down. An overturned shoebox lay on the floor. Kneeling down, Jo flipped the box over. It was Tony's memory box. Most of its contents scattered across the lounge rug.

A woollen scarf, a neon plastic necklace, a Tamagotchi keyring.

An odd feeling of disquiet struck Jo as she gathered up the closest items. The same unnerving sensation she'd experienced the first time she had discovered the box. But now she knew the reason. Most of these items easily postdated the nineteen seventies. Meaning; they could never have been owned by Tracey Babcock.

A sudden rattle drew Jo's attention across the studio. The sound echoed with a hollow resonance, like a plastic beaker bouncing off a hard surface. Shocked by the unexpected noise, Jo froze in mid-crouch, still clutching the retrieved items in her hand. 'Hello?' She could feel her body tensing as she waited for a response.

Nothing.

Rising to her feet, Jo took a tentative step toward the hallway. 'Tony?' Her voice was barely a whisper. The closer she got to the darkroom, the more intense the burning glow from the safelight became. Reaching the darkroom door, she lent into the room.

'Shit, shit, shit!'

Instinctively, Jo's hand covered her mouth but it did little to muffle her strangled scream. Staggering backwards she bumped against one of the framed photographs hanging on the studio wall, sending herself and the frame crashing to the ground.

Fumbling with her phone, it slipped through her fingers, landing on the floor. Scrabbling to retrieve it, Jo caught another glimpse of the twisted body of Roy Norris laying on the darkroom floor, his contorted face and lifeless eyes gazing blankly back at her. Fighting a frenzied wave of hysteria, Jo snatched up her Blackberry. Crawling backwards away from the darkroom, she slammed up against the bottom of the kitchenette counter.

Reeling on the floor, Jo spotted a piece of bloody gaffa tape stuck to her boot. Repulsed and sickened, she began franticly clawing at the tape, only for it to adhere to her fingertips. Shaking it off, something glittered in the moonlight. A metal clasp on a piece of red string.

Lila's wish bracelet.

A stark image formed in Jo's mind. Lila had been here in the studio. Tied by her wrists with tape.

Trying to avoid the sight of Roy's contorted body, Jo glanced back at the darkroom. There were still traces of gaffa tape stuck to the legs of the developing table.

Jo's head spun. Why would Norris bring her here?

But then, of course he hadn't. Jo recalled Roy's phone message.

'I s-s-s-saw what happened to L-l-l-lia Mishal. He t-t-took in the van; her father's van.'

It had been Belo's van alright, but it hadn't been Belo driving it. It had been Tony. He had stolen the van and lured Lila to it. She must have struggled free of her jacket during the attempt to snatch her. Roy had either witnessed the attack or had discovered the jacket soon after. He must have followed Tony back here. It had been Roy's bicycle in the loading bay. He had climbed the fire escape just as she had. It had been Roy who had broken the window to rescue Lila. And now he lay dead in the darkroom.

Jo could hardly breathe. She could feel herself careering toward utter panic. Forcing her mind to focus, she attempted to construct a likely scenario of events. Tony had taken Lila. He'd held her here in this studio. But why had he taken her?

Lurching to one side, Jo vomited onto the sanded wooden floorboards. Spiting bile from her mouth, she pulled herself upright again. Gazing wildly across the studio, she caught sight of the black and red striped scarf she had gathered from Tony's memory box. It was lying on the floor where she had dropped it while fumbling for her phone. Reaching for it, she realised where she had seen it before. On the local news report, during the police reconstruction. This had been Ashley's Hooper's scarf. The scarf she'd been wearing the day she disappeared. A dull realisation struck Jo as she scrutinised the other items scattered across the floor.

The eighties neon bracelet hadn't belonged to Tracey Babcock, but it hadn't belonged to Ashley either.

'I've been searching, so long. I don't know what's real anymore.'

Placing her hand over her mouth, Jo fell back against the counter in numb shock. She felt faint. Pulling herself to her feet, she staggered over to the open window. Thrusting her head out into the night, she gulped a mouthful of cold air. She had to call the police; call Lila's parents; tell them what was happening.

But tell them what?

That Lila was no longer here?

An overwhelming sense of urgency gripped Jo as she squeezed the thin wish bracelet in her hand. What would Tony do now? He had just killed a man in his own home. He'd be panicking and desperate. He had taken Lila with him, probably in Belo's van. Where would he go? Now he no longer had anywhere to go to? Jo took another deep breath and tried to calm her mind.

In the distance, a thin chain of lights moved silently in the darkness.

Of course. He would go to the one place he always went. The place he'd never left.

***

Mid-eighties video recording: A young man, in a plain institution t-shirt, rocks gently back and forth in a moulded plastic chair.

The timecode in the corner of the screen is reads:

14:18 17:10:1987

'Tony, do you understand what has happened?' a male voice asks from off-camera.

Mumbling to himself, Tony twists in his chair.

'Do you know why you are here?' the voice asks.

Tony's rocking becomes more agitated. 'Tracey, I want Tracey.'

There's a brief pause while the unseen man contemplates Tony's statement. 'Tony, you know that isn't possible.'

'I want Tracey!'

'Tony; you do realise your sister is no longer with us?'

Tony shakes his head violently. 'I want Tracey. Where is she? What have you done with her?' As he attempts to stand, a stocky ward orderly appears in shot and tries to return him to his seat. As Tony struggles, another man appears from behind the camera and both men attempt to restrain the young man together. Barging the orderly backwards against the camera, Tony lets out an agonising scream, 'Tracey!'

As the camera topples over, the image cuts to black.

20. Ghostly Apparitions

A physical manifestation of a spirit or entity; these phenomena are extremely rare indeed, but can take many forms: Human-shaped mists or transparent human apparitions; or the most rare of all: Full-bodied apparitions. Human forms that look as real and solid as any living person, but disappear completely once they move from your line of sight.

These full-bodied apparitions are so rare they're considered the 'Holy Grail' of paranormal investigation.

***

PC Jack Barnett could barely keep up with the fleeing woman. Pushing through a tangled mass of fallen boughs and brambles, he marvelled at the resilience of the panicking woman. At her ability to force herself through the mare's nest of knotted thorn bushes and tangled undergrowth, while constantly struggling with two hysterical children. Jack wheezed as a sharp stabbing pain cut through his side. Gasping deeply and struggling for breath, he felt tempted to let the woman go.

Where the hell did she think she was going, anyway? Wearing only slippers and a flimsy dress. She couldn't get far, not in her current state. If it wasn't for the fact the woman was now attempting to flee alongside an active train track, he would have long since given up the chase. But with a hysterical woman and two young children running loose on the line, the already fraught situation could only get worse.

Scrabbling up the steep embankment, Jack emerged at the mouth of a tall railway viaduct. Over which the frantic woman was now lugging her young son, pursued by her teenage daughter. With little space on either side of the rails, if a train passed now, they'd all be trapped. Jack glanced anxiously over his shoulder. Still no sign of George. Probably still back at the burning house.

'Fuck it!' Jack growled. How the hell has it come to this?

Just a short while before, he and George had been sitting in their cosy, warm patrol car, eagerly counting down the last few minutes of their night shift; when they had a received an urgent call concerning a domestic disturbance in a nearby street. George had muttered a string of blunt expletives as he had shoved the car into gear. A seasoned veteran of the district, he was all too familiar with the address and the family that lived there. Jack had also heard of the Babcocks. Their names had been all over the news for months now, but being new to the division; he had yet to meet the infamous family.

So it had been with an exasperated sense of duty and a curious expectation that both officers had arrived outside number twenty-seven Clifton Close, only to be greeted by a scene of utter chaos. Fierce flames had flickered behind the soot stained widows of the Babcock house, while turbid black smoke had billowed from the front door. As distressed neighbours streamed across the street, a distraught teenager in a nightdress had run out in front of the patrol car. 'Tracey!' George had shouted from the window.

Tracey Babcock had frozen at the sound of her name. Clambering out of the patrol car, George had gripped the young girl by the shoulders. 'Tracey, where's your mum and dad? Where's Tony?' Wide-eyed and dazed, the girl had turned toward the burning house. There was movement behind the darkened windows. 'Fuck it!' George had growled. Pushing the girl toward Jack, he had turned toward the patrol car. 'Hold her there while I call the fire through.' But George had hardly taken a step before Tracey had wriggled free from Jack's loose grip. 'Tracey, no!' George had bellowed as the young girl had disappeared back into the burning house.

Whether out of to pure instinct or sheer panic, Jack had raced after the girl. Blundering through the open front door, he had heard George's exasperated cry behind him. 'No, Jack!'

While still untouched by the fire, the hallway inside the Babcock house had been a vortex of choking black fumes. Having lost Tracey in the billowing smoke and already regretting his hasty decision, Jack had pushed blindly forward. Spluttering and coughing he had stumbled into the kitchen to discover a scene of unbridled carnage. A barefooted man, in a pair of dirty jeans had been slumped against a cabinet on the kitchen floor, his vest top stained with blood and gore.

Paralysed by an immediate sense of shock and horror, Jack had gawked at the body. Nothing so far in his career had prepared him for the sheer ferocity of the scene before him. In fact, he probably would have remained completely transfixed by the scene if George hadn't suddenly burst through the wall of smoke behind him. 'Christ almighty! It's Chris Babcock!' George had sputtered. Spotting a trail of bloody footprints leading out the back door, George had slapped Jack on the shoulder. 'Get after her,' he had barked, forcing Jack out of his numb paralysis.

Jack had darted from the house, driven by both his duty to catch the fleeing girl and also his need to escape the horrific scene in the kitchen. Staggering out the backdoor, he had glimpsed Tracey Babcock disappearing into the dark woodland at the far end of the garden.

Jack had followed the sound of shrill screaming into the dense thicket. Evidently, Tracey had been chasing after her mother and brother. The children were shouting and calling each other's names, while their mother cursed and screamed in the night. It had been utter madness.

Now, as the early dawn broke over the treetops; Tracy Babcock had finally caught up with her mother. Midway across the viaduct, she was franticly attempting to pry her brother from her mother's steel-like grasp. Lashing out at her daughter, Ruth sent the girl stumbling backward over a rail. As Ruth reeled from her daughter's attack, the young boy slipped from her grip. Tumbling to the ground, he rolled across the track, screaming hysterically. Ruth took a faltering step toward her son before catching sight of Jack rushing toward her.

Racked by indecision, Ruth's face contorted into a grim effigy of pained anguish, before she spun away from the boy. Lashing out afresh at her elder child. Grasping Tracey's hair and clawing wildly at her face, Ruth began hauling the terrified teenager across the gravel, toward the side of the viaduct. The girl's bare knees scrapping across the jagged stones. Mauling and grappling, they fell exhausted against the metal guardrail. With mother and daughter now trapped against the low parapet, Jack pulled his run up short. 'Just stay where you are, luv,' he panted, holding his hand out toward Ruth. 'There's nowhere to go now.' He flinched as the stitch in his side reasserted itself. Twisting his torso, Jack attempted to regain his composure. Although she'd stopped running, there still remained the small matter of getting the hysterical woman and her children off the line before the morning service begun.

Fiercely gripping her daughter's hair, Ruth began muttering and cursing. Her words, a mad jumble of incoherent ramblings and obscenities. As Jack edged forward, she jerked backwards, stepping up onto the metal guardrail. Her wild eyes bulging with madness. 'Don't move!' Jack shouted as Ruth teetered ever closer to the edge. Craning his neck to see over the parapet, Jack's heart leapt. Although far from the viaduct's highest point, a fall from this section of the overpass would still be fatal. Gripped by a renewed sense of urgency, Jack took another step forward, prompting Ruth to tug Tracey even closer to the edge.

'Fuck, fuck, fuck!' Turning, Jack stared back down the railway line for any sign of George. But the track was still empty. Taking a deep breath, Jack tried to calm himself. If he could just contain the situation a little longer. 'Don't do anything stupid love!' He heard himself saying, as Ruth blurted out a long stream of vile cursing, while Tracey screamed franticly in her arms. The girl's face and neck, a bloody patchwork of ragged cuts and scratches, gouged by her mother's broken nails. Consumed by indecision, Jack took another faltering step forward, causing Ruth to clutch her daughter closer.

Wrestling in her mother's grip, the young girl freed an arm. 'Please!' she screeched, thrusting her hand out in a direction beyond Jack. Bewildered, Jack turned, hoping beyond hope that George had just appeared on the viaduct. But to his surprise, it was the girl's younger brother standing behind him. 'Tony!' the girl screamed, as the young boy's bewildered expression transformed into a mask of utter horror. Glancing back Jack caught a brief glimpse of Ruth and Tracey, as they disappeared over the top of the parapet. Moments later, a sickening thud echoed from the base of the viaduct.

Then everything stopped. The world fell silent. For what felt like an eternity, Jack stood staring at the vacant space where the pair had just been standing. Until finally the silence became too much to bear.

Jack turned around. The young boy hadn't moved. Transfixed by numbing shock and sheer incomprehension, he stood staring at Jack. His pitifully gaze searching for something; anything. Any explanation that his traumatised young mind could hope to grasp.

But PC Jack Barnett had no answers for him.

The sky is swathed in vibrant swirls of purple and gold. The tree branches dance in the morning breeze. Turning my face to the sun, the pain evaporates, as a sense of expectation consumes me. I feel at ease, my mind feels clear. I have control again.

'Tony!'

My name cuts through the haze, fracturing the calm. The world tumbles back in on me and I'm back where I started. Back where it all started. I glance over the crumbling parapet at the wild overgrowth below. A dark tangled mass of thorny vegetation, where lush rippling grass once billowed in the evening breeze. Tracey trembles in my arms. 'Don't be scared,' I tell her as I gently stroke her cheek. She looks terrified. The incident with Norris has upset her. She's not herself.

Nor am I, come to that.

I can sense the uncertainty returning. I thought I understood. Now I'm not so sure. Something about Tracey's desperation. Somehow, everything seems worse now. It all feels wrong. I stare back at the trees. Back toward the horizon. Hoping to find myself in that moment again. But it's gone. I've lost it. Suddenly, everything feels so hopeless. I twist Tracey around and push her towards the parapet. Struggling, she falls against the scaffolding, knocking a rusted pole free. It rolls over the side, spinning into oblivion.

'Tony! Don't move!'

I turn and look back across the viaduct. Kalman's on the cycle path. She's panting and out of breath. She looks petrified. 'Keep away!' I scream. 'Don't come any closer!' A sudden surge of anger swells inside me. I want to reach out and grab her. Punish her for being here, for interfering. But if I do that; Tracey will escape.

Tracey will escape?

This realisation hits me like a cruel stab to my heart. I stare down at Tracey's distorted tear smeared face and I'm repulsed. After everything I have done for her. How ungrateful can she be! The anger swells within me. Tugging Tracey's hair, I pull her closer to the edge. I've waited too long. We need to get away from this madness. Then she'll realise, then she'll understand. She moans in my arms, and there's panic in her eyes.

What have they done to you, Tracey?

'She's frightened Tony. Let her go.' Kalman bleats.

'No! She wants to stay with me!' As I pull Tracey closer, I stumble backwards, knocking against the loose scaffolding. It creaks under our weight. 'She wants to be with me!' I sob. Tracey struggles with her bindings. She knows Kalman is here to take her away. She's scared and panicking. I rip the tape from her mouth and twist her around to face Kalman. 'Tell her! Tell her you want to stay with me!'

Tracey's stubbornly silent. She can be like that. Sometimes she can remain quiet for days on end. But I need her to tell Kalman the truth. Explain what is really happening here. But she just whimpers in my arms. Her silence only makes me angry. 'Tell her!' I shake her by the neck as Kalman edges closer.

'Tony, please! You're hurting her.'

Christ! She sounds pathetic. 'Hurting her! I'm saving her! Do you hear! I'm saving her...' But even to my own ears, these words sound hollow. I glance over the broken guardrail as my courage fades. There's just too much emotion to deal with. Everything is just so tangled. 'I tried so hard!' Tears well in my eyes. My failure is now obvious, but I can't let Kalman see me cry so I turn away, nestling my face against Tracey's neck. 'She gave everything for me and I couldn't help her.' My voice breaks. 'I couldn't do anything.'

Kalman's voice softens. 'It wasn't your fault. You were just a boy.'

'I watched her die and did nothing.'

'Tony, come away from the edge.' Kalman's voice falters. She's more scared than she's letting on.

'I can't go on,' I tell her. 'Not like this. I can't keep doing this, over and over again...'

'But this is not the way.'

'Why not!' I scream. 'Why can't you leave us alone? Why can't it be just the two of us?'

I shuffle backwards. There's fresh panic in Kalman's eyes. 'You know why,' she splutters.

I shake my head. 'Why?'

'Because she's not Tracey!' she yells, her frustration spilling over. 'You know this don't you? Deep down you know she's not Tracey?'

Suddenly, I can't move. Every muscle in my body is refusing to respond. 'No, no, no,' I mutter. My mind's spinning in circles. 'You're trying to confuse me!'

'Look at her Tony.'

I know she's lying, but I can't bring myself to look. I can't be wrong. Not again.

'It isn't Tracey. She made everything up.'

'That's not true. This is Tracey!' I clutch at Tracey's hair and she squeals in my arms. 'It has to be!' My voice sounds strained and uncertain.

'She isn't Tracey,' Kalman repeats. 'Just like Ashley wasn't. Or the girl from the university. None of them were ever Tracey.'

'No, no, no!' Images of other faces clutter my mind. Of twisted, pleading faces. I can't concentrate. I'm losing control. It's all slipping away again.

Kalman takes another step forward. 'Tony, you have to trust me. It's going to be alright.'

For a moment, I want to believe her. I need to believe her. She reaches out a hand and all my defences fall away. Maybe if I just let her... The sound of a police siren echoes through the trees. Glaring at Kalman, her expression betrays her guilt. 'They're here to help you. I had to call them.'

But I'm not taken in by her phoney pleading. 'I knew it! You're just like all the others. You just want to take her from me.'

'Tony, that's not true. It's not like that. I want to help you.'

'Help me!' I snort. 'By lying to me!' I pull Tracey closer, slamming against the scaffolding. She screams as the whole frame shudders. 'Why won't you just leave us alone?'

Kicking wildly at a scaffolding pole, it swings out over the edge. Kalman's expression is now one of absolute panic. 'Tony, don't do this. Please, I'm only trying to help you!'

'Why? Why would you want to help me?' I push Tracey toward the gap in the parapet. 'Why are you always trying to help me?'

'Because…' she falters.

'Because what!'

'Because; you're my little soldier.'

At last, Tracey's voice. The voice I remember. The words she used to say to calm me. I stare down at her in my arms. Her lips are quivering. Her face is a mess of mucus and tears, but she isn't speaking.

'I told you, I'd always be there for you. No matter what.'

It's her. I don't understand. I turn back to Kalman. She's smiling. Her expression is soothing, understanding. My mind's spinning. 'Tracey?'

She steps forward and touches my cheek with her hand, staring deep into my eyes. 'I said we'd always be together. I wrote it here in the book didn't I.' She pulls a notebook from her coat. It's the book she wrote all our plans in, the book with all the pictures in. The pictures she drew to keep me strong. I take it in my hand, my tears falling upon the crumpled pages.

'Is it really you? Are you really here?'

'Yes, Tony I'm here.'

My whole body is trembling. How could I have not known? In an instant, the pain washes away. I stare down at the snivelling creature in my arms. The dumb child with the smeared makeup and snot defiling her face. I'm repulsed by the sight.

'Let her go, Tony,' Tracey tells me.

How could I have been so mistaken? I drop the baggage to the ground and push it away. Someone will find it there, snivelling in the dirt.

'I'm so confused. I don't know who I am anymore.' My shoulders sag and my legs shake as I struggle to stay upright. Tracey takes my hand in hers. It feels so soft. 'I've been so alone for so long,' I sob.

'It's okay, everything is going to be alright' she pulls me closer wrapping her arms around me squeezing me like she used to.

'I haven't been myself.'

'I know Tony, I know.'

'I let you go.'

'It wasn't your fault,' she strokes my hair, pulling me closer. 'There was nothing you could have done.'

'I'm sorry. You said we should stay together and I let you go.'

'It doesn't matter anymore.'

'You're right, you're always right.' Tears are rolling down my cheeks. I'm ashamed. Crying in front of my big sister.

She's waving the creature away from the edge. She doesn't want her here any more than I do. The thing scuttles away in the dirt. Now it's just me and Tracey.

'You didn't leave me. I knew you wouldn't leave me.' I want to laugh. For the first time in years; I want to laugh out loud. Tracey smiles and my heart feels light. 'We're together again.'

'Yes, we are.'

'For always.'

Tracey actually looks surprised as I grab her wrists and pull her toward me. For a moment, it even feels like she is twisting away from my grasp. But I'm not letting her go again. Not now. Not ever.

I feel the freedom as we both topple over the scaffolding. The exhilaration of speed. As we fall, she cries out. It sounds like a scream, but it's a cry of joy, a cry of exultation.

A final cry of release.

Lila opened her eyes; but her gaze failed to focus on the gap in the crumbling parapet. Or the tangled overgrowth covering the edges of the cycle path. It failed to comprehend the damaged guardrail or the broken scaffolding. Instead, Lila stared blackly across the deserted viaduct, her legs drawn up into a tight ball.

She felt safe like this. Protected from the outside world. Removed from her surroundings. She didn't want to think about what lay beyond the broken guardrail. Or on the ground far below. She didn't want to recall the events that had brought her here. Or the terror she had endured. Instead, she let these images blur in her mind. Allowed them to transform into vague translucent illusions, as a familiar, creeping numbness spread through her consciousness. Despite her earlier panic and desire to escape. Lila found she no longer wanted to move from her huddled position. In fact, her brain seemed incapable of fashioning any kind of command her body appeared willing to comply with.

Gradually Lila lost all interest in her own senses. She no longer cared what she saw or heard. She didn't even acknowledge the lone policewoman racing up the cycle path toward her, or the sound of the distant ambulance siren drifting over the treetops. For Lila, the policewoman and the ambulance had become detached and separated from her own existence. There was no need for acknowledgements.

Because none of this was real anymore.

The summer sun glistens through the overhanging branches. The leaves jostle and flutter in the breeze, splitting the sunbeams into a riot of cascading splinters. Tracey lays opposite in the long grass, her battered yellow Dragstar gleaming in the sunshine. The scent of summer hangs in the air. A lawn mower echoes in the distance. Birdsong drifts through the trees. All the years of pain are gone. The past is empty. Like a half-remembered dream, my old self feels so removed. So distant. Suddenly I'm afraid. As I sense my consciousness slipping away, the panic returns.

Then Tracey smiles and I know everything will be okay. The warmth in her gaze comforts me and all the fear evaporates. I'm at peace. For the first time; everything is how it should be. All the terror. The anger. The dread of leaving this place. It's all gone. Now I know we'll be okay.

We don't have to go anywhere. We can stay here together; Tracey and me.

***

Contemporary news footage: With her thermal jacket fastened tightly around her neck, a local news reporter addresses the camera directly. Over her shoulder, a solitary police officer stands idly by a police tape cordon, as a light drizzle falls. Further in the distance a tall railway viaduct rises above the treetops.

'Once again tragedy has struck at a renowned suicide hot-spot in the Ashwood Park area. Early this morning an unidentified man and woman plunged from the Ashwood Viaduct. Police have confirmed that one person was pronounced dead at the scene, while a second is being treated for life-threatening injuries.

A spokesperson for Ashwood Borough Council stated earlier today that a fresh enquiry would be setup concerning the Ashwood Viaduct and that all appropriate safety measures would be taken in the meantime. The names of the couple involved in today's incident have yet to be released, as police are still attempting to contact their relatives.'

The reporter holds her last pose until she receives the 'all clear' signal from behind the camera. As her body relaxes, a look of dogged satisfaction appears on her face. 'Okay,' she says, 'Let's get out of here before it really starts pissing down.'

The shot drops to the ground, freezing on a muddy patch of grass, before cutting to black.

A Final Word

Most of the phenomena listed here can be explained quite rationally when examined individually. But they're much harder to disprove when they occur repeatedly, or in conjunction with each other. Especially if they've been observed by multiple people or at different times.

Now, before you jump to any hasty conclusions, remember to look for rational explanations first. Chances are, you'll find them. The truth is; actual paranormal activity is very rare and it's much more likely that you're not experiencing it than you are.

After considering all the above, if you still suspect your house to be haunted and you've already tried all the documented counter ploys; burning sage, cleaning the floors, sprinkling holy water, etc. Here's what you need to do about it.

Call a reputable medium with spirit rescue experience. Let them see what they feel or sense in the property. If there does seem to be a presence in your home, they should be able to give you appropriate advice. Or alternately, you could contact a reputable paranormal investigator if the situation becomes more pressing. They'll have a much better understanding of the phenomena and will deal with it in a more immediate and professional manner.

There is, of course one final solution you may consider. You could simply accept the ghost into your household. Admittedly, this may be difficult for most people to do. But many ghosts will simply leave you alone if you just acknowledge their presence and reassure them they're welcome in your home. Remember ghosts react badly to negative emotion, so by directing positive energy toward them instead, it can have surprising and effective results.

Who knows given time, you might actually grow to appreciate your ghostly lodger.

Acknowledgements

I would like to express my gratitude and thanks to following without whom this novel wouldn't be what it is today.

Peter Alexander, Ian Brimble, Tony O'Calahan, Dr David Corcoran, John & Ladi Da Prato, Ilaria D'Elia, Andy Hallett, Annie Hulley, Tony Longhurst, John McArdle, Ian Puleston-Davies, Jimmy Osborne, Diana Van Proosdy, Russell & Louise Richardson, Jemma Stephens, Georgina Slowe, David M Warn, Steve White and Frank Williams.

My 'writing buddies' Hugo and Milo.

And most of all my wonderful wife Lucia, for her patience, love and advice.

Printed in Great Britain
by Amazon

43098405R00270